THE GODDESS OF FORTUNE

A NOVEL

ANDREW BLENCOWE

978-1-927750-45-2 (paperback)
978-1-927750-46-9 (eBook edition)
Also available in German and Japanese.

Published by Hamilton Bay Publishing
publish@HamiltonBayPublishing.com

Dedicated to the memory of William Troeller

Contents

Preface

ON A VERY HOT Sunday morning in June 1914, Gavrilo Princip ducked into a sandwich shop in Sarajevo for an early lunch a little before noon. Earlier that day he had failed to kill Archduke Franz Ferdinand. Outside the sandwich shop quietly eating his cheese sandwich, Gavrilo could not believe his luck: the large limousine carrying the royal couple stopped directly in front of him. Princip dropped his sandwich, took three steps forward, and fired just two shots, killing both Arch Duke Franz Ferdinand and his wife Sophie. Had the sandwich shop been located two doors further down the street, Princip would have been too far from the car.

This is not to say that the proverbial powder keg of central Europe in 1914 would not have exploded from another spark a little later. But who knows, and who knows when? The Second Balkan Crisis of 1912-1913 had been resolved peaceably. Perhaps the tiny spark that started the catastrophe of the First World War was the location of the sandwich shop.

Another one of these situations was the Japanese Imperial Navy's arrogant and sloppy overuse of French Frigate Shoals—the Japanese Navy had used this small Pacific atoll to launch ineffectual and gratuitous raids on the Pearl Harbor naval base located on one of the two main American possessions in the Pacific. The Japanese used French Frigate Shoals to refuel flying boats by tanker submarine.

The sole purpose of these useless raids was to puff up the reputation of desk-bound admirals in Tokyo, nothing more.

But the ever-astute Chester Nimitz had noted Japan's repeated use of French Frigate Shoals and had placed an American destroyer there as a deterrent—the Japanese having needlessly alerted the Americans to the critical strategic value of French Frigate Shoals with the useless raids.

When the French Frigate Shoals were truly needed for the critical refueling of the reconnaissance flying boats prior to the battle of Midway, there was an American destroyer sitting there. Had the destroyer not been there, and had the reconnaissance flying boats been refueled, they would have reported what Yamamoto most feared—that the American aircraft carriers were not in Pearl Harbor. As it happened, the Japanese went into the critical Midway battle blind, lacking this key piece of intelligence.

Andrew Blencowe
Tuesday, 4 February 2014

Prologue

ON THE 84TH STREET of Manhattan on this glorious Monday morning in September the sun into my study is streaming. On days like this I think how it was just a few years ago when Germany and America almost went to war. Fantastic though this seems now, I want to explain to the new generation of readers how this seemingly impossible situation could have almost occurred.

This afternoon I will be taking a short trip to the Empire State Building at 34th Street to meet the German Chancellor, my close friend, Alfred Jodl. Alfred is my only true friend in politics—on either side of the Atlantic. A friend in politics seems like a contradiction, as we politicians are all just sharks circling looking for the weakest to eliminate. Tomorrow we will be travelling by train to meet President Truman to discuss, among other topics, the situation in French Indochina.

As this is Alfred's first trip to New York (his previous two trips were just to Washington), I promised him we would visit the Chrysler Building, so he could see for himself the stainless steel terrace crown designed by Van Alen.

The steel was a special order by Walter Chrysler himself to the Krupp works—only the best German Krupp steel (the patented Enduro KA-2 austenitic stainless steel) was good enough for what many consider the ultimate icon of the Manhattan skyline. I know the details as I was the architectural consultant to Van Alen. Every time I look at the Chrysler Building, I think of Krupp.

Alfred is arriving on the new zeppelin Paulus filled with the German invention of Hydrolium—a special uninflammable mixture of hydrogen and helium—safe, but with 80% of the lifting power of hydrogen. It's fitting that the German Chancellor is travelling on an airship named in honor of the victor of Stalingrad and Persia, whose bold audacity captured the Suez Canal from the British, and who hastened the end of the terrible war with Britain. The Empire State Building's old zeppelin mast has been re-engineered to take the new German automatic mooring cables.

As most people know, Alfred took over from me as chancellor, after I served my term following the signing of the Armistice of '42. But this is all water under the bridge—now you can read for yourself how our two great countries came so close to the brink of a disastrous—and completely unnecessary—war.

Albert Speer, Manhattan
Monday, 13 September 1948

1: Meeting An Old Friend

THE SUN SLOWLY SET in the late summer day but the heat was still on the lake. Lake Léman—"Lake Geneva" as the moneyed classes liked to call it in Geneva—was its normal quiet self: modest, still and bland, just like the Swiss themselves. Julius Stein wandered about his apartment in his old purple and yellow dressing gown, the gold braid ends of the belt having been almost completely chewed off by the short-haired dachshund that respectfully followed his master. Julius slowly made his way to the small interior bedroom for his ultimate luxury—his afternoon nap.

The bed was really an elevated tatami mat holding a pale orange futon with a small Japanese buckwheat pillow at its head. The Asian bed blended into the room that was conventionally decorated by Julius's very conventional German wife in what she boasted to the rich Iranians living in the apartment below was a "Japanese motif." Sophie so loved to use the English word "motif," a word she had recently discovered in one of Julius's precious copies of the American *Esquire* magazine, which, for reasons never explained, Julius kept and very occasionally re-read; the February 1936 issue was always in his study, with a slip of paper to mark an article by an American writer.

Julius laid down and thanked heaven for his tiny, small corner of peace and calm in the world. Every minute of every day back in Germany there was a tension in his chest and in his stomach, a sense of anticipation—actually more a dread—of the knock on the door, or even the tap on the shoulder as he rode the slow and squeaky elevated railway around Alexanderplatz—his and other Berliners' beloved "Alex." A dread of him and his family being taken away by the security service to disappear into the night and fog, to have their names recorded in the horrible and antiseptic SD books with only the terrible initials of "NN" beside their names. It had happened to his friends, it could have happened to him any day he was in Germany; this was the reality of the "New Germany."

Julius knew the Swiss: they were dull, they were boring, and their lives centered around money and prestige, but they were fair in a world rapidly losing all sense of fairness. And he loved the sense of security he felt in Vevey.

Now, a glorious warmth slowly wrapped its soft feminine fingers around him, caressing him like a mother does to her child, nothing more important to her than to see the little smile and the tiny eyelids slowly drooping.

In the warmth and peace of the small bedroom, Julius could actually sense himself slowly falling asleep, a sensation he had never experienced in Germany. Soon he and the dog at his feet were asleep, both quietly snoring.

As the large, dark navy blue Mercedes descended into Vevey from the surrounding hills, the light rain ended and was replaced first by gloom and then, increasingly as they descended, by sunlight, at first feeble then increasingly bright and warm. The smell of chocolate announced the arrival at the home of the Swiss chocolate industry, with the cows in the surrounding verdant hills providing the milk.

The car quietly moved to the parking reserve of the Trois Couronnes—the Three Crowns—a typical Swiss five-star hotel: discreet, spotlessly clean, self-effacing and, of course, extremely expensive. The fresh coarse gravel made little noise as the car came to a rest after its long journey. The motor, now at rest, sang out occasional metallic pings as it cooled after its long labors.

A tall and sparse figure left the comfort of the Mercedes—the custom-made rear seats were astonishingly restful—seats made by the custom maker Kurtsmann's who specialized in bespoke coach work for Mercedes' arch-enemy Auto Union, but in this case had been persuaded by the effortless guile of the balding young man.

Unobtrusively, the modest man made the five-minute walk from the hotel to the first group of apartments up the slight incline by the lake. He looked like any Swiss bourgeois—a small business owner perhaps—dull in dress and self-effacing in appearance and demeanor.

The small gate was painted a shiny piano black with three brass hinges, unevenly spaced, in the north Asian practice, where the two top hinges bore all the weight while the lowest hinge acted simply as a rudder. Closer inspection showed the gleaming paint to actually be baked enamel—"God is in the details," the visitor smiled.

Stopping for a moment, more out of habit than necessity, the man looked for the name—this was not his first visit. Pressing the button marked Stein, after a delay of a few minutes, the heavy wrought iron front door opened, and the familiar face of Professor Julius Stein peered out, still slightly befuddled from this nap.

Clarity returned and Stein exclaimed, "Albert! What a joy!"

"Professor."

"Please, please come in, and please no more 'Professor!' "

Albert entered.

Sophie, Julius's wife, coldly greeted Albert and then disappeared into the modern but quite small kitchen.

After Albert left she complained, "They are all the same;" Julius gently reminded her of how both of them had avoided the camps or worse.

It was Albert who had persuaded the Swiss—initially against their will—to accept, perhaps "tolerate" was more accurate—the former head of the political economy school at the University of Berlin. Albert had pointed out to a number of Swiss departments, in particular the security people, the benefits of having Stein as a local consulting expert: his cosmopolitan world view; his expertise and knowledge of all things American; his encyclopedic knowledge of economic history.

And Albert had an ulterior motive. While it was true that he could have gotten safe passage for the professor and his wife to England or America, Albert wanted to retain access to Stein and his insights; so quiet, bucolic, boring, and nearby Switzerland was the perfect choice.

An example of Stein's mind was the searchlights; it was Stein who had initially suggested the searchlights. As a canny and effective business man in his own right, Stein was thoughtful and surprisingly imaginative when it came to projecting the image of a company (or even a country) and this he discussed with Albert one bitterly cold evening in Berlin in '35.

"Albert, you should consider something truly spectacular for the next one of your so-called party rallies. While I obviously detest your Chancellor's internal policies, I have to admit I begrudgingly admire his use of radio—it's as effective as the American dictator Roosevelt's. (Stein retained a deeply cynical streak when it came to all politicians, especially those who came across as caring; 'they are the worst thugs of all', Stein had told Albert numerous times.) And these mass rallies are the modern-day *panem et circenses* that the ancient Romans did so well—sadly the average person wants to be told what to do and is happy to comply if his belly is full."

4

It was with this comment that the two men created the idea of the Cathedral of Light (or rather Stein explained and Albert listened). Against the rabid complaints of all, Albert had collected every searchlight in Germany—there were 130 working searchlights (eight others were still being constructed) —to be combined to create the Cathedral of Light lighting spectacular in the '37 Rally of Labor in Nuremburg. Albert got the credit, but both Albert and Stein knew it was Stein's Berlin idea on that bitterly cold winter's night that generated this breathtaking extravaganza (photographs of which got as far as the 1600 Pennsylvania Avenue and the Imperial Palace in Tokyo).

Stein led Albert to the living room with its glorious view of the lake.

"After such a long and arduous journey, I am sure you need some sustenance. Come, Albert. Eat."

Point be made, Albert was hungry after the trip, but he was also concerned the food would simply make him sleepy.

So Albert asked for Italian coffee.

"Espresso, it is to be then."

Turning to his wife, Stein quietly said,

"Sophie, why don't you let me and Albert catch up on old times? Does that make sense?"

"Does that make sense?" This was the phrase Albert had heard Professor Stein say a thousand times—"Does that make sense?"

This was precisely the reason for Albert's visit—does that make sense?

Stein lead Albert to a very small study—no desk, books alone three walls, a large dull brown overstuffed club chair with a small table to the left side—Albert recalled Stein was left-handed.

Albert settled on the small sofa, the only other furniture in the room.

Stein looked at Albert and smiled.

"So I suppose you're interested in knowing what Germany should do when Japan attacks America."

Stein's delivery was like a Vevey tram ticket collector's "that will be one franc, please."

Try as he might, Albert was unable to contain a gasp.

Stein laughed.

"Albert, dear Albert, you are still so easily shocked, and after all these years as a high functionary."

Stein remembered one warm Sunday afternoon lakeside stroll they had made together, and how Albert was so shocked by the discovery of the detritus of Saturday night's activities of courting couples' lovemaking in the park that he ran all the way down to the lake.

Albert looked at Stein directly.

Stein shrugged.

"Albert—a blind man can see this. And here I am all alone, without my brilliant students, all alone in this beautiful apartment you created for me," Stein raised his hand at Albert's objection.

"Albert, you—you, Albert—you alone got us the two Swiss passports and the money and the papers—you, it is to you to whom Sophie and I owe our lives. Of course, I do not have words to thank you."

Stein looked at Albert as he spoke, and Stein was at an age where he could be honest without being mawkish.

"So, Albert, how can I help you; how can I repay you, if ever so trivial?"

Albert leaned back and looked at this man—tall, still handsome, generous, and erudite. Sometimes Albert sat and wondered about the "master race" gibberish and asked himself, what was the Austrian's game?

Albert sighed and said,

"Professor, as always—as always—you're more than a few steps ahead of me. Actually, I wanted to get this point in about two hours' time, after I had my knights and bishops in place. But as you've squared my rook, as you so often do, I will be brief."

Stein's warm eyes did not move from Albert.

"You are correct. We do expect our fair-weather oriental allies to attack the Americans. We are not sure where or when, but it will be soon."

Stein, matter-of-factly, said,

"When and how does not matter—the Japanese could attack San Francisco, or Seattle, again, this makes little sense, or San Diego—that does make a modicum of sense. Of course, instead of the United States, the Japanese may attack the American possessions of the Hawaii Islands or possibly the Philippines. When is also not critical. Personally, I expect it before May or June of '42, because that is when the Japanese will run out of oil. But it could be tomorrow, or it could be August in '42. My guess is sooner, rather than later, it will be before August 42 as August is the start of the typhoon season in north Asia."

"Well, back to your question: when the Japanese attack the Americans, what does Germany do?"

Stein had been waiting for this question since he opened the front door.

"Nothing," Stein replied.

"Nothing, Professor?"

"Albert, let's be realistic. You know I spent '20 and '21 at Harvard, along with students from China, Japan, Britain and Austria."

Stein had spent two years teaching at Harvard, and another six months seconded at River Rouge in Michigan working with a Senior Vice President, who reported directly to Henry Ford. Stein had hosted a number of trips for his Harvard students.

"Please don't take this the wrong way, but Europe is on a steeply declining parabola. We're done for. The 14/18 war has sapped all our vitality—the Germans, the French, the English, the Italians, the Russians, all of us—kaput. When I was at The Rouge, as the Ford manufacturing plant is called—and it's more a small nation-state than a factory—I realized Europe was doomed."

Stein explained to Albert how coal and iron ore and rubber entered one end of this behemoth and cars spewed out the other end,

"'Total Manufacturing Integration' is what the Ford executives called it. And it makes Krupp look like a Lego factory."

"Do I think Germany will be successful when the *Reich* attacks Russia? Possibly, and much as I hate the current claptrap that I read in the German newspapers, the Slavs *are* peasants, and they need to be defeated. Stalin is just the latest in a long line of tyrants.

Gorky was correct when he said about the Russians that '*All the dark instincts of the crowd irritated by the disintegration of life and by the lies and filth of politics will flare up, and fume, poisoning us with anger, hate, and revenge; people will kill one another, unable to suppress their own animal stupidity.*' And the Russians have a history of five hundred years of pogroms and remember the Czarist Black Hundreds groups who hunted down and killed all the Yiddish-speaking people they could find.

Russia never changes—my friends at the Swiss security department have some extremely disturbing recent reports about what Stalin is doing in Russia—secret trials, mass executions, widespread starvation as a weapon; food rations have been cut to 1,000 calories per day; the minimum for an adult to survive is 1,400 calories. It is truly horrific and, remember, *pogrom*—the mass killing of Jews in Russia—is a Russian word that means *devastation*. And while I hate to say anything good about the regime you serve, it is actually the lesser of two evils. It was the American newspaper the

New York Times that stated about the Soviets, '*For the first time in history, a nation has undertaken a general crusade against religion.*' That was 10 years ago, but it is even more true today according to my Swiss friends."

It was clear that Stein detested—and feared—the idea of a Soviet hegemony of Europe.

Stein continued,

"But America, that is a very different proposition—the Americans have an amusing phrase 'a whole different ballgame.' "

Albert's confusion showed.

"Have you been to America, Albert?"

Albert had not.

Albert was becoming more and more concerned with what he was hearing, "So what can Germany do?"

Stein explained the two essentials, and Sophie joined them with the much-delayed espresso. The first critical step was to distance Germany as much as possible, and as quickly as possible, from Italy and from Japan.

"The Italians have wonderful coffee, and nothing else—*il Duce* is a clown, and a very stupid clown at that, albeit with some very colorful uniforms. I am sure you are aware of this from your friends in Berlin, and from fat Hermann's transcripts." (At this Albert looked very closely at his mentor).

"The Italians are totally unprepared for war, even a small war. Pomp and bluster aside, they're children. Remember how Musso headed nine of the 22 Italian departments, including the merchant marine and how he forgot to tell his merchant ships to put to sea when the Italians finally declared war against a prostrate France and a weakened Britain—a quarter of all the Italian merchant marine tonnage was immediately interned by the British. Of course, the smiling Italian sailors were completely happy to be imprisoned in safe and civilized Britain on the Isle of Man."

"Think of it as swords: Germany is one of the Saracen's finest swords, England is a rapier, but America is the largest of terrible broadswords."

"And Italy?" Albert asked

"As a child did you ever play pirates with an eye patch and hat and rubber sword?"

"Well that is what the Italians are like—amusing and entertaining buffoons at best, very serious liabilities at worst."

"The Japanese?"

The professor said nothing. He stood and went to the bookcase. He lifted a humidor elegantly decorated in mother of pearl. Silently, he opened it to Albert.

"Albert, Cuban Cohiba—your favorite."

"Let's go onto the terrace and I will tell you a story."

The two moved to the terrace. It had a large retractable shade, which was partially extended so the terrace had all the warmth of the glorious late summer day, but no direct sunlight.

The Cuban cigars were less than four weeks old, their dark brown leaf was soft and fresh—no aged hardness, just moist, inviting, and tender. Albert wondered how, then remembered Julius did some very quiet consulting for the Swiss Federal Government in Bern.

With the nubile young cigars lit and smoking happily, the Professor continued.

"One of my students at Harvard when I was teaching there in '20 and '21 was a very bright and very funny chap everyone called Six Fingers. He was Japanese, actually descended from samurai. Spoke perfect English and went on to become a naval *attaché* in Washington after his time with us in Cambridge."

"He was in the party of students I took on a tour of The Rouge when I was there. I will tell more of that trip by and by, but I got to know Isoroku extremely well, and we exchange letters to this day. In fact, I'll give you his Christmas gift to me as my Swiss doctor prohibits me from drinking spirits and I know you're a whiskey man."

According to Six Fingers, Japan is being controlled by much the same people you work with—boldly aggressive, highly nationalistic, but petite bourgeois in the worst possible way: fanatical about rank; always wanting to be nearest The Palace; all having the finest and youngest mistresses; taking slight at the smallest issue; and constantly stabbing each other in the back.

Albert looked at Stein, and said, "Sadly, that does strike very close to the quick, very close indeed. Replace 'The Palace' with 'Berghof' and actually it's an exact parallel. Only last week, Paul related to me that when they were recently touring northern France, there was a caravan of 18 huge Mercedes—you know the dual axle type you see in all the newsreels. According to Paul, they were all competing to be the second car. Of course, for many in the procession their stomachs got the better of them and they stopped for a three-hour lunch."

"Well, according to Six Fingers, the problem in Tokyo is that the Army and Navy are at loggerheads and the Navy has built this huge fleet."

Stein learned forward for emphasis, "A huge fleet that is sucking the country dry of oil."

Stein explained how after the Washington Naval Agreement of 5/5/3, the Japanese were outraged when they were treated as the junior partner—Britain and America could lay down five times the amount of new tonnage to Japan's paltry three times. The Japanese contemptuously referred to it as 'Rolls Royce/Rolls Royce/Ford'. The Japanese had simply ignored the limitations—as had America—and had built, overbuilt actually, a navy fit for a celestial emperor, not just a mortal one. But this created a huge problem by consuming scarce and very expensive imported oil at an even faster rate.

"They have built huge oil tanks, but with no oil to put in them, these tanks are useless. A blind man can see the Japanese with their so-called East Asian Co-Prosperity Sphere need all the oil of Malaya and the Dutch East Indies. This is their only option—I doubt they can go through the Canal and sail up to Texas and the American Gulf states and ask for a few spare hundred million gallons, especially now that the Americans have unilaterally and illegally banned all Japanese ships from what they like to call 'their' canal."

"It does not take much to read between the lines of the letters from Six Fingers to see this."

"Yes, he is proud of the navy his country has built in less than twenty years, but he is a realist—they have this huge navy and no oil. At least we have the Romanian fields."

Albert inwardly smiled at the Professor's choice of pronouns.

"So?"

"So the Japanese are a far greater liability to Germany than the Italians, odd though that sounds."

"So America is the enemy of the *Reich*?"

"Not at all—the Americans are no one's enemy at present, but I think it likely they will become Japan's enemy soon."

"And the outcome?"

Stein ignored the question and asked,

"Albert, do you remember how the Russians fought before their surrender in 1917? To remind you, they had one rifle for every four solders, so one soldier would race toward our troops, be shot down dead, and then the second Russian soldier would jump up and snatch the dead man's rifle—a baton race of the dead as it were. That, my dear Albert, is what you are facing when your Chancellor turns to the East, as he will sooner or later. The Slav peasants all fear everything, from the crowing of the cock at sunrise to the gentle dusk. But, in spite of all these fears—or perhaps it is because of all these fears—they all passionately love Mother Russia, regardless of whom the current autocrat is."

Albert rose and thanked his host,

"With your permission, I should like to return tomorrow to discuss this further Professor."

Stein scowled at Albert, "Only if you call me Julius."

They both laughed.

Albert left his mentor's apartment and walked back down the slight hill back to the Trois Couronnes. In the distance on the left he could see the simmering lights of Avian, famed for its baths and waters and at the other end of the lake the early evening lights around Geneva with its banks and casinos and whores.

Albert's mind turned over the idea of Japan's feet of clay and the possibility of America having the power of Hercules. Stein had no reason to dissimulate; there was no motive—or benefit—Stein could gain. Actually, the opposite—wise and prescient counsel could only help Stein.

Albert returned to the hotel. In the early evenings the hotel was the epitome of Swiss dullness. Albert was greeted by the concierge, a man Albert had hand-picked for the job four years early; Albert was nothing if not thorough.

"He's in room 301," the concierge whispered.

Albert nodded.

The lift was the old-fashioned type with the pair of wrought iron doors.

Closing the wrought iron doors himself Albert rotated the long brass control arm clockwise and took the lift to the third floor.

Albert found 301 immediately—across the archway from the lift, it was the first door on the left.

As Albert reached the outer door of the suite, the door was opened by one of Berlin's leading actresses, a personal favorite of the Propaganda Minister—"Suzanne" or something like that, Albert vaguely remembered—Paul had mentioned her, actually gushed about her, but Albert had not been in the mood to listen.

"Suzanne" smiled at Albert and left along with another actress Albert recognized from the Berlin stage.

Albert entered and greeted his guest. Lord Nasherton was a tall man in his forties. His family had made its fortune in Scotland with patented inventions centering around bobbins and spools for automatic knitting machines. Over time, the Scots had moved south. Nasherton retained his Caledonian cautiousness regarding money and had handsomely improved the family fortune.

Albert asked after Lord Nasherton's two daughters.

"Yes, both bonny. Shiny coats and wet noses."

Albert remembered Nasherton's tedious habit of referring to his daughters in terms of a dog's health.

"And young Stephen looks like he will be going to Sandhurst this year. I understand there is something of a European war going on at present—hate to see Stephen miss the party."

Both men laughed.

Albert sat down and Nasherton poured Albert a very generous whiskey—a single-malt that Nasherton favored.

Small talk, idle gossip for a few minutes about Nasterton's subterfuge about travelling to Spain and then to Italy and finally to Switzerland.

The single malt warmed Albert and he guessed Nasherton was already sufficient relaxed after the actresses and now the Scotch for Albert's spiel. Nasherton's German was as good as Albert's.

So Albert got to the point immediately, which was: England was bankrupt after the Great War, same as Germany, not quite as apparent as Germany's penury, but real just the same; France was a whore, and a disheveled whore at that—a Montmartre strumpet, not a nice, fresh, young, polite "niece" who you could readily take to polite society; Russia—not Germany—was England's natural adversary—the Slavs had created a crazy patchwork quilt of Europe's races that make the place a constant powder keg; dealing with the Americans would surely spell the end of the British Empire

Nasherton listened pensively; he had the gift of quiet. In some ways an odd man—just moments ago carousing with two of the *Reich's* finest ladies, and now he had smoothly shifted gears and was giving Albert his complete attention.

"I agree, but what on Earth can we possibly do?"

Albert explained that the thinking in Germany—meaning what Albert and some of the senior military types suspected—was that the biggest obstacle to an immediate cessation of all hostilities between Germany and England was Churchill. With Churchill gone, progress could be made; a peace could easily be brokered, the Empire saved, and Germany could get on with the business at hand, which was the annihilation of the hated *Bolsheviks*, and the final stabilization of Central Europe.

Nasherton stood and walked to the window. He looked out over the lake to the lights of Avian and then to the mountains in France—in spite of it being September, tiny swatches of last winter's snow were still visible on the highest peaks.

He turned to Albert.

"Of course, I completely agree. How could I not agree? Winston is rum, he's always been rum, always will be rum. Just look at the '15 disaster in the Dardanelles. Last year, God only knows why we didn't get Halifax. Churchill is as brave as a bulldog, but with about the same amount of brains. (Albert, have you ever noticed how Winston actually looks a lot like a bulldog? Of a certain bastard line, a miscegenate line. Have you ever noticed that?) And he deludes himself that he has the Yanks in his pocket—he's in for a rude awaking there; that is for certain. Actually, Albert, it just *may* be possible to get rid of Winston—just kick him up stairs somewhere—just as he himself did to poor old David Windsor. As for David, well his only problem—his only weakness—is that he loves to have *that* woman's mouth over his you-know-what. But nevertheless, how in God's name did the King of England fall for that Baltimore tart, a blind man could see she was a slut of the worst sort."

Albert smiled thinly, but only to be polite.

Albert had heard that the former king loved Wallis Simpson's attention, and—from a different source—that she was renowned throughout Europe as being without equal at being able to get the dead to rise to life again. It was said she had tricks with her mouth for her most prestigious lovers, tricks she had learned before her marriage to Mr. Simpson when she worked in some of the very finest brothels in Shanghai.

Nasherton went on, "And Winston is far too friendly with the frogs—damn French had done little or nothing for England, simply whine all the time. Look at this total rout three months back at Dunkirk—what a total cock up."

"But, be sure Albert; we'd have to play our cards very shrewdly—a little too early and one or both of us find ourselves swinging from the end of a rope—remember 'treason' is often defined as 'premature truth,' so timing is of the essence."

Albert agreed.

Nasherton returned to the PM,

"It never ceases to amaze me that Winston has the gall to spout the nonsense he does. In reality, he is the opposite of what the press and the cinema newsreels portray. Truth be told, he is a bully and he becomes a violent and bitter bully when drunk, which essentially means any time after two in the afternoon. And his friends are so ill-chosen. Add to this that he is constantly in debt—he does not have a bean to his name."

Nasherton then expounded on the wisdom of a coalition, possible with Halifax as the new PM. On and on the two men planned and plotted.

After an hour of extremely useful conversation, Nasherton suggested a detailed plan of campaign.

"Well that's damn well done it—I think we two have done a fine job of reshaping the map of Europe here in quiet Vevey this evening."

Albert fell silent but thought Nasherton was not overstating the case.

Nasherton said, "I always find that playing Bismarck makes me so extremely randy—no chance of calling back those two Berlin sweeties, is there Albert?"

Albert simply smiled, and lifted the telephone receiver. Nasherton couldn't quite make out the instructions, but his curiosity was satisfied five minutes later when four exquisite Japanese young ladies quietly glided in. They were four of the most beautiful women he had ever seen. All in the Fall/Winter '41 Chanel. The four were all extremely quiet and moved as if any sound was an insult to their hosts. Only later did Nasherton learn that their classic geisha training forbad them from talking while they walked—they could only speak when stationary.

It was clear from their carriage and demureness that they were very different from white women—all four affected a shyness (and perhaps they truly were shy?). They all looked like models from Paris, but with soft almond eyes and the most delicate soft skin Nasherton had ever seen—their skin seemed to have no pores. They varied in height tremendously—the tallest, in heels, was taller than Nasherton, who was a good six-foot, while the shortest, even in heels was only of modest height.

What both men noticed was the four girls were already excited. This was to be expected; whereas men are excited simply by visual physical beauty, women are far more sophisticated in this area—power, and the confidence to wield that power are what excite all women. In fact, the nipples on the short one with the very large 33EE bust were already boldly standing forth even through her Chanel jacket, not just minor bumps that could be occasionally glimpsed for a second in a perfect light by a timid, blinking schoolboy, but rather two hard pebbles proudly standing clear for everyone to see.

Nasherton was an old hand at this; he had handled—"entertained" was his euphemism—four girls simultaneously on a number of occasions; in Paris as well as in Capri. Paris had been disappointing, and Capri was as bad, for in both cases the white girls clearly had no interest and were simply watching the clock; if whores could only realize that the way to a men's heart is though his trousers—an investment of just a few weeks of carefully concocted amorous attention could easily lead to a very expensive divorce in a year or two, but most working girls only wanted to leave they second they were paid.

Nasherton thought these Japanese girls looked different. Time would tell.

"Oh my, Albert, you have truly outdone yourself. I thought the two German starlets were outstanding, but I have never seen women such as these. How on earth did you get hold of them?"

Before Albert could answer there was a polite knock on the door.

Albert opened the outer door of the suite. The Swiss waiter from the restaurant on the ground floor rolled in a table covered with a starched white linen tablecloth. On the table were four servings of the house's specialty—Vevey chocolate cake.

Also on the cart in an ice bucket was a bottle of Dom Pérignon 1921. Nasherton whistled, "Oh God, a '21; that's got to be one of the finest years ever."

Albert agreed.

Ever the connoisseur, Nasherton explained the importance of the 1921 vintage to the girls, who looked to him like they were dutiful school girls cramming for an important examination. Nasherton himself took a sip, and confirmed the glorious bouquet of the '21—the vanilla and sandalwood. But Nasherton did not linger, he—like Albert—realized the goal was to relax the young ladies to make them all the more excited, and all the more pliable.

"So ladies, enjoy this wonderful vintage and your cake, we have some men's talk to do. But please take your time to relax and enjoy the wonderful Swiss chocolate cake. Please, take your time."

Albert and Nasherton repaired to the other room in the suite.

"I say old boy, those girls are all absolutely first rate. You must explain how you came across them."

Albert explained,

"I've put Gabrielle Chanel up at The Ritz. She's getting her own suite in a few weeks, but she is currently in suite 254, and I've made sure she is completely happy—you know these fashion types are actually very simple to please, once you get past the initial pretensions and bombast. Her current suite is the one used by the American writer Fitzgerald, to write his book *The Great Gatsby*. I had the girls spend a few weeks with Gabrielle, for just a little more polishing: hair, shoes, and all those things that makes for a perfect lady, not really necessary with these Japanese girls, but could not hurt. One thing you will notice tonight is the exquisite softness of these girls' skin—and that no Japanese woman ever suffers from cellulite. I don't know the reason, perhaps it is the diet with all the fish. I don't know but compared even to the two starlets, these girls are head and shoulders above. And compared to white women, these girls' skin is amazing, as is the level of excitement."

"The other thing you will notice is how all these Japanese women love men and more than anything love to pamper men. I've never seen the like—the mentality of Japanese women is so refreshing. Not only are they raw sexual animals under that facade of demure shyness, but they simply *know* so much more than white girls—these Japanese girls know of hidden pleasure points on a man's body that you don't even know you have. And they can excite a man far more intensely and for a far longer period of time; they are simply sublime. Their attitude is based on the greater pleasure they give to the man the greater their self-esteem—essentially the opposite of white women."

Albert paused and looked into the middle distance and smiled one of his rare smiles as Nasherton listened intently.

After a decent interval, the two men returned to their guests.

The four girls all thanked the men for the wonderful cake and the delicious champagne.

The one with the very large chest had taken her jacket off. While doing so, both men noticed her nipples were now larger than ever, and she could see the two men saw this and this made her even more excited to show off her raw excitement to them. It was like a bullfight in extremely slow motion, the teasing and the toying and the languid passes of the cape.

Nasherton meandered over to Albert who was by now standing at the window smoking a cigar.

"I want the little one first."

Albert looked at him, "The one with the huge tits?"

Nasherton nodded.

"Yes. Yes, wise choice as she is the hottest of the four, but I suggest you have her last," Albert said with an air of authority.

Nasherton wryly smiled, "So, you have vetted all, have you?"

Albert smiled and said, "James, do you expect me not to have ensured all are of the first water?"

At this Nasherton laughed, "You are one of a kind, Albert."

"She loves it front or back and she loves two men at once. Get her on her back some time tonight and watch her tits move—they are like two eggs in a frying pan as the pan is shaken. When you're on top, grasp her arms, as circus acrobats do, so you can pull her towards you. She loves that, and she is extremely loud. Their loudness is one thing that differentiates these girls from white girls."

"Two eggs, yes, I know what you mean. Loud, that's wonderful," Nasherton acknowledged.

"By the by old boy, what are the girls' names?

Albert explained, "Masayo is this short one with the huge chest; Mikui is the tall one; Suki is the one with the blonde highlights; Yuki is the one with the extremely pretty face. But you can forget about their names, as you will shortly see."

Nasherton frowned good-naturedly, "If you say so, old boy."

The room was extremely large. By the windows was a small writing desk. Looking out on the lake were two pairs of tall but narrow glass doors that reached from the floor to the ceiling, closing both pairs of doors blocked all sound from the outside. The room was dominated by a huge bed—it was large enough to comfortable sleep eight, but it was designed to *hold*, rather than sleep, eight.

Nasherton commented on the bed's size, "Christ Alive, Albert, that's a monster—we really need it all?"

Albert smiled and simply said, "Yes."

The four girls finished their cake and the bottle of champagne had been emptied. One of the girls had put the bottle upside down into the ice bucket as she had seen Albert do at the Ritz in Paris. Albert—ever the technocrat—said to Nasherton, "the chocolate excites them and they weigh half as much as a man so it's the same as if they had shared two bottles of champagne wine."

Nasherton piped in, "and of course, bubbly is absorbed very quickly, so these four are all chomping at the bit, if you forgive the metaphor. I think it's time to strike the colors."

Albert nodded.

Nasherton went over to the girls—"like the cake?"

"Oh yes, it was the best we've ever had, sir—even better than in Paris," said the tall one.

The "sir" made Nasherton more excited.

"Now why don't you girls take your shoes off and all sit on the bed together? Then I have a little game we can all play."

The four girls complied and before too long all four were giggling and sitting on the bed, all looking—and feeling—very relaxed and comfortable.

Nasherton turned off all the lights in the room apart from the small light on the writing desk by the window. Nasherton had opened the bottle of Bordeaux white wine the waiter had brought earlier with an ice bucket.

"People generally don't appreciate the white Bordeaux, this white wine is so often ignored—say 'Bordeaux' and everyone always thinks of the reds," he said as he poured himself and Albert each a glass.

"Now, girls, the champagne has relaxed you and it is warm and safe here. What I want you to do Masayo and Suki is to remove the jackets and undo the blouses of the other two girls to entertain Albert and me, but very, very slowly please. You must go very, very slowly. We are not in a race this evening, you understand?"

This instantly led to four pairs of hands in front of four faces, and more giggling. It was, as all in the huge room knew, the protocol of graceful—but entirely artificial—innocence. It was play acting of a reluctance that was completely false—the four girls were each dying to feel a man inside them and deep inside them—"to hit the top of my roof" as one said later.

With a speed that made a lie of the giggles, the two girls started undressing the other two girls.

By now James and Albert were sitting on each side of the small side table, sipping the chilled white Bordeaux.

Nasherton confided to Albert, "This is the part I love most, the slow teasing. And this is where you really see the quality of the girl—all can get on their backs and do the completion, but few can properly *tease* a man. This is the start of the gold medal event, like in Berlin in '36 at your games."

It was clear to Albert that Nasherton was both experienced and knowledgeable.

The two girls had removed first the jackets and then the creamy white blouses of the other two, but then there was a change to the plan: the other two then removed the blouses of Masayo and Suki, so all four girls were sitting on the bed in the brassieres and skirts— it was a very arousing sight.

From across the room, Nasherton said, "ladies, please take the shoulder straps of your brassieres down, very slowly please."

This time there was no giggling as the soft light combined with the champagne had made the four young women even more excited. Now they wanted to exhibit themselves, to excite a man, to be ravished, to get the men to do what men are supposed to do to women. So Suki gently pulled her brassiere straps down and then, without being asked, she took her brassiere off. She had been sitting on the bed with her ankles crossed. When she removed her brassiere she uncrossed her ankles and put her right hand on the hem of her skirt, and she proceeded to pull her skirt up a little at first, and then more so the clips of her garter belt were showing. The very slow and elegant teasing was working; Nasherton smiled.

The other three girls did the same. Now the female carnal competitive instincts stirred—this was what the two men had been planning, and had been expecting; both men said nothing.

Far more than most men realize, women are sexually extremely competitive. This is especially true when two or more women are dishabille—they compete to entice the male to mount them first, and they will do just about anything to get the Téte de Cuvée of the man's seed. And this was the case of the extremely randy four Japanese beauties—each wanted to be the first to get the full load of seed inside them, they all wanted the full load, not a paltry second, or the dribble of a third.

In less than a minute all four girls were sitting upright on edge of the huge bed wearing only their garter belts, stockings, and skirts. And by now all four had hitched their skirts up. Masayo's skirt was all the way up to her garter belt and while her knees were getting further and further apart as she got more and more excited. She was clearly inviting the men to ravish her, and to do so now. And her nipples were like two very large peas—so round and hard.

All of this the two men took in and enjoyed, savoring their wine. The men's lack of action now teased the girls. "My pearl was aching so much, she wanted to feel a man inside her," Masayo later confided to Albert.

Little in life could match this incandescent level of pleasure—the power the two men felt as they watched the four girls vie with each other for the men's attention.

(And as both men knew from experience, it was going to get very loud, very soon.)

It had started with Masayo, but very soon all four girls had hitched their skirts up to their waists. As none was wearing panties, their dark shadows were clear to see, even in the modest soft light of the writing desk's lamp.

Nasherton stood and walked over to the bed.

The first girl—it was Suki—looked up and brought her knees up, her hands were now on her knees and she opened her legs. Her breasts were round, sagging the slightest amount, and her breathing shortened; she was more than ready.

Nasherton then walked around the foot of the bed to the other side, to review Masayo who was in same position. Nasherton could not help but notice a small dark patch on the strict and starched white hotel sheets. James smiled—Masayo was so excited that some of her juices had already made a small wet spot—there were no panties to absorb the wetness. As Nasherton approached, Masayo slowly moved her hands from her knees, up her inner thigh to her garter belt. It was easy for her to use her fingers to open her lips. At the top of her lips Nasherton could see her large round pink pearl. James smiled—he had seen some large clits in his time, but this was by far the largest, and all of her lower lips were dashed with wetness. Nasherton decided she would be the last one "in the rotation"—by forcing her to be last she would be begging for it, just as Albert had recommended.

This mock inspection took minutes and the girls were getting more and more excited.

Albert, still seated, then said, "Girls, please show James our little surprise."

This time their level of excitement (and their desire to be serviced, and serviced as soon as possible) trumped any faux modest giggles.

The four girls stood up from the edge of the bed and removed their skirts, placing the skirts in a neat pile on the large chair in the corner of the room. All four girls wore identical white garter belts and white stockings.

The four girls stood naked apart from their garter belts and stockings. Nasherton noticed a curious thing: their feminine hairs had all been trimmed short, but even more curious was that they had been shaved in such a way that they each had roman numerals from "I" to "IIII."

Nasherton laughed at this piece of theater, and said, "Albert, this reminds me of one of my trips to Hong Kong. I was at one of the better whore houses in Kowloon where all the girls wore just an enameled medallion with a number hanging around their necks on a brass chain. I seem to remember I had Number 5 and Number 17 that night. But your approach, Albert, is more in keeping with the spirit of the event."

"Thank you ladies, please sit down on the bed together, please," Nasherton requested.

The two men could see each of the four was slowly going mad with desire to feel a man inside her.

Nasherton smiled and said, *sotto voce*, "we are driving them crazy."

Albert nodded. Nasherton poured more white wine, and said,

"Leave the girls stew in their own juice, as it were, for a moment."

(He knew that the forced delay would make all four lubricate even more.)

26

✠ ✠ ✠

The two men's attention now returned to the four girls who were now so excited that they were all giggling and panting. Nasherton noticed with approval that the presence of these two powerful men had affected the other three girls as well: the three other girls now all had tiny wet dots under them, although they all tried to hide their wet spot—Power As The Ultimate Aphrodisiac.

Albert asked how they liked meeting Coco.

At the mention of Gabrielle Chanel's name, the girls burst into a plethora of thanks.

The room was not cold, but now all the girls' nipples were taut and erect. The teasing phase was the one all men enjoy the most. And knowing that the sensation would be one of a very smooth entry into an extremely wet, but at the same time young and tight, Japanese gem.

And the girls were so excited, as they constantly crossed and uncrossed their legs, not out of modesty, but to be able to increase their excitement by squeezing themselves.

Albert sat at the writing table with the still chilled Bordeaux white, smoking. He was interested to see Nasherton's play acting with the girls. After a long while, Nasherton removed his suit jacket and sat on the bed evenly dividing the girls into two pairs. Masayo—the short one with the huge chest—was first to act, which was not surprising as she was already starting to pant, and the panting was not light—her breathlessness was not forced and the panting made her huge chest rise and fall ever so slightly. She was panting just from anticipation—neither man had actually touched her. Uncontrollable desire on her part made her recklessly—her hand on Nasherton's knee as a matter of formality. Then, instantly, she slid it all the way up and she was confidently stroking him. She wore her hair in an elegant Parisian page-boy bob; the color was a very dark brown with the slightest hint of some blonde highlights, the overall effect was dazzling. The instant she started stroking Nasherton—and Nasherton was very hard—Masayo's panting increased and she leant over and kissed Nasherton's neck, brushing against him with her nipples.

During this foreplay and teasing, the other three girls were undressing Nasherton so his hands were free to first cup, and then squeeze Masayo's huge breasts. Nasherton found them to be soft but surprisingly firm, and he himself was getting even harder. After Suki had wiggled off Nasherton's trousers, after first having removed his shoes, Masayo got on her knees and put Nasherton into her mouth. At first, just the head, and then all the shaft—she loved that slight gagging when a big man's head reached her throat. Naturally enough, Nasherton had some early milk, which she licked with the tip of her tongue—a little salty but not unpleasant, she thought.

All the time Masayo was on her knees she was moaning loudly, as the act of sucking was exciting her even more.

As Albert had explained to Nasherton earlier, all Japanese women think it an honor to be allowed to "dine." And the ultimate delight was to be able to swallow all of a man's milk.

"They're very different in that respect to white women, aren't they?"

Albert agreed, and went on, ever the analytical German,

"There are other major differences as well. For one thing, Japanese women all climax four or five times and you can often feel the early contractions and pulsations the moment you enter. More and more these days, white women cannot complete—they get close but then you have to stop and they are forced to resort to the crude and primitive act of using their own fingers. In contrast, these Japanese girls are essentially walking, slightly chilled, orgasms."

Nasherton smiled at Albert's use of the adjective—"Only slightly chilled, Albert?"

Ever serious, Albert continued his lecture,

"Oh yes. They have this extremely demure front and modesty because they are all firecrackers ready to explode. Diametrically opposed to white women, who are typically bluster on the outside but frigid on the inside. When I recruited these four beautiful young girls in Paris, I took them in pairs to dinner. They had not met me or each other beforehand. And both pairs thought it completely natural and normal to reward their host that night, and reward their host mightily. All four lack the white woman's posturing, the whining, and the thinking she was God's gift; no, none of that, just a sophisticated two hours of a half-dozen female climaxes by each girl. Then the expected nap."

Albert continued wistfully,

"Yes, I like the Ritz in Paris, as the beds are so large there. On the night I interviewed Masayo and Suki, after the nocturnal frivolities the two girls had a bath together, both chattering away like elegant little sparrows. Looking at them against the soft pinks and peaches of the marbled bathroom, well I can tell you that that alone was very exciting and had I not been previously completely drained..."

Albert smiled as he remembered those delightful times in Paris with these glorious Japanese women.

✠ ✠ ✠

Masayo's mouth had worked almost too well, as Nasherton had to pull her off him. She was panting loudly and she got up and lay on her back on the bed; she took her fingers and again opened her lower lips. Normally, Nasherton felt this common female guile was a little too anatomical for his tastes, but the way this Japanese girl did it, it seemed perfectly natural. Immediately he pushed himself completely inside her, up to the hilt. Her almond-shaped soft eyes opened in shock, then surprise, then delight. Just as Albert had predicted, her contractions started pulsing immediately. She was panting loudly now and had her hands behind him and she was pulling him in, deeper and deeper. All the time, she was speaking Japanese in a high-pitched but soft voice saying, *"iku iku; iku iku; iku iku; iku iku; iku iku."* Albert later explained the precise translation was the opposite of the European phrase—the Japanese girls say "I am going," meaning "I am going out of control," which in the case of Masayo was certainly true.

While Nasherton thrust inside, Masayo pushed herself up; her eyes opened wide and she was quiet for a second or two—she let out a deep guttural moan as Nasherton felt her grip him like no other woman ever had.

"It was not just the power, but also the duration—she was like that for ten seconds—her wide eyes stared at me and she seemed to be in a state of suspended animation. All this time the noise came from her. Then she relaxed. Before she relaxed I could not move in or out she gripped me so firmly. Amazing. Then there were a series of rapid but very light and soft contractions. Then it was over for her. She just lay where panting. I noticed all her body was covered with a sheen of perspiration; her back was dripping wet with perspiration."

✠ ✠ ✠

The effect on the other three girls watching Nasherton on top of Masayo was to make them all as excited as Masayo. All three got on their hands and knees on the bed, and Suki asked Nasherton, "please sample all of us and tell us which one you prefer."

In contrast to Nasherton's prior experiences with four girls in Paris and Capri, this was *crème de la crème*. In his life, Nasherton had never experienced such excitement as this evening, as these three girls unselfconsciously—and with complete naturalness—offered themselves to the Englishman to be ravished. And Nasherton observed one other thing: these girls were enjoying themselves more than he was. That truly shocked him, and it went a long way in explaining Albert's love of Japanese women on his visits to Paris.

After the excitement, Albert bid *adieu* to a very tired, but extraordinarily well satiated, Nasherton and quietly retired to his suite.

2: Jules Verne's Spaceship

THE NEXT MORNING, ALBERT had an early breakfast of crois-
sants and real coffee in the spacious restaurant on the ground floor
overlooking the lake. There were just a few small sail boats on the
lake, all slowly crawling along the lake's edge like sleepy beetles.
There was no sight of Nasherton and there was only one other table
occupied—the four girls all flattering Albert with admiring glances.
On his way out, he went over to their table and thanked them for all
the "hard work" the previous night. Amidst the giggles, a flurry of
hands to faces and downturned eyes resulted.

"Actually we were going to thank you and Mr. Nasherton for
such an exciting evening," Masayo said.

Astonishingly, her nipples were already visible at eight in the
morning at the breakfast table.

Albert smiled to himself at the unlimited carnal energy of these
young Japanese women—he was reminded of Nasherton's comments about the somnolent ways of plump English girls (Nasherton
had actually been more explicit), and Albert was also reminded of
the complete absence of cellulite.

✖ ✖ ✖

After saying goodbye to the four young ladies, Albert leisurely strolled up the path to the professor's apartment. In the bright sunlight of the cloudless morning, the church bells called the faithful to worship.

Once at the front door, Albert knocked and the professor opened the door, this time bright and alert.

Conspiratorially, Stein confided that his wife had left to visit her friend in Geneva and, so—slipping into his American patois—Stein quietly proclaimed, "The coast is clear."

Sitting on the terrace sipping coffee, Albert asked about America and the current state of its economy.

Stein said, "Wait here please."

He left the terrace, returning a moment later with a magazine.

"Here is the most authoritative source we in the field of political economy have. It is a magazine that rather pompously likes to call itself a 'newspaper' so as to differentiate itself from the likes of Luce's meretricious *Time* magazine and to associate itself with the quality broadsheets like *The Times* of London, and the *Financial Times*, and even the rather parochial *New York Times*."

Stein opened the issue to the page he had marked with a slip of paper.

"The gist of this comment is that in 1930 the income of the average American was one-third greater than that of the average Britisher, but now at the end of the decade it is at par—the average American's income is now the same as that of an Englishman. This is just 10 short years. And remember, apart from coal, Britain is devoid of natural resources, natural resources that the United States has in abundance. The magazine has recently commented that the United States seems to have forgotten how to grow. It also notes that in the five years from 1933 to 1938 Roosevelt has spent more money than the total money spent by all his 31 predecessors combined, and those presidents had to fund a terrible civil war as well as the Great War."

"Really, more than the previous 31 presidents, combined? Are you sure, is that really possible?" Albert said, clearly very surprised.

"Yes, it's rather amazing, isn't it?"

Clearly warming to his subject, Stein continued, Socrates-like, "Is there hunger in Germany, today? What about America?"

"Sadly, there is hunger in all countries. Sad, little children go to bed hungry in all the world's countries. I would like to think that in Germany since '33, we have improved the lot of our people, at least I hope we have."

"And I think you have improved the lot of the average person in Germany, at least as far as their belly goes. And I agree with you—sadly, there is hunger in all countries. So let me put you in a spaceship from Jules Verne with engines made of the finest Krupp steel, and take you to a planet where there is hunger but the state dictates that six million pigs be slaughtered and destroyed and wasted. Or that farmers are paid *not* to grow food, even while honorable young boys in Brooklyn hang themselves so as to not be a burden on their starving family. Or that a farmer who wants to put an acre under crop needs a government license or is fined $1,000 a day. Or that chefs are told how they must make macaroni. Or that a housewife buying a chicken cannot select the bird, but must by law be given a chicken at random. So on this fantastical planet, housewives lose their primal right of selecting the food with which to feed their family. What would you say about that place?"

"Six million pigs wasted. Well, Professor, you're right, it is science fiction—no such place could possibly exist."

"Albert, I have described exact events that have happened in America in the past ten years."

Stein smiled at Albert's frown.

"Bizarre though it sounds, since 1933, Germany's economy has been freer than that of United States. Obviously I am speaking strictly about just the political economy, not about personal freedom, as Germany's one-party dictatorship is just that—a dictatorship, and like all dictatorship it is a terribly brutal one: Kristallnacht; the endless hounding of Jews; the copying of the Britishers' concentration camps of their South African wars of the last century—the list of brutalities is endless.

"But in purely political economic terms, there is less regulation and less harassment of German business men today than on the other side of the Atlantic. The wasting of the six million pigs was mandated by Roosevelt in an insane attempt to increase farm prices. Of course, that's just another way of increasing hunger and starvation—the government told poor people to pay more to help farmers. And take the treatment of Henry Ford. When Ford refused to sign the so-called Blue Eagle code of Roosevelt's NIRA and follow instructions that he must *increase* the prices of his cars, he was mercilessly persecuted. Ford was threatened by the brutal commissar, an impetuous bully named Hugh Johnson, a man Stalin would admire, both for his drinking and his explosive temper. About Ford, Roosevelt actually said at one of his press conferences that '*we have got to eliminate the purchase of Ford cars from all government tenders;*' these are his own words, the words of the current American president. And when Ford bid on a contract for 500 trucks for one of Roosevelt's alphabet soups—I think it was the CCC—his bid was $169,000 less than the nearest rival and yet it was rejected.

"Now Roosevelt did not start the Depression, that dubious honor is reserved for his predecessor, President Hoover, whose nickname was the 'Boy Wonder.' Actually the Republican Hoover was much closer to Roosevelt's ideas than most people realize: Hoover's backward view was that 'high wages creates prosperity.' Obviously, the opposite is true. So before Roosevelt, after the crash of '29, Hoover forced companies to keep unsustainable and artificially high wages; these companies did what any rational business man would do, they simply laid off employees, which had precisely the opposite effect of what Hoover wanted. You see Albert, Hoover and Roosevelt both think that government is wiser than the market place. The Republican Hoover was the opposite of his predecessor, the Republican president Coolidge. Whereas Coolidge thought government interference caused more problems than it solved, Hoover loved to jump in, to 'do something'—to do anything at all, no matter how bad. But the problem is that the things that Hoover did were hugely damaging. In the last stock market panic in '21— before Hoover—companies laid off workers and business improved with the increased efficiencies, and then they hire back the workers, and more workers as well. One of the many things Hoover did that was so damaging in the '29 Panic was he forbad companies to fire people, so many companies just went broke and shut their doors. And Hoover forced the railroad companies to spend one billion dollars, and this was at a time when the entire U.S. government budget totaled just three billion dollars."

At this juncture the two men were joined by Sebastian, Stein's faithful dachshund, who wandered onto the terrace and after approvingly sniffing Albert's shoes, proceeded to lie in the patch of sunlight.

"He will get too hot in a few minutes and then will move back inside."

Sure enough, after two minutes Stein's prediction came true.

"Albert, you see, these days governments around the world believe that business men are more immoral than politicians, when in fact the opposite is actually true. A business man is only interested in one thing, namely profits, but politicians and their kow-towing minions in universities are only interested in power, hidden under the pretense of 'helping people.' Academics the world over all think they are greatly superior beings, blessed with superior intellects, conversing with superior colleagues, discussing superior topics, holidaying in superior locales, ineffectively lusting after pretty young waitresses. Fortunately, academicians are generally ignored. But politicians nowadays believe that only they can manage their country's political economy, and that the normal and natural cathartic effects of busting of periodic bubbles with panics are unnatural. Politicians and my fellow academics don't realize that they do more damage in the long term by trying to change human nature. And business men and especially investors are driven by the contradictory emotions of greed and fear. It would be nice to have the ideal of the 'rational man' but sadly people are not rational; they are primeval and crude and unpredictable; this will never change.

"Now, the Jules Verne space ship stories are all true stories from America. Both Hoover and Roosevelt believe in action and in gambling with taxpayers' money. Most important of all, they both believe in bigness, especially bigness in government. While the government of Hoover created the depression, the government of Roosevelt has made it the Great Depression. Hoover's government encouraged farmers to over-produce, which they were happy to do. Of course, the inevitable happened and farm prices collapsed—as there was more supply than demand. So the Hoover government put an infected and unclean bandage on another infected and unclean bandage and wasted 500 million U.S. dollars in the process trying to fix this disaster.

"And here is the most interesting point: in the same country, with the same workers, but with a different government in the decade of the 1920s, the country boomed. As you know this is a period that I have written about extensively and, of course, I observed the early years of the decade myself first hand when I taught at Harvard. In this period, President Coolidge was extremely conservative and believed that not interfering with the American economy was the best approach. Coolidge kept income tax rates low so that successful businessmen could plow back their profits into their businesses, which business men love to do as they generally treat their companies as their own little babies. And with these low taxes, Coolidge was rewarded with a robust economy. Of course, human greed took this too far, as it always does, and the American stock market became irrationally exuberant—the wild 'animal spirits' took over. For example, common people started to gamble on stocks and often did so using borrowed money called 'margin' and this was not investing for retirement but rather gambling.

"They were able to do this only because the Federal Reserve flooded the market in 1927 with cheap money. At one stage in 1928, the amount of this so-called 'margin' was equivalent to 18% of the entire American economy. Of course, with all this loose money, stock prices increased at an unnatural rate—from spring of '27 to summer of '29, the stock index, called the 'Dow Jones' doubled from 200 to 381. So when the selling started in late 1929, the second human emotion of fear took over, and the stock market collapsed faster than it had expanded in the prior two years. Now this extremely unpleasant—but essential—purging would have been relatively short-lived, but for the all-knowing politicians and the Federal Reserve, who continued to interfere. The only way to tame animal spirits is by people losing money, not by government rules to 'regulate' the markets—until the last trumpet sounds, people will always be driven by greed and fear.

"Albert, if you see people are oversized children, as I do, rather than as rational beings, then it is clear that these children need to be chastised rather than pampered. And farmers are a perfect example. In all countries, farmers are the greatest whiners—they complain about everything. The best solution is not to cave into their complaints, but rather to ignore them. Let the weaker farmers give up or sell out, this is called the marketplace, and the marketplace is just a formalization of human nature."

"The marketplace is simply an abstraction of humanity, of human behavior, of greed and of fear, of the very nature of people with their strengths and weaknesses. While politicians and their toadies in academia are convinced they can rise above this baseness, they are wrong. Politicians like to boast on the radio that they can quote 'make the world a better place;' actually, it is business that makes the world a better place, but the process is an ugly one, and people's loathing of this ugliness is what politicians prey on. Politicians all promise to 'control,' to 'regulate,' to 'improve.' Their fanciful schemes often do generate a short-term euphoria, but this drug quickly wears off, and like the person running down stairs, more and more is needed—it is simply an addiction. And as the addiction rapidly grows, it needs to be fed more and more."

3: Cold Comfort for Fatso

THE SUN FEEBLY STRUGGLED—and failed—to warm Haus Wachenfeld. The SS guards tried to convince each other that the winter was not as bad as the ice winter of the previous year—the winter of '39 was the coldest in living memory: canals froze; hearty livestock died in the fields before they could be shepherded to barns; and airplane engines refused to start. But the current winter was just as severe.

A roaring fire in the great room burnt brightly. In front of it, and hogging most of it, stood a very fat man of medium height wearing the extravagant uniform of *Reichsmarshall*. He looked like a colonel from a Latin America banana republic, his chest was so encrustulated with medals. In his right hand he held a jewel-encrusted baton. He was explaining—or rather pontificating—to the very small man standing beside him how his baton was a full three centimeters longer than any other in the *Reich*. The other man succeeded in appearing impressed, and flattered the fat man by saying that it was not just his baton that was longer. The fat man liked this phallic reference and laughed.

"So, Paul, why are we here? I was planning to hunt mountain goats at Oberlech for the entire week. Couldn't this meeting wait?"

The small man said nothing.

Presently, their host entered and approached the fire. He was careful not to catch the fat man's eye. The host suggested they move to the secure room in the second basement. At this, the fat man's smile disappeared and he started to sense trouble, as one of his Austrian mountain goats senses danger even before picking up the scent of the hunters.

The three walked to the lift that Bormann had had installed in a single 24-hour period when the owner was away in Berlin. When the host first saw the miracle, he simply shook his head and smiled, and without thinking, said to all how he could never do without Bormann; a remark Bormann repeated one hundred times over the next few months.

The three men entered the lift and the host inserted the key in the brass control panel of electric push buttons and pressed the button for the second basement, which could only be accessed via the lift and only by someone with the key (Bormann held the only other key.)

Silently, the Siemens lift descended and the three men walked to the first room. The entire second basement was uncharacteristically spartan—it was like a prison, or more accurately, a dungeon. Unfinished concrete marked the walls of the corridor and even the room itself was sparse—a large desk, four arm chairs, a moving picture screen and a new electrical phonograph were the only furnishings. The room was well lit by electric lights and heated by two three-bar electric heaters.

The fat man's unease increased.

"I hope you two are not going to do me in here," he laughed, trying to get a reaction.

The complete lack of response from the other two really alarmed him. After all, these were two of his oldest comrades in the Struggle, and why he had marched with the host in Munich in '23.

"Please sit here, Paul has something to show you. But before we start, I'd like to ask you just one question: do you know a man by the name of Prodromos Athanasiadis Bodosakis? Here is a photograph of this man."

At this, Goering blanched and started to sweat, a little at first.

"Well, I meet lots of men. Why Paul, this chap looks like your nemesis from the old times in Berlin—the old police chief who persecuted you."

Even the reference to the hated Bernhard Weiss generated no response from the slight man.

"It's a simple question, Hermann," the host asked, almost plaintively.

"Do you know him? Yes or no?"

The fat man realized his comrade from the old days was trying to help him.

Goering said nothing.

After a moment, the host said, with no enthusiasm, "Paul, run the film please."

The little man walked to the film projector and started the film. The film was very grainy and the sound was at times inaudible, but the film showed the fat man and the Greek in a hotel room. The room was clearly a large and expensive suite in the old style of a grand hotel of Vienna or Paris or even Rome.

About a minute into the film, Goering was heard to ask about "the second payment." The Greek told the fat man that the money was already in the fat man's bank account in Switzerland. On the film, Goering could be seen rubbing his hands—like a stereotype of the greedy avarice of the bankers he professed to hate.

"Carinhall needs more work, so this will be most useful" the grainy figure was heard—and seen—to reply.

A few seconds later the film ended.

"So I met this fellow, he was simply a business colleague, what of it?" Goering lied.

The little man handed Goering a folder of a dozen sheets of paper.

Goering opened it and looked.

"Fuck—what is this, who forged my signature?" the confused fat man first confessed and then tried to bluster in the same sentence.

"You supplied the fucking Republicans with arms which they used to kill German soldiers. You arranged for the fucking ship *Bramhill* to deliver 19,000 rifles, and 100 machines guns, and 28 million rounds in '36. You're a fucking traitor. Brave Germans soldiers you helped kill, you, you fucking piece of shit, you fucking animal, you coward, you killed German soldiers in Spain."

On and on went the rant, and the host was screaming. His face red, the veins in his temple throbbing.

The little man said nothing.

"Do you realize, you piece of shit, what would happen if my enemies got this folder. Germany as we know it would be finished— the *Wehrmacht* are just waiting for me to make a mistake like this. It would be '34 all over again, but not Röhm this time, it would be me. You're finished, it's over, you piece of shit."

By now, Goering's hands were shaking.

"Wolf, Wolf, look, you're right, you are always right. I was wrong, but look, no one other than the three of us needs to know," Goering pleaded using the host's nickname that only the host's closest intimates used.

"Are you a complete fucking moron, you fucking idiot—what about the French who filmed this, what about our agents in Switzerland, what about those cocksucking Swiss bankers, and what about that fucking Greek—he is a total whore, just like you? Just one of these needs talk and we are all fucked—you, me, Paul, everyone. You're done, it's over, and you, you fucking moron, are finished."

Suddenly, Goering remembered the meeting—it was in Paris in '36. He was in real trouble. That fucking Greek cunt.

"I can retire, I will go quietly. Paul can tell the world I am ill."

Without saying a word, the host moved to the desk and pressed a hidden electric buzzer. Four SS guards entered the room; the host nodded. With the authority of the German Chancellor, the four lifted Goering bodily and stood him against the cold concrete wall.

Goering's eyes opened wide.

"You can't be..."

Before he could finish his sentence the four had discharged their Lugers. The corpse of the former Great War flying ace—leader of the late Red Baron's Flying Circus—slumped to the floor.

"Get rid of him," the host said flatly, as if ordering one of his favorite cream tarts.

"Bury him behind the greenhouse. Use the picks to break the frozen ground."

Paul and the host left, taking with them the folders.

Once back in the great room, the host said,

"What the hell was he thinking; did he not realize the implications? With your radio work and my performances, we've neatly been able to trick the world. The rest of the world wonders openmouthed at the power and the solidarity of the German juggernaut. Damn, if the world actually knew how frail we actually are, how brittle this spider's web I try to hold together. Jesus. Remember when we marched into the Rhineland in '36? I know those fools in the *Wehrmacht* were ready to skin me alive if the democracies so much as farted. But as the British and French did nothing, our Struggle survived to live another day. Do you think the British are weak and as brittle as we are? Surely not—they cannot be that frail and fragile. For one thing, they have a wonderful ruling class. And that big moat, of course. But we have to be so, so careful. You know, I loved Hermann, and he had so many great and redeeming features, but perhaps it was the morphine for the shoulder. Perhaps it was the loss of his Swedish princess. Perhaps it was... God, I don't know. He was such a tower of strength. Such a titan."

Paul nodded at the host's puerile musings. Business-like, as always, he said,

"Well, we'll announce that he was killed by the Resistance while visiting France. Always good to bank some grievances, real or imagined. If the truth ever does get out, we will simply deny it; we should be safe for at least six months. Now regarding these files, I see absolutely no reason to keep them or the film. Yes, of course you are correct, there are other copies—those fucking French can be depended on to try to fuck us, but thank goodness we found this out now and not later."

Back in the great room, Paul fed one sheet at a time on to the fire. Even the plain, buff-colored manila folders themselves were burnt. The cellulose film burnt with an acrid smell and filled the great room with lachrymose fumes. After a few minutes, all that remained was the charred steel spool.

"My sister is going to be livid when she cleans the fireplace on Monday," the host said referring his sister who managed the household and who insisted on cleaning the fireplace herself, in spite of having over two dozen servants at her disposal.

4: Sasaki's Franklins

Tokyo
Wednesday, 8 January 1941

THE SNOW HAD STARTED TUESDAY, just before midnight. By mid-morning most of it had melted, but at dawn, for two hours in the soft morning pastels, the city had taken on a new and softer character. At nine o'clock that morning, two blocks from the sprawling 845 acres of the Imperial Palace, Kaito Sasaki looked out the window from his third-floor office. An organic chemist by trade, Sasaki often wondered at the vicissitudes of life that had transported him from his simple and not entirely unpleasant job at the leading paper maker in sleepy northern Hokkaido to the center of power at the Bank of Japan.

"It's all about the paper," his boss enthusiastically explained an hour later to the assembled meeting of bored generals and admirals.

"You see, gentlemen, it is the paper that makes a banknote and we're fortunate to have seconded Mr. Sasaki from the Hokkaido Fine Paper Mill Company. Sasaki is the world's leading authority on mixing textures and rags from different mills and has written extensively on the topic and the related topic of the varying levels of acidity of rag-to-paper mixtures. I will not bore you with pH levels, but believe me, Sasaki is the expert."

While trying to politely stay interested, the assembled admirals and generals were fast losing interest.

"Please open the envelopes in front of you. Inside, you will find ten American 100-dollar bills. Please examine each and make two piles to tell me which are the ones Sasaki and his team here at the Bank created and which are the genuine American bills."

This request suddenly reenergized the meeting and the four admirals and five generals each opened his envelope and enthusiastically examined all ten bank notes. The bank notes varied from pristine to worn, ragged, and torn. As Sasaki expected the two piles were made based on freshness, and the testers proclaimed—to a man—that the Japanese forgeries were the fresh ones, while the old and tattered bills were the real American ones.

Sasaki's boss smiled slightly and nodded his head.

"I see, so the clean new bills are the ones Sasaki printed and the old ones are the American ones. Of course, this is a completely reasonable and logical conclusion."

"It is also a completely false one;" this announcement got everyone's attention.

"You see gentlemen, every bank note you have in front of you was printed in the basement of this building here in Tokyo.

The liberal Admiral of the group—only 49 years old and one of the youngest Admirals in the Japanese Navy—asked,

"Excuse me, but can you tell me the cost of printing these bills?"

"I think I will let Sasaki answer that as it was he and his team that made these earth-shattering weapons."

The room turned to Sasaki who rose and bowed slightly.

"These bills have a total cost of about three yen each, or, if you like, three American cents."

"Oh," the Admiral said.

Sasaki continued,

"That includes the ink, the paper, the electricity for the printing and cutting presses, and I added one-tenth of a yen for rent of the building."

The Admiral laughed, "Well, we must never forget the rent."

Everyone laughed. Some so as to not stand out, and some to appear to understand. Those who did understand instantly saw the astonishing new weapon Sasaki had built.

Sasaki showed he understood the Admiral by adding,

"So, one million U.S. dollars consisting of 10,000 bills would cost about 30,000 yen or about 300 real U.S. dollars.

"Fuck me," an old Admiral from the days of Tsushima said in the succinct way that all navies speak.

"Indeed, gentlemen, indeed. Do remember gentlemen all this paper money is actually just paper. It has no value. It is not like silver or gold, that have real value and value across the world—one country's 100-dollar bill is just another country's toilet paper," Sasaki's boss politely explained.

"Look at this," he said as he passed around another American 100-dollar bill.

Frowns ensued.

"You see this is also an American 100-dollar bill, but this fragile piece of paper was issued in 1864 by the rebel southern states. And its value today is, of course, zero. It's an interesting relic to people like us here at the bank, but it simply serves to remind us of the completely worthlessness of paper money. Here is another, this one is a 100-billion *Reichmark* note from 1923. Again, just another silly slip of paper."

Sasaki's boss turned philosophical,

"Remember what the Russian revolutionist chap V. I. Lenin liked to say, 'The best way to destroy the capitalist system is to debauch the currency.' Well, Sasaki has created an amazing weapon that we can use to destroy the enemy with paper, ink, and a printing

49

press. Gentlemen, I will also remind you that in most parts of the world the American 100-dollar bill is the *de facto* currency, and that 80% of all U.S. currency is denominated in 100-dollar bills. Moreover, all the paper, ink, plates and printing machinery are Japanese. And with the development in 1939 and 1940 of the New Trunk Line—the Shinkansen—modern steam locomotives now being developed that travel at 200 kph. So the time to carry the paper from northern Japan to Tokyo has been compressed to under 10 hours. And with our presses in the basements of this building we can create silly slips of paper with the nominal value of one hundred million U.S. dollars per day."

Sasaki's boss paused, and then said:

"Our respectful suggestion at the Bank is that we supply our Army and our Navy each with 100 million dollars' worth of currency each week. You gentlemen can use it for whatever purpose you see fit."

A doubting voice asked,

"This is all well and good, and this is a wonderful plan—or perhaps I should say 'scheme.' But we in this room are not experts—will these bank notes be accepted? Are they good enough?"

Sasaki's boss smiled,

"A very, very wise question. Since January of last year, we at the Bank have been supplying Sasaki's new weapon to our agents in the American possessions of the Hawaiian Islands and the Philippines, as well as to the American cities of San Francisco and New York. In total, close to seventy million dollars of Sasaki's currency has been spent, and not one bill has been rejected."

This raised eyebrows.

The doubter congratulated Sasaki who quietly rose and bowed deeply.

Another voice asked about the old papers,

"If these bills were made recently, how is it that some of the bills look so old?"

Sasaki explained it was actually a simple process; the first step was agents in the United States collected 1,200 real Franklins of all grades (here Sasaki inadvertently slipped into jargon). By tabulating the dates of the bills and then grading each bill, Sasaki's people could determine the average life of a real U.S. 100-dollar bill to be between seven to nine years. Sasaki smiled and explained that the early Japanese bills' paper was a little too robust and the rag content had to be reduced to better mimic the bills printed by the U.S. Treasury—the Sasaki bill lasted longer than the genuine ones printed in Washington. Sasaki had printed bills with dates from 1928 to 1939. To age the bills, the Bank had bought and installed 200 of the latest Bendix automatic clothes washing machines, all bolted to the floor on the second basement and third basement of this very building. Sasaki smiled and explained that these machines had been bought in San Francisco and shipped to Tokyo in 1938 and 1939 had been paid for with Sasaki's own notes. At this last revelation the room burst out laughing.

Sasaki continued,

"So once cut, we dry the newly printed bills in an array of air dryers. Once completely dry, we then wash the bills in the Bendix machines one or more times with a small amount of water and a tiny amount of white vinegar to mimic human sweat. Then we dry the bills again in dryers that rotate and tumble the bills to create a used appearance and texture."

Until this meeting, just about everyone in the room was aware of the terrible and wasteful bickering that never stopped between the army and the navy. As one of the older admirals had explained to one of his military cohorts,

"It's like a scab—you know you should not pick at it, but you cannot help it.

The senior general listening to this agreed,

"God alive, we're all Japanese but we're constantly doing this. It's all because we have too much time and too little to do, but these times are when we should be using this precious time for planning, not fucking fighting."

This meeting might just heal this canker and end the scratching—a printing press more powerful than the world's largest dreadnought.

5: Kobayashi's Friday Night Soirées

Mexico City, the Old Town
Friday, 31 January 1941

KOBAYASHI ALWAYS MISSED NAGANO this time of year; most of the season's snow would be in the mountains and the cool and clean air of winter would be a pleasant change after the hot Japanese summer. But in Mexico City, the air was dry and chilly and the altitude was always trying, especially for Kobayashi's wife Akiko who hates the thin dry air of the Mexican winter.

On the last day of January, Kobayashi had received his first shipment of boxes from Tokyo. The labels specified "phonograph records," and that was true—each of the five boxes when opened did present the viewer with a collection of 78 rpm phonograph records, each of Bakelite and about as thick as a man's small finger. However, removing the three phonograph records in each box revealed the real contents—two million U.S. dollars in used $100 bills.

Before sending some of the first batch of bills from the Bank of Japan, Kobayashi had the embassy buy and install an old-fashioned safe with only three keys. One key he gave to the urbane ambassador, hidden inside his beloved original German copy of "On War"—he knew the ambassador would lose the key if Kobayashi had simply given him the key, so the book ruse seemed sensible. The second key he kept. The third key he buried in the yard, while his wife watched. The frost was in the ground so it took time with the gardener's pick, but after 30 minutes the job was done.

The five boxes arrived each month at the end of the month until Kobayashi telegraphed Tokyo to send no more—he was collecting boxes faster than he could buy favors, and favors were cheap in Mexico. At the peak, he counted over 46 million dollars in his safe—enough to buy a small country or start a war, he mused.

Thus, Kobayashi set to work and was busy throughout all of 1941 dispensing gifts large and small to just about all the Federal politicians and most Federal judges in Mexico City.

It did not take very long at all to establish "friendships" with the Mexicans. Actually, once word got out about Kobayashi's "stipends," "consulting fees," "honorariums," and "speaking fees," people—and influential people at that—had actually started to drop by the embassy unannounced to visit with the Senior Diplomatic Attaché, to offer him any services he may be in need of.

"Nothing is too small, and if you need my help, well you know we Mexicans are all friendly and peace-loving people. We just want to make our country stronger."

Starting in April, Kobayashi and the ambassador started hosting getting-to-know-you dinners, initially once a month, then twice a month and by July, once a week—the Friday night soirée quickly became the event to be seen at. All recipients of Kobayashi's generosity would appear at least once a month, and sometimes once a week. Here, the bait was not Mammon but flesh—Kobayashi ensured there were always at least 30 girls—his "geishas" as he called them; mostly Mexican, with a few bored blonde adventuresses from Europe. Kobayashi had provided all the girls with false, but realistic looking, business cards that the girls could readily pass out to a potential client in full view of the client's wife or current mistress.

THE GODDESS OF FORTUNE

Then on the following Monday or Tuesday, the client would drop by, "strictly on business, you will understand Señor Kobayashi," was the most common refrain.

This worked very well with one minor problem when one of the girls—against Kobayashi's express instructions—had been moonlighting and caught a particularly nasty dose of the clap from three U.S. sailors, which in the small and intimate circle of Mexico City's diplomatic elite spread like wildfire. The girl was cured, and then fired. With little difficulty, Kobayashi was able to divert the blame to the ambassador at the Canadian embassy, whose wife was known to be extra-ordinarily ugly.

By July, Kobayashi had established an "institute"—more of a clubhouse actually, but the title on the brass plate outside the double glass doors with the black wrought iron institute monographs (designed by Akiko), was "Mexico-Japan Institute for Trade and Friendship." The office Kobayashi had chosen had itself made the newspapers as one with the largest and most spacious lobbies—the lobby was a full two stories high. The leading quality paper, El Universal, sent two reporters and a photographer.

In the middle of the back wall sat two receptionists who had been selected because of their height—in flats both were a good head taller than Kobayashi, and they towered over him in when they wore heels; a second requirement was having the most beautiful legs in Mexico City. Kobayashi dressed them in black sling backs and the tightest knee-length black pencil dresses imaginable. From the knees down, visible to all the world, were the finest calves ever to grace womanhood.

Kobayashi paid the two women three times what they requested and expected, and he received complete loyalty and discretion. Needless to say, the recipients of Kobayashi's gifts dropped by in droves, sometimes singularly, but more often in twos or threes, to crudely ogle and whisper. A few had the courage to request an introduction from Kobayashi, but Kobayashi would simply shrug and tell the requester it was—sadly—not possible.

On the third floor, Kobayashi had hired a team of five people, a salesman who formerly sold Cadillac cars to the Mexico City elite, three lawyers, and an advertising man. All Mexico City-born and -bred, and—apart from the salesmen—all with university degrees. From this group, Kobayashi created what was to become the "Peace, Friendship, And Fidelity Agreement Between Mexico And Japan." On the 1st of October, the President of Mexico welcomed the Prime Minister of Japan, Mr. Konoe, and both signed the agreement. When Konoe asked Kobayashi about the astonishingly warm welcome he had received, Kobayashi simply told the Prime Minister that all Mexicans were very friendly. What neither premier knew was that the agreement had a secret annex that stipulated that Mexico would attack the United States and would reclaim Arizona and New Mexico if any form—the secret annex was quite clear about this—if *any* form of hostilities should break out between Japan and the United States. Also stipulated in the secret annex was the provision of 20 million per month to Mexico, in U.S. 100-dollar bills, of course.

Regarding the meeting of the two premiers, the *New York Times* carried one column, on page eight.

6: Big André's Suggestion

Montreal
Thursday, 6 February 1941

KOBAYASHI'S COHORT IN MONTREAL, Oonishi by name, could not be more different from Kobayashi—tall, gangling, thin, a chain smoker, never married and a lover of whisky, with or without the "e." Akiko knew from experience that three small glasses of sake and her husband's face would glow red like a glowing coal in a winter fire; Oonishi, in contrast, seemed to live on whisky and he was not choosy—Japanese, naturally enough, was his favorite, the 21-year-old Suntory Hibiki as his personal favorite, but American bourbon, Irish and Scotch all were welcome friends to Oonishi. Oonishi's strategy was the same as that of Kobayashi—buy favors. But Oonishi's tactic was the opposite. A formal agreement was not possible, especially after Canada's 1935 trade agreement with the United States. But what was possible was to stir up the embers of the Québécois discontent. Discontent that was often barely hidden, and sometimes not hidden at all.

With Oonishi's friendly, boozy ways, he was seen by one and all as safe, friendly and unthreatening, albeit a little loud at times. But Québécois in their rough ways did not resent this in the slightest; actually, it made him a welcome change from the Anglos from Toronto and Ottawa with their superior airs. Paradoxically, Oonishi's

French was that of the upper class of Paris, and while this seemed in direct contrast to his plebian manner, the Québécois were quite taken by it, as their French was universally ridiculed by Parisians, as all Québécois well knew. The paradox was rewarded with Oonishi's nickname—*Bien-Aimé,* as in Well-Loved, the people's name of Louis XV of "Après-Moi-Le-Déluge" fame.

"Bien" trolled the bars near the Army transportation depots and near the roundhouses of the Canadian Pacific railroad. Striking up friendships, well lubricated by the unexpected luxury of top-shelf liquors, was simplicity itself—these bars were strictly male and strictly working class. Occasionally—on the anniversary of a mythical ancient festival Oonishi would concoct—it would be open bar all night long, and all bar owners loved the way Oonishi would pay the day before the Honorable Anniversary in American currency. It was child's play itself for a trained and disciplined agent like Oonishi to simply listen and grade the grumbling of the working men. Most complaints were dreck, but occasionally Oonishi detected a speck of gold. This was the case with Big André, a very short man with big shoulders, and—like all short men—a chip on his shoulder.

In Oonishi's one-time cipher reports to Tokyo he described how André's complaints were systemic, not simply operational—into his cups, André would complain about the hated Anglos and the "Yankees" as he always called the Americans, "you know, Bien, the Yankees are the bosses in Canada, it is the fucking Yankees who control Canada, they tell those ball-less wonders in Toronto what to do and the Anglos simply do it. Total piss-ants. We French need to do something, 'cos the fucking Anglos will do dick."

Oonishi nodded, said little, apart from agreeing with these words of profound wisdom.

"Yes, many Japanese feel the same way—that the Americans are trying to rule the world."

"Right! Rule the fucking world, that's just what those cunts are trying to do; fucking cunts!" André pounded his fist on the bar.

Oonishi sighed, "If there was just something we could do."

"Don't worry Bien, I will think of something."

Oonishi ordered another round—André was drinking his beloved Molson, while Oonishi, in a patriotic flourish, was drinking—or pretending to drink—Canadian Club. Oonishi steered the conversation to André's favorite topic, and a topic that he genuinely did know well: Walschaert versus Stephenson valve gear, or more specifically the wonders of Walschaert.

To make engineer, André had to bribe the examiner with $1,000 of Oonishi's money as Andre was well under the minimum height requirement. As making engineer was André's life-long dream— "since I was five"—Oonishi was now André's very best friend—"ask me to do anything and I will do it for you."

André expounded on the manifold benefits of Walschaert valve gear,

"You see, Bien, with the Walschaert valve gear, a steam locomotive is more efficient. We engineers (he paused for effect), all want to save as much coal as possible, while still keeping on time. With the old Stephenson gear, it is hit or miss—no control."

Oonishi waited for the obligatory barb, and did not have to wait long,

"Of course, those fucking southern cunts only adopted Walschaert after we Canadians did."

Oonishi listened intently, not because of his agent training in working an asset, but because André held more than a spec of gold.

"The valve gear is the brain of a modern steam locomotive—all else is just steel and brass and copper, but the control is all in the valve gear. Disable or damage the valve gear and the locomotive is dead."

On hearing this last sentence, Oonishi looked up at the door as a rare woman entered. She was a working girl from the docks on the river, well past her prime, and she made her way to a table at the back where four lumberjacks sat.

"Yes, that is fine, but removing a piece of the valve gear is of no use, even your American friends are not that stupid—they could easily replace it."

André's face instantly flushed,

"No, no, no. Totally wrong. Totally wrong, Bien."

"You see, the trick is to add a holed coin to the upper oiler."

Oonishi played the fool and looked as stupid as he could, "So?"

"So? Fucking so? I tell you what-the-fuck so."

André assumed a conspiratorial crouch over the bar and moved just a little closer to his benefactor.

"I can make a coin that will allow the loco to get onto the main line, travel for two or three hours. And then..."

Oonishi's face was that of a timid 15 year old school boy getting a tutorial from the senior master.

"And then," André smiled, put his fists together and made a motion as if to wring a chicken's neck.

"But how can you be so sure?"

"Look, I am an engineer (another pause for effect) and in advanced training class we are trained on the flow rate of lubricating oil for all points of the valve gear. As a warning to all of us, one of our instructors started the valve gear on the training chassis in the morning class and he reduced the oil flow to the upper oiler by exactly one-third. Sure as Yankees are pigs, the upper oiler seized right on time at two in the afternoon."

"So these are special coins, right?"

André looked at Oonishi as if speaking to a simple child, he sighed, "Yeah, really special—take a Canadian quarter, drill a 3/8th inch in hole in it, and Bien, you have your special coin."

"Oh, I am sorry Engineer Maloit, I am just a lay person, you are the engineer," Oonishi said with as much candor as he could muster. Enunciating André's formal title was all that was needed to make the little man Oonishi's marionette.

The engineer simply nodded, "That is fine my friend, you are not an engineer, you could not possibly know this."

They went back to drinking as the whore left with two of the lumberjacks.

While a completely reasonable assumption on the part of André, in this case the engineer was wrong—two years earlier this precise illustration had been given to Oonishi in the test area of the sprawling locomotive works in Yokohama. And on that day, the instructor had used an American quarter and had even used a 3/8th inch drill—from one of the two drill sets in the locomotive works that was not metric. The results were the same.

Next to his beloved locomotives and drinking on Oonishi's wallet, André's other fascination in life was greyhound racing, or more specifically losing money betting on three-legged greyhounds. As fate would have it, André lived within walking distance of one of the two indoor greyhound tracks in Montreal. It was not uncommon for André to seek out his friend on a Monday evening and seek "a little loan," which Oonishi was more than happy to provide. By Thursday the loan had been forgotten. Oonishi slowly fed André's habit with a simple expedient:

"André, could I ask you do to me a favor? Could you take this $100 and wager it for me. With you, it is more like an investment than a wager."

André would always beam at this, and would happily agree. In this way, Oonishi encouraged André to attend every meeting.

By late November, Oonishi friends in the bar warned him that André was "owing some very nasty people a lot of money, so be careful, Bien."

While working André, Oonishi also recruited five other engineers—one for each of the other mainline roundhouses of the Canadian Pacific railroad. In addition, at the bars servicing the thirsty mechanics of the army motor pool depots, Oonishi had slowly recruited 12 mechanics, and like all men, these men had their own foibles and not a few of these foibles were weaknesses: one mechanic was running a wife and three different mistresses at the same time; one was always drinking at work, and always getting caught and always surviving only because of Oonishi's "loans" used to bribe his accusers; one loved to steal from the depot—"everyone does it"—and the depot police would visit his house at the most inopportune times (the depot police got anonymous tips by telephone, the caller speaking impeccable French); one loved the high life in Montreal where he particularly liked to employ the services of the high-end whores, generally more than one at a time.

Of course, like the six engineers, the 12 mechanics were each in their own cell—independent and self-standing agents; the loss of one would in no way impinge on any other agent.

Like André and his Walschaert gear, the 12 mechanics all had their own ideas about the best way to disable a truck, from the simple to the fantastic. As was to be shown on the second week in December, one of the most effective approaches was simply to snip the bowden cable of the truck's choke with a small pair of bolt cutters—wire cutters could be used but in practice it proved to be difficult, whereas a small pair of bolt cutters—it was the proverbial hot knife through butter. In the frigid Canadian winter, trying to start a gasoline engine without a choke would typically flatten the battery and with 48 trucks in a pool, all trying to be mustered at once, well the effect was chaos.

Three of the other mechanics used the tried-and-true sugar in the fuel tank. This worked extremely well, especially after Oonishi had specified the finest icing sugar—poured faster and dissolved faster than regular sugar. A patriotic variant used by two other mechanics was Canadian maple syrup.

Running and protecting and nurturing and controlling all these agents was exhausting—Oonishi was out every night, sometimes visiting two bars in one evening. However, Oonishi's little black book was full. All he needed was the signal from Tokyo.

7: The Well-Read War Plan

Washington
Wednesday, 2 July 1941

THE CITY WAS UNCHARACTERISTICALLY QUIET as the exodus from the capital was all but complete for the Friday holiday. A few stayed in the sweltering heat and humidity of the middle of the torpid summer. After lunch, the President was talking to his two favorites in his Brains Trust—Harry Hopkins and Rex Tugwell, seconded for the next six months from his day job working for the Little Flower in New York City. The discussion moved to Japan and the possible actions the Japanese might take.

Professor Tugwell was describing how he had just re-read Senator Beveridge's 1900 speech.

"That old GOP war horse?" the President snorted.

"Yes, Mr. President, but his views are actually close to your own."

The President's always-moving eyebrows rose.

"Do tell, Rex."

"There is a copy here for you. I've underlined in pencil the more important passages."

"Rex, I am a politician. I talk, I don't read; you tell me why that old codger's speech is important, and get me a drink while you're up."

Tugwell proceeded to do both, after giving the President a dry martini; it was his third for the afternoon.

"Beveridge's gist is that the Pacific is the ocean of commerce, the most important ocean in the world, and as such is critical for the U.S. to dominate. The loss of control or even the impingement of control of the Pacific would be a disaster for this country. As Beveridge stated, '*the Pacific is the ocean of the commerce of the future. Most future wars will be conflicts for commerce, for example for oil. The power that rules the Pacific, therefore, is the power that rules the world.*' I have to admit that is astounding prescience for something written over 40 years ago. With the current situation, his words ring true."

Roosevelt said nothing for a moment, then impulsively he picked up the telephone.

"Have Johnston come in, please. OK, then send him in."

There was a knock on the door and a man entered. It was Johnston's junior that all three knew by sight.

"Send over WPR please." the President said.

The man nodded and left.

Tugwell and Hopkins looked at each other, it was clear neither knew what the President had just requested.

In retrospect, it was hard to say if it was the martinis or just the President's natural impulsiveness with all things, from the national economy to the government's Hyper Secrets.

The President smiled,

"By rights, I should not be showing either of you this material as it is graded HS, but I think in the current circumstances it is justified."

Both men knew that Hyper Secret, or "HS" as the President called it, was a rare grade of document above Top Secret. Both were secretly thrilled to see this document as neither had seen a Hyper Secret before.

✠ ✠ ✠

After the President's request, the duty officer called B3 of the Archives and requested WPR be sent to the White House immediately.

The request caught the archivist by surprise as requests for Hyper Secrets were rare.

The archivist in turn called the transport pool and spoke to the officer in charge,

"I need a Locked Wrist to go to 1600."

The transport officer swore under his breath—he and Hoffmann were the only two Locked Wrists on duty, and he sure as hell was not going to do it; for one thing, a Locked Wrist was duty bound to stay at the White House until the President was finished with the document, and he still remembered the time in '37 when he was the Locked Wrist and the President had forgotten to return the document and had gone to bed—he waited all night at the White House until 9 a.m. the next morning.

"Hoffmann, you've got a LW for 1600. Go to B3 and get the documents. Here, take this."

The officer passed Hoffmann the key to the wrist bracelet.

"Obviously, keep this hush hush as I should not be giving you the wrist key, but these Locked Wrist assignments are a huge pain in the ass."

Hoffmann knew as the officer often regaled him with the horror of the night in '37 and how the briefcase locked to his wrist had been a millstone when he tried to relieve himself—"God, it's like having one arm cut off" the officer had told Hoffmann. Hoffmann nodded.

Hoffmann locked the bracelet to his wrist, dropped the key into his left-hand pocket and departed.

On the way out, Hoffmann dialed a local Washington telephone number and let it ring three times.

✠ ✠ ✠

Those three rings electrified the man hearing it. The special phone had only rung twice in the past year. The man jumped up and ran down the hallway.

"Sir, we just got a three-ring."

Schneider, the cultural attaché of the German embassy, looked up.

"We are very lucky today," he said with a smile.

"Alert the team and have Louise come to see me."

The man nodded.

Louise Koch's title was Deputy Assistant Cultural Attaché and, like her boss Schneider, she was a security agent—a polite word for spy.

While Schneider was starting to run to fat, Louise personified the German ideal of womanhood: tall—in sling backs she was half a head taller than Schneider, blonde with blue eyes. But all men's attention was drawn to her body—her legs were model-thin but her chest was a breath-taking 36 with a C cup that actually was closer to a D. And her breasts were uncommonly firm and taut—she wore a brassiere not, as most women do, for support, but rather to tone down her appearance.

For this assignment there would be no brassiere and under her skirt just a garter belt and stockings—"commando" was Schneider's term. Only 24 years old, her judgment was surprisingly good, and she knew how to control just about every man. Schneider was an exception and she liked him a great deal for his professionalism, which was just another term for his organizational and training skills.

When she had first arrived at the embassy, he had spoken to her in depth about controlling the men who were her targets, and they both had enjoyed the "training" in his office—she loved the feel and smell of men and she liked to be able to combine this pleasure with the training with Schneider. He had shown her a few secrets that she had already put to good use. However, his training on responses to accidents was the most useful. She herself had never thought about—and was thus embarrassed by—accidents; she did not know what to say. He had taught her how glib and superficial most men are and how just a few choice words were all that were needed: for an early completion: "Oh my God you made me come so hard, please stop now or I will have an attack of the heart;" for a very small man, "that's too big for me;" for a fat man, "thank God you're not all skin and bones;" for a skinny man, "thank God you're not fat—I hate it when a fat man is on top of me and often I cannot feel him inside me."

They both laughed when she had recounted to Schneider how these lines of flummery were perfect—"they always work," she said, surprised.

She was proud of her body and found it exhilarating to use it. Even as she walked into Schneider's office she was already excited and aroused; her nipples broadcast as much.

"This is a big one, Louise, so take your time. It is Washington, so it is a safe and simple town. The standard approach."

And as an afterthought,

"And do enjoy yourself, you can tell me all about it later."

This last remark reminded her how lucky she was—she had come to love having two or three men in a day; together was good, but separately indulged her dreams of misbehaving. And she loved to feel Schneider inside her while still wet from the target. She thrilled to think about his soft, gentle, but dominating techniques.

The main team had assembled in the back court of the embassy. Louise had already left, walking five blocks before hailing a Checker for the Willard.

✠ ✠ ✠

The transport pool driver drove Hoffmann first to the archive building and then to the White House. Hoffmann was pleased to see it
was Jones, a dim-witted boy from Biloxi, Mississippi. It seemed
Jones's main interests were disposing of his wages as quickly as possible in illegal poker games, and as Jones put it, "dames."

Hoffmann chatted to Jones as Jones drove the dun-colored
Packard.

"With a car like this, you must get all the dames."

"I wish, sir."

"Well, you'll get lucky sooner or later. All the pool drivers tell
me the dames love just to sit in the back and they are always very
generous."

Jones snickered.

"Maybe I will get lucky," Jones said in an accent so thick
Hoffmann would not have understood had he not started the
conversation.

Hoffmann entered the archive building and took the elevator
to B3, where the WPR folder was placed in the security briefcase.

"No idea when I will be back," Hoffmann said.

The officer simply grunted, "Yeah, God knows."

Hoffmann made his way to the White House and told Jones to
wait for him behind the Willard hotel.

"I will meet you there—make sure to behave and don't do anything I wouldn't do."

Jones laughed.

"He's a nice boy," Hoffmann thought.

On entering the White House, Hoffmann was taken directly
to the Oval Office. The President gave the security key to Hopkins and asked Hopkins to unlock the case and remove the thin,
bright-orange folder. Hopkins complied and Hoffmann left to wait

in the basement cafeteria while the great men upstairs pondered the contents.

An hour later, the call came to return to the Oval Office. The President was, as before, sitting behind his desk. Hoffmann placed the brief case on the table and discretely averted his eyes. Hopkins placed the folder in the case and locked the peripheral locks.

"All set, Captain, and thank you," said the President.

"Yes sir, Mr. President," and Hoffmann gave his best parade-ground salute and left.

Jones had dropped off Hoffmann and drove the one block to the Willard, almost getting into a traffic accident in the process. Jones parked behind the hotel, locked the car, and sauntered into the hotel, not that he had the courage to even order a cup of coffee, but he liked to look at all the high-class "dames." Like many, he heard that the Willard was a favorite area for politicians to meet their mistresses. Whether true or not, Jones did not care, he just loved to gawk. He summoned up the courage to change two dollar bills for the Willard Coins—the Willard cleaned all coins they collected in huge vats in the basement and gave all who asked for change these sparkling pristine coins, "just like the moment they were minted" was the hotel's boast. Many years later the St. Francis in San Francisco adopted the same practice, but by then "Willard Coins" was part of the American vocabulary.

After an hour and lots of unfriendly looks from the concierge, Jones left to return to his car.

As he turned the corner, he saw what he first thought was someone trying to break into his car. He panicked for an instant, then he realized it was a "dame" using his side mirror to touch up her lip stick. The captain had been right—it was his lucky day. The car was parked so Louise could not see Jones approaching but she knew exactly what would happen—a ham-fisted and painfully obvious pass.

"You know there's a law against that—it's called illegal use of government property."

Louise gasped and turned.

Jones eyes went directly to her nipples, as she knew they would.

"Oh please, don't report me," she said.

"You know there is a much bigger mirror inside; let me show you."

Louise smiled, demure and vulnerable, as Schneider had taught her.

Jones unlocked the car and opened the door for the lady. Louise entered, making sure her pencil skirt rode up her legs to mid-thigh. None of this was lost on Jones, who showed her the larger interior side mirror.

"You're so kind, but why does a military vehicle have mirrors at all? I mean you soldier men are warriors and fighters."

This last sentence she asked with just a hint of breathlessness. Then came the fluttering of the eyelashes, the look down at his baggy serge trousers, and the mandatory touching of her hair—the universal sign of a woman in heat. Jones's inexperience made him miss this last sign, but he was already well and truly hooked.

Louise—like all experienced women—loved to tease, to flirt, and to tempt a man-child like Jones. She was expecting him to be a 30-second man. No matter, Schneider would make her climax four or five times when she returned to his office—she could already smell the leather of his chair on which she would be forced face down—she loved to be taken from behind by a confident and forceful man. Power.

"Well, Miss, you see here in D.C., we drivers drive not just military men, but also their wives and..."

"Their mistresses," excitedly Louise finished the sentence.

"Oh God, that is so exciting; do you ever get excited doing this, you know driving these girls—does that excite you? Driving the mistresses? Driving these young women who love to do it for money? You know, do sex for money? God, if it was me, I would be so excited. I would love to be paid for sex. Tell me some stories, what have you seen? You must have seen a lot, right? Gosh, that is so exciting. Have you seen things?"

Her breathlessness was genuine—"just think about it and start touching yourself—excite yourself and you will excite him," were Schneider's words. And Schneider's advice worked.

While asking, Louise was ever so slightly rubbing her legs, not just for poor Jones, but also because she was getting genuinely aroused and she could squeeze herself to deepen and extend her excitement, just as her mentor had said.

Jones told her the story of when he picked up a four-star general and his 19-year-old "niece"—"actually, here from the Willard." The general was a desk soldier in the quartermaster corp or some other backwater.

"Well, he was three sheets, no make that four sheets," he said, laughing at his own description.

The girl looked at Jones in the rear view mirror and their eyes meet.

"It was as if she was wishing it was me in the back," Jones said with a rare flash of insight.

"Go on," Louise said.

"Well, she disappeared from view for a minute, and then I could see the old general close his eyes and start to moan."

With this, Louise pulled her dress up and started touching herself. Many men think a woman touching them is the most exciting element in foreplay, but as Louise knew so well when she touched *herself* the man watching was instantly aroused. And Jones was no exception. He looked at her. He was about to say something when she panted, "Keep going, please."

Jones continued and Louise could feel herself starting to get very excited—"enough of this, back to work" she said to herself.

Rasping, she said "I want to be the girl; can I?"

Jones nodded.

Before he could change his mind, she had him in her mouth.

Clean, uncut, reasonable size, she noted.

She could taste a little early juice and knew if she wasn't very careful it would be all over very soon, and she wanted a gift for Schneider.

"You must fuck me—please put that cock inside me and dump all of it inside me, please, please, do it to me, I need your cock today. I never get enough cock. Never enough."

The last two statements were true—the more men she got, the more she wanted; today she would need more than Jones.

As expected, Jones was a 30-second man and Louise had her "come back," as she liked to call it, ready.

"God, that was so good; thank goodness you stopped—I thought my heart was going to stop."

Jones smiled, the conquering hero.

"Sir, I have one more request, can you bite my nipples, but bite them a little, not too much, just a little."

Jones complied and Louise did actually climax.

"I don't know about you, but I need a cigarette, you got any, sir?"

As Louise told Schneider later, the "sir" made Jones putty.

Ten minutes earlier, Hoffmann had left the White House and had walked toward the Willard. But instead of going behind it to the car, he kept walking for another three blocks. In the quiet back street was a truck, nondescript with a few streaks of rust on the side.

Inside sat a man doing the crossword puzzle from the day's *Washington Post*. Or at least that is what he appeared to be doing to the casual observer. In reality, he was watching the two side mirrors. He saw Hoffmann turn the corner. Hoffmann got into the passenger's side, taking care to lock the truck door. He silently unlocked the wrist lock and passed the brief case behind him through the truck's internal window into the main body of the truck. Schneider's hands took the briefcase.

The inside of the truck was like a tiny, well-lit factory. Along one side of the truck's wall was a table and standing beside the table were three men all wearing white cotton gloves. Schneider held a roll of 20 keys—all the keys, in fact, for all Locked Wrist cases made in the past 15 years. The army in its admirable quest for frugality had issued tenders for the locks and like all governments worldwide had not blinked an eye when the tender was won by the Chicago company of Neumann and Braun, a renowned locksmith company, a subsidiary of its German parent. That the bid was under half of the second lowest bidder raised no eyebrows; why should it?

The fifth key opened the two peripheral locks.

Schneider removed the folder, passing it to the team. The first man in the team removed all the pages and then passed each page to the center man, who placed the sheet under a mechanical apparatus that looked like a huge black steel spider. The center man pressed a button and a flash of light indicated a photograph had been taken. Then third man took the sheet from the second man and reattached it to the original folder. The entire process took under five minutes. The case was passed back by Schneider to Hoffmann.

While the photographing was being done, Hoffmann chatted to the driver, secure in the knowledge that he was legally on German soil. Any inquisitive policeman who happened to wander by and ask unwanted questions would have first been told that Hoffmann was simply enjoying a chat with his brother-in-law. If that failed, Schneider would have then appeared and threatened fire and brimstone. True, Hoffmann would have to have been repatriated to Germany but better this than facing a firing squad. In any event, no policeman appeared and Hoffman left the truck and walked to the street behind the Willard.

Hoffman angrily knocked on the rear door of the Packard; Jones started.

"What the fuck are you doing Jones; who the hell is this woman?"

Jones started to splutter.

Smoothly, Louise said, "Captain, it was my fault; you see I asked this gentleman for help and..."

"Out!" Hoffmann commanded.

"What the fuck were you thinking Jones?" Hoffmann asked on the drive back to the archive.

Jones smiled weakly and turned for an instant, "You were right captain—I did get lucky."

Hoffmann relaxed and laughed, "You fucking lucky dog, she looked like a Hollywood movie star. You have to tell me your secrets."

Actually, there was no time to tell any secrets as Jones was transferred two weeks later to Bataan in the Philippines.

"You will like it," said his CO, "It's just like Mississippi weather."

The rust-streaked truck returned to the Germany embassy. The rear of the truck opened and the men emerged.

"Get the film developed," Schneider said, somewhat needlessly.

The camera operator nodded.

✠ ✠ ✠

After her "lucky escape," Louise walked to the front of the Willard and entered, slowly walking to the bar she knew so well. She could feel some of Jones's milk starting to run down the inside of upper thigh; she always loved this feeling. It made her feel so slutty and so alive. She made her way to the bar and sat down, easily crossing her now well-lubricated legs.

"A glass of champagne, please Peter."

"Sure thing, Louise," said the smiling barman who was thrilled to be on first names with a woman like Louise.

"Now Peter, there is no need to tell me again the stories of President Grant sitting here at the bar and in the lobby, and how the vernacular "lobbyist" was coined by Grant's visitations here," she frowned in mock disapproval.

Peter looked like a little boy who had been discovered wetting his bed.

"Oh, Peter, don't look like that. They are wonderful stories, and I am sure they make a lot of luck for you with the officers' wives and mistresses, but remember you told me them all before."

At this moment an Army colonel sauntered over to the bar, "Hey, barman, gimme two fingers of Jack, and give this lady a drink while you're at it."

No "please," just a command from God to a peon.

"So, honey, you here on your own or what?"

"No, colonel, I'm with someone, but thank you for asking." The quiet sarcasm was missed by God.

"Whoa, that's too bad honey, 'cos I could show you a real good time.

"Say, barman, where are the phone booths in this dump; I got to get me some action for tonight?"

Peter politely pointed and God left.

Louise paid for her drink, giving Peter a large tip.

"See you later, Louise."

Louise left and had the doorman hail her a cab to the small bookstore called Boyles, which was down the street from the embassy. Louise wasn't sure if it was habit or just tradecraft that made her do this, but she always walked the wrong way for a minute and then suddenly turned looking for any tense missteps.

Like all men experienced with women, Schneider had trimmed his fingernails so there was no nail extending at all on any finger—"nothing to irritate or hurt any female delicacies," he smiled, thinking to himself. He also checked his chin and lips—not the slightest sign of stubble; Louise did so love his mouth while lying on his desk, legs wide, wide apart. Sometimes she would let her legs dangle, while other times she would hug her knees, all depending on her mood.

In the back of the taxi, Louise had mopped up the excesses of Jones that had been slowly dribbling down her leg. It was one thing to excite Schneider, it was another thing to be sloppy for her "second."

Schneider was smoking a cigar when Louise entered. By his relaxed demeanor, it was clear the mission was a complete success. Schneider rose and bowed slightly, then quietly applauded, "Perfect. You were perfect, my dear."

"Some cognac to celebrate?"

She nodded.

Louise loved to have sex when she was drunk—it seemed to heighten the pleasure.

For almost half an hour, Schneider debriefed Louise. It was slow and pleasant and each knew the other wanted sex and so each teased the other, very slowly.

"He was a 30-seconder, as you predicted."

Schneider remarked he was not surprised.

"So the material is good?"

"No, it is not."

Louise frowned for a second until Schneider raised his hand, like a policeman stopping a car while directing traffic.

"No, the material is not good. The material will change the path of world history in a significant way."

Louise felt her nipples tingle, she was starting to get aroused again. Her skin was alive.

Schneider continued, "What the President of the United States reviewed today is a plan for the Americans to attack the British Empire, starting with an undeclared attack on Canada."

Louise's mouth sagged opened and she stared at Schneider.

"That can't be true—the Americans are allies of the British."

"At the moment, but the gods have an amusing sense of humor. Remember what the Britisher Palmerston said, '*Nations have no permanent friends or allies, they only have permanent interests.*' "

They had been sitting on the overstuffed burgundy leather club couch, Louise sitting with her legs crossed. With Schneider's pronouncement, she uncrossed her legs without thinking and moved forward on the seat. She was lubricating intensely.

"Oh my God, that is the most exciting thing I have ever heard. I hope you are not going to tease me too much longer."

Then she suddenly said, "So we will announce this to the world now, right?"

"Well that would be the best way to expose and destroy our source. Would that be a good idea?"

Schneider explained that with material this powerful, it was essential that nothing leak.

"This is like fine wine, we need let it age a little. In a month or two, and after a few more Locked Wrists using people other than our source to the White House, then we will be safe to use it. This material will not go bad with age."

Changing the topic to what she was most interested in, she simply said, "Fuck me now, please."

Schneider realized Louise had understood.

Louise was a beautiful young woman, but Schneider's experience was such that he felt not a twinge of nervousness, the opposite of young Jones.

He kissed her on the lips and she forced her tongue into his mouth. "The assignment has done all the preparatory work for me," Schneider thought.

Louise grabbed his trousers and unzipped them. She had her elegant hand around his hardness and was squeezing and took her thumb and rubbed it over the tip. She was pleased to feel that oily wetness that always excited her. She had opened her legs and his hand was teasing the now wet area of her upper thigh.

"Oh for God's sake, stop teasing me, put it in me, now. I want to feel it in me now. All the way."

Schneider rose and took her to his desk. He had already moved the ink well and blotter, so the area was clear. She lay on her back with a sigh of anticipation and opened her legs to their fullest extent. Schneider slid inside; she was astoundingly wet, not just from Jones but also from her own body.

"God. Jesus that. Oh yes, that. I want that. All the way. Put it in all the way. I want it all in. Deep. Dump it all in me now."

He could already feel the small contractions starting, and her juices were running down her legs and bottom to the desk. He slipped his left hand under her and lifted her a little. Her contractions were rapidly increasing in both strength and frequency. She was squeezing her nipples though her blouse. She was fast approaching climax. Schneider was pumping so hard that the front of their pelvic bones were hitting at each thrust. "About 20 seconds," he thought. At this stage, when she was too far gone to complain, Schneider gently but insistently slid his index finger into her back door.

Her eyes widened, her mouth opened for a second and no sound came, then, "Oh my God. Yes. Fuck me. Fuck me."

She closed her eyes and was moaning louder and louder.

Her head was wildly moving side to side. When his finger was all the way in, she stopped moving, and got up on her elbows on the desk. She opened her eyes wide and looked at him, a look of shock on her face.

"A big one," is all she said.

Then she started to climax. While she was contracting, he worked his finger backwards and forward; as the contractions started to weaken, he moved the tip of his finger more and more. He could feel himself through the walls of her body. As the tip of his finger moved more and more, her weakening contractions started again to strengthen. He continued this for two minutes.

Finally, he thought he should stop. He gently withdrew his finger and with his other hand stroked her brow.

"You're safe, just relax, honey. Let me get you some water."

Louise's body was uncontrollably twitching on the desk, her legs were quivering. She had her hands to her mouth. It was as if she was crying, with light, defenseless pants.

"Just stay here," he whispered.

Quickly he slipped in to the small bathroom at the corner of his office. He washed his hands and poured two glasses of water and dampened a hand towel with warm water.

Returning, he found her a little less distraught.

After a moment, she opened her eyes.

"What was that?"

"Hmm, little different to the American Jones?"

Her breathing returned to normal, and she put her hand to her forehead.

"I have never felt like that before. What in God's name was that?"

Of course, a gentleman like Schneider was never going to explain to a lady the explicit details of what he sometimes referred to as "the plumbing." Such details would destroy the romance; years ago while serving in a Freikorps, he had been given some photos—"saucy," as he called them—of French ladies. Some of these were so explicit they seemed to belong in a medical doctor's text book. How, he asked himself, could such photographs be considered erotic when they removed all the mystery.

Actually, Schneider had kept the photographs as a test; he would show them to candidates for his department with the threadbare excuse that he had them thrust upon him by a soldier, and "what do you think of these?" The answers always fell into one of three categories: "do you have any more" (instant rejection), or—at the other end of the spectrum—"these are horrible" (instant rejection), or "interesting, but frankly, I find these images destructive of romance and more suitable for education of medical students" (possible). His recently-hired aide, Herman Jäger, had expressed the third opinion.

It was with Jäger over brandy one evening that the conversation had moved to the female "plumbing" and Schneider had for some reason explained the technique.

"Jäger, you see, in every woman's backdoor there is a spot, about this far in," he held up and extended his index finger.

"And this special spot when stimulated correctly increases the strength and the duration of her climax. Done properly—and it does take a lot of practice—a woman's climax can be extended to one minute, or even two full minutes, or even longer."

From Jäger's face, it was clear this was new to Jäger, and he frankly said, "Herr Schneider, I did not know that. I will try this at the next opportunity."

Schneider quickly offered some warnings,

"Jäger, ensure your finger nails are all trimmed right down to the quick. Also do not start this until the lady's motor is already running and warned up. Down cold, as it were—too early—the effects can sometimes be of revulsion. Use her nipples as a judge. Of course, women's nipples vary tremendously in shape and size, but the common point of observation is the change in the size of the nipples. I've known some women whose nipples in normal life are actually dimples, but always—always—when aroused the little buggers come out of their hiding places to stand up over-sized to proudly take their place in the world."

Jäger laughed at this last comment, and nodded his head, as he too had observed the same phenomenon. Schneider thought Jäger too young to be told of the time in Peking when Schneider entertained a Chinese lady, whose nipples grew to two centimeters in length and moved like worms; Schneider was so dumbstruck at this that he quickly and politely moved to *à chien*—those two worms were very off putting.

That evening, after Louise had leisurely bathed and pampered herself, Schneider took her to the main dining room at the Willard, in part because the food was excellent, and in part to let Louise relive the afternoon's adventure.

The waiters had cleared the table and the restaurant was mostly empty because of the upcoming national holiday.

"You see my dear, women are delicate flowers that need to be treated gently and carefully, else the petals be damaged. But inside all women there sleeps a tigress, and that tigress can be awoken, and when aroused she is a wild animal. What happened in my office, is I simply awoke your tigress. And once unleashed your tigress can roam for a very long time."

"I have never experienced anything like that before. How long was mine—I was so crazy I lost track of time?"

Schneider replied, "A little over two minutes."

"I thought I was going to die."

"Yes, I know; that is why I stopped."

"You mean it could have been longer?"

"Oh yes."

Louise sighed.

"That is why you slept on the couch for an hour. Your body was in shock and needed time to recover."

Louise said nothing, lost in thought.

"How can I thank you?"

"Thank me? Why the pleasure was all mine," Schneider smiled.

"Schneider, it's a curious thing, but the more men I have the more men I want. Is that the same with you with women?"

"Yes, but Louise you will find that it becomes addictive. But it's a nice and entertaining addiction. And you are in the happy position of it being part of your job."

Louise smiled slightly.

"You know I could do it again now, I am getting excited. Is that unhealthy?"

"No, it is completely normal. What I suggest is you go to the bar; I will take you there and then leave. When the detritus at the bar see me leave, they will swoop on you like eagles on a lost lamb."

As promised, after dinner, Schneider took Louise to the bar of the Willard, but not before Louise had briefly adjourned to the ladies' room to, as she said, "remove one unwanted undergarment." So freed, she whispered her thanks to Schneider, and also that she was starting to "get wet there again."

"I must be crazy."

Schneider shook his head, "The more you get, the more you want. That is all. You are not crazy. You are simply healthy."

Perhaps because of the holiday, in contrast to the restaurant, the bar was unusually crowded for a Wednesday night. Schneider assumed some were bachelors with nowhere to go, as well as some married officers who were escaping the boredom and tedium of suburban home life for a few hours. He ordered champagne for both of them. Peter was still on duty and smiled at Louise who returned his smile with a genuine one of her own.

After a decent interval, Schneider asked for his hat. Kissing her on the cheek, he whispered, "I will want a full report tomorrow." Louise simply smiled.

As he had predicted, even before he had reached the front door, a red-faced and slightly drunk officer, and without being invited, sat down next to her.

"Say, what's the idea of your boyfriend leaving you alone in a place like this with all us wolves?" he laughed.

Louise had the ability to force a smile that was indistinguishable from her genuine ones that she gave to Peter and Schneider.

"Oh, he's not my boyfriend, he's my boss," she answered, with just a tiny hint of breathlessness, to create the illusion of "my, your army uniform sweeps me off my feet."

"Your boss, eh; then he should really know better. He should be protecting his most valuable troops. That's what we officers always have to do. So what do you do? As you can see I am protecting the country against our enemies, whoever they are," he laughed.

"Well, I am a reporter for a Chicago business newspaper," she said.

"That's interesting," he lied without bothering to try to hide his lack of interest.

Schneider had explained to Louise that reporters were the perfect cover, as their job was to ask questions, and that a business reporter was the best of all, as questions about millions of gallons of sulphuric acid, or number of trains to San Francisco, or aircraft production, all seemed like reasonable questions that a hard-working business reporter would ask.

Louise quickly finished her drink, and the officer—he was a quartermaster as it turned out—snapped his fingers like a little Caesar and ordered her another without her asking.

Then she started her slow little pantomime routine she had honed with Schneider. First came the hair toss; next was running her hand through her hair—"even the most stupid man should pick up this signal of a woman in high heat," Schneider had explained; then the brief gaze into the eyes—"only for half a second, otherwise he will think you are completely drunk, or a whore."

Then, the most important of all: "Then put your hand on his knee. Just tell him you are getting a little drunk."

Truth be told, Louise was getting a little drunk and loved the feeling of teasing this nonentity.

The nonentity—like most men—was deluding himself that his wit, charm, and personality were winning over Louise. And Louise's slow encouragement was only amplifying this delusion. In reality, he had no wit, no charm, and very little in the way of personality, but he did have a bulging briefcase at this feet which he would periodically and ostentatiously move.

"I am writing a piece for the paper on rubber production in Ohio; you know anything about that?"

Suddenly he was nervous, "You know, honey, we should not talk shop here."

"OK, if you don't know, then you don't know."

He moistened his lips, and said *sotto voce*, "Well, what's in it for me?"

Louise said nothing but answered by lightly grazing his crotch with her hand.

"I want all your milk on my face. All of it."

She could see he was in two minds, but as expected, lust won. "Room 1511."

He left carrying his bulging briefcase.

By now Louise could feel her own juices restarting.

After five minutes, she left and took the elevator. Knocking on the door, the officer, now relaxed, opened it.

She entered and he asked, "So what's your name, honey?"

"Well by an amazing coincidence, my name actually is Honey, at least for tonight. And I am going to call you 'Major Sir,' if that is acceptable, Major Sir. And, Major Sir, I have been a very bad girl. A very naughty girl. I need to be punished for being bad. Can you do that to make me a better and pure girl again, Major Sir?"

He smiled. "Some brandy?"

She nodded and sat at the writing table. She lit a cigarette.

"Sir, I hope you are going south of the navel line, but to do so you're going to need rinse your mouth as brandy and spirits sting my feminine charms."

He smiled at the way Louise could be both lady-like and grossly carnal at the same time.

"Why don't you have a quick shower so you're fresh for me?"

He hesitated, but she read his mind,

"And here's your big briefcase that you likely need to read why you're showering," she said as she lugged the travel-worn bag into the bathroom.

After the bathroom door closed, Louise stood up and unzipped her skirt at the back, stepped out, and placed the skirt neatly on the lounge chair beside the bed. This done, she resumed her seat and had her long legs crossed. Her garter belt was canary yellow, from Germany—the American ones were all so dowdy, either arc-light white or a sickly pinkish color. The stockings themselves were the palest possible yellow. While her hairs around her "charms" as she called them were wispy, she had dyed them to darken them to help them standout—she so envied girls with a large dark triangle of black hair, as she did not like her lower lips to show.

Major Sir quickly emerged from the bathroom and even without Louise's little show was already heavily tumescent. Louise suspected that he had helped the process along in the shower—he wouldn't be the first man to do so. Louise stood when he entered and turned around to show him the full cache.

He was a strong and crude lover, about the same size as Schneider, but with none of the skill and little of the attention of her boss. She gently added her teeth when he was in her mouth, and he was initially surprised—she assumed that for all the bluster he was actually fairly inexperienced with women. She could taste a little of his early juice as he got extremely excited and she was forced to curtail the sucking to prevent the much-feared 30-second man from raising its ugly head.

Her recommendation of her lying on her stomach on three of the pillows on the bed was happily accepted by the mildly surprised Major Sir.

"Whoa, this is kinda clever, ain't it, Honey," was his succinct comment.

Schneider had taught her this position and Louise immediately took to it as she did not have to kneel on all fours as in traditional *chien*. She could simply lie there relaxed, arms and legs outstretched, with her feet just grazing the carpet. Even better, the solid base of pillows meant the man *du jour* (or was it man *de l'heure?*) could get in far, far deeper—the traditional version of this position allowed for far too much movement, and the only corrective step was for the man to firmly grab Louise's shoulders, but this was always limited in its effectiveness; "Schneider's position," as she called it, was effective, relaxing and, best of all, extremely arousing.

She enjoyed the crudity of the officer; he was simple, strong and had surprising stamina. And she liked the hardness. But she thought it best to relieve her tension sooner rather than later, so she concentrated on his animal grunting—the sounds a manmade were always the most exciting aspect of the act for her. Once in Berlin she had entertained a beautiful blond Adonis from the Berlin Ballet, chisel-face, glorious long blond hair; it was a total fiasco as he was mute as a mouse, she could not get aroused even as be pumped and pumped his milk inside her. She had to resort to the standard moaning and that-was-so-amazing lies.

The start of her quite genuine contractions had—as she expected—turned the soldier's horse onto the home straight. But to be safe she completed most of her climax *before* starting her standard stream of "oh, I love your big cock," "pump all that juice inside me," and the never-fail "fuck me harder." And he was—like her—clearly an aural animal. Her legerdemain worked as expected, and as commanded, he did indeed pump inside her, and she was—as a professional—impressed by his completion.

She said, "Well, now it's my time to use the shower and I don't need your briefcase."

She had removed her jacket and standard-issue cream blouse before taking up the "Schneider Position." Wearing only her brassiere and garter belt, she walked to the bathroom. She showered and reentered the suite to find the officer smoking the obligatory post-excitement cigarette. He lit one for her and they chatted for 10 minutes. It turned out that he was a nobody, in charge of soldier hygiene supplies. She dared not ask for any details. After her leisurely cigarette, she dressed and, with a peck on the cheek, left.

In the cab back to the embassy she was completely satiated—she leaned back completely relaxed; it was having three men in the one day—having two was exciting, but three in a day was satisfying beyond belief. Schneider was correct: the more she got, the even more voracious was her appetite.

8: The Urbane Gentleman

SCHNEIDER CALLED LOUISE into his office.

"I have an important assignment for you, Louise. Through an intermediary, I have arranged for you to be part of a dinner group that interviews one of the most important men in the country this evening at the Willard at 8 p.m. Henry Morgenthau is Roosevelt's Treasury Secretary and as such is obviously extremely powerful. He is hosting a dinner for five European reporters and you. This man is one of the main forces behind Roosevelt's New Deal program and I am very interested in you getting the details of his thinking and his current views on Roosevelt. Interestingly, he is Jewish and is actually only the second of that faith to be in an American administration. In spite of all the whining we hear about our *Reich*, the Americans don't do much themselves. I want you prim and proper but still very feminine. I have prepared a list of questions I want you to ask Mr. Morgenthau. Spend one hour reading and memorizing these questions and then you can do a mock interview with me."

With that Schneider gave Louise three pages of hand-written questions.

Louise took the questions and left and room and went to the embassy library.

One hour later, Louise returned and the tedious but valuable dress rehearsal started.

"The secret to these meetings is to be demure and in no way threatening. The other five reporters are all men, and they will all try to outshine each other early. I want you to simply smile and ask just the first two questions until desert is served. By that time, Mr. Morgenthau will be thoroughly sick of the men and with a little gentleness, Mr. Morgenthau can be shown you are his friend and not simply someone who desires to score points and to get some very printable quotes. You have a room booked for the evening at the hotel. It is extremely unlikely that Mr. Morgenthau will suggest anything—from all reports he is a very boring man. And this assignment is not one that requires your female charms, gorgeous and munificent though they are. If that does occur, then that is good, but it is neither required nor expected."

Louise listened intently and understood.

At seven p.m., Louise checked into the hotel and after a quick review of the room, made her way to the bar. Her favorite, Peter, was on duty and she gave him a huge grin. Clearly, her appearance had made his evening. They chatted and Louise loosened herself with a single glass of champagne.

Early as always, Morgenthau appeared and was seated in the central table. No reporters appeared, and so Louise walked over and introduced herself. Mr. Morgenthau, for all his modesty, could not but happen to notice Louise's smoky sexiness and her genuine charm.

"Well, the White House never told me I would be in the company of someone as lovely as you, my dear."

"Mr. Secretary, you are far too kind."

Schneider's drilling of correct titles of address was already paying off, "For God's sake call me Henry."

"I rarely get to Washington, as I work out of Chicago mainly and it's such a wonderful city. You know, I love all the big American cities, they are so much more vibrant than cities in Europe," Louise said, careful not to mention Germany.

"I see, so you don't live here?"

"Oh, no, I came to this very important meeting, I am staying here and I return to Chicago tomorrow morning on the *Chicago Spirit*."

"OK. I see."

"But I have a friend here, Peter the barman. I always have a nightcap."

As she finished her sentence the group of male reporters descended on them.

Returning to his formal Mr. Secretary mode, Morgenthau said, "Welcome, gentlemen. Let's get started, shall we?"

It was clear from his manner that Morgenthau was as bored as the reporters were excited—it is not every day that a humble foreign correspondent gets to interview the American President's right-hand man.

For two hours, the reporters droned on, asking a wide array of questions, from the perceptive to the ridiculous. It seemed to Louise that the reporter from the London *Times*, a chap named Harold, was by far the most astute. His stutter was a little off-putting at first, but he was intelligent and charming, as well as very handsome. He said he had reported on the Spanish Civil War for the *Times*. One of the other reporters at the far end of the table seemed to refer to him as "Tim," but Louise suspected she may have misheard.

Most of the questions centered on the success of the President's New Deal. Towards the end of the dinner, the Englishman asked about the books that Morgenthau read and had been influenced by.

Deftly, Morgenthau turned the question around, back to the English reporter. At this stage, the reporter had downed a little over a bottle of wine, and three small tumblers of port, and instantly he replied "Feuerbach." Morgenthau looked at the Englishman very directly and simply said, "Interesting choice."

"But, but, but, but simply from a purely philosophical viewpoint, none of it much applies to the real world," the English reporter was quick to stutter a disclaimer.

Louise was pretending to write notes, and looked up at Morgenthau; he was looking directly at her; she smiled.

The dinner ended and the reporters all thanked the Treasury Secretary. The men made their way to the lobby, while Louise went first to the ladies' room, and then to the bar. Peter was delighted to see her. She had only sipped her wine and had taken no port.

Sipping her glass of champagne at the bar, she was not surprised to see the Secretary of the Treasury of the United States of America amble over and sit down beside her. As it was a quiet Tuesday, the bar was empty apart from the two of them and Peter.

"Here is a confident gentleman with brains and charm; while he is not going to *try* to sleep with me (all he needs do is ask), he clearly enjoys female company," she thought.

"Peter, how are you this evening, I understand you are lucky enough to know this beautiful young lady?" Morgenthau asked suavely.

Peter nodded, "That I am sir."

"And Mr. Secretary, what would you like this evening?"

He ordered a brandy.

"And Peter, call me Henry, please."

Louise compared this true gentleman with the other men she had met at Peter's bar.

"So you were very quiet at dinner, were those the only two questions you had?"

Morgenthau restated Louise's two questions with precision.

"Well, sir, my real interest and the interest of my readers is what is the man behind the wonderful voice like? I understand that, like me, you are a great admirer of Mr. Roosevelt."

"That is an understatement—I am the President's greatest fan and I think everyone knows that. I have the highest respect and regard for Franklin. He is a man of extra-ordinary talents and unequaled political skill and acumen. People often call me his Yes-man, and I suspect I *am* too pliant at times, but yes, I am a huge admirer. And his use of radio is unequalled, that glorious baritone voice, so smooth and powerful, like an iron fist in a velvet glove."

"So you mean he is a saint?"

Morgenthau laughed, "Oh, by no means. He is human and he is sometimes all too human."

"So give me one of his human foibles. Nothing too indiscrete, just something of interest."

"You are in a sticky situation here, because I can do one of two things, I can speak on the record, which you can print, or I can speak off the record for background for you, but you can print not one word. So what'll it be?"

Louise's choice was obvious, but she tried not to rush it.

"OK, well let's sit over here at this table by the window and I will give you some background."

"Peter, one more of these, please."

Peter nodded at Morgenthau.

The two sat down. Louise and made a show of putting away her reporter's notebook, she then asked,

"Mr. Morgenthau, can I ask you why you are doing this. I mean why are you sitting down with a young reporter, and a woman at that? And I work for an obscure Chicago business paper."

"Well, I think some things need to be aired, and a change of direction or an adjustment to the course needs to be taken, and I think foreign newspapers can lead the way, and you are an outsider. Franklin has the White House reporters at his press briefings in his pocket and he is such an operator—he never forgets their birthdays; for his favorites, intimate dinners at the White House and little snippets before the press release is made public," Morgenthau said without the slightest hint of malice.

As Morgenthau had explained to Louise, he felt the White House reporters were far too chummy with the President. And while pleasant was not necessary a bad thing, too friendly *was* a bad thing—the White House reporters had tended to lose all objectivity and to see the President's policy as fact, rather than a political agenda with its inherent strengths and weaknesses—for the White House reporters it was all strengths. And Roosevelt was breathtaking—and unequalled—in his ability to control and connive and con the White House reporters. Some sunlight, especially if it came from foreign reporters, could be useful, or so Morgenthau thought.

"So I think the airing of a slightly different opinion is healthy. You see, my dear, I am a little worried, no, concerned would be more precise. We've run up a huge deficit and unemployment is still very high; we've increased the tax rate from 24% to 79% but we're getting in fewer total dollars," he stopped, first looking at his drink, and then at Louise.

What put Louise into the top rank of agents was her ability to very quickly instill confidence. Mostly, she did this simply by looking and smiling and saying nothing.

"I don't understand, Mr. Morgenthau."

"Henry, for Christ's sake," he laughed.

She was getting very aroused this close to real power. Not a "Major Sir," but real, genuine power—the Treasury Secretary of the United States of America. She felt herself getting excited, she could feel her nipples swelling. It was so typical—the powerful men are suave and quiet, the water beetles are loathsomely noisy.

"So... Henry... what is the man really like?"

"Well Franklin is an odd old bird in many ways. As a business man, before he became governor of New York, all his ventures failed. He tried a live lobster business and lost a lot of money; he tried vending machines and that was a complete catastrophe; he tried farming in Georgia at Warm Springs and lost his shirt. My good friend Henry Wallace, who knows Franklin as well as I, told me that he would have no business dealings with Franklin because Franklin lacks the essential patience that all business men need to succeed. In other words, Franklin does not think methodically but just jumps to conclusions—he is like an impatient child who loves to try new things. So should we entrust the nation's economy to a failed business man? That itself is very disturbing."

"In contrast, my own father is a very cautious and therefore very successful business man. What many people do not realize is that most business men are patient and very careful—it's their own money after all. So when the naive and feckless attempt to mimic the success of a business man, they take wild and sudden gambles, just like what they see on the silver screen at the talking pictures. But the Hollywood image of rapacious business men is mostly fiction. That's not how successful business men operate. All of them that I know are far more careful than the average man on the street. They hate risk, especially risking their own money. Now while Franklin is a great leader, what I find most disconcerting is his ability to fly off on a tangent. He is dangerously impulsive and too much of a gambler. This is especially true when his so-called Brain Trust is present. No idea seems too outlandish. He also has a very dangerous sense of luck."

Louise turned her head to one side, as if to ask a question.

"Well here's an example: he and I were in the White House setting the price of gold one morning and I told Franklin it had to increase by between 18 and 22 cents, so Franklin said, 'OK, make it

21 cents'. I asked him why, and he said, 'well that's one of my lucky numbers, it's three times seven.' I thought to myself what would happen if the world knew that the price of gold in the United States was set by one of the President's lucky numbers. And he has lucky shoes and lucky hats and lucky dates. As my father taught me, true business men never believe in luck—many of them don't even buy lottery tickets. Also, Franklin's sense of the truth is a little hazy at times. He said when he was campaigning in 1920 that he had personally written the Haitian Constitution. The truth is that he had nothing to do with it."

Louise gave Morgenthau a taste of her sophistication and elegance by uncrossing and re-crossing her long, long legs. Not to suggest anything, but she knew that while the Treasury Secretary was a devoted man of the people he was also a man.

"Like most politicians, especially those with lots of power here in Washington, Franklin has a very hazy sense of money—he seems to think money comes out of thin air. So when he creates yet another of his jobs programs that costs say 100 million dollars, the money has to come from taxes, but Franklin thinks I just have to run the printing presses a little longer. And that is a major problem. Here's an example for you. Let's assume that all of the 100 million dollars in tax comes just from taxing Mr. Ford. In other words, Mr. Ford had to give up that 100 million dollars of his own money in taxes to fund the jobs program."

Louise frowned, "So what is the problem with that... Henry?"

"Well let's say Mr. Ford gave up 100 million dollars to create a government jobs program. Now if it was still Mr. Ford's 100 million, do you think Mr. Ford, who is known to be a scrooge, would watch his—his—100 million dollars very, very carefully? Of course he would, it's his own money after all. But if it is assigned to Rex's old agency, or another bureaucrat's agency, do you think they would look after it so carefully? No. All these government people think I create the money with a printing press. You see, government never really creates value or worth, it simply re-distributes wealth generated by the real creators, like Mr. Ford. Government simply taxes, it does not go into the marketplace and battle with competitors. It just makes pompous laws made by government people who see themselves as superior beings to the roar and rabble of the business men, who they see as poorly educated, crude, and vulgar."

"Yes, but Henry these people in the job's program spend money, which is good for the economy, right?"

"Of course, but the same would be true if Mr. Ford paid them."

"So what is the difference? Both Mr. Ford's people and the job's program people spend the 100 million, so that is the same?"

"Actually my dear, it is not the same. Let's assume the 100 million dollars is used to make cars, cars made by Mr. Ford or cars made by government factories using the 100 million in tax money that was extracted from Mr. Ford. Now in the case of Mr. Ford, he can produce let's say 100,000 cars, while the government with its red tape, and political appointments, and inherent inefficiencies would only produce 50,000 cars.

"Here's an example: I know for a fact that Mr. Ford sends his mechanics and engineers to scour junk yards around the country to minutely examine his old junked Ford cars. And these men all have to tell Mr. Ford what parts and components are still in good condition, so Mr. Ford can reduce the cost of those over-built and wasteful components. You see, my dear, Mr. Ford's goal is to have all the car wear out at the same time. By doing this he can reduce the price of the car to the customer, as it is cheaper for Mr. Ford to make these cars. Now that is pure American genius at work—no government official would ever have the imagination to consider such an idea—not in a thousand years. All these bureaucrats think of is the pecking order in their department and how they can get to the next rung on the bureaucratic ladder. And because Mr. Ford is a skin flint, and because it is his money, he watches it carefully, and he fires lazy and incompetent and inefficient workers. But Rex and his brethren will simply smile benevolently and will indulge the lazy and slothful, rather than fire them. Do you know that no CCC or WPA worker has ever been fired?"

"So you mean Mr. Ford will make the 100 million dollars work harder?"

Morgenthau smiled, nodded, and leaned back in his chair.

Louise's elegant eyebrows rose.

"You see, it is not just in Germany that politics is a dirty business. I know for a fact that without WPA workers, the '36 race would have been extremely tight. Two Gallup polls as late as July, 1936, had Landon—he was the Republican candidate—winning the Electoral College. But then Tugwell, Hopkins, and the other Brain Trusters opened the spigot. And the results were that Franklin carried the Electoral College by 523 to eight—one of the greatest landslides in American history."

He opened his jacket pocket and removed a cigar, "Do you mind?"

"Of course not."

Smoking made Morgenthau more reflective. He said pensively,

"Actually I think the election of '36 has changed the country permanently and I am not sure for the better. I've spoken to both the Democratic National Committee chairman, a man named Farley, and his right-hand man at the DNC, Emil Hurja, and they both actually *boast* about spending money for votes—they boast about buying votes; they're worse than the late Louisiana Kingfish ever was. Now you may call me old-school, but I think that is wrong. What these two did was to promise projects to marginal states. So if a state was borderline and especially if it held a lot of electoral college votes, then—hey presto—lots of additional New Deal projects were announced in the five months leading up to the November general election.

"The worst of it is that now the average person thinks government money is simply printed by my department. Unfortunately all I print is little bits of paper with some ink on them, bits of paper that have no value. What gives these bits of paper value is the guarantee that the U.S. government will honor the bits of paper. And the only way any government does this is by being solvent, and the only way to be solvent is to increase its own income by taxes. You know that is the reason the President repealed Prohibition, so he could tax booze. And if you want an example of what happens when a government is not solvent, look no further than what happened in your country when the bloody-minded French invaded the Ruhr in 1923. So that is why I see the prior election in 1936 as a watershed."

Louise asked, "Why is that a problem?"

Morgenthau looked at her and said,

"You are an exceptionally beautiful woman, and you've got more brains than most men. I hope you plan to stay in the United States, as we need people of your caliber."

Louise blushed at this kind and genuine compliment.

"Let me tell you a story. Once upon a time, there was a big country that I will call the 'Middle Kingdom' and the people in the Middle Kingdom were very advanced and they made many items that Europeans wanted, such as tea and silk and porcelain. And the emperor of the Middle Kingdom did not like foreigners at all and tried to stop all trade, as he saw trade as immoral and dangerous. Of course, this did not work, and the trade with the Europeans, especially the English, flourished. With good reason, the Middle Kingdom did not trust these 'foreign devils,' and the Middle Kingdom insisted that the Europeans pay in silver. Now this was particularly burdensome for the English, whose currency was based on gold not silver.

"Nevertheless the somewhat desperate English went along. Then some bright spark at the British East India Company had the idea of introducing opium grown in British India to replace the silver. Needless to say the Emperor was justifiably outraged at this—trying to destroy the lives of millions of his subjects for 30 pieces of silver, as it were. And opium is terrible—it is a highly addictive and extremely dangerous drug. It always amuses me to think that Christian England would think it fit and proper to destroy the lives of millions of people. Whole villages were destroyed as the villagers all 'chased the tail of the dragon,' as smoking opium was called. Crops were left to rot in the field. As often happens, we Yanks got into the story a little late in the game, and the largest opium trader in the U.S. was the Boston firm of Russell & Company. And the young star of the company was a 24-year-old Yankee named Warren Delano."

Louise was bored, "And?"

"And young lady, that is what we are now doing—we have turned our American voters into addicts. Under President Roosevelt, now voters *expect* entitlements. They are starting to expect the Federal government look after them in all ways. The wonderful ideals of independence, of personal responsibility, of thrift, of hard work, and of self-reliance are all being dissipated and destroyed. So the very principles that made this country great—the pioneering spirit of the people in covered wagons and the like—are being reversed. People are now trading their freedom for their own personal opium and for serfdom. But rather than being Russian serfs to the czar 100 years ago, now they are serfs to the President's dictates; farmers now need licenses to farm; manufacturers are banned from competing; prices are fixed and rigged."

Confused, Louise asked, "Delano is the middle name of the President, isn't it?"

Morgenthau nodded.

"How is that?"

Morgenthau smiled, "Warren Delano was Franklin's grandfather."

Louise eyes widened, she was about to speak, but Morgenthau beat her to the punch,

"Yes, the President of the United States has a grandfather who destroyed the lives of millions of people by selling them a vile and despicable drug. In short, President Roosevelt's grandfather traded in death and misery of millions."

Morgenthau was lost in thought wondering how close the President's morality was to his grandfather's.

For the first time in the evening, Louise looked directly into Morgenthau's eyes.

Hesitantly she said, "Does this relate to these notes from the Congressional Record?"

She passed him two small sheets of cream note paper she had taken from her sky-blue crocodile Hermès handbag.

Both were typewriter written; the first read,

> "Now, gentlemen, we have tried spending money. We are spending more than we have ever spent before and it does not work. And I have just one interest, and if I am wrong, as far as I am concerned, somebody else can have my job. I want to see this country prosperous. I want to see people get a job. I want to see people get enough to eat. We have never made good on our promises. We have never taken care of them."

The second typed sheet of note paper read,

> "And as I say, all I am interested in is to really see this country prosperous and this form of Government continue, because after eight years if we can't make a success

*somebody else is going to claim the right to make it and
he's got the right to make the trial. I say aftereight years
of this Administration we have just as much unemployment as when we started."*

Morgenthau smiled, "I see your typist even copied verbatim
the error of 'aftereight' from the record, a nice touch."

"This is when you made an appearance in front of the House
Ways and Means Committee in May 1939, right?"

Morgenthau nodded.

"Is this still your view today, sir?"

Louise deliberately said "sir" to make herself even more
excited. Her nipples were almost painful in their enduring excitement. She smiled to herself that dry economic theory could do this
to her 24 year old body, then in the same second she realized that
it was actually the proximity to power that was making her so wet,
not the theory of production and arcane politics. She had sampled
a large number of men since arriving in America two and a half
years ago; now she got excited very easily and she needed constant
scratching of her new itch. Back in Germany, she was a healthy girl
with healthy appetites, but under Schneider's tutelage—and practical training—she had become insatiable; she needed to feel a man
inside her every day; in contrast to her decorous way in Germany,
now she had become the aggressor. And it was a feeling she adored.

"How old are you?"

"I am 24 years old. But 25 at my next birthday in three months."

Both of them laughed at the comment that all six-year-old
boys make.

"You have to be careful here in Washington. For a woman who
is so scintillatingly attractive as you, well, I feel like your father giving you advice."

"You are very kind and sweet... Henry."

Louise was madly lubricating.

"Just be careful, my dear. I have to go and see Franklin now, so I am afraid I have to leave you now. But, you know, you should meet Rex so he can give you his perspective himself. I can arrange that if you like. Give me your card and I will have Rex's secretary arrange a *tête-à-tête* with Rex for you next time you're in Washington."

Louise realized she had hit another seam of gold, "That would be wonderful."

"It's the least I can do, and I owe it to Rex to let him put his views to you directly."

With that "Henry" rose and shook her hand. He left. Louise sat and marveled at her good fortune to meet such a gentleman.

Louise was dripping wet; she could actually feel her juices starting to run down her inner thighs; thank God her skirt was black and knee length; she was sure there was some of herself on her skirt.

But the proximity to such power, and such eloquent power at that, had aroused her more than she wished to acknowledge. She knew she needed to be satisfied. She smiled to herself: the benefits of banking friendships. She walked over the bar, it was empty.

"Peter, you get off work in 30 minutes, don't you?"

9: The Little Flower's Helper

Washington
Monday, 21 July 1941

IT HAD TAKEN HENRY MORGENTHAU only a few long-distance telephone calls to New York to summon Rex Tugwell to Washington. The overt reason Morgenthau gave Tugwell was to review some ideas the Treasury had; the real reason was for Rex to meet the reporters and especially Louise. While Tugwell was nominally based in Manhattan, his own personal opium once tasted could never be forgotten, so Rex agreed with alacrity. Truth be told, the Wall Street crowd—with their constant demands for real results and profits—had bored Rex, and his work for the Little Flower was tedious and his policies were being blocked. Any excuse to return to his beloved Shangri-La in Washington was a welcome relief.

The same five reporters met Rex Tugwell at the Willard, and many of the questions were actually repeats from the previous dinner with the Treasury Secretary. The handsome British reporter was present. It seemed to Louise that he was more subdued and his entire intake that evening was a single glass of wine. Perhaps his boss had slapped his wrist? Still charming, just sober this time.

For Louise it was a re-run of the first dinner; Morgenthau had told Louise when she had called long-distance from Chicago what to do. (Schneider had sent her to the office in Chicago, which consisted of one bored, but dutiful, German frau who answered the switchboard with a charming German accent.)

Sadly, Peter had his night off, and the bartender who served Louise was a short, fat surly man of Spanish extraction who was losing his hair. Hector fetched Louise her standard glass of champagne, but the man had the conversation ability of the Egyptian Sphinx. Louise was relieved when Tugwell sauntered over and suggested a table by the window.

Louise immediately noticed two things about Tugwell: that he was handsome, and that he was "interested." The second did not mean that she was expecting a pass, but that if a pass came, she would not be surprised. His handsomeness consisted of a number of features—his thick, wavy hair; his open, honest face; his liking of a cocktail; and his genuine sense of adventure. All these things were apparent. The trained agent in Louise later noted with approval that he had downed four martinis with dinner.

Rex explained, with a little too much pride, his history since Washington,

"My office at American Molasses was at 120 Wall Street, that's just past Water Street; that used to be the old shoreline of the East River, thus the name 'Water' Street. So I crossed the Styx, as it were, and joined the underworld. That job was OK, but I prefer working for the Mayor."

To none of the reporters' interest, he laboriously explained that "Fiorello" in Italian actually meant "little flower," and that at all of five feet in height it seemed to fit Rex's New York boss perfectly.

The dinner droned on and on. A sense of horrible boredom descended on the table, it was like a school class on a dreary, wet Wednesday afternoon when the classroom was filled with the smell of wet and dank clothes. Finally, the dinner finished; the reporters were all relieved; Tugwell didn't notice the tedium as he had been going on and on about his favorite subject—the President of the United States. The five reporters thanked Tugwell and they left.

Louise sat at her now familiar perch at the bar. The Spanish bartender studiously ignored her, which was just fine with her. A moment later, Tugwell sat down next to her; clearly Morgenthau had briefed him.

With no introduction or small talk, he announced,

"I still come to Washington from time to time. I met with Henry this afternoon. I think you know Henry."

Louise nodded, and quietly asked,

"So Mr. Tugwell, what is President Roosevelt really like?"

Tugwell, ever the fever-eyed evangelist, skipped the obligatory "call-me-Rex," and started his spiel,

"He is a genius. It's that simple, he is a genius and he is kind and gentle, while being tough at the same time."

Turning her head a little coquettishly to one side, Louise asked,

"So why did you leave?"

As Louise confessed later to Schneider, her question was the height of stupidity. Yes, Tugwell was well and truly liquored up—and this is all that saved her—but the question was too strong, too early. She cursed herself when Tugwell, flushed and flustered, started to spit out a senseless collection of words. Louise saved the situation by quickly answering her question,

"I suppose all your work had been completed with the NIRA and the Relocation Agency, and your great success with the green belts, like the Greenbelt in Maryland, and I suppose you must have felt a little like Alexander the Great when he wept when he realized he had no more worlds to conquer."

With this reference to antiquity, Tugwell did relax, and the martinis in his gut also helped to calm him.

"Yeah, I guess you could say that. Yeah, that's the ticket—'no more worlds to conquer.' Yeah."

Louise made a mental note to thank Schneider for Schneider's complete case book notes on Tugwell. Without this knowledge, Louise would have been sunk. And Louise would reward Schneider in the way that Schneider most liked.

"Well, you know, Miss Koch, you hit the nail on the head," Tugwell said, emptying his brandy. He ordered another, and asked Louise if she would like more champagne; she shook her head. Desperate to recover the conversation, Louise smiled her most alluring smile and sat back in her chair so as to give Tugwell the full effect of her body and her clearly visible nipples though her peach-colored silk blouse.

Her stars being aligned that evening, she was able to get Tugwell back to his beloved President,

"So Mr. Tugwell, tell me more of this extra-ordinary man."

At last she was blessed with the "call-me-Rex."

"Well, let me show you these snapshots."

He removed a small black lizard-skin photograph wallet and from it he took out two photographs, which he passed to Louise. Both photographs had the regular variegated edges. Both showed the President, but the two photographs could not have been more different.

"Here is the man in all his glory, and these two snaps show the two extremes of his being. Both are quite old, from '33 as it happens. The first is with the British Prime Minister during a conference on setting money policy, while the second is in Virginia," Tugwell explained.

"That's you on the right of the one in Virginia, isn't it?"

Tugwell smiled and nodded.

Louise studied the two photographs and Tugwell was correct: in the photograph with the Prime Minister, Roosevelt's countenance was one of boredom bordering on insurrection. Neither he nor any of the 15 other men were smiling. In contrast, the photograph in Virginia had been taken at a lunch table where Roosevelt and his group are seated; behind the seated men stood 40 beaming young men, reveling in the fine weather and their proximity to their President. At the table, all the suited men were also beaming and at the head of the table, Roosevelt, leaning on his left arm rest, was actually elevating himself half a head higher than his lunch companions. His massive shoulders and fine head of hair clearly evident with that trademark gay smile that charmed all, from prime ministers to that crusty old curmudgeon, Irving Fisher of Yale University. On his nose he wore an old-fashioned pair of pince-nez, far too small in proportion to his large beaming face.

"What's this round thing?"

"Oh, that was the microphone. President Roosevelt had just finished addressing the camp when the photo was taken."

"These young men all look so fit and happy and healthy. It reminds me of the youth groups we have back in Germany. Why this blond boy at the back looks pure German."

"Actually you're right. He was an exchange student from Münster. This camp was one of our Civilian Conservation Corps, what we call CCC. It is a huge success and very popular."

"So tell me more about this remarkable man, Mr. Tugwell," Louise said with prim formality, but happy that Tugwell had been stealing glances at her chest.

"Well, I guess the best part of the man is he is so generous. He wants to share the wealth. Like me, he sees private wealth as a sin—why should all Americans not share in the wealth of this great country? This is why he increased income taxes. Why should any person ever need more than $100,000 per year? It makes no sense. It's just pure greed. With the American frontiers now closed, the wealth should be spread around more. And people like Ford are all just crooks—they never do what the government tells them to do and they do all kinds of crazy things. You know, Ford and his gang go off on a tangent."

"But can't he do that?"

Tugwell had finally gotten a head of steam,

"Not now. Today we have to think about everyone, not just a greedy few. A man who wants to make a lot of money is not a decent man. It's immoral. Take Ford. One of the worst things Ford does is to *decrease* prices on his cars. And that can only lead to national economic ruin. You see Louise, when prices go down farmers are hurt and then everyone is hurt, and wages go down and then it is a terrible downward spiral. Ford broke the law, the law of the United States, the law of this great country."

Now Louise was genuinely confused,

"But in the '20s didn't Ford double his workers' wages and reduce the price of his cars from $3,000 to $500? As a woman, of course I am not good at mathematics, but isn't that a six-fold improvement? And doesn't cheaper food help the poor? So they can buy more food and better quality food?"

Ignoring Louise's point about poor people not going hungry, Tugwell steamed ahead,

"Oh, yeah, with Ford that was last decade, you know in the Roaring Twenties. But that's ancient history now. And that was under the Republican Coolidge—'Mister Do Nothing.' You can't even compare that time to this time. And Coolidge's financial guy, an old miser named Mellon, actually decreased tax rates so rich people kept more money."

"Oh, I see now. And by now increasing taxes the government gets more money for your camps, right?"

Tugwell changed the topic. This was what Louise expected as Morgenthau had admitted to her that canny Mellon's tax cuts in the 1920s actually *increased* total tax revenues. In contrast, the tax increases of the Roosevelt regime had—unexpectedly—decreased the total revenues. Morgenthau ruefully had admitted to Louise that when taxes increased, rich people simply worked less and invested less, and by investing less, companies got less money to grow, so Roosevelt's administration was forced to create more and more make-work alphabet soups, and more and more camps. But none of this Louise mentioned to the zealot.

"You see, Louise, we're no longer afraid of bigness, and unrestricted competition is the death, not the life, of trade. This is a new world and we're just doing what Mussolini in Italy is doing, but we're doing it in an American way. You know, comprehensively and completely and frankly better than Mussolini, who I've met by the way. You see, some people are stubborn and some people just don't want to change. But with his glorious fireside chats, the President has been able to convince people. When I was here in Washington we would listen on the radio to the President and my God, what a voice. Calm, deep, reassuring—why, he can talk the birds out of the trees. It's like he can make a dream come true. Any dream."

He paused and looked at her,

"He can create a new reality for the new world we're building. Yeah, sure there will be some unhappy people, especially the greedy people, like business men. But the President understands all the people's needs, not just the rich people, not just the investors. And yeah, we'll keep increasing taxes. You know that is why the President repealed Prohibition—so we could raise more money taxing booze—it all counts. And we can get a new NIRA without those damn Brooklyn Jews complaining. Everything is possible now; there are no human limits when the government can control things. We just have to keep experimenting. We cannot let people decide for themselves in this ever-more complex world. It's madness to think so."

Louise found Morgenthau to be genuinely very attractive, in part due to Morgenthau's not trying to bed her; in part due to Morgenthau's innate sense of propriety; in part due to Morgenthau's intelligence; and in part due to Morgenthau's honesty. In contrast to Morgenthau, Louise found Tugwell to be identical to some of her father's friends back in Germany—too many of her father's friends were just as narrow-minded and as bigoted as Rex Tugwell.

Louise stood and shook Tugwell's hand,

"Absolutely fascinating. My God, you're the cleverest man I have met in this city. You're amazing. I don't know how to thank you."

Completing these classic Schneider phantasy lines, and before Rex could suggest one, she left the table and walked to the front door. The doorman waved and the first Checker on the rank pulled up.

"What a total asshole," Louise thought.

10: Mr. Horikoshi's Confession

THE PRESIDENT WAS LEANING BACK in his wheelchair smoking a Cuban cigar. He was always very careful to only be photographed with a cigarette in his famous cigarette holder—always the common man, at least in public.

Harry Hopkins said,

"In light of our discussions on the HS document a few weeks back, I have since reached out to a friend at Sullivan & Cromwell. You know John Dulles, Mr. President?"

"He's a fucking Republican," said a startled Roosevelt with a frown.

"Yes, that he is, and he is well-travelled, intelligent, and experienced in international affairs, which I suppose makes him unique among that ilk."

Roosevelt laughed.

"OK. So what does this fellow Dulles say?"

"Well, he's a lawyer, and a very successful one at that, so he does tend to speak in circles with every sentence a conditional, but over dinner last night he said that Japan, not Germany, is this country's greatest adversary, not only now but in the future. And he does have an excellent grasp of history."

"According to Dulles, by 1970 Japan will be the first supernation in history—150% of U.S. GNP; we have to do something now, or they will be unstoppable and the white race will be doomed."

"Oh, for Christ's sake, Harry, get a grip of yourself—the Japs ahead of us?—impossible. I am not sure if you know this but the average Jap has no balance—they are carried around on the backs of their mothers and this completely destroys their balance—they can barely drive an automobile let alone fly a fighter 'plane. Probably couldn't drive my fucking prison-on-wheels," said Roosevelt referring to the wheelchair he hated so much.

"Perhaps, but we need to stop them now," Hopkins retorted

"Dulles says we don't have a lot of time—they work like Trojans, but with the brains of a white man. Their weakness is their lack of oil; we need to nip these Nips in the bud, now."

The President of the United States smiled at Hopkins's pun.

Hopkins leant forward, opened his small black briefcase and extracted a nondescript and well-worn manila folder. From inside the folder he removed three copies of a report. He passed one first to the President and the second to Tugwell.

"This is a report I was given last night by John. It is from his brother, Allen, who, as you know, is currently in Switzerland. This report is a translation by the Swiss security office of a report from a German flyer who toured the Mitsubishi Heavy Industry plant in Yokohama in May '39; Allen is apparently on very good terms with the Swiss security people," Hopkins said with a smile.

"This report is from a German in their Condor Legion in the Spanish Civil War, he was one of the leaders of the devastating air attacks in July '37 in the Battle of Brunete; it was the German air support that won that battle, and much of that war. Anyway, please turn to page five, starting at the second paragraph." Hopkins read aloud,

THE GODDESS OF FORTUNE

From the hotel to the factory by car I was driven. At the main gate the manager and five of his senior staff greeted me. The main gate and the factory itself were both modest and spotlessly clean. Two small green shrubs in earthenware tubs were the only decoration and two ladies had just finished the daily trimming, these ladies proudly stood beside their wards. The manager and the five staff all wore the same dark blue uniforms which I take as the color of the factory. The translator explained how the factory was honored to meet an ace who had flown the famous Messerschmitt 109 so successfully in battle. I was surprised to learn how much they knew; during the tour, the armorer specialist offhandedly remarked on my change of the ratio of my cartridges from 30/70 to 50/50, armor to incendiary. This really shocked me as I had forgotten this change myself.

The factory itself was extremely well lit. But what first struck me was the complete absence of wood—back in Germany all our factories, including aircraft factories make extensive use of wood for shelving, and even for support and construction jigs for wing assemblies, and so on. In this Yokohama factory there was no wood to be seen. One of the senior managers—a Mr. Horikoshi— explained that wood was not used so all workers would come to see light alloy as their natural wood. I walked over to one of the shelves holding cylinder heads and was shocked to see that even the light alloy shelves had been carefully painted with a clear shellac lacquer.

The factory was divided into four sub-factories: two lines for 'plane assembly; one—the largest—for engine building and testing; and one for radio and navigation.

"Galland-san, we have studied Fordism and have, we like to think, in our own little ways, improved it. Mr. Ford is a great man and he is our inspiration," the manager told me. I was shocked how the workers were so efficient. As we passed each of the 22 stations on the line, the workers would pause, and all bow together to me. I must say, I felt like a feted virgin.

As a pilot, the construction of these 'planes—called the 'Zero'—was of greatest interest to me. The wing construction was of particular interest. When I examined the wings assemblies being fabricated, I was shocked to see the extremely lightweight nature of the wings and I frowned. Mr. Horikoshi seemed to read my mind and he explained that his company had initially withdrawn from the competition for the Imperial Navy's new fighter, but by working with Sumitomo, Mitsubishi was able to use a special new alloy called Extra Super Duralumin. Even as a lay person and not as metallurgist, it is clear to me that the Japanese are clearly well ahead of us in metallurgy. And there were even more startling revelations to come.

Eventually, we came to the final of the four sub-factories where the radio and navigation equipment was assembled and tested. In the navigation assembly area we passed through three separate air-tight doors and I had to remove my shoes and put on cotton slippers, and a cotton cap like a lady's shower bath cap. If the rest of the factory was clean, this assembly area was like nothing I had ever seen—the air was specially manufactured with the humidity and temperature both strictly controlled.

At one of the light-alloy benches, Mr. Horikoshi passed me a pivot pin used in the compass of the 'plane. It was an ordinary looking pin, one millimeter in diameter and about 40 millimeters in length. I examined it and passed it back to Mr. Horikoshi who smiled enigmatically. He took the pin and clamped it to a small clamp under a huge lense. Beneath the clamp was a small electric light. After a moment or two of adjusting the clamp's vernier screws, Mr. Horikoshi invited me to look. "Shit," is all I said. All the Japanese laughed.

Under the magnification of the huge lense, I was able to see that there was a tiny hole that had been drilled the entire length of the pivot pin. The shock on my face was genuine, and I started to splutter, not making any sense. A few seconds later, I regained my composure.

"This is the most astonishing engineering feat I have even seen; how is this done?"

Proud of the praise, Mr. Horikoshi was happy to explain,

"These critical pins are made at three special factories in northern Kanto. The locations of these factories were selected based on the quietness of the ground there. As you know, Japan is on edge of the Pacific Rim and is thus prone to earthquakes, but most of the time the ground in northern Kanto is very stable. Our engineers conducted micro-seismic studies and surveys for six years before building the three factories. The hole you see is able to take a strand of a young girl's hair, but it is a very tight fit."

I simply shook my head.

"Galland-san, we have a demonstration I think you will find entertaining."

After this, I doubted I would be surprised, but I was wrong.

We walked to the engine test area.

In the middle of the floor were two blocks of ice, each about twice the size of the ice block used in domestic iceboxes in homes in Germany. Each block, waist high, sat on a cotton mat about five centimeters thick, and these mats in turn sat on light-alloy stands with four splayed legs. On a large table lay two swords, one was a sword from the Middle Ages. I recognized it immediately from my school boy outings to museums in Germany as a Great Sword, a massive two-handed affair about one and half meters long and weighing at least eight kilograms. In contrast, the other was modest: about half the length, slightly curved, and beautifully decorated with intricate engravings running the entire length. One could easily be forgiven for thinking it a work of art, rather than a weapon. Mr. Horikoshi explained this was a traditional Samurai sword.

Standing beside the table was one of the workers from the factory, a slight chap who was almost a head shorter than me. Beside him stood the largest Japanese man I have ever seen, not fat, but all muscle. It was explained to me he was the current All Japan National Amateur Wrestling Champion and I had no reason to doubt it.

Apparently, he worked in the factory and he towered over his companion.

Mr. Horikoshi asked me to take the huge sword and to cut a block of ice in two. Obviously I was extremely hesitant to do this, but, of course, I could not decline after all the wonderful hospitality afforded me. So, somewhat hesitantly, I lifted the monster with both hands, and it was even heavier than it looked. I staggered a little and the two Japanese men had wisely moved well away. Mr. Horikoshi advised me to swing it in increasingly vertical circles, making the motion himself of what to do. With difficulty I was able to swing the sword, and after six rather unstable swings was finally able to bring the sword crashing down on the block of ice. I felt a terrible pain as the shock ran up my arms. A few chips of ice flew from the ice block. Then Mr. Horikoshi instructed the wrestler to take the sword from my hands. Free from this burden I examined the block of ice—it was essentially undamaged. The wrestler's swinging of the Great Sword made mine look puerile. After seven or eight swings the sword came down on the ice block. The entire table shook. I was pleased to see that his efforts were just as ineffectual as my own. The wrestler bowed and replaced the monster sword on the table. The pain in his arms must have been extra-ordinary but he did not grimace at all.

At this stage, the small worker stepped forward and took the Samurai sword. But rather than swinging the sword as we had done, he took three very large steps backward away from his block of ice. He held his sword in both hands and raised it above his head. He stood motionless, standing like a statue for almost a minute.

Then, suddenly, with a shout, ran at the block bringing the sword down with such speed the steel became a blur. Just as suddenly he retraced his three steps and held the sword above his head, as if preparing to strike again.

As he resumed his statue-like pose, the two halves of the block of ice hit the concrete floor. Uncontrollably, my mouth hung open. Mr. Horikoshi smiled, and said, "Galland-san please inspect the matting."

I did so and was shocked to see that the cotton mat had itself was deeply cut, cut so much that the bamboo padding was exposed.

I said to Mr. Horikoshi, "I said before that I have seen the most amazing engineering. I was wrong. This is even more amazing, and this technology is over 600 years old."

Mr. Horikoshi, bowed deeply and said, "With deepest respect, Galland-san, this Japanese technology is older than the Christian Jesus. This particular sword is over 500 years old."

I simply shook my head in disbelief. Had I been asked before the display, I would have been completely confident in predicting the outcome, and I would have been completely wrong.

But there was still one more shock left for me that day.

I thanked Mr. Horikoshi, and said, "your factory deeply impresses me, and I am amazed at the design on your new fighter. The designer is a man of extra-ordinary talent and foresight."

Mr. Horikoshi said in a very quiet voice, "Galland-san, I am the designer."

Roosevelt looked up and said, "so, we're in a fight."

Hopkins nodded, and said,

"And remember, Mr. President, the Japanese are a people who plan in terms of decades, not days. And they have such a love of country that they will bear any burden, or meet any hardship to preserve the honor of their country."

These words would ring in the President's ears in December.

But then, just as suddenly, the momentary thoughtfulness evaporated, and the demagogue returned,

"Well, I have provoked them as much as possible. Why, if I had been provoked half as much, I would have started a war. These fucking people have the patience of a fucking saint. I started the oil embargo; I've stopped them from using our Canal. You know, I've played all the cards."

Hopkins knew this would happen, so he plowed on,

"Well, we need to do a number of things, according to Dulles: put our war industry on a crash rebuilding course; build up the West Coast now, not next year, but now; we need a war and we need a war we can win. The Alaska Territory is our ace in the hole—the Hawaiian Islands to Japan is 4,110 miles, but Dutch Harbor to Japan is 3,583 miles and we have a land bridge—no huge Pacific Ocean to cross. By building up Alaska we have a strong, stable northern base that we can completely control. We build a rail link from Seattle and we can run express trains up there. It would be a dagger pointing at the heart of Japan. Especially if we cut a deal with Stalin. With Stalin on board, we could even lease some bases in eastern Russia like we did in Cuba in '03. And, keep in mind, the Soviets still remember 1905, so there is no love lost between the Russians and the Japanese."

Hopkins paused for effect.

"And, if we promised Stalin war materiel, he could use his railroads in western Russia to bring it east, safe from the Germans."

"Hmm," Roosevelt could see the reasonableness of the approach.

"Of course, Winston would not be happy."

"Yes, but the British are finished; why even the Irish have defeated them and they're not exactly the smartest race on the planet. So it's only a matter of time before the colored countries of their so-called Empire do the same as the Paddies have done."

"Well, that's a little far-fetched, don't you think?"

"Perhaps, but look at what the Japanese are doing to the Europeans in Asia and the last time I looked they were not white."

"Mr. President, here is the problem with Asia: with the defeat by the Germans of the Dutch and the French, their colonies in Asia are 'fragile,' and fragile is putting it mildly. Our possession of the Hawaiian Islands is stuck out in the middle of nowhere; Australia is the other side of the world; we have no friends—not that we want any—in South America. While not a state, Alaska is ours and with it a land bridge—no subs to sink convoys. We need to plan on attacking and destroying Japan now, not tomorrow. And we don't know how long Stalin can hold out. According to our intelligence, the Germans have moved over 700 miles into Russia in the past month. And frankly, Stalin is very weak at the moment. Now is the time to cut a deal—he's desperate for help."

Then Hopkins unsheathed the knife, "and what is the current unemployment percentage?"

Roosevelt flushed with anger and was about to speak.

Hopkins, in a move unprecedented in the history of the Oval Office, put his hand up to signal the President to stop.

"Excuse me, Mr. President, but as of last month, the number was 10.4% and it is not going down. A crash rail building program to Alaska when combined with similar effort for war industries out West could drop this to three or even two percent, now, today. Ridiculous though it sounds, we could build a special high-speed line. Last night, Dulles reminded me of an English engineer from last century who actually built a railroad with a seven-foot gauge. By using a gauge of seven- or even eight-foot, large sub-assemblies could be shipped from the Boeing aircraft plants in Seattle and from California."

11: The Seasoned Campaigner

Haus Wachenfeld
Saturday, 26 July 1941

AS THE OWNER WAS BUSY INSPECTING the new complex recently completed for him in Poland, the mountain house had been closed down for July and August—ever the Austrian penny pincher from Braunau am Inn, the owner saw no reason in wasting a pfennig. From the pile of reports Bormann had gotten from his obsequious and terrified informants and sycophants, the new Polish complex was a horror—hot, damp, fetid, and mosquito-infested; at night the air conditioning was so noisy that it left everyone tired and listless the next morning; the mosquitos were amazing in size and their ability to raise painful bites—Bormann's Chief had bored everyone by going on and on with boring jokes about how the *Luftwaffe* was at fault for these obnoxious airborne interlopers.

Bormann expected the owner to return, by Auntie Ju, to the mountain house in early September after attending to party business in Berlin; Bormann did not for a minute believe any of the malicious gossip about a new busty peroxide blonde that the hated little poison dwarf of a propaganda minister had introduced to Bormann's boss.

As far as Paul himself went, he was always a joke to Bormann. The amazing combination of Paul's stunted right leg and his breathtaking intellect—he was a Doctorate of Philosophy after all—made for the oddest man Bormann had ever encountered. Once Paul had confided to Bormann the approach he took to dalliance: "First, I have the lady over for a nice meal at my house by the lake, then I play my piano for three hours (I favor Chopin), and then I ask how she feels about the music and does she find it ethereally soothing" Bormann, the former farm laborer on a pig farm, smiled at Paul and asked, "Why don't you do as I do?" Paul fell into the trap and politely asked what that was. Bormann laughed, "Tell the bitch to sit on the couch; sit next to her; command her to open her legs; tell her to start sucking, and that the sucking better be good." Bormann laughed at the combination of shock and horror on little Paul's face.

"Paul, the difference between you and me is that you *chase* women, whereas I just tell them what to do. You're like all the others I hear here at the house, talking fancy words, but never getting any cunt. Whereas I have no fancy words, but more women than I can handle. Believe me, women all need to be told what to do and *like* being told what to do."

Paul glowered and said nothing.

The house was entirely empty—no kitchen staff, no butler, no gardeners. Even the SS Life Guard—resplendent in their new Hugo Boss uniforms—had been excused; a lone pair of sentries remained at the main gate, and that was a good ten minutes' walk from the house. Only Eva remained; what she did all day Bormann did not know, nor cared to know.

Bormann had—as always—taken a few liberties. He had stocked his prized new Electrolux Einstein-Szilard refrigerator in the nearby pantry with his favorite weizen bier, without realizing the inventor of the new 'fridge was a German physicist who had fled to America; no matter—the wheat beer was ice cold—that is all that mattered to Bormann; Bormann was a practical man.

He had checked on Eva that morning and found her in her room and as they were the only two living souls in the house had told her to find him if she needed anything. And the house was as if it was in the city of the dead; the birds outside were the only sound of life. It was a pleasant and relaxing change from the bustle and constant activity when the Chief was at home.

After checking on Eva, he roamed the empty house, it was like a deserted ski hotel that had closed for the summer—a little musty and damp in the carpets on the stairs. He entered the master bedroom and snooped and spied, opening drawers as he had done so many times before. Regardless of how often he did this, he always felt a small frisson of excitement at this petty sacrilege. He proceeded to the master bathroom, a very small and boring affair for such as great man of state as his boss was. He weighed himself on the Chief's bathroom scales, and, leaving the door open in an act of petulance, he proceeded to use the Chief's toilet to move his bowels. Afterwards, he weighed himself again on his boss's scales and was pleased to see he had lost almost half a kilogram.

It was hotter than Hell—the day was one of the hottest of that very hot summer. Bormann sat at the long table in the great hall. The monster was a full four paces long and had six, not four legs, and the surface was a deliciously cool marble, not one slab but three triangular pieces the Chief had personally selected from a very, very nervous Swiss stone merchant; what was the Swissie frightened of—the Swiss had been neutral for over 200 years? The delicious coldness of the marble was a refreshing contrast to the day's heat.

The great hall where Bormann sat was still, cool, and completely silent. At the long table, he had set up his store of ledgers and pencils; he never used ink—too hard to change. The large table sat along the far wall facing the picture window; he had used the electric switch to automatically raise the steel shutters so he could enjoy the panorama of the mountains from the huge floor-to-ceiling picture windows. Not for the first time sitting alone in the long room, he imagined himself as the lord—as the king of the manor, and why not; he was the Chief's right-hand man, after all? Here, he slowly and carefully checked the figures of deliveries and of produce delivered; "you can never be too careful with peasants—they are the shiftiest of all of God's creatures." In truth, he was simply playing at working—he had succeeded in terrifying all the peasants with threats of damnation or worse if Bormann was overcharged by as much as a pfennig.

A noise at the door made him look up. It was Eva. Apparently, she had been exercising on the small side terrace under the shade of the long canvas awning as she was wearing her customary silk gym slip and top—a delightful soft peach pink.

"I hope I am not disturbing you, Martin. Am I?"

He stood up at the table, and bowed slightly.

"Of course not, Miss Braun; how can I be of assistance?"

(*Always keep the tone with heavies very formal*, was a Bormann dictum. He always kept this slightly stilted formality even when they both knew they were the only two in the house.)

"Oh, I was just so hot and thirsty so I thought I would ask you for a glass of water from the pantry."

"Certainly, would you like some ice, Madam? It's so hot today."

He knew his boss was a very busy man, busy with the affairs of state, busy with international affairs, and—understandably—had no time for the softer affairs of the heart. On a more practical level, Bormann knew from the housekeepers that the owner rarely, if ever, made any visits to Miss Braun's room—"you can always tell if two people have slept in a bed," the grizzled head housekeeper had confided. The sad truth was that the chief's eye had moved to the more buxom starlets in Berlin that little Paul was able to supply in large numbers as controller of the *Reich's* film industry. As happened with many men, Bormann's boss was able to maintain the little wifey at home while getting a roster of new, fresh and exceedingly nubile young starlets in Berlin, all looking to please to further their careers; "after all, it is just the same as eating or shitting," one of the girls from the provinces had proclaimed with charming candor.

Even from the doorway, Bormann could see Eva was already excited and Bormann loved to savor the observation of an excited woman. Thousands of conquests let him sense it like a prize fighter relishes an opening in his opponent's defense. Some boxers were close to perfect with just a tiny flaw, but that tiny flaw—if exploited properly—would put them on the canvas, or at least put one knee down. In Eva, it was her modest chest, or more specifically, her nipples—the light reflected on her silk top and he could see clearly two bumps which she made no attempt to hide. Why should she—they were completely alone?

And he knew from the housekeepers' discrete observations that Eva's monthly was only two or three days off—she was in high heat, like a cat screeching at night for relief.

"Madam, would you prefer a cold beer? I have an exceptionally good cloudy German wheat beer with an excellent after-taste." (Bormann had heard Albert drone on and on about wines. So Bormann had decided to use the same approach with his beloved beers—it would certainly make Bormann look smarter; at least Bormann thought it would.)

"Oh yes! My husband told me he loved the German wheat beer when he was in Munich in the early days. He was drinking this beer with chicken the day when that terrible, terrible thing happened with his niece in his apartment. But that is all in the past now, isn't it? I mean my husband has you and me now, doesn't he?"

Eva used "husband" all the time around the house to everyone from the maids to Bormann, even though there had never been any ceremony. It was her way to assert an ascendency over all in the house. And it worked with everyone apart from Bormann, as he was the Chief's right hand, and Eva knew this.

"You know, beer is far more refreshing in summer," he lied.

He rose and returned from the pantry. He brought a coaster as well. I was one of the cheap, coarse leather coasters he had made by the hundreds, with the party insignia and "Wachenfeld" stamped on it. As with all supplies to the house, Bormann skimmed his normal eight percent.

"We have to give the tourists something to steal," he had told his boss. When the *Duce's* party had left after their last visit, all these coasters—and a lot else—had disappeared. "They are Italian," he told his boss, as if that explained their mendacity. The Chief nervously laughed briefly at Bormann's comment—perhaps it was a little too close to the truth.

Eva sipped the beer.

"You are right, this is *so* refreshing."

Bormann noticed how she had emphasized the adjective.

Then she did the classic action of a woman on the prowl—she brushed her hair slowly with her free hand, then touching her neck as she slowly rotated her head, affecting the appearance of bearing the problems of the world on her shoulders—Atlas had no burden compared to poor Eva.

Bormann smiled to himself—he should write a book on women; for all their artifice and haughty distance, they were as transparent as petulant children.

She put down the beer and started sliding up and down the huge room. She was still wearing the ballet slippers she wore when exercising, and she slid on the polished marble floor of the great hall like an ice skater.

"Martin, you know we are the two luckiest people in the world, do you know? You and I are the Chief's right-hand man and his right-hand woman."

He expected a giggle, but none was forthcoming.

Instead, she slid over to the table and leaned forward, to give Bormann his first clear view of her *décolletage*. Her nipples were slowly getting larger. While she was looking at him, he looked directly at her nipples so she could see him looking. He loved this part of the seduction, when the woman was so excited and was trying so hard to tease, and to please, but her excitement worked against her—they both knew what she wanted and he was far too seasoned a campaigner to make any rushed moves.

It was like when he was playing checkers with the other farm hands before the Struggle had started; some days he could look three or even four moves ahead, it was as if he was a machine and his hands simple implements to move the pieces on the board.

She knew this as well, and his sense of control—and thus power—made her more excited. She sat down in the large green chair at the end of the table, and how she sat did start to stir the old trooper in him.

When the boss was home, Eva played the Vestal Virgin perfectly—often not even making eye contact, but soft, sweet, demure, innocent and pure.

But now, alone in the huge house—the house that could now rightly be called the center of the great new German empire—she sat with her legs splayed. For the first time since she entered, Bormann could see the clear outline of her camel toe, and she made no effort to hide it; clearly there was nothing under the pink silk gym shorts—she was a screeching cat and she could not help herself.

She sat there slowly drinking her beer. She was teasing herself as much as she was teasing him—she knew as well as he did what was about to happen.

While she offered herself to be ravished, Bormann leaned against the wall, as the table was next to the wall with cushions in the old Austrian farmhouse style; the instructions given by the owner to Albert were "simple but friendly;" Albert—as always—succeeded in hiding his disdain of the "taste" of the Austrian peasant, who had flattered Albert with "the greatest genius the world had even seen" and such like nonsense.

"You look like you need another," Bormann said after a while.

Eva readily agreed.

Bormann went to the refrigerator, which he insisted on calling "his icebox" and fetched two more bottles.

He poured another beer for Eva.

He had brought a bottle of schnapps,

"Madam, would you like a little of this as well?"

"Oh yes, but just a little."

He loved this part of the seduction, when the woman's first volley had come to naught. He thought about what her next tack would be. Even while thinking this, Eva started,

"Oh, beer with schnapps always makes me so lightheaded." (The oldest retort in the play book, Bormann thought.)

Bormann said nothing.

The alcohol was starting to work its effects, as she asked, "Martin, you remember Berlin in the '20s?"

Bormann said he did, not that he did, but this was clearly a lead-in to more.

"Hoffie is such as bad man, you know he took me and Sally, his other assistant, to some nightclubs. Do you know the Pink Diamond?"

Bormann said he did, another fib.

"Hoffie took us there; it's a nightclub, you know? And Sally was such a randy little minx—she always embarrassed me, she was so forward." (The ubiquitous I-am-pure-but-she-is-a-slut play.)

"Well, we were all there one Saturday evening—it was hot like today, but it was pouring rain so everyone in the club came in drenched, and before long it was like a Swedish sauna—so hot and steamy. And there was a stage and on the stage there were three women from the East, you know Slavs, and beside them was a huge Negro man with massive muscles—he was very tall and he was very black, black like ebony, and under the lights you could see how much he was sweating, but that is not what most people were looking at."

She paused for effect and for more beer and schnapps.

Bormann knew what was next and could fathom what she was leading to, but like an actor who had practiced his lines a thousand times, he replied.

"Oh" (short answers showing no interest at all teased these vixens more than anything.)

"Down there he was so big." (Obligatory giggle.)

"You were looking?"

"It was impossible to miss—it was so big—more like one from a horse than from a man. And Sally said to Hoffie, 'God, think of that thing inside you'—Hoffie just giggled, and now I know why he giggled. Actually I was getting tingles all over looking at it, and he did it to all three girls on the stage, one after the other, you know from behind and you could see it going into them and each of the girls cried out in some Eastern tongue as it must have been so extremely painful."

She looked at Bormann. Bormann could see her eyes looked like she had a touch of fever.

"Actually, I got the tingles then," she laughed.

"I have to tell you, Martin, that I even get tingles now all over again just telling you about it."

Bormann waited for the next question—it was just like checkers at the pig farm.

"I've heard you have done that, too; is that true?"

Quickly, she added, "I mean with proper German girls, not impure Slav whores, but three or four at once, is that true, Bormann?"

This was the part of the ritualistic Morris Dance that Bormann really enjoyed—making his minx-of-the-day "tingle."

Coyness was always the best counter.

"What do you mean, Miss Braun?"

With the alcohol, the months of neglect, and her imminent period, there was now no stopping her, she raced on and on.

"Oh Martin, for God's sake call me Eva. I am Eva to him. I can be Eva to you. Today, I can be Eva to you. Well, I have heard that you, that you sometimes have three or four girls from the village and from other places at your house at the same time. Do you ever do that? Tell me all about what you do with these women. Are they sluts or nice ladies. Are they all German? Are any married? Do they like it? What is it that they do for you? What is your secret?"

Just as suddenly as she had started, she paused.

"Do you mind me asking you, Martin?" she said, overcome with nervousness.

"Would that excite you, Eva, if that was the case? Should I tell you?"

"God, yes, I need to hear, I need to hear. Tell me, please. Please."

"Certainly. I will tell you. But just tell you—it has to stop at that, Eva; my boss, the Chief, trusts me and I would be betraying his trust."

"My husband tells me he trusts you more than any man alive, that you are a good man, an honest man, and that I can get from you anything I need. When he says *anything*, he truly means anything I need at all, and today I am very tense after my exercise, and remember it is just the two of us alone in this huge empty house. So can you help me today, Martin, I mean, with what I need today? To be relaxed today. Can you remove my tension? My tension is terrible today."

Bormann said he could. He stood and moved to the back of the chair. Without hesitating, he pinched her shoulder muscles very hard. He got the usual "that feels wonderful." He was looking down at her small breasts as he squeezed her shoulders.

"Eva, now you know today has to be a dream; it is just for today and never again, and I will destroy you if you mention this to anyone."

As expected, this threat excited Eva rather than frightened her.

"So here is what I do. I do get girls at my house up the hill when the boss is in Berlin, and I relax with them. Actually, for me it is more like work. First, have the girls up to my house while my wife is at the baths at Baden or somewhere else."

Eva's eyes opened a little at this announcement that Bormann's wife helped out from time to time.

As if ordering a load of potatoes from a local farmer, Bormann went on.

"I play some gramophone records, we have some beer and schnapps, it is normally early on a Saturday afternoon when it is quiet and slow here in the mountains. I relax the girls. Some of these country girls are extremely shy while others are very eager—women all vary, some are bashful, but all are very excited to be with a powerful man of the *Reich*; the young mothers are the most randy, must be Nature telling them to breed more. Then I slowly play with each of them in turn, with them fully dressed at first, touching them, teasing them. Then, very slowly, I slide my hand up their dresses. They are all so wet, so excited at this slow teasing. You see, I like to tease them, very, very slowly—what's the rush, we have all Saturday and Saturday evening? Only twice have I been forced to ask one to leave."

"To leave?"

"Well, even with the two of them still clothed, I could smell them on my fingers—it was like opening a can of Norwegian sardines. But, this is so rare as German womanhood is so pure—not like the animalistic Slavs. Only two German women in over 300 have I ever told to leave. All the others were so wet and clean and so, well, 'panting' I suppose is the best way to describe it. And they are always so wet. Must be the mountain air. And with all these pure, German women, the teasing is the best part, don't you think?"

With this Bormann lightly rubbed Eva's arms, and she reacted by taking the cold beer glass and brazenly rolling it over her nipples. She was drunk and very, very randy. Her pink top was now wet and when she put the beer glass down, she opened her already uncrossed legs. When she did this Bormann could clearly see his goal for the first time.

"Go on. Please tell me what you do next—what do you do next?" she said, lightly panting.

"Then I take them to the big bedroom—you've been to my place. Well, it is the big bedroom that overlooks this house and all the way down the mountain. I like to do it from behind and with their dresses on, just hitched up. I think doing it to a woman with her clothes on is the most exciting way. I do one, then the next, then the next one, in turn."

Now Eva was panting heavily, "You do it in each of them?"

"No, no, no—that never works. Do that and you have lots of dissatisfied customers. No, the trick is to hold back, otherwise a man gets soft right away. And the German schnapps helps keep a man very hard. No, you have to wait. So I entertain each one for a few minutes, I like the girl to complete so I can feel her clamping on me. But not too much, you want to her to want more for the next lap. You have to be very careful because if the girl completes too much then it is too exciting for the man, and it's easy for the man to complete too early if you are not careful. It's extremely exciting to see all these girls lined up on all fours on the bed—four in a row, dresses hitched up over their bodies."

"You have a real system, and these girls are virgins?"

"No, no, no—never virgins. Virgins have the obvious benefit of being tight, but they have no idea of what to do, and it is too much trouble to teach them. And virgins are often nervous. No, the best are young, randy wives who love getting it every day, but with their husbands away in the army, they are all very tight from lack of use. And there is always the promise of a safe and friendly assignment for their husbands. And there are a lot I do on a Return Ticket—you know, out and back, they come back again and again for more."

"You make it sound like work."

"It is half and half; half work but also fun—you would not believe the noise—four young, randy German women all in heat and completing (they often use their fingers on themselves while waiting for me to properly relieve their itch). You see, what makes all women most excited is when they see other women getting excited, it excites all the others and then the first one gets more excited, and so on. The noise is like a Stuka attacking—you know our new dive bomber with the screaming airbrakes. It is always very loud; that is why my wife is at the baths in Baden and I dismiss my servants for the weekend. But I like it. It's a good way to pass the time; who knows—the British or Russians might invade any day and kill us all."

"You see, when women are in a group like this, they immediately become raw animals who all want to be next, they like the act, but even more, they want to get the power. They start competing for the man. Whenever you get two or more women together, even in a social environment in a bar, instantly they start competing. Even when I worked on the farms years ago, on a Saturday night I would take the ugliest girl I could find into town, and just her presence would attract other women like moths to a candle. It works every time. This is why when you have four women all kneeling on all fours on the edge of the bed, they get amazingly excited and they make so much noise when you're inside them because they have never been so excited—Mother Nature is making them be the one to get the man's seed. This is why they are so wet, and why they try to make you complete in them and not the other girls. And to be the winner, they actually will do anything and they say the wildest things—things I cannot even imagine."

Eva was too excited to let this last idea disrupt her. Later, Bormann doubted if she even heard it.

She then did the standard procedure of girls like her—she stood and walked to the far end of the table, the end with no papers or pencils, she bent over the table and she turned her head to the side.

Looking at Bormann, she said,

"Martin, please show me what you do to them. Now."

"Eva, this is what I do and this is what other men don't do to you."

While she may have been envied by tens of millions of German women, and on the cover of countless women's magazines, the fact was that she could not remember the last time she had been entertained by her "husband." She later confessed to Bormann that she did not understand if she had lost her appeal to him or what it was.

Eva was panting breathlessly and demanded it rough—she liked a little pain; actually, she liked more than a little, just like the three Slavs with the huge Negro at the Pink Diamond.

Eva was deliciously tight—very wet like any experienced woman, but oddly tight—almost like a virgin. Immediately, Bormann felt her starting to tighten and contract, and the contractions came faster and harder very quickly. But before she completed for the first time—and to ensure her heat continued—he stopped and he lay on the floor.

Once on the floor, he had Eva do all the work, perched above him bobbing up and down like a cork on a fishing line. She was so tight that when she descended fully for the first time, he felt her start to complete, so he thought no reason in waiting and he dumped all he had into the First Mistress Of The New *Reich*, or as she preferred to think of herself, the First Lady Of The New *Reich*. His extra lubrication made her climax deepen. Bormann smiled to himself at the thought of someone interrupting them—the insanity of the event, the shock. But, what the hell? He would lie his way out of it as he always did. But no one appeared and he stood her up and with Eva facing the picture window, he hardened again and took her from behind. This time, very roughly and she made a lot of noise; clearly the forced abstinence made her like it even more.

After 15 minutes, she collapsed.

"Oh my God, I needed that. We need to do this more often. I miss it so much. You know, I am a normal girl with normal desires and needs. Once, when I was very randy just like this, I had Hoffie relieve my tension, even though he is a homo. You know, it was like a dream—once I saw that slut Sally stroking him and teasing my boss in the office and I knew I had to have Hoffie, it was like an invisible hand of some primitive spirit that made me force him to put his thing inside me first, and complete inside me first. I don't know what it was, it was just that he had to do me first to give me of him before Sally got any. It was madness. I need this more often."

Bormann shook his head, "No, Eva, this is the first and last time—too many problems."

She nodded, sad and wistful, "Yes, I suppose you are right."

As it happened, Bormann's boss—his beloved Chief—was never again to see Bormann or Eva or the large table.

12: The Wingless Eagle's Last Flight

Haus Wachenfeld
Monday, 1 September 1941

THE FIRST DAY OF SEPTEMBER was the hottest day of the hell-ish summer of '41. And at a mountain house, it was a real tar burner. By nine in the morning, the sun had already turned the terrace into a furnace, the alpine elevation doubling the sun's power. It seemed like every blade of grass had given up the struggle and decided to turn brown, as if it was a wounded animal feigning death.

Breakfast, normally served to the guests on the terrace, had been moved to the great hall. Bormann had the "manufactured air machine"—his dated term for the air conditioning plant located in the lowest basement of the mountain house—running at full capac-ity. Like a prized Pekingese, he moved from guest to guest to annoy each of them in turn with his self-important chatter, mentioning to each in turn how hard he was working—"Like a draft horse. No, worse actually, as animals get Sunday to rest; for me there is never any rest."

"And less brains than a draft horse," was Albert's unspoken thought.

Albert move to the balcony and sat alone, allowing the heat to envelop him. But, even with his second excellent double espresso, he was getting just a little sleepy. Nevertheless, the glorious view of the mountains and the sound of the birds made Albert feel completely at ease—no squabbling petty officials with their fastidious attention to their shirt cuffs and the precise knotting of their ties, and their vacuous arguments about why they should be the sixth car in the entourage—"not stuck in the back in car 17"—oh, the horror of not being in the top eight.

His brief reverie of calmness was broken when Jodl greeted him, accompanied by Milch.

"Well, it is one for the record books today," Milch said.

His two companions agreed.

On the terrace the three men sat under one of the light-blue-and-white-striped umbrellas. They were alone except for the occasional cack-handed spying exercises by Bormann who would periodically patrol to inquire if they needed anything: Would they be having lunch with us today? Did they need any more coffee—it is real coffee here? His inane list seemed endless.

Jodl was universally known for two traits: the extreme ugliness of his wealthy Swabian wife and his ears. He was pitied for the first and named "Wing Nut" for the second. Regardless of these two trivialities, Jodl possessed the greatest tactical, and certainly the strongest strategic, mind living, with the possible exception of his British counterpart, the dour and modest teetotaler, Ulsterman Field Marshal Alan Brooke.

Jodl was a swarthy and earthy Bavarian with a very quiet demeanor that belied his outstanding intellect. It was Jodl who had held his nerve during Narvik while his leader, whimpering and vacillating like a whipped dog, changed his mind by the minute. It was

Jodl who rapped his knuckles with each word until they were white on the massive oak table in the conference room, as he stated, "In—times—of—extreme—pressure—a—leader—needs—to—lead." The nine other staff officers in the room each inwardly gasped at the audacity of this act.

At the end of this statement, there was a very, very long pause; the leader straightened, and actually pulled down the tails of his uniform jacket, as nervous young cadets the world over do. Careful to been seen studying the map and avoiding any contact with Jodl's eyes, he asked the plaintive question, "Jodl, so what do you recommend?" showing Jodl's dominance over the Austrian. The effect on all of the professional military men present was to cast the very first seeds of doubt about the so-called supreme commander, whose only real experience was as a very brave but very lowly message runner on the Western Front in the Great War.

"Let's go to the lookout," suggested Jodl, "Fewer ears there."

The other two nodded.

The trio made their way down the stone path Bormann had created two years earlier.

The lookout was a collection of three Austrian gazebos Bormann had had built the previous year. Rough-hewn, they were in the traditional Austrian mountain style so favored by the owner.

Once seated, Jodl offered his cigar case—from Dunhill's of London.

"A gift from a Swiss colleague," Jodl explained.

Both accepted.

Albert was not a great cigar smoker, but he was the greatest chameleon of the *Reich*. On the other hand, Milch loved to smoke—"Cigar" was one of the two nicknames his staff had given him; "The Diplomat" was the other, as he was probably the least

145

diplomatic commander in the *Reich*—"totalfuckinghorseturd" was his mildest statement of reproach.

Five minutes of small talk followed about the quality of the Cuban cigars.

Albert moved the conversation to France of the previous year. Jodl said,

"Yes, sitting here is a far cry from the dust of France in last May. Last year in France, we were constantly on the move. There was no quietude or stillness. We covered so much ground. The French collapse was astonishing. It was like watching snowflakes land on a red-hot stove—they were gone in an instant. I've never seen anything like it. I can't image it happening again in my lifetime."

There was a thoughtful pause,

"I suppose this is what 1870 must have been like, when the Krupps destroyed the French in an afternoon."

Albert said nothing. His extensive dealings with officers had taught him that getting them to start speaking was the hardest task. And while a few were buffoons, his experience was that the senior *Wehrmacht* ranks were far more sophisticated, better educated, and above all, more thoughtful than the shallow politicians who were their nominal overlords.

"The Russian campaign seems to be going splendidly, would you agree Jodl?"

"It is going very well, actually a little too well, but Russia is not France, and the Russians are not the French. In spite of the early success, I have some very disturbing reports from my commanders that many of the Russians refuse to surrender—they simply keep fighting, they never surrender. When out of ammunition, they simply charge our troops with their bayonets. From a military viewpoint, this is very disturbing to be facing soldiers with such spirit. I start to see what Napoleon was faced with 130 years ago. And there are so many of them—the Russian divisions seem endless."

"So, the notion of 'All You Have To Do Is Kick In The Front Door And The Whole Rotten Edifice Will Come Crashing Down' is not true?" Albert asked.

"I am not sure what the Chancellor was thinking when he made this truly odd remark," Jodl replied.

No one spoke as they each tried to determine what the other two were thinking.

"My concern is when we face reversals, how we will react. As Schlieffen liked to remark, 'a war without a crisis is simply a skirmish,' and that is my concern. The Swiss military men I speak to from time-to-time mention that we Germans seem to lack the coherency that we had in France last year."

"I share that concern," Milch added thoughtfully.

Albert said, "My concern is this, my thesis, as it were, is: we are very strong at home, but we have no foreign policy at all and we are lumbered with extremely brittle allies. The Chancellor seems to be completely under the spell of the *Duce*, who I see as weak and vacillating. What is your view of Italy, Jodl?"

"In two thousand years of war, there is probably no worse ally than Italy today—they are just harvest hands, nothing more, nothing less. Remember how they waited to declare war until we had done all the fighting last year in France?" Jodl blandly replied.

Albert asked Jodl to elaborate.

What made Jodl so impressive was his complete detachment— he was like a chess grandmaster: always cool and clear; never flustered; never emotional; never theatrical. He simply analyzed the situation as if reviewing the position of pieces on a chess board, and for him they *were* pieces on a board. With Jodl there was no shouting, no pouting, no insults, no threats as there was from someone who proclaimed to all the world that he himself was a military genius.

"Mussolini is essentially an overgrown and exceedingly pompous boy scout. He lacks all the basics. He is a typical Italian dreamer,

147

he dreams of a new Roman empire, with him as the new Roman emperor. Look at Abyssinia in '35—God help us, he actually had to resort to poison gas against native tribesmen. And I've seen firsthand his deployment in North Africa and it makes me shudder—he has his camps much too far apart, so they can be picked off piecemeal by a wily opponent, and while the British are currently on the back foot, the Italians are asking for trouble. Our German attachés have tried to warn him, but the Italians are so proud and vain, proud and vain that is until they suffer their first defeat, when they simply surrender *en masse*."

"In addition, their commanders are all inept. Here is a perfect example of basic rules that our friends in the south break: German field commanders eat only after their men, to ensure their men are fed first in case the food runs out; German commanders share the same rations; German commanders share the same privations. In contrast, the Italian officers eat superior food, they even get wine, and they get special tents, some with electric fans that are run off the trucks' electric batteries. I can think no better way to create discord, and the Italian fighting men are clearly not of the same caliber as our soldiers to begin with. But we can never broach any criticism of the *Duce*. Italy could very quickly become a millstone around our neck."

After a fractional pause, Jodl corrected himself,

"Will become, it is simply a matter of time. And remember, the Italians soldiers are all babies—they all lack the guts of the German soldier."

Jodl smiled. Observing Albert's natural coolness, Jodl continued: "I am sure these stories and military points bore you, Albert."

Albert shook his head.

The gazebo was five paces from the edge of the vertical cliff. The largest of the three gazebos was the size of a German workman's house, typical of Bormann's complete lack of proportion. It was another brainchild of Bormann who seemed to have an endless list of projects all designed solely to curry favor with his protector.

Ever the diplomat, Milch asked Jodl: "Forget that fucking horseshit; how is the Russian campaign actually progressing?"

Jodl said nothing for a moment, looking at the ash forming on the end of his cigar, and then replied,

"It's far more brittle than we expected. As I said, our biggest problem is a lack of clear objectives. And our intelligence has been woeful."

Jodl was couching his words, as he did not know how much he could trust his companions.

No one spoke. Albert broke the silence,

"I have an old professor who now lives in Switzerland. It is his view that the *Reich* is over-extended."

Jodl turned his head to look directly at Albert.

"The old Jewish chap?"

"Yes."

"But he is an economist, he knows nothing of military strategy. Don't tell me I have to deal with yet another fucking amateur?" Jodl asked, making a not very veiled reference to the owner of the mountain house.

"Yes, he is the economist and as he says—and I agree—modern war these days is now primarily an economic battle, not a battle of swords and shields, or men and aircraft. I visited him recently. He pointed out that we are very poorly positioned for a long war—if we do not end this war in '42, we're done for; for one thing we simply do not have sufficient labor for our factories. His point was that America is a huge and untapped powerhouse. While they are neutral at the moment, their presence in this war will likely lead to a German defeat. They don't even need send any troops, but if they start supplying *en masse* then Russia could become very sticky for us. We simply lack the labor and we lack the oil."

Jodl said, "At present we are out-maneuvering the Russian commanders, but one thing my training has taught me is that enemies start to adopt the winning tactics of their opponents, and Stalin is a wise old bird, the opposite of Mussolini."

Albert thought and said,

"Our immediate goal should be to keep America out of the war. The Germans and the British are natural allies. The Far East is unstable, and the American President Roosevelt is trying to provoke both us as well as the Japanese. The Americans are the winners with a bankrupt Britain and a prostrate Germany, and that is precisely what Roosevelt is trying to create. As far as Japan is concerned, sooner or later the Japanese and the Americans will be at war. When—not if—when this happens, if we throw our lot in with the Americans, we get a strong ally, we isolate Russia and we stir up a hornets nest in London. But, we have to plan for this now, and we have to be ready for this inevitable Pacific war, and we have to declare for America, not Japan."

Jodl decided he needed to take a risk, "Well, he may be correct. Milch, what do you think?"

"I agree, but in the current political climate, I don't see how the fuck any of us can change anything."

The "current political climate" Milch referred to was the current Chancellor.

"Albert, you have more sway with him than me or Jodl; can't you speak to him?"

Albert said, "I hardly think he will listen to his part-time architect."

There was silence.

"Our leader is hale and hearty, apart from his chronic bowel problems," Albert continued.

"Not if you speak to Morell," was Jodl's cheeky reply, referring to the Chancellor's disgusting and obese doctor, who was universally considered a quack by all, apart from his "Patient A." Milch often told the stories of how Morell would poke two of his fingers (with filthy black fingernails) into an orange and them proceed to suck out the contents of the orange, or how he would plunge his dirty and hairy hands into a glass bowl of ice cubes and grab some ice for his drink, or how he bathed once every two weeks.

"Nevertheless, our host's general health is good—for now. But if this is an empire for a thousand years, what happens when he is no longer blessed with such good health, which must happen sooner or later? 'All that live must die, passing through nature to eternity,' as the old play has it. And health aside, his choice of comrades is based solely on loyalty and his ability to manipulate them—look at our good friend Martin. And there is the little matter of the oath."

At this statement, Jodl's demeanor suddenly changed—"that fucking oath, total fucking madness—the German army swearing total alliance to a fucking foreigner. Christ Alive! Next, we will be swearing alliance to a French queer—there are enough of them these days."

It was true that the German army's swearing of the oath in 1934 had raised the hackles of all of the officers—to swear an oath to one person—not to the country, or even to an office. And to someone who was not even a German citizen until 1932, for God's sake.

Jodl's fuming subsided a little. Keeping to the safety of the hypothetical, as any good academic would, Albert went on,

"Just imagine for one terrible moment that the leader suffers a heart attack; how would Germany continue?"

The bishop had just been moved to determine the outcome of the match—both grandmasters said nothing, but both appreciated they were playing at the highest level.

Jodl's reply was shocking in its directness and simplicity, "There would be no difference."

Jodl drew on his cigar.

"Look, Albert, all three of us are adults here. I know precisely what you are asking me, and I would not trust this to another civilian. But you have a brain between your ears, so as you have been frank with me I will return the compliment. There are three military-types who run the *Reich*: me, Milch and Donitz. That's it. Milch can speak for himself, and I know Donitz and I think I can speak for him. He is no more enamored with the current regime than I—the murderers, the criminals, the fucking *Gauleiters*."

Jodl stopped, but the point had been made.

Albert probed, "So, if the terrible occurred and the leader was suddenly incapacitated or even died?"

Albert paused for effect, which was completely ineffectual on Jodl, who simply looked directly at Albert and waited for the obvious question.

"So, what would happen; I mean, what would be the mechanics?"

Jodl paused, looked out at the mountain range in the distance and said:

"The Untersberg is truly magnificent today, isn't she?"

Albert could not believe that Jodl was toying with him, but it both impressed and reassured him.

Albert smiled, "So, what happens?"

Albert had deliberately changed the tense as he sensed Jodl was clearly with him. Jodl drew in a deep breath and started to explain as if lecturing young cadets,

"Clausewitz teaches us the nation state needs a political structure, like a ship needs a command superstructure. Everyone agrees on this. What they do not agree on is the form of that political structure. We could discuss that until Jesus returns, if that ever happens. But for now we will agree a structure is needed. Today, we essentially do not have a structure. What we do have is a foreign dictator from Austria who is a superb actor and who is marvelous at reading people and especially good at detecting and exploiting their weaknesses. Remember how he played that homo Röhm in Operation Hummingbird—Operation Fuckingbird would have been a more appropriate name for the purge. But at running a country?"

Jodl turned up his face, and knocked the white-gray ash off the end of his cigar and continued—his blood was up:

"I have seen it for far too long. Have you seen him write a note—the man is almost illiterate? His handwriting like that of a child—that is why he never writes anything. That is why he *dictated* that pile of horse manure, 'On Five Years of Struggle Against Lies, Morons And Idiots,' or whatever the original title was. It's unreadable shit—total shit, and until his rise to power it had sold 971 fucking copies—the first edition sold 971 copies, then it became our fucking bible, a bible of shit. He cannot write; he cannot organize. And my army has a fucking oath to this man. Christ all fucking mighty, whose side is God on for the sake of fuck?"

Unfazed, Albert simply stated: "so if the leader died or decided to retire, you, Milch and Donitz could take over?"

Jodl paused, "Albert, you do not understand—we *are* already in control, *our* obstacle is the current political structure."

The treasonous talk petered out. And the conversation returned to the current situation in Russia.

Jodl expanded his explanation, as much as a review for himself as for the other two:

"Our problem is oil, or more specifically the lack of oil. We're in much the same boat as the Japanese and the dago shit-eaters, our so-called fucking allies to the south." Jodl hated the Italians with their posturing, their laziness, and worst of all their desire to leave brave Germans soldiers unsupported when even the weakest enemy appeared.

The strategic genius returned,

"It's the simplest classic problem of military logistics: every kilometer we advance into Russia is one more kilometer our tanker trucks need cover. And in contrast to our tanks, these oil tankers are thin skinned—even the simplest raid by enemy 'planes can leave a critical oil convoy in shambles."

"And as I earlier said, our intelligence has been poor for Russia. It is true that in the early weeks we made amazing progress—Leeb reached Dvinsk; Smolensk was in our hands; Rundstedt was at the gates of Kiev. In contrast to our leader's proclamation about kicking in the front door, he should have quoted his beloved Frederick the Great: 'You have to shoot every Russian dead twice, and still turn him over to make sure.' That is our problem."

No one smiled at this stark truism.

"The Russians are precisely—precisely—the opposite of what we were led to expect. Sometimes they charge our machine guns armed with pitch forks or axes. It's medieval, not 1941. And much of Russia is trackless. I feel we are the Romans fighting in the northern forests in 9 A.D.—and we all know how the three legions were massacred in the Teutoburg Forest; it's the same today in Russia. This whole campaign is a massive gamble—France was a bad enough gamble, but a loss or a stalemate in France would not have been fatal to the *Reich*. And we started the current campaign in Russia with all of 10 divisions in reserve. Guderian told me that the Chancellor had said to him four weeks ago, 'Had I known the Russians had that many tanks, I would have thought twice about attacking.' Wonderful. Fucking wonderful."

A neutral assessment by the Swiss intelligence service after the Armistice of '42 ranked Jodl with Alan Brooke as the two outstanding strategic thinkers of the European war, followed—a long way behind—by Rundstedt, Student and Guderian. His next statement showed the Swiss were correct.

"In Russia, we face two unrelated problems. The first is lack of focus—against all that Clausewitz taught us about 'maximum force on the minimum front'—we are trying to do everything. The second is the civilian administration—using the more brutal elements of the Gestapo, and the clowns—the fucking clowns—that are being assigned."

Jodl simply shook his head,

"It's like Poland all over again, but a thousand times worse. Here's an example: in the Ukraine we are being welcomed as liberators. Our German officers attend church services with the local worthies. But with the 17 July dictat, fucking Koch is in charge—Koch that fucking moron. He's so fucking stupid."

Here Milch interrupted,

"In Berlin at dinner one time Koch said to me 'If I meet a Ukrainian worthy of being seated at my table, I must have him shot.' I agree with Jodl completely—the man is a complete moron. Koch went on to tell me—in the most emphatic way—that quote, 'these Ukrainian peasants need to be taught to count to 400, learn the days of the week and the months of the year,' unquote. What an idiot."

Jodl said,

"It is people like Koch who will lose this war for us. The Ukraine is huge; it is almost twice the size of Germany. If properly managed, it can become a semi-autonomous *pāgus*, as the Romans did with Gaul. And the fucking Ukrainians love us and they hate the Russians with a passion. They love us—the fucking Germans—they love us. And so what do we do? The Austrian appoints a horse turd like Koch? The Ukrainians want to fight for us—for us, the fucking Germans—for Christ's fucking sake. And how do we reward these people? We give them fucking Horse Turd Koch."

Jodl shook his head. Jodl's level of irritation was easy to judge by the increase in the level of his profanity.

Jodl fumed and then started to return to his normal analytical calculating engine,

"The first problem is my problem—already, we are spread too thin, just as Albert's professor said. And why in the name of fuck are we attacking Leningrad? Well, I will tell you why. Solely because it is the birthplace of *Bolshevism*, for that sole reason, no other. No military significance is attached to it. And we're running out of time. Today is the 1st of September, and we're two years into the war. But in northern Russia—like Leningrad—the very first part of winter starts in 30 days' time. Last night, I was re-reading Napoleon's diary entries for his campaign in 1812 and it goes like this: 7 September: 'glorious weather, my troops are happy;' 14 October: 'first snow;' 7 November: 'freezing cold, my men are dying like flies, and I am losing 100 horses a day.' I will remind you gentlemen that the seventh of November is 68 days from today and 22 June is 70 days in the past. We are provoking the Fates in a very, very dangerous way."

Speer looked at the Diplomat, and then back to Jodl.

"So you suggest what?" Albert asked.

"Well, there is a simple solution—move south. Simple. Move south. Stalin's Achilles heel is oil—just as it is for us. And so we should attack south, protect our Ploesti oil fields and capture or destroy the Baku oil fields in the Caspian. We should collapse the current elephantine front to a line running from Brest-Litovsk to Kiev down to the Crimea and to Baku. I've discussed this with Rundstedt and he agrees. This line means we protect and strengthen Ploesti and Romania as a whole. We can also ferry fuel across the Black Sea. And it is warm—no fucking snow. With a line like this means we can have Turkey enter on our side, and if they don't, then fuck them—we're in a strong position to take Turkey by force. And with Turkey, we're in a very strong position to take the Middle East and then..."

Albert finished the sentence,

"The Suez Canal."

Jodl smiled.

"One of our biggest problems is that the current Chancellor is a political animal who deludes himself that he is a military expert. Lawyers kowtow to local hick politicians who promulgate the laws. Regardless of how bad these laws are, the lawyers take the laws as sacrosanct. Politicians are the same, they kowtow to the perceived leader, and because of the March of '23 to Rome, the Chancellor is enthralled by the short fat one in Rome. And this strutting Italian is the same as Koch—he is entirely capable of losing the war for us, and in a few months, not years. While the Italians fought well in the Great War, they have decayed into a gutless mob. Just look at last year in the Western Desert—what a fucking joke those dagos are. This insane love affair with Rome will cost us dearly, mark my words. But if we attack overland we do not need these worthless monkeys. I agree with Albert's professor—oil is the key to this war, not people, not armies, and certainly not cities. When we take or control Baku, Stalin is done for. But this is just a pipe dream in the current political climate."

From the main house, Jodl's ADC came running down the stone steps. In his hand was a sheet of pink paper—an urgent wireless message.

The ADC bit his lip and said nothing and passed the flimsy to Jodl.

"Thank you, Schäfer. Keep this strictly to yourself, and put the army on full alert on my authority. Get in contact with all the batons and tell them to expect to get a Category One message from me in 30 minutes."

The ADC saluted and raced back to the house.

"What is it?" Milch asked with rare curiosity.

Jodl passed the urgent wireless message on pink flimsy to Milch.

Milch jumped to his feet.

"Holy fucking shit."

The paper was passed to Albert.

The message read:

```
*** URGENT ***
FLIGHT D-2527 CRASHED ON TAKEOFF STOP
NO SURVIVORS STOP
REPEAT NO SURVIVORS STOP
*** URGENT ***
— 00 —
```

"Well, this does change the landscape a little. Doesn't it?"

Without meaning to, Albert laughed at Jodl's massive understatement.

"Blessing in disguise," Jodl said.

"Yes, yes it is, it truly is. He did so love using Fatso's old Ju-52 with the red markings of von Richthofen," Milch replied.

"Well, gentlemen, this event has changed our country's destiny; I will tell both of you that Russia is a problem and will be our downfall. I have wanted to make these changes, but I have been overruled. But now, the situation has suddenly changed, or should I say improved?"

As Albert and Milch contemplated Jodl's comments, a disheveled figure was seen running down the steps.

"The news. The news. The news. It is terrible. It is the end of us all. He's gone. He's gone."

Jodl was the first to speak, "Bormann, whatever do you mean?"

"He is gone. Gone. He is gone."

"Who is gone?" Jodl asked, teasingly.

"The Chief, the boss, the Chancellor—he's gone."

"Gone where?"

"He's dead"

"Who is dead?"

"The boss, our leader—killed."

"No, not possible; here man, sit down, enjoy this fine sunny Bavarian weather, enjoy yourself."

"Enjoy, are you mad? Are you living in cloud cuckoo land? He's gone. Look at this message."

Bormann passed a garbled telephone message from one of Bormann's lackeys.

Bormann sat down in the gazebo, making no sound.

Milch stood and quietly walked two steps behind Bormann. Jodl looked up and without changing his expression gave the slightest of nod of agreement. The bullet from Milch's luger chipped the left incisor of Bormann's lower jaw as it left his skull and proceeded to nick one of the granite flag stones on the late Bormann's gazebo. Bormann's body slumped forward, like a marathon runner exhausted after finishing a grueling race.

The Diplomat replaced his luger in its holster, puffed his cigar and said,

"Of all of the many, many cunts in this *Reich*, this cunt has to have been the cuntiest cunt of the worst fucking cunts, a total cunt of cunts."

Jodl smiled, "Not a fan?"

Slightly nervous and nonplussed, Albert asked,

"But what if it is not true—we're all in deep horse shit?"

"Why? He is just a casualty of war. Come on, dump him over the cliff. I am sure my flimsy was correct. If it isn't, we've done the country a service. If the flimsy is false, just deny it when asked."

"He's right, dump the cunt," Milch added.

With that, the three men manhandled Bormann's body over the cliff. For a brief second they could see it cartwheeling as it fell. A small sound a few seconds later was heard indicating Bormann had reached his final resting place.

"It's over 900 meters down there and the foxes will clean up the body and it will be weeks before it is discovered," Jodl said with without a modicum of emotion.

Jodl was wrong. It was not until '47 that the body was eventually discovered. As luck would have it, the body fell into the high branches of a pine and lay tightly wedged there for six years. And the body was discovered by—of all people—an American photographer on assignment for the *National Geographic* magazine hired to photograph the birds of southern Bavaria. The photographer climbed the tree in question and thought first he had come upon an elaborate nest. Only when he saw the bleached bones did he realize this had once been a man. The photographer almost fell out of the tree. The entire affair was by then ancient history.

"Let us assume the gods are not playing a trick on us, what do you gentlemen suggest are our next steps?" Albert asked.

"A list," was Milch's instant reply, withdrawing his ever-present small note pad from the left chest pocket of his uniform. (Milch was famous for his note taking—most photographs show him with ever-present cigar, scribbling away like a Teutonic Edward Gibbon.)

"Yes, I agree," said Jodl.

Albert's frown was addressed by Jodl.

"Actually we need two lists. First, a list of the political changes needed. Second, a list of the military changes needed. For the first, we need to stabilize the country—at the moment the country is more like 1748 than 1941—cabals of half-mad princes all struggling for power and influence. This must change. And this crazy and hare-brained campaign in Russia must be corrected today, now, this afternoon, not tomorrow."

"Until one hour ago our problem was a very simple one—Emil's luck was that of a beginner, or more specifically, amateur's luck. In 1940 in France we were weaker along the entire front line except for the Ardennes. We did have the benefit of fighting the Poilus. You know, the 'hairy ones' as the French *populi* called the undisciplined, unwashed and filthy French soldiers who were so often drunk on cheap wine. But the Ardennes attack was a huge gamble, a massive gamble, and a *breathtakingly dangerous* gamble. I am still amazed we got away with it. It was only the army's superb leadership that pulled it off."

At this last comment, Milch added,

"Albert, this is completely and absolutely true. I spoke to my pilots of the so-called Storks—the very light observation aircraft that can land on the top of a tobacco tin, and they were universal in their praise of our army. Of course, this was against the decadent French, who always prefer surrender to honor."

Jodl continued,

"In the Ardennes, a single column of our armor, end-to-end, would have stretched 1,600 kilometers. The foreign press created this mad word called 'blitzkrieg'—lightening war they called it. A better word would have been 'Lucky-German-And-Badly-Led-French.' And in France we just got through by the skin of our teeth— the French had more tanks, bigger tanks, better tanks, more pow-erful tanks. But the French were so gutless and so weak, we would send four, or six, or even eight of our little baby tanks to attack one of their behemoth Char B monsters. With this tactical superior-ity, we won, but it was a damn close run thing. Of course, we were more than happy to take the laurels, and the French used it as an excuse for their breathtakingly incompetent generals. Do you know that the French commander-in-chief Gamelin did not even have a telephone at his headquarters; all messages arrived by motor-bicy-clists, and no messages could be delivered for two hours at noon—they were having lunch?"

"Shit," was Milch's succinct comment.

Jodl continued,

"So after the May '40 campaign in France, all of our political leadership caught that most dangerous of diseases—Victory Disease. A rank amateur gains the confidence of the people and bombasts the armed forces, and aided by his shit heads—like that wingless eagle we just tossed over the cliff—he took control of the nation and dominated all military planning. There is a difference between the actor—which all good politicians are—and an actual leader. Albert, you know as well as I do how the late Austrian had four departments in Berlin all doing the same work, just so he could set one against the other. This is no way to manage a country. And remember, the flashier the leader, the more completely full of horse shit he is—Stalin is boring, the short, fat dago is pure show and nothing else. And who are we attacking?"

Jodl's comments were ended by his ADC, this time walking, making his way to the huge gazebo.

"General Jodl, all Field Marshals have been notified."

"Good, we shall be up to the house shortly."

The ADC left.

Pensively Jodl said,

"Life is so odd—moments ago we were talking about the correct but unattainable goal for Russia, then suddenly it is now completely attainable. I suggest the following steps: First, the Army occupies all the towns. Second, the Gestapo leaders are arrested and all Gestapo offices are sealed by the Army. Third, after these first two steps, we tell the poison dwarf to broadcast to the nation, from here. Before his defenestration, Bormann mentioned to me that little Paul was coming here today to do his typical brown-nosing of his beloved master. Now, the small matter of the new chancellor. I suggest the three of us are announced as the interim committee. This way the Army will be assured, the Air Force will be assured, and the foreign press always liked Albert."

Jodl was rewarded with one of Albert's rare smiles.

"I can tell you, gentlemen, that I feel a huge weight has been lifted from my shoulders," Jodl said.

The three men made their way back to the main house.

It was a pleasure to watch Jodl working in a crisis—it was as though it was just a weekend chess game in the park; no emotion, just clear and concise instructions. But for Jodl—with the superb training of a senior *Wehrmacht* officer—it was not a crisis. Just a change in plans. First, he spoke by radio to the commanders at the front. As expected, all were cautious—the Röhm purge was still a recent memory. But to a brother senior officer, they were also frank in their relief; they all hated the little Austrian with false teeth, bad breath and chronic flatulence; the quiet, conspiratorial jokes about his endless farting and terrible odors were legion. Then, Jodl spoke to all the regional commanders and told all to secure their cities, but as a first step they were to seize the local Gestapo offices and lock up everyone they found inside; this scum would be dealt with later.

Goebbels arrived in the early evening in a panic about rumors he had picked up on the road.

There were many—Albert was one of them—who wondered how Goebbels had survived Kristallnacht, the insane mob's attack that almost destroyed the *Reich's* finances and had successfully turned all the world against Germany—Roosevelt, Halifax, and a host of others saw the Ninth of November as the Rubicon. As the *gobemouches* told it, it was only little Paul's wife that saved him— "her ovaries rattled whenever she was in the presence of Paul's boss," was the commonest view. But, for Germany it had been a disaster— America's ambassador recalled; worldwide horror; the real and justified panic at the *Reichsbank*.

Goebbels became apoplectic when he saw Jodl, Milch, Albert and the commander of the local SS unit all smoking cigars and drinking champagne in the great room with their boots on the low coffee table—the highest act of sacrilege.

Until that day the coffee table had acted as a sort of tiny shrine to the British aristocracy, covered as it was with back copies of *The Tatler* magazine with photographs of smiling corgis and their happy, albeit very dim-witted, masters. The magazines were devoured by the late host until they were dog-eared. In the photographs of the smug, smiling, supercilious faces, there was the superior caste rightly destined to rule a great empire; at least this was what the poor peasant boy from Linz wanted to see. But in spite of his boyish phantasies and dreams, all the magazines actually proved was simply the desperate need for a second Cromwell, one this time that would do a proper and complete gutting.

"What are you doing, what are you doing—you know smoking in the great room is forbidden? It's a deep insult. When I am asked, as I surely will be asked, I will have to tell the truth."

"Well that will be a first," said Milch, who detested Goebbels.

"Are you all mad?"

Albert passed the small pink piece of paper to Goebbels.

"Oh God, it is true. God, we're doomed, we're all doomed."

"What the fuck do you mean?" Milch said with real vitriol.

"The Army has occupied all the towns; the Gestapo scum are already under lock and key; and I have extra flights flying and reporting to the local Army commanders. God is in his heaven and your late boss is probably in the other place."

Jodl rose and walked over; putting his arm around little Paul's shoulder, he said softly,

"Paul, this is what you are going to do. Albert has put together a small announcement, which you are going to read, now, from the broadcast room down stairs."

Goebbels read the hand written note, and reflexively said,

"I cannot say this, I will need to clear this with...," then he stopped as he realized the completeness of the situation for the first time.

"But."

"Paul, look, here is the situation: Albert, Erhard and I together are the new chancellor committee—we are your new bosses—we're the ones with the power. So let's all go and make the announcement; otherwise Albert will, and if Albert has to then, well, that will not be good for you."

Ten minutes later Dr. Paul Goebbels, *Reich* Minister of Propaganda, broadcast to a shocked nation and an even more shocked world. He told the microphone that the late leader had specifically asked for no memorial and no special services. Of course this was completely false, but Albert's goal was to erase immediately from the German consciousness and psyche any memory of the bitter, petty and vindictive Austrian in hours, not weeks.

Then the good doctor, somewhat reluctantly, called editors of all the German and Austrian dailies and told them to lead tomorrow's front page with a large piece about a sudden snow fall in Kitzbühel and how this was the first time since 1822 that such an amazing event had occurred in September. As the editors had no information, the papers' accounts varied wildly to a comic degree—in some it was a light dusting at the start house; for others, it was ankle-deep on the Rasmusleitn. And the happy phrase "September

Snow In Kitzbühel" entered the German language as an astonish-ing—but not completely unwelcome—event.

13: A Gift For Ayinotchka

Barcelona
Monday, 15 September 1941

ALBERT ARRIVED IN THE EARLY AFTERNOON. The streets were dozing fitfully in the afternoon heat. He had taken a taxi from the train station to the Grand Caudillo hotel, frantically renamed to honor the short and pot-bellied conquistador, who had conquered Spain from his exile in Spanish Morocco courtesy of the German *Luftwaffe*—it was said that without the *Luftwaffe*, Franco would have remained exiled in that foul and desolate hell hole.

The lobby was almost empty with just three sleepy bellhops and a single officious concierge, who brightly greeted the modest German businessman, looking for a tip. The two resident whores seated in the lobby drinking coffee glanced at him for a second and judged him boring and not worth approaching—no Latin heat there and no interest or desire for a mid-afternoon dalliance, however exhilarating.

The senior bellhop carried Albert's single modest case to his suite on the top floor. After tipping the bellhop, Albert surveyed the suite. It was typically Spanish—extremely high ceilings to counter the overpowering heat of the Spanish summer. The huge bathroom was deliciously cool in white marble with small, square, white tiles on the floor. The bathroom was dominated by a large, old-fashioned white enameled bath that proudly sat in the center of the room on its cast iron claw feet. Out of professional interest, Albert briefly ran the cold and hot water taps—water gushed out of both in a torrent and the hot was indeed very, very hot; the massive bath would only take a minute or two to fill.

Satisfied with his inspection of the bathroom, Albert returned to the main room and picked up the telephone and called room 353.

"I've arrived, please come over when you are ready," he said into the instrument.

Five minutes later there was a sharp knock on the door.

Albert opened the door, and a woman entered.

"Albert, so wonderful to see you, I have been waiting to see you again for so long," she said in a thick Russian accent.

"Mrs. O'Connell, wonderful to see you. Please, come in."

"Oh Albert, you always call me Ayinotchka, do you not?"

"Please take a seat; how are Oscar and Oswald?"

The woman smiled. She was short, with the wide hips that one associates with the East, perhaps Leningrad. She gauchely wore a somewhat odd outfit topped with a white triangular hat that more suited an effeminate Napoleon than a woman. Her dress was plain brown and did not flatter her mannish body. She had the round face of a friendly Russian peasant. Her dark-brown hair was cut short, in the style of a 1920s flapper, in a forward-slanting bob. However, what Albert—and what all men—noticed were her eyes: deep, luminous, hypnotic and magnetic.

"I have brought you a present."

With that, Albert opened his small suit case and gave her a box wrapped in brown paper, inside there were six boxes marked "*Panzerschokolade.*"

She opened it and gasped,

"Oh Albert, you shouldn't have. Or perhaps you should have."

They both laughed.

"You know I love tank chocolate, and it will help me complete the book. You know I am just a writing machine and this is the most wonderful gift. There is just so much more to do."

"Well, when my friends at the Spanish embassy passed me your letters from America, I thought it might come in useful."

"Well, you know how I write, constantly and often throughout the night. I try to squeeze out a few more hours at the fountain of creativity each day by wearing wet towels stuffed with ice from my ice box around my neck. But your sweets will be far more effective to keep the juices of the Muses flowing. You know, I am just a channel for the Muses, just their poor servant ever. The Muses are everything, I am nothing. I just write what the Muses tell me, I never edit, or review, or change, or tamper—it just comes out like a stream, a cascade, a torrent. Any change would be a sin, a cardinal sin, a mortal sin."

Albert ignored her harping about the "Muses" with aplomb.

"So how is the book progressing?"

She placed a new cigarette in the long, curved, black cigarette holder,

"Well, I am making progress, but with all the events in Europe, it is a little distracting. But I am sure this trip to Spain will be worth the trouble. I have checked and re-checked my premises and found them all to be entirely and completely sound. I found it very interesting to observe Spain on the train from Portugal. Thank God the communists have been defeated, but I am afraid the Spanish have replaced one horror with another—Christianity is just the kindergarten of communism. And it seems the new leader is very communistic in his own way, regardless of how he professes to hate the Left—a central government council that stymies creativity and innovation by taxes and government thugs with guns, and this could go on for decades, long after he is dead. The *Caudillo* seems to be using the standard approach of all dictatorships of the Left and

Right by telling the people they need to work together, 'for the common good,' that 'we need protect the weak.' What utter hogwash. He is bribing them. No, no, that is too vague. Actually, he is drugging them with a cascade of entitlements created solely by the transient power of his currency's printing presses. He seems to be copying precisely what Roosevelt is doing, so lazy losers are elevated at the expense of producers. You know, I saw one poster at a train station that exhorted, 'Prison To Those Elements Who Demean Spanish Sustenance Tickets.' When I asked a fellow passenger, he explained Sustenance Tickets were food tickets given to people who did not work. I suppose there is no better way to generate unemployment than these Sustenance Tickets—why work when the government encourages you to take handouts from government moochers? And one pack of moochers encourages another. The American President certainly has a lot to answer for. Who with any honor would demean themselves by taking such dreck as these Sustenance Tickets? I mean, what noble and honorable producer would stoop so low? Only the moochers would do this, am I correct, dear Albert? With this collectivist nonsense sooner or later the producers will go on strike—why should they work when the fruits of their sweat and their efforts are stolen from them? And the gentleman on the train explained another weird, collectivist insanity. In 1938, the *Caudillo* required all Spanish government mortgage institutions to approve 30% of all mortgages from poor people who did not qualify, people who the banks would—quite intelligently and reasonably—not lend to because their credit was unacceptable; last year he raised it to 55%. The overt reason was to 'help the poor;' for the sake of Saint Peter, what a crock. The way to help the poor is to show them the way not to be poor through thrift and self-reliance, concepts gone from this planet now. The real effect of this government meddling, of course, was to create a bonanza for the looters, who did precisely what the government told them to do and fabricated millions of phony mortgage applications, which the mortgage institutions were delighted to approve—after all they were just doing what the government told them to do. According to my gentleman, the stock market is reaching new highs every day as these bogus loans are packaged into tranches and are happily sold to even happier banks throughout Iberia and South America. Now, the looters are valuing beach shacks in Spanish Morocco for 10 or 20 or 100 times their actual value. But—at least for the moment—everyone is happy to live in this Fool's Paradise as the looters get to print free money (citizens of Spain are forbidden to hold gold); the government struts it success; the bankers, like all leeches worldwide, are happy to get their commissions selling the tranches; the investing banks get a glorious return; and God is in His heaven. Well, that is, until this house of cards collapses. Think Dutch tulips, but just no pretty flowers. I am surprised the Americans have not thought of this diddle, as they tend to be at the forefront of government thievery, as America now has the humorless fascist Roosevelt as emperor, albeit sans clothes—'Washington' should be probably be renamed 'Moocherton.'

"For part of the same train journey, I shared a compartment with two men. And these two men could not be more different. One was tall and thin and a natural athlete; he told me that he favored the decathlon and the marathon; he spoke approvingly of the purity of athletic competition, of how athletes require discipline and self-denial. The other man was his opposite—short, very fat, and seeming to be jolly, as so many fat men seem, at least at first blush. But just beneath the surface of this superficial conviviality was a bitter man who loved power solely as a compensation for his fatness and laziness; instantly, I could sense he was a moocher, but I was willing to give the very fat man the benefit of doubt. But then they started speaking and all was suddenly clear. Both were of the Right, not that I think there is much of the Left in Iberia these day.

But the handsome athlete was modest and disciplined and even-handed, while his companion just barely hid his vitriol, but after a few minutes the very fat man's hatred became apparent. Whereas the athlete advocated self-discipline and had the gall to suggest that government was 'thugs with guns' (as you know one of my favorite phrases), the very fat man vehemently disagreed and was most earnest in his advocating of government and government surveillance as both good and necessary, that individual liberty was a sin and at the cost of the collective good. How could a man who professed to be of the Right even contemplate such a transgression—that government was more important than the individual? He went on to state—most emphatically—that every time there was a storm the government should compensate the victims who had so stupidly built their houses too close to the shore. Albert, is there any better way to encourage reckless and immoderate behavior—well, is there? The very fat man is a lawyer for the government while the thin man is a doctor, specializing in diseases of the eye. I smiled to myself at this natural contradiction between the moocher and the producer. The journey was a long one—the total time was 15 hours—so we three children of philosophy had bags of time to check and re-check our premises and to review the position of our opponent. But suddenly, just before ten that evening, the very fat man became extremely agitated and suddenly ejaculated that the dining car was about the close and that he must have his dinner. At this outburst, the thin athlete calmly asked if the ethereal mind was not more important than the baseness of the belly. The very fat man's lawyerly coarseness emerged and he said it was unhealthy not to eat. The athlete asked the very fat man if the very fat man lacked the discipline to withstand a modicum of discomfort. The very fat man did not reply. At which the athlete asked the very fat man how many pushups the very fat man had done that morning. The very fat man looked startled and was about to speak, but the athlete beat him to the punch (the fat man sparring seemed then, as it does now, ridiculous). 'I did my daily one hundred pushups, how many did you do?' The very fat man's mouth opened but no sound was emitted. 'You see, all you fat people are lazy, and as lazy people you want to be given government pork and this so-called social contract makes you feel superior.' The very fat man looked at this opponent with spitting hatred in his eyes. He stood up and finally exclaimed, 'The government will find you and prosecute all the people like you, the people who are—*ipso facto*—anti-government. You know we will find you, all you people who promulgate these insane notions of personal freedom and liberty, these crazy and outmoded and insane ideas. Now, I will leave you two anti-government idiots and take my dinner; I do hope I am not too late.' With that he stood and waddled out. In complete silence, I looked at the athlete and he looked at me. Then suddenly we both burst out laughing at the same time. Water was coming from my eyes I was laughing so hard. For a moment I feared I was going to destroy my ladylike composure. Fortunately, this embarrassing event was avoided. After we calmed down, the athlete said to me, 'You know, my rule is that love of authority is directly proportional to weight—my slogan is 'Thin People Love Freedom, Fat People Loathe Freedom.' And as countries become fatter, so too will the moochers thrive.' I looked at him and saw his premise was correct. And you know how intelligent men excite me so, and therefore we locked the door to prevent the return of the moocher pig and I had him take me and to take me roughly and without end and with no regard and with pain that slowly changed into pleasure and a pleasure that was sublime in its radiant purity."

Albert listened in silence.

Mrs. O'Connell's eyes were big and black and glowed with energy. Their luster radiated a powerful sexual magnetism. Her mouth was sensual, round and prominent, with beautiful lips. Not for the first time, Albert sensed the erotic power of this woman.

"There is a lot of sex in that face," he thought. And in turn, she could sense his interest. Later that afternoon, she first uncrossed her ankles and then very, very slowly moved her shoes apart. The effects of the Spanish Rosé wine was working its effect on both of them, and just as slowly, Albert realized her broad hips and frumpy clothes mattered less and less. She was in heat, as was always the case when she spoke to intelligent men. Albert knew that Mr. O'Connell, in spite of his movie star looks, drooped in this area and she was always looking to be satisfied from other men; she stalked men she deemed worthy of being worshipped. Of course, it would all end in tears for her, as she took no exercise (apart from that taken lying on her back); all too soon she would become a short, stout, and very roly-poly elderly Russian woman. But that was in the future, and for now she was a conquest Albert wanted very much.

Like a runaway train, she raced on,

"Albert, it is glorious to see your country has grasped the nettle and is purging the world of the pus that is Russia. It's a graveyard there and the sooner you cauterize it the better. And the collective drivel of Versailles, with its bizarre premises, can finally be ended. You see Albert, people generally look through the wrong end of the telescope—their basic premises are wrong and so all that follows is equally false. The theory of knowledge is based on language. This is what people never seem to understand. The language defines how people think—the Germans and Japanese think clearly *because* their language is clear and unambiguous; the Spanish on the other hand never stop talking as Romance languages are all cluttered with flowery nonsense. The extreme case is the Australian aboriginal language, where counting is limited to three words: 'One,' 'Two,' or 'Many'—not much chance of Leibnitz's calculus being invented by these Stone Age primitives, is there? Here's another example: the worthies at Versailles mandated the creation of what they laughingly call 'countries.' Now what is a country? Well, a school boy would say it is a geographic area, such as the island of Ireland. But, as Ireland proves, this is a false premise. A country is really a group of likeminded people who share a common language and a common belief structure. So, to say there is a country called Germany is really a false premise. What there actually is what I will call a supra-country—you can call it the *Grosse Reich*—that consists of all German-speaking people in central Europe. Now that is a logical premise—not lines on a map, and certainly not these bizarre monstrosities created in 1919. The single most important component of a nation is its common language, without a single shared language, the so-called country will sooner or later collapse. This is what makes America strong, and what makes both Greater Germany, and Japan so strong. This is why the Soviet Union would have collapsed even without your act of preemptive self-defense. A nation needs a common language, the Soviet Union is really just a renamed Czarist Russia dominating its distant serfdoms by brutality—there is no common language and no common beliefs in the Soviet Union. For example, the people of the Ukraine are Orthodox Christian. Therefore, the Soviet Union is a false premise and as such will collapse, sooner or later. Compare that graveyard in the East to the British Empire, where the English language is the glue that holds the whole thing together; this is how they are able to control India—before the British, India was riven with hundreds of languages, now it is part of the greatest empire since Rome. But, back to Ireland. The second requirement is common beliefs. The North with its Protestants imported from Scotland sees itself as British, while the Catholic South sees itself as Irish. There will never be peace until this is resolved, probably by force. By examining our basic premises, we can see what the yellow press call 'countries,' such as Czecho-Slovakia, are not really countries at all—these are just artificial play-words.

"Regarding the book, it is moving forward, and your tank chocolate will help a lot. My husband occasionally helps me with a little of the dialogue, but it is all my work. The basic premise of the book is to take Nietzsche's idea of the lone creative Superman and write it in such a way that when all the little people read my book they will each quickly and easily identify with the hero. They will see their own weaknesses and failures as *proof* of their greatness and to reverse these weaknesses to prove their hidden creative talents. So, all these sheep say 'yes, yes, yes—that is me.' It's as if they were back in kindergarten and they all got gold stars on their work every day, and every day the lady teachers told each and every one of them they were extra-ordinarily talented and creative. Think of my new book as a sort of bible for the mediocre, as a phantasy where the reader is a gallant and brave knight from the tales of Ivanhoe, whereas the reality is my readers are all a bunch of lazy, fat, and farting moochers who pine over their lost 'greatness' as they identify with the book's heroes. As you can see Albert, the sheep will love their portrayals as Olympian heroes. Philosophical novels are where the money is, Albert. The secret of my book is to create a duality of us versus them, of the noble outsider versus the insiders, of the blessed versus the damned."

She paused, concerned she had given a little too much away, so she changed tack,

"The mob never created anything—the light bulb was invented by one man, not a government department; the telephone was invented by one man, not a government department; the flying machine was invented by two men, not a government department. Are my premises sound? Yes, they are. As a fellow artist, you know this Albert. And you know the Muses only appear when you are alone. All artists need quietude and being alone. 'Being alone with your thoughts' is the goal of all artists. For most artists the results are disappointing. But ideas alone survive, and we artists are simply the conduits and the channels of ideas. There are three traits of the real and true artist: Aloneness—the artist prefers solitude, and prefers to be alone; Focus—the artist is rude when told of his social obligations, 'you need visit aunt Mary in the hospital, she is very sick,' the artist's polite reply is 'I am sorry, I am working that day,' the less polite reply is 'let her die, she is a nobody;' and Unstoppable—the artist's work is truly his life, for most people, for most slugs, work is odious, it's the old saying about Italians and Germans, the former work to live, while the latter live to work. A person's creativity can instantly be judged by how much they like to be alone. The true artist works alone, and loves being alone, otherwise the crass looters frighten off the timid Muses. And God knows, the Muses can be timid bitches at times. No one said genius was 'run of the mill.'

"Since my time in America, I have seen that many Americans call themselves artists as if the act of calling themselves an artist makes them an artist. This is most common in California where I was writing screenplays. Truth is these are talentless empty vessels—they are nothing more than very loud empty vessels of shit. In contrast, the true artist demurely says, 'read my book.' "

For two hours, the novelist from New York kept up her monologue. It was clear to her that she had Albert's complete attention—he interjected the occasional question or comment. His interest, bordering on fascination, aroused her like few other men could. His power in his country, his good looks and his gentlemanly manners—all combined to make her want him. And she did not just want him, she wanted him to dominate her, to take her spirit and do whatever he wanted, however he wanted. There would be no boundaries, no limits, no petty bourgeoisie niceties. She wanted it rough—very, very rough. She was one of those women that love the slow, teasing increase in intensity, so that pain and pleasure combined as one.

She kept teasing Albert with her speeches about "false premises." The wine helped. As the day lengthened and shadows entered the room, she ineluctably opened her legs, so slowly it was like ice melting on a pond on an early bright spring day. Her dress obliged and rode up her legs. For the duration of the monologue, Albert had been sitting in one of the two large armchairs opposite the sofa.

"Come and sit next to me, Albert, I have a secret to impart," she commanded in the language of a bad novel.

Albert obliged.

He took his right hand and put it up her dress. She was naked under her dress.

"I want you to completely dominate me. Do whatever you like. I want to feel pain. My premise is that pain is often a sexual concept. I want to worship you, Albert. Dominate me and do whatever you want to my body. I want it now. And I want you to slowly pain me so the pain is overwhelming and I feel nothing but heat and I want to feel pain."

Truth be told, Albert had never felt a woman so soaking wet. It reminded him of one night years ago in his university years when he had drawn the shortest straw of three at a whore house, and had to patiently wait his turn. But even then, the girl that night was not as wet as the Russian novelist.

Expecting this outcome, Albert had taken the earlier precaution of buying the understanding of the hotel's staff about "some possible disturbances." The concierge politely smiled and said, "I shouldn't worry, sir—the hotel is mostly empty this time of the year."

Nevertheless, the two young whores in the lobby shook their heads in disbelief as the novelist's increasingly insistent demands and moans were heard down the central open stair case; how could such a meek German be capable of generating such noises from this woman, or from any woman; what in God's name was he doing to her? The next evening the two gaudy young beauties found out for themselves, and neither of them was disappointed.

14: Isaiah's Message

Washington
Sunday, 21 September 1941

THE THIRD SUNDAY IN SEPTEMBER was a blustery one in Washington with the police reporting five trees uprooted in the District. The Police issued a flash radio bulletin just after *The Red Skelton Show*.

In the Oval Office, the President was discussing with Harry Hopkins the previous week's fireside chat. Hopkins was Roosevelt's closest adviser and the President was aware how Hopkins was key to the President's New Deal.

So it was odd when Hopkins suggested that the President meet Louis Brandeis.

"Brandeis, Old Isaiah, that cunt—are you out of your mind—he and his fucking cunt buddies on the Supreme Court almost killed my ND?" (By this stage, Roosevelt had developed an addiction to abbreviations—'my alphabet opium' he called it, forgetting how his grandfather had made his fortune destroying millions of innocent people with the selfsame drug.)

"That cunt and his buddies on the Supreme Court killed my NIRA."

It was true that the center piece of Roosevelt's New Deal was his National Industrial Recovery Act or NIRA. Roosevelt had designed the NIRA to give him almost unlimited powers to dictate how American industry would be organized. And Brandeis had infuriated the President by telling one of Roosevelt's aides, "go tell your boss that the world already has more than enough dictators—we don't need another one, and certainly not in America." The balls on this sick old man.

"That cunt, that fucking cunt!"

On and on went the President.

Hopkins put his hands up, as though a trainer in a boxing ring training a promising fighter with pad work, "He's outside."

"Outside, outside where, outside here you mean?" the President asked, a little startled.

"Yes, I think you need to speak to him."

"What, now?"

"Yes, now, and I think you will find what he says very interesting."

Roosevelt sighed.

"Alright, bring the cunt in."

While Hopkins went to the door, Roosevelt wheeled himself over to the low table in middle of the room. On either side of the table was a long sofa upholstered in yellow damask; the pattern was a Greek bull wildly but ineffectively tossing its horns at the heavens.

"Louis, so wonderful to see you, how are you?"

Hopkins's manner was impassive—he'd seen Roosevelt pull this *volte-face* hundreds of times—wailing in private then all smiles in public.

"Mr. President, I am sorry to bother you on such a stormy night, but I wanted to show you and Mr. Hopkins a document."

"OK, but what is so important? And why can't it wait until Monday?" asked the President, who was known for his very short attention span, short even by politicians' standards.

The President was sitting in a magnificent maple and birch wheelchair, with polished stainless steel spokes and hard-polished solid brass handles. In his hand he held a cigar from Havana (attached to the wheelchair was a glass ashtray that could quickly be removed for his "official duties" and for photographs).

Like many skilled politicians, Roosevelt's public persona was very carefully manipulated to project a down-home image, a "man of the people," just as the *Duce* was photographed bare-chested "bringing in the harvest," whereas in reality the short, rotund Italian had never cut a sheaf of wheat in his life.

"Please, have a seat, Louis, and let's see what you have."

"Say, would you like a drink?"

"No thank you, Mr. President, my doctor tells me at my age my drinking days are over."

Roosevelt noticed that Brandeis's lips were an unhealthy crimson.

"This document comes from a very close friend in the Swiss army who is the ADC of General Guisan, the head of the Swiss Army. Just to give you a little background, in July 1940, Guisan spoke to the entire Swiss officer corp where he outlined a plan of defense against a possible German invasion. As part of this, the Swiss have infiltrated the German and Italian high commands. They have had extremely limited success with the Germans—all too professional and too closed-mouthed, but with the Italians it is the exactly the opposite. As you know, the Swiss cantons speak French and German, as well as Italian."

By the look on Roosevelt's face, it was clear to Hopkins that this was the first the President had learned of this.

"Is that a fact? I must admit I did not know that."

"Yes, Mr. President, so infiltrating the Italian military was very simple and the big weakness of the Germans is that they are forced to share at least some of their intelligence with the Italians, and the Italian foreign minister, Count Ciano, is Mussolini's son-in-law, so the Germans are forced to tell Ciano more than discretion suggests is wise. So, the weak link is the Italians."

"Fucking Wops, and they almost cost me Chicago," the President muttered a little too loudly.

Brandeis was startled, but continued.

"So, here is a three-page summary that I got today from the Swiss embassy, it was in the diplomatic pouch. I have briefed Mr. Hopkins on the contents earlier this afternoon."

"OK, so what is it?" the President said, becoming irritated at the clear but lawyerly description.

"I have translated the document from German for you; as you know Mr. Hopkins reads and speaks fluent German and I went to school in Germany."

Hopkins spoke,

"Essentially, Mr. President, this document, if true—and like Mr. Brandeis, I believe the veracity of this document—this document makes three points."

"First, that the burning of the synagogues on the so-called Kristallnacht or Night of Broken Glass was seen by the late German leader as a huge mistake—a public relations disaster; he correctly predicted the world's reaction. Dr. Goebbels was almost dismissed. Second, that Hess's flight was very carefully planned by Hess, Hitler and Goebbels. And third, relating to the second point, the Germans are eager for peace with England, and the Germans have no professed interest in the British Empire, the Royal Navy, or the British Isles themselves."

Roosevelt leant back and puffed his cigar, "Fuck," was all he said.

"Mr. President, you can see why I thought I should bother you and Mr. Hopkins on such a vile night."

"Yes, indeed."

"But I don't get it—if the Hess flight was not the 'mad-man-in-a-Messerschmitt,' why portray it as such? Why not simply come out and state it?"

Hopkins fielded this loose ball, "Well, the Germans are in a bind—they had to come up with this pipe dream for precisely the reason why it has been rejected by the British—they would seem weak even before their June invasion of the Soviet Union."

"OK, but if this is the case, why the hell don't the British settle?"

Brandeis and Hopkins looked at each other; neither spoke. Then Hopkins said one word, "Churchill."

Until now, Roosevelt had kept his professional politician's masque on, but the brandy was starting to work its effect.

"That pompous asshole thinks his shit doesn't stink."

Brandeis ignored this and went on, "In the Jewish community, there are two opposing views of how to deal with the current situation: the majority view is that the Germans need be defeated and actually destroyed—that Germany needs to be turned into farmland. The minority view is that the re-creation of a Jewish state is a better idea. As you know (all lawyers say this when the listener does not know), this is called Zionism. I am an adamant proponent of the second view. Actually, I am prominent in the American Zionist movement, and I believe this to be a better solution because it requires less bloodshed and frankly central Europe is Germany's backyard, and the crazy and brittle monstrosities of Versailles, such as Czecho-Slovakia, made no sense in the real world. These checkerboard so-called countries only exist solely to hem in the Germans."

Roosevelt professionally hated Brandeis as the main opponent to the glories of Roosevelt's New Deal, but at a personal level Brandeis was impossible not to like: modest, polite, well-educated and intelligent.

Although addicted to lucky numbers, and lucky shoes, and lucky hats, Roosevelt was not unintelligent. He thanked the elderly Justice.

Brandeis slowly rose and left the room.

Roosevelt looked at Hopkins and said, "Interesting."

15: Milch's Boffins

AS THE LIGHT SNOW FELL SILENTLY on the stone terrace of Haus Wachenfeld, Jodl explained to the assembled group how the new Brest-Litovsk-Kiev-Crimea line was succeeding better than expected. To create a complete break with the Berlin brawlers and thugs, Milch had rather wisely suggested that the late Chancellor's mountain house made an ideal command post,

"With today's advanced wireless telephony, this is the ideal place, or would you prefer the mosquitos of Rastenburg in summer and the 20 degrees of frost of winter?"

Jodl had simply smiled at this question, remembering the marshy, malaria-infested hell hole in East Prussia.

To the group of Field Marshals, Jodl explained,

"I can tell you the mercury is reading 20 degrees of frost in Leningrad according to our Finnish friends. But, it is actually very hot in Moscow."

Gerd von Rundstedt looked up, surprised.

"Yes, it is a sweltering 17 degrees of frost in Moscow."

The room exploded in laughter.

Rundstedt said, "Terrible shame about the September crash."

It looked like Kurt Student was going to choke to death laughing.

Loeb said, "Careful, Rundstedt, you're going to kill Student if you're not careful."

Jodl smiled and said, "Time for dinner gentlemen, and I understand it is wild turkey and pig's trotters. Well, it should be, as I ordered the dinner for this evening."

Since the events of the 1st of September, Jodl had implemented Milch's suggestion, installing the centralized command of the widespread front at the mountain house. And he had ensured all vestiges of the former owner were removed: the complete staff was replaced; Eva had moved back in with her sister, and her room had been repainted; and the vegetarian's greenhouse had been replaced with a concrete pad for howitzers (and thus, Fatso's bones were permanently interred, or as Jodl once joked 'interned'). Cigar smoke wafted through the mountain house and meats of all kinds were the standing order for all meals.

Standing alone in front of the fire, Albert absentmindedly gazed at the orange of the flames. He now realized how the country was so lucky to have men like Jodl and Milch in charge: sober, modest, and above all, professional. He wondered were the past few years just a horrible cruel nightmare? And the elimination of the bitter, hateful Austrian bile that all Austrians seemed to be poisoned with—the blind malevolence they spat was as bad as the Slavs' centuries of pogroms and the Soviets' mass execution of millions of their citizens.

As Albert thought about Jodl and Milch, his thoughts turned to Professor Stein and Stein's comments about Germany, and how its strength—its backbone—was its private companies, based on Stein's emphatic statistics of a professional economist: how German companies averaged 140 employees, while southern Europe's average was just ten employees, and Stein's always-prescient insight of how this radically affected the calibration of the political order of the day—the stable, professional and educated middle class versus the hard-scrabble petty prejudices of marginal corner shop owners.

Then Albert recalled Julius's initially odd comment about German private companies' fear of debt. Albert had checked for himself and found his mentor to be completely and entirely correct—it was true that private German companies disliked—almost feared—debt. And how this caused them to lose three percent in growth each year, but, at the same time, these modest private German companies were the most stable in the world, and many were over one hundred years old.

As Albert pondered this, he could finally see how Germany would—in one form or another—survive a thousand years. And slowly, with the patience of a true German craftsman standing at his work bench, Germany would expand throughout Europe like a flower blossoming in spring—slowly, imperceptibly, but with unstoppable inevitability. And the superiority of Germany's education and training system and its ethic of work would dominate the world far more effectively than anything that could have been done by the strutting, chaotic and flatulent Austrian with chronically bad stomach, rotting teeth and blind hatreds.

After dinner, the leaders of the *Wehrmacht* and *Luftwaffe* chatted contentedly over cigars and brandy.

Jodl said,

"With the immediate executions of Koch, Greiser, and Himmler, the *Reich* is starting to be purged of the poisonous elements. Also, executing Rosenberg was quite useful—the man was like a mad Nietzsche."

All listened in silence, then Rundstedt explained how the Ukrainians were shaping up well,

"As we discussed in early September, German NCOs have been promoted and have been promised small lots to farm after we gain an Armistice. They have been instructed to show the Ukrainians how we Germans are their friends against the Russians, who they all hate to a man. Of course, we did have a few rotten apples, as all armies do, but we removed them—men who have drank a little too much from the poisoned chalice of Übermensch. But, all in all, extremely good progress. And the same goes for the Baltics. We only have to look to the Roman Empire and how it expanded by having the Roman NCOs marry the local girls to increase the breeding stock. Worked for them, no reason to believe it will not work for us. Just as the Romans made Latin the *lingua franca* of the time, we can today do the same with German."

Jodl continued,

"Romania is in a very strong position now with the addition of the German troops freed from the madness of trying to take Leningrad and Moscow in the North in the middle of the fucking winter; there was never any reason to repeat the little Corsican's disaster of 1812. And in the south, Paulus and his Sixth Army are doing very well—it's hard for the Russian tanks to attack us when they have no fuel. Our own fuel ferries across the northern Black Sea are working well—we moved to the Black Sea all the Kriegsmarine submarines operating in the Mediterranean and half of the Atlantic wolf packs attacking the American convoys to Britain. Our U-boats are sinking any Russian surface raiders in the Black Sea—in the last convoy, not one German oiler was lost. Field Marshal Milch's Condors are providing excellent intelligence for our U-boat commanders in the Black Sea."

At this last comment Milch beamed and added,

"Next week we intend to start attacking rail links from the Baku oil fields directly from our forward bases in Maykop. We have specially modified the Ju-88 with extra fuel tanks and we've removed all the armor and armaments. As there are little or no Russian aircraft, this seems a reasonable approach, and they will be accompanied by flights of 190s. And this will stop all oil to the Russians, while preserving the oil for our aircraft and tanks when we reach Baku."

Jodl disclosed,

"And Turkey is close to entering on our side. Of course, with forward aerodromes in Turkey, we will be able to go south to what is now called Iran, as well as to the Suez Canal. Our strategy is to strengthen the southern flanks of Bulgaria and Romania to fight the British on our terms on our ground, not in Egypt and Libya where we have to depend on the Wops to ferry fuel across the Mediterranean where the British Royal Navy is still strong and still dangerous. And we can always depend on the Wops to be undependable, so we need consider the Italians as our adversities. I have assigned a tank commander to Bulgaria who did well last summer in France when he forced the crossing of the Meuse with his 7th Panzer—the *Gespensterdivision*, as it is called. He's a bit of a showman, but there is nothing wrong with that. And I think this man—Rommel—will provide useful support for Paulus's right flank. This will be even more the case when Turkey joins us. Also, the Romanians are morally weak, like the Italians—I've seen reports of some Romanian army staff officers wearing rouge and propositioning young boys on the streets of Bucharest; they make the French look pious and devout."

Jodl shared with all the other officers an abhorrence of this depravity—how the late, unlamented Chancellor could stomach the likes of Röhm was beyond his understanding.

As a young officer, Jodl was told of the horrors of one evening in '01 when the Kaiser was entertaining Fritz Krupp. The centerpiece of the entertainment for that night was the brilliant and scintillating performance by a ballet dancer in a glorious pink tutu that was finished with the most magnificent mock sapphires. Around and around in the center of the huge parquet wooden dance floor the dancer twirled. Up and down the room, teasingly towards the two men who sat together on a small elevated stage. Fritz whispered to the Kaiser the joys of such a performance. God was in his heaven and the two men were so very happy.

Then, as if the devil was watching and had decided to destroy this simple human joy, the dancer—now in the middle of the room—stopped twirling, looked first at Fritz for a brief instance, and then at the Kaiser and then let out a terrible, muffled moan. Grabbing his chest the dancer dropped to the floor. Dead. The ten men in the room made no sound. Then the Kaiser commanded them to get the Field Marshal out of this tutu and back into his uniform. There was a horrible delay of twenty minutes until the dead Field Marshal's uniform was eventually located (he had secreted it in the back of a locker in the Ladies Gowning Room). Then, the real disaster started—rigor mortis had already set in and so it was impossible to dress the Field Marshal who was massively corpulent and whose uniform had to be specially made in Berlin at a tailor who specialized in the extremely obese. For reasons of decency, Fritz Krupp and the Kaiser had left while the other eight men tried—and failed—to dress the dead Field Marshal. Remembering that terrible evening, Jodl understood why the British at the time called these perversions the "German Disease."

"Of course, I am getting daily telegrams from the *Duce*, who is alternating between threatening and begging, but we can safely discount him. I think it might be worth doing a small Italian Anschluss when the time is ripe—I know from our agents that the Vatican would welcome that, especially if we bribe the Pope with significant power in a new Italian puppet government, thus returning the

Italians to their natural order—a cabal of back-stabbing city-states so clearly described in *The Prince*. I will now let Milch tell you of his excellent progress."

Milch had spent too long associated with the politicians to remain completely untainted. Like his late boss, Milch liked the good life, but at a human level, not the caricature that was the dead *Reichsmarschall*. Milch provided a sea change—he was competent, modest, a good listener, and above all, worked well with the *Wehrmacht*.

"Just as Jodl has done with the *Bolsheviks*, so we started our little circus by asking one question: In today's modern, scientific war what are the enemy's greatest weaknesses: civilian morale, lack of soldiers, our U-boats, lack of planes, what? My *Luftwaffe* research department boffins have come up with a three very interesting— and I think quite surprising—answers."

He paused to ensure he had everyone's attention.

"The boffins say: 'RDF, airfields and 100-octane fuel.' "

"The British have invented an apparatus called 'Range and Direction Finding' or 'RDF.' This equipment lets them see, on a special glass electronic screen, illuminated green dots that indicate aircraft. RDF cannot tell the size of the 'planes, nor can it tell if they are friend or foe, but if you see 12 dots taking off in France and crossing the English Channel, then it's reasonable that is our boys on one of their party outings to London. So, the British RDF is the eyes of the British air force. Now, this new apparatus requires very tall radio masts and the British have built a series of these stations dotted along their southern coast. So, in today's modern war, removing this critical and central facility is our first job—it is not, as my former boss used to endlessly boast, about shooting down enemy 'planes, and the glories of flying circuses, etc. That may have been how it was done in the dashing and glorious days of the air knights of the Great War, but in these modern times, the economic aspects are the most important."

"The second area we have identified is a simple one—the air fields themselves. If the enemy 'planes have nowhere to land, then that will be a problem for them. This affects their bombers more than their fighters—it is often possible to land a modern all-metal monoplane fighter in a decent sized meadow, but even then it becomes the time-wasting task of refueling the fighter that can take a full day or two, and jacking up the wheels that have sunk into soft meadow grass. So after we cripple the RDF stations, we will attack the enemy airfields from a height of just 1,000 meters. Both JU-88s and Stukas will attack in waves. The goal is to destroy the entire length of the enemy runway, not just create one or two pot-holes. For maximum effectiveness, we will attack in the very early morning when the English bombers are returning from their raids on Berlin and the Ruhr. These English bombers will all be low on fuel and with a very small margin of error. And in contrast to the enemy fighters, the bombers only crash land in meadows, as bomb-ers are far heavier than the fighters, the bombers dig in on contact, the whole thing goes arse over tit—the enemy heavy bombers must land on proper runways."

"The final one is 100-octane fuel. The backbone of the RAF is the Rolls Royce Merlin engine—they use it in just about everything. Most important are their heavy bombers and their Spitfire fighters. Now, these engines were originally designed and tuned to run on 87-octane fuel. But we know from our Dutch friends at the Shell company in Holland that the RAF has been working since 1937 to convert all the Merlin engines to run on 100-octane. And the per-formance improvement is significant; according to the Dutch, the British have gotten a 50% increase in boast pressure, which trans-lates into about 200 extra horsepower. And our own pilots have compared 87 to 100 in the 190s and they too all report significant improvements, and these were blind tests as well—our pilots did not know if they were using 87 or 100. The only thing stopping the British in completing this conversion is lack of 100-octane—they've converted about one-third of the engines."

"Now, the British get their all 100-octane from the Americans and from Trinidad. They offload this 100-octane spirit in Plymouth and Liverpool, then it is transported it to the various aerodromes in the South East of England by rail. After the first two phases are complete, the *Luftwaffe* will begin attacking Plymouth, not with bombers but with special flights of 190s. In each flight there will be 12 aircraft; nine will be conventional, while three will be equipped with a 45 mm cannon. To allow for the extra weight of this armament and to maintain the performance all the machine guns have been stripped from these modified machines."

"The plan is to send a large armada of bombers to London in three streams. Even without the RDF stations, the British will scramble their fighters to intercept this raid. While they are flying North, the special flights will race over to Plymouth in the South West corner of England, and will destroy the main storage facilities in Plymouth. Of course, these tanks are all thin walled, and in contrast to heavy oil used in tanks and ships, 100-octane aircraft spirit is extremely volatile—a single hit from one of our 45 cannons and the huge tank explodes. Our plan is to strip Britain of all 100 octane fuel in four weeks—of course, this means the one-third of the 'planes already converted to 100 will be forced to run on 87 and this will cause many problems—our boffins have done experiments and have found the engine life is halved, assuming the engine does not explode in mid-air from massive pre-ignition."

Jodl smiled, "And then?"

Matter-of-factly, Milch said, "we start back at the first phase as rebuilding the RDF stations will be the Britishers' top priority. I discussed this with little Paul and he wisely pointed out that we can create a huge news bonanza by telling all neutral countries that we are now eschewing all civilian targets. The British cannot respond in kind as the Ruhr is so old that the workers' houses are cheek-to-jowl to the various Krupp works. In Goebbels' view we can get a great deal of sympathy."

Milch immediately caught himself, "Of course, what he does is fine, but it is my job, gentlemen, to ensure no enemy aircraft ever attacks the *Reich*—I don't want to have to eat a broomstick."

The generals and field marshals roared their approval at this inside joke.

Milch's simple, three-pronged approach worked far better than he could know. Churchill had a slight collapse after spending 15 minutes in a drunken fit screaming at the head of Fighter Command, Hugh Dowding, at the Whitehall underground command bunker. Dowding had not said a word during the unconscionable tirade, but had made it clear to Jock Colville that his retirement was effective the next day. Once sober, Churchill tearfully plucked and pleaded with Dowding, but to no effect. Alan Brooke, who witnessed this outrage, had told the repentant prime minister than one more such episode, under any circumstance, would result in Brooke's own resignation.

A scandal of this size could not be kept quiet for long in the fish bowl that was the London clubs. And sure enough, before the week was out Stimson had been given all the gory details. Stimson's source was not a surprising one—Lord Halifax, the British ambassador in Washington, and Churchill's former rival for the prime ministership.

16: Mimi's Sparrow

Cristobal, Panama
Saturday, 29 November 1941

FOR MIMI, SATURDAY was always her favorite day—no school and no painful kneeling in church for an hour recalling her sins for the past week. Not yet a teenager, Mimi struggled each Sunday to find sins to confess to her mother's God; she hoped as she grew older it would be easier—her eldest sister Maria, 18 years old and already married, assured her that shortly Mimi's sins would blossom.

Over the past two months, every morning Mimi would rush to open the blinds of her room to say hello to her two new friends, which she had christened Mama and Quick Fox. Mama rarely moved, just gently swaying, always calm and serene, while Quick Fox was the opposite—never seeming to stop moving, darting here and there, never still.

But to Mimi's surprise and sadness, Mama was gone. Mama had grown to be a silent friend to Mimi. Mama had arrived after church on the first Sunday in October, that foul day of rain and lightning and thunder, when the clock on the tower of the Town Hall had been hit by lightning and had stopped. Mimi leaned out her window and looked from one end of the bay to the other, but there was no Mama. Quick Fox was there, dashing around as usual, like a fly caught in a glass jar. Mimi would ask Father Koannes tomorrow about Mama—the German Father was wise and gentle to her and all the children of the parish.

Mimi was not alone in her disappointment about Mama's sudden disappearance—just about everyone in the town had been pleased by the arrival of Mama and Quick Fox. The townspeople knew of Mimi's two friends more formally as the aircraft carrier *Tancho* and the destroyer *Suzume* of the Imperial Japanese Navy.

A year before the arrival of the two ships, three Japanese bars had been established on the waterfront. For the first few days, the existing bars had naturally seen these newcomers as competition that would have to be shut—one way or another. But before any action could be taken, the three spotlessly attired Japanese proprietors had entered each established bar as a group and bowed deeply. The Japanese explained—speaking beautiful Spanish—that Japanese tradition demanded that the Japanese compensate their honorable colleagues for any lost business. The leader of the trio explained that the Japanese would like to pay 500 U.S. dollars each week as "Honor Rent" to each of the established bars.

"Would this be acceptable?"

The established bar owners could not believe their luck. Like clockwork at noon every Wednesday, the leader of the trio would appear at each of the bars, bow deeply to the amused owner, and pass over a small brown paper envelope containing the "Honor Rent." A local gang had planned a robbery of this arrangement, but Little José of the Spanish Mermaid had heard of this and had the leader's legs broken—"just to tell all what would happen" if anyone had ideas of hurting the golden Japanese goose.

The three Japanese bars became the focus of drinking on the waterfront, not only because of the cleanliness of the bars—"my God, even the heads are clean," marveled one U.S. Marine on shore leave—but also because the prices of drinks were the cheapest in the town. Between themselves, the local fishermen mocked the dimwitted Japanese who always paid top-dollar for the fishermen's catch, and the Japanese always paid in cash, and always in U.S. 100-dollar bills—no more pleading with the local bar owners. Over time, the Japanese opened a restaurant specializing in seafood, which attracted people from all over town. And the Japanese were wonderful hosts; when news reached them of a local family in need, the local parish priest was dispatched with a meal of fish and a small red packet of three U.S. 100-dollar bills, enough for the family to feast every day for six months.

So when the Japanese announced two war ships of the Imperial Japanese Navy would be visiting, a sense of excitement filled the town.

When the *Tancho* and the *Suzume* arrived, the first act was a visit by the two captains and the ships' officers to the mayor at the town hall. The captains and officers lined up in front of the mayor and bowed deeply. The leader of the three Japanese bars from the waterfront acted as translator and explained the nature of the goodwill visit, and suggested to mayor that the town be paid $2,000 per week for anchoring rights in the bay. This delightful surprise raised the mayor's eyebrows and he smiled, showing the gap of his two missing front teeth. The translator had been careful to ensure the two editors of the local papers were present, but "no photographers please, as we Japanese believe taking photos is bad luck." As with the phantasy of the "Honor Rent," this silly explanation was not questioned, especially as the Japanese had become the largest advertisers in the two local papers, and they always paid in cash, "even before the ad runs," marveled the editors.

It was an ideal arrangement: the Japanese officers had the Japanese bar owners buy fresh fish each day from the fishermen as well as fruit and vegetables from the local farmers. The editors had made some very tentative suggestions about touring the ships; the officers explained that, sadly, this would not be possible and instantly the matter was dropped.

From the shore the sailors could be seen painting and cleaning the two ships; initially, this was seven days a week, but after a priest had mentioned that working on the Sabbath might upset many of the devout local people, Sunday work was immediately stopped. The townspeople could see sailors in different uniforms moving about. Little did the watchers know that the *Tancho* held only a skeleton crew of 60 sailors who would change their uniforms three times a day to create the illusion of a full complement. Not that this was of concern—the locals were all benefitting from presence of the Japanese and their bottomless supply of dollars; all 100-dollar bills, or as Sasaki had called them, "Franklins."

News of Cristobal's good fortune spread quickly. Then the curious news came back to the town that its sister city at the other end of the isthmus had experienced similar good fortune. At first, the local townspeople dismissed this as simple boasting in the truest of Spanish *machismo*, then some local merchants returned to say, "No, it is true—Vacamonte has a big, big Japanese warship, also accompanied by a little sparrow. And there were also the new Japanese bars—two in this case. And these Japanese bars were as clean as the ones in Cristobal, and the Japanese business men were just as naive and inept as the ones in Cristobal."

17: The Swede's Bridegrooms

Nogales, Mexico
Monday, I December 1941

JOSÉ RODRIGUES SHIVERED as he stood by the black walnut tree in the forecourt of the compound. It was already past ten in the morning and the thin sheet of ice on the pond across the road had just melted. But it was still cold; this was Mexico—wasn't Mexico always supposed to be warmer than his Spain?

It was the first of the month and he was looking forward to a visit from his exotic visitor from Mexico City. Sure enough, the dust indicated the arrival of the tall Swede's white car. The 12-cylinder Cadillac came to a stop in its regular parking place. The Swede emerged from the back seat and greeted José,

"All ship shape, eh, José?" (Always, it was this greeting.)

José nodded. The Swede was something to do with the Swedish embassy in Mexico City. José never quite knew and thought it wiser not to ask too many questions as the money was very good and regular and plentiful, and after the past five-year's torment in Spain, this was a very pleasant change indeed.

"Well, let's get on with it, I have a second meeting after this."

José knew of this meeting, as the Swede was distinctive in appearance and had been seen entering the Hotel Centrale, according to some of the other Spaniards. The Swede kept a full-time suite there as well as his three Mexican girls, all under 18, who he frolicked with after the duties of the "Bus Company" were completed. And the Swede made no attempt to hide it—as a diplomat, albeit a corrupt one, he had complete immunity, and more importantly, his dollars were always plentiful to everyone with whom he came in contact.

Together they climbed the external stairs to the catwalk that ran along one side of the building. From the catwalk the Swede could see the progress of the work on the five buses. Later, he would inspect them in detail. But first he needed to check the morale and the state of his "troops," as he called them.

On the ground floor a single large office occupied the corner by the large double doors. In the office stood 50 men. When the Swede entered, they snapped to attention.

"So, how are my bridegrooms of death today?" he smiled.

The question was a rhetorical one. José, whose slouching by the black walnut tree had been replaced with a physical strictness of the professional soldier that he was, answered for the company.

"The *Caballero Legionario* are all excellent, thank you, Commander."

Two men stepped forwarded and saluted.

"All five transports are ready, Commander. The new engines have been fitted and tested as have the new tires," the first man explained.

"The dynamite, limpets and the magnesium flares have been tested and all are completely acceptable," the second one stated.

"Excellent," the taciturn Swede replied.

"Time for a dress rehearsal and then equipment check," the Swede stated, feeling slightly odd using such a feminine term as "dress rehearsal."

"Are there any questions about the missions?"

The silence was what the Swede wanted to hear.

The men marched out leaving José and the Swede alone in the room. The Swede opened his satchel and withdrew two envelopes, one bulging as it held 50 smaller envelopes, each containing five U.S. 100-dollar bills.

"Here are the men's pay and your expenses. Do you need any more?"

"No, thank you, Commander, this is more than satisfactory."

José and the Swede descended to the garage floor for the Swede's "dress rehearsal." For the next hour, the company presented their uniforms. First were the uniforms of two well-known private security firms. Then, a little more sinister, uniforms of track workers for the Southern Pacific Railroad and the Central Pacific Railroad. Most sinister of all were the uniforms of the U.S. Navy.

From his satchel, the Swede extracted a large map, which he pinned to the wall. He took a broom and unscrewed the brush. He handed the broom handle to each of the company commanders in turn and had each Company commander explain his mission, so all 50 men understood. From time to time, the Swede grilled a soldier at random about any of the three missions. All the company had to understand all the missions so there was "depth on the bench" (he particularly liked the American football expression, one of a number he had learned while stationed at the consulate in San Francisco in the early thirties).

After the mission plan was completed, the Swede examined the buses. They were defrocked Greyhounds, externally tired but with fresh engines and new tires. The Swede had selected these buses as they were extremely common in the West of the United States and would not draw a second glance. His agents had gotten Texas license plates. Last, but by no means least, the Swede inspected the dynamite, limpets and magnesium flares cached inside the false sides of the storage area of the buses.

Satisfied, the Swede thought it time for his speech,

"Gentlemen, all of us are mercenaries and so we fight for money. But we all know it is not as simple as that. We also fight for a cause. We have all seen—most of us first-hand—the enemy ogre; you have seen how our beloved Spain was ignored by the Americans in her hour of need. Spain, the motherland for most of you and my adopted motherland (here the Swede was gilding the lily ever so slightly). This treachery cannot go unpunished. And, we few, we happy few, are blessed with the power to strike a fatal blow to show the world—and to teach the world—that Spain must never be allowed to suffer again. Without men like you, the *Bolsheviks* would have overrun and destroyed Spain. I earnestly pray all of you, my bridesmaids of death, return safely. The mission is a simple one, we have trained very hard for four months, and most important of all in any battle, we have the advantage of complete surprise. Kickoff is at 0600 tomorrow and I will return to greet all of you on the Tenth."

José thought, "He may be a prick at times, but this Swede did the same training with the men, humped the same pack, and never pulled rank."

The men nodded.

✚ ✚ ✚

True to his word, the Swede was there on Wednesday, the tenth day of December, and he greeted each of the returning men. All 50 men returned safely—their missions had all gone off flawlessly. *Train Hard, Fight Easy*, the Swede had inculcated in them time and time again, and it was true; true as the dictum that *Surprise Is the Greatest Weapon*.

Each man had received his mission pay, and for those who stayed in Mexico, a regular stipend of 10 Franklins each month. And when the cost of the finest Mexico City whore, the very crème de la crème—young, tight, with large, soft brown doe-eyes, and a firm and enticing bust—was ten U.S. dollars, the men lived very,

very well on a thousand dollars a month, or as Sasaki would have costed it, around 30 yen or about 30 American cents (assuming one-tenth of a yen for rent of the building per Franklin.)

18: The Valve Maker's Observation

ON ARRIVAL IN OTTAWA, Schneider and Louise quietly left the train from Washington. It had been a wonderful trip so far. Earlier that afternoon they had dined on oysters, caviar, and ice-cold *Dom Pérignon*. Louise liked to encourage Schneider to get her drunk—it appealed to her lascivious side. She was wearing her favorite pair of patent leather nude sling backs with the black highlights on the toe. At the heel were two separate skin-colored straps rather than the traditional one, and these two independent straps made the sling backs far more comfortable to wear. Also, they made it less likely to slip off in a moment of sudden passion. As was her custom, under her knee-length silk skirt she wore just her garter belt holding up her cream-colored silk stockings. Wearing just her garter, she was completely open and available to any man; that alone made her start to lubricate—to be walking around with all these men, and virtually exposing herself. And the pleats in her light silk skirt did their part by swishing and exposing her legs. And her excitement fed on itself—the more excited she got, the more she lubricated.

She loved to be taken fully clothed and she loved to look down at her nude sling backs with the black toes still on her feet, legs splayed wide apart, while Schneider pushed deep inside her. (In a moment of unladylike sauciness, she told Schneider that she called these sling back heels her "fuck shoes." With the effects of the champagne, she giggled like a naughty schoolgirl.)

They travelled as Mr. and Mrs. Holtz, upstanding American citizens; their passports were nicely scuffed courtesy of the forgery office in the basement of the embassy. Naturally, the customs officials did not look twice at them—in Chicago Germans made up the largest ethnic minority, and both Schneider and Louise spoke flawless English.

Schneider was posing as a Chicago economist specializing in the "Depression within the Depression," as his typewritten paper proclaimed. To "live the legend," as he preached to Louise—as well as to his acolytes—he held forth to her in the dining car. He had told her to emulate interest. And he droned on and on, louder than was really necessary, but it was just cover after all.

"Dear, here are the points I will make at the lecture." (Of course, there was no lecture; Schneider was just living the legend.)

"Point One. In '37 the unexpected consequences of the new Undistributed Profits taxes meant that companies no longer could keep rainy day funds, and so when it did inevitably rain and sales decreased, these companies had to shed employees instantly. Actually, the headline on Friday the 27th of August, 1937, in the *New York Times* was *Levy on Profits Halts Expansion*, which discussed the unexpected consequences of this tax. But you need remember, dear, most governments are run by lawyers who never imagine—and are always shocked by—the unexpected consequences of their actions; often government fiats generate precisely the opposite of what the bureaucrats expect. The Undistributed Profits tax is a perfect example.

"Point Two. On Monday, 18 October 1937, the bond market collapsed. Bonds are a measure of the future growth of an economy, as bonds are the cost of borrowing money for future growth, and if people are not borrowing money it is because they see no hope to grow in the future.

"Point Three. On the same day—Monday, 18 October 1937—as the bond market collapsed, a seat on the New York Stock Exchange was sold for $61,000—the lowest price since 1919—no one wanted to be a stock trader any longer.

"Point Four. I was reading a newspaper that had printed a letter from the clever English economist John Keynes. In the letter, Keynes said, 'it is a mistake to think business men are more immoral than politicians,' and I have to agree with him. I disagree with most of this man Keynes's ideas, but this remark did seem germane—his ideas on the Paradox of Thrift are typical of English homosexualists and the mad notions they screech from the roof tops, as they see themselves as intellectually superior to mere humans. Keynes wrote his letter in '37; this is the same year that the New York Stock Exchange dropped precipitously because business men were unsure of what Roosevelt was going to do and so they wanted to keep their money and not invest until the outlook was less uncertain."

At this point, Louise interrupted and asked, "Is that Englisher the one who told his lady friend Lyn that she should go to Tunis because that is, quote, 'where bed and boys were also not expensive,' unquote. Is that the one?"

Schneider, slightly annoyed to be interrupted (but quietly please that the legend was now truly being lived), corrected her,

"My dear, it was actually to a man that Keynes wrote this reprehensible suggestion. The man's name was Lytton Strachey. The letter to this man was about replicating Keynes's own visits to the Maghreb to exploit poor, bewildered, and terribly frightened little boys of 10 or 12. These English homosexualists thought nothing of abusing young boys of 10 for their own weird sexual satiations. Actually, hard though it is to believe, some of these terrified young boys had been castrated to better appeal to these English homosexualists. It's so odd that these self-same people are so keen on talking about economic exploitation, yet seem oblivious to this far more horrible attack on a child's innocence. These pompous and pious homosexuals consider themselves to be a class of their own—just as the U.S. government today does; Roosevelt thinks he can exploit people, just as these English homosexuals think they can destroy the innocent childhoods of these tragically poor and terrified young boys in Tunis.

"People call this Keynes fellow '*Pozzo*'—like a sewer—as his private conversation is often scatological. And this pedophile Keynes harped on about what he calls the 'Higher Sodomy.' You won't find it listed in any library's card index of course, but while at Cambridge he and this Strachey would prowl for young undergraduates to corrupt. And they thought it a great lark and adventure to visit Tunis to permanently injure these sad little boys who were not even teenagers. And this Keynes is highly thought of in the United States and worshipped in England. What is the world coming to?"

Louise looked at Schneider; she had struck a nerve, a deep nerve that she felt uncomfortable exploring. Fortunately Schneider almost instantly resumed his cover, his legend.

"Point Five. Stock flotations on the New York Stock Exchange in the Calvin Coolidge era were about 1,000 million dollars a year, but now during the current Roosevelt regime, where they have sunk to just 50 million dollars a year.

"Point Six. And this is the most important point. Government bureaucrats do not realize that businesses are fragile flowers that are more often than not created by irascible and driven fanatics whose own identity is in these companies—a company is often the founder's child. And what these fragile flowers hate most—and fear most—is uncertainty. So when President Roosevelt gets on the radio and boasts of 'unbridled experimentation,' and changes his mind daily, then my dear, companies become frightened by this uncertainty."

"I hope you will not say 'my dear' to the professors," Louise teased.

She smiled.

At the next table in the dining car, a tall, slim man with aquiline features rose and walked over.

"Excuse me sir, I hate to be rude and interrupt, but I couldn't help but overhear your lecture notes as you read them to your exceedingly beautiful wife. I must say that it is as if you are inside my own head. I am a manufacturer of valves for cars and my company makes the finest valves in the world. Inlet valves, exhaust valves, high-temperature valves for racing engines at the Brickyard—my gosh, we make just about all kinds of valves. I work with all the big companies in Detroit. And I am proud to say I have met Mr. Ford himself on a number of occasions. And Mr. Ford is a very stern taskmaster, a martinet as it were. Yes sir, he is tough and demanding. I have to tell you that the points you just made are so true that I want to shout 'Hallelujah' out loud for you, sir, are a man who truly understands that uncertainty is the killer of enterprise, and that the current President and all his highfalutin know-nothing experts are killing freedom in this country. I just had to tell you that, so thank you, sir."

With that the man bowed and left the dining car.

"Well, looks like my lecture may be a success after all, my dear," Schneider smiled.

Louise nodded. It was clear from her demeanor that she felt she had done her duty as the spy posing as the dutiful wife, and that now she expected her reward. A reward that was a little more down-to-earth than all this economic jargon. In short, she wanted to be fucked hard.

On arriving at the station, Schneider hailed a Checker to take them to the Majestic. Once ensconced in the hotel, and after one very quick but highly satisfying standup, Schneider told her to rest then to go shopping at the hotel's boutiques, which were open until 8 p.m. He would be back about 9 p.m. She nodded.

Schneider left the hotel and took a cab to the printing company. The company was very small and in the industrial part of town. Even for an early evening it was still bustling and he was just another man—a travelling salesman with a samples case, perhaps? On entering the printing works, Schneider greeted the old German, Heinrich, and his three brothers. The printing business was a family affair and that is how Schneider liked it. Schneider was a welcome visitor and the packages he had arranged to mail each month from Chicago had helped to smooth the partnership. Each package had contained twenty U.S. 100-dollar bills. In Ottawa, as in all of southern Canada, U.S. currency was readily accepted by all.

Of course, the bills were all from Schneider's close friend Hiro, of the Japanese embassy in Washington. The arrangement was mutually beneficial, not only did Hiro encourage Schneider to keep half of the notes Hiro supplied, but Hiro also paid for all the visits to their favorite whore house on K Street. Hiro spoke reasonable English, but was a little shy in public, especially as the bashing of Japan by the American papers had escalated over the past months. So Schneider made the running, and Hiro slip-streamed in behind. Louise was not aware of his visits to K Street, but would not have cared had she known—powerful men active in one area of life are active in other areas, she would have quite reasonably concluded, and after all, Schneider is her boss and a very, very generous and accommodating boss at that (her mind pleasantly drifted back to thoughts of his desk in Washington).

At the printing company, Schneider passed the suit case to Heinrich who in turn passed it to his youngest brother, who curtly nodded and disappeared into the plate room to create the plates. Schneider had tried to find a newspaper press, but as Heinrich explained these were rare and more importantly took almost two dozen pressmen to operate. After discussions with Hiro, they had compromised on Heinrich's small and very discreet press.

Two hours later, the press was running and the first pages were being printed. In reality, it was the last page of the report. As Heinrich explained, they would print the pages in reverse order as this made the collating machine's job easier.

By eight that evening, the first batch of 5,000 copies was completed. The two middle brothers then left to each steal a car. The two stolen cars appeared 30 minutes later and the five men loaded the first two thousand copies into the back seats of the cars. It was cold and a snow had started to fall, which suited Schneider—fewer pedestrians to watch their nocturnal deliveries.

Schneider bid the brothers farewell and returned to take Louise to dinner.

The cars made their way on the two well-rehearsed routes. At each Catholic church on the route, the rear door opened, and a brother dashed to the front door carrying a bundle of 25 copies in each hand. Each bundle was loosely tied with twine—easy for even the oldest parishioner to open. The brothers dropped bundles at each front door. Once, they were disturbed by a startled priest, who was too shocked to do anything. Completing their church run, the two stolen cars were dumped in a grocery store parking lot. The entire operation had taken under four hours.

Returning to the Majestic, Schneider shaved and showered. He also carefully trimmed his fingernails.

19: The Smell Of Burning Rubber

Washington
Thursday, 4 December 1941

AFTER A LEISURELY BREAKFAST, as the President was pushed in his wheel chair from the residence along the veranda, the Marine Honor Guard snapped to attention. Call it professional bias if you will he thought, but my jarheads are the best: best saluters, best marchers, best uniforms. He allowed himself the indulgence of the pronoun. In reality, he was Commander In Chief of all the armed forces, not just of the Marines.

Rex Tugwell ordered coffee for the Commander In Chief.

"Rex, what is that God-awful stink?"

"Well, Mr. President, from what I understand there has been some sort of fire in Ohio."

"Ohio, what sort of fire?"

"Some rubber tires, I have been told."

The President sniffed, "Well, the sooner it burns out the better, but Ohio—that's hundreds of miles from here."

"Must have been one hell of a fire, hope the fuckingthingburnsout," the President chuckled, the last four words sounding as one.

In truth, "the fire" was actually two separate fires in Akron: one at the Goodyear dump and the other 25 miles away at the Goodrich dump.

The "fucking thing" did burn itself, or rather, themselves, out—in February. Yet another of the usual Washington cover-ups followed—an inquisition followed to protect the guilty and torment the innocent, much along the lines of the original one in Spain, and with about the same level of veracity and honesty. The official title was the "Secretary of War's Review Panel of the Ohio Rubber Fires," less reverentially referred to as the "Rubbers Report." The report conjectured that a number of men—"possibly of an Italian or Spanish persuasion"—had surreptitiously entered the two massive dumps and had planted "up to 100" magnesium flares. These flares burn with temperatures approaching the outer surface of the sun. Or as one reader succinctly described it, "very, very fucking hot."

The fire had destroyed 60% of the U.S. reserve of rubber, and—a little more importantly—the ability of the U.S. to wage war.

But that was the least of the President's problems.

20: Roosevelt's Sacred Magisterium

Washington
Friday, 5 December 1941

"**BAD BUSINESS, THAT TIRE THING,**" the President remarked to Rex.

Rex nodded, but looked ragged and nervous.

"What is it, Rex?"

"Sir, I'd rather wait for Mr. Hopkins to join us."

Roosevelt's ever-sensitive antennae twitched, "Rex, when you say 'sir' and 'Mr. Hopkins,' I know something is wrong, so out with it."

Tugwell looked at the floor hoping for some form—any form— of salvation.

At this moment, salvation did arrive in the shape of Harry Hopkins.

"So, Harry, give me some good news."

"Well, sir, the Canadians are no longer whining about the fires in Akron."

"Good, so I hope those no-good, fucking gutless Northern monkeys have stopped their bitching. Have they?"

Saying nothing, Hopkins moved to the President's desk and laid out the late morning issues of three Toronto morning newspapers.

"United States Plans To Invade Canada!" was the headline in end-of-the-world type; these six words were the front page of each of the dailies.

"What the fuck is this nonsense?" the President asked.

Hopkins took a very deep breath; Tugwell was still staring at the floor, praying he was anywhere but the Oval Office.

"Well. It seems the Canadians have gotten hold of War Plan Red. And so too have the English, and the Australians, and so on, and so on, and so on. And they know all about our proposed poison gas attacks as part of the plan."

"How the fuck could this happen? WPR is a fucking HyperSecret—that means, Eyes Only, no fucking copies."

"How the fuck could this happen?" by now Roosevelt was screaming, well beyond merely shouting.

Hopkins quietly said, "It gets worse."

"Worse, worse, how much fucking worse can it get? Are you fucking joking—worse?"

"Well, the Canadian papers say there is a handwritten note from you to Stimson that is supposed to say, 'Henry, as we discussed, we need to make these dopey northerners the 49th state ASAP—this cuts across party lines, Franklin.' And these papers say they have had the hand writing analyzed and it is ah, conclusively, ah, yours, ah, Mr. President."

Hopkins prayed for an earthquake to swallow up the White House, or at least that he would be struck dead; neither happened.

Roosevelt said nothing, then simply asked—himself more than the other two—"How the fuck did this happen?"

"So, what should we do, Mr. President?" Rex asked feebly having finally summoned the courage to speak.

Roosevelt, the consummate dissembler, reached for a cigarette.

"Do? We do nothing, we do dick, zero, nothing, nada. We don't need those fucking Canadians cunts. If they whine, fuck them, we will cut off all the milk and honey to Mr. Winston and see who needs whom then."

Even before finishing this sacred magisterium, Roosevelt's finely tuned calculus engine was already turning, and he returned to master manipulator politician mode.

"Pour me a drink, and take one yourselves, if you like." In spite of it being two minutes before 11 in the morning, both did likewise.

"So who does this help? Obviously, Berlin, but also Tokyo. So it must have been one—or both (Roosevelt chuckled at this). I have to say, I thought I was the wiliest cunt in the henhouse until today. But these people make me look like a Hudson River hick."

The straight Scotch steadied—if only a little—Tugwell's nerves, and he realized he was playing at the top table—here the President of the United States was making a brief study that would please even Niccolò.

"So Berlin is clearly the first winner, but Tokyo also gains if those dozy northern cunts take umbrage. But we really do not need the ball-less wonders." (Tugwell was reminded of the President's frequent conjecture that "All—no, that's not fair—let's say 97%—of Canadian men were born without testicles.")

The President chuckled, "We live in interesting times."

How could he change so quickly the two men wondered?

21: A Fine Social Contract

San Diego
Saturday, 6 December 1941

THE RAIN SQUALLS HAD STARTED a little after ten that evening. By midnight, the wind had picked up and the rain was so heavy a man could not see more than 30 yards in front of him, and with the rain and wind came the cold. To Harrison, who had served in Minneapolis, this was mild weather. But still he did not like it—give him Galveston any time. Now there was a sweet town: warm, lots of booze, and lots and lots of girls who just loved a good time—a good time that almost always ended in what he liked most, what he called a "bed whacking." But this cow town out West, you could take it, and you could keep it.

As the leader of the hourly patrol, he was strongly considering a slight variation in procedure, namely, a quick whip around the fuel tanks to ensure that no Mexicans had loaded them onto their donkeys and had stolen them. Then, over to the garage, which was always warm, dry and quiet. True, there was none of what he most liked, but poontang would be in abundance when he got he got his 48-hour liberty on Tuesday. Down by the docks, he loved to entertain the girls who had made their way up from Baja. To compete with the local girls, these Mexican senoritas were always cheaper, hotter and, most important, younger—many *looked* like innocent virgins. While it was true none of them were tight—after all, they were hard-working girls—they did get (or seemed to get, he could never quite tell) more excited than the local girls. And excitement and noise and wetness, as the girls all know, are what excite all men the most.

Harrison left with a two-man squad, "This will be a cursory and summary inspection."

The two soldiers in the squad looked at each other, not understanding his words.

Slightly exasperated, Harrison explained, "We will look at Tank 1, then go to the garage. I doubt the Mexicans will be stealing the tanks tonight."

Both men smiled and nodded.

Five minutes later, they got to the garage. It was typical—dark, bottle-green and over-painted, with signs dispensing such nonsense as "Let's Prevent Noise By Ourselves" and the ubiquitous "No Smoking While Dispensing Fuel."

The three men opened the side door. From the outside floodlights, they could see the dark shadows of the pool's trucks and jeeps and they could smell the stale grease. They walked to the drivers' inner waiting room and sat down. The small room was a sanctum of quiet. Scattered about were copies of *Life* and the *Saturday Evening Post*, and a few magazines that his mother back home would call "rude" with smiling ladies all beaming at the reader, nipples brazenly erect, occasionally with a hint of pubic hair.

The drivers' waiting room was not the cleanest place in the world, but there was a two-burner electric stove, an icebox, and most important of all, hidden behind the wood paneling above the icebox, a fifth of bourbon. The established protocol was: *Drink It, Replace It.* But for a fifth of a gallon of the best southern bourbon, this was a fine social contract.

The three sat down, and three glasses were found. Not that the glasses were the cleanest, but—what the hell—the whiskey would kill all the germs.

Outside, under the cover of the driving rain storm, ten men emerged from a hole in the chain wire fence at the top of the compound. All were wearing Navy uniforms. The rain was the last thing on their minds. At the last moment, the idea of carrying mock wooden rifles had been discarded, not because the rifles did not look real, but rather because they would be of no benefit if the men were captured. All ten entered through the hole in fence at the north of the compound—the highest point—as the Swede had explained that, "This gives us a small advantage in case of discovery—the opposition will have to run up hill, and this will slow them, especially while carrying rifles."

The troops nodded and appreciated his thoughtfulness about their well-being—their Spanish commanders in their civil war could have learned from the Swede's thoughtfulness and planning and consideration for his troops.

The rain was a godsend but had they not rehearsed for the week prior back in Nogales, they would all have been lost. And, Holy Maria, these tanks were huge—in training, the men could not believe the circles of lime the Swede had marked on the four soccer fields in Nogales. But now they could see these monsters for themselves, each wider than a soccer field's width and higher than a ten-story building; inside each, enough fuel for one of the giant American aircraft carriers for a month of cruising. And there were ten of these monsters.

Each man half walked, half ran to his designated monster. Placing the first of the two limpets on the uphill side of the tank, he then moved to the opposite side—this was the dangerous part as now the man was in the lights.

In far less time than they dreamed of, all ten men reunited at the hole in the fence. In reality, it was just four minutes. The ten scrambled through the fence back to bus. Once they reached the bus, they scrambled on board, like very nervous and frightened school boys who had successful robbed a candy store for the very first time at the start of their promising young criminal careers. The inside of the bus was dark—just three red bulbs dimly glowed, just enough dull glow to not trip over the steps. All ten stripped off their uniforms and placed them in two cream calico bags. While they were doing this, the bus had jumped into life and had slowly and carefully started on its slow journey back to the safety of Mexico. Two hours out on the highway, they stopped and dumped the two calico bags on the side of the road into a ravine. They all talked about the mission and their rewards for four minutes of pure, breathtaking exhilaration—imagine actually being paid to do this.

In the drivers' small waiting room, the two electric burners glowed red and while their glow was somewhat feeble, the room was very small, and soon it was warm. In addition, the bourbon was having its effect. Harrison and his tiny army were all feeling no pain. Harrison rose and was starting to say they should make some coffee and get going back to the barracks. Just as he made this slightly garbled announcement they heard a muffled noise from the top end of the tank farm, then a second later, another, then the sounds of six more. Startled, all three looked at each other.

Two seconds later, the pool garage and the inner sanctum of the drivers' waiting room were swept away by a flood of nine million gallons of heavy fuel oil. Enough fuel oil—as the quickly convened inquisition, the "Naval Review of the Loma Fuel Farm

Attack," pointed out—to fuel the US Navy's entire aircraft carrier fleet for 74 days.

Or as one slightly more astute analyst pointed out: with the loss of Loma and the Hawaiian Islands oil farms, the American carriers best use would soon be to be scuttled as artificial coral reefs; Yamamoto pondered this as he thought about the time his Emperor had mentioned to him the need for more coral reefs for his Emperor's son's beloved fish.

22: Sato's Cherry Blossoms

Cristobal, Panama
Sunday, 7 December 1941

AT SIX IN THE MORNING on the bridge of the *Tancho*, Admiral Sato looked at the sky. Broken clouds masked much of the full moon. An hour earlier, all 60 men had squeezed into the ward room designed for 20 officers.

"Well, men, today we will make history for our nation. I can tell you that our countrymen are about to attack the American possession of the Hawaiian Islands in the Pacific."

A gasp swept the room; Sato waited for it to subside,

"And with that attack, we will start to fulfill the Emperor's destiny to be the ruler of the Pacific, our Pacific. But our mission is just as important. And we can cripple our enemy—cripple it without the loss of one life, either Japanese or anyone else."

Sato moved to a large map on the wall of North and South America. Two red lines showed distances from New York to San Francisco. The red line going through the Canal had the distance listed beside it of 8,370 kilometers, while the second one, around the Horn, had the distance listed as 20,900 kilometers.

"Gentlemen, as you can see from these lines, the Panama Canal is the most vital strategic resource the Americans have. Yet, in spite of this, they have decided not to reinforce it in any way. Such a sweet little virgin cannot be wasted." (All present knew of Sato's predilection for Yokohama virgins; it was common knowledge that in this very ward room Sato had deflowered seven girls—"just there where you are eating your udon noodles"—he would remind many a blushing midshipman who stared at the table. "Clean, sweet, innocent and above all, very, very tight," Sato would smile.)

Sato was loved for his wit, his love of wine, his *joie de vivre* and above all, how he cared for his sailors.

"But seriously, gentlemen, we have been blessed. So here is the plan: we will weigh anchor at midnight and will slip out of this very congenial port. Silence is key. Our hosts will mostly be in their beds, but there is no reason to tempt the Fates. We will steam due east. Our agents up the coast have indicated there are no commercial vessels at the mouth of the Canal. Then we will turn 180 degrees and steam into the mouth of the Canal. We will travel at just six knots, and even at that, it will be damn close as the Canal is only three boat widths wide in the entrance. The depth reading our fishing boats have taken over the past year as they have 'accidentally' strayed into the Canal have suggested we can drive at least five kilometers, possible as far as seven kilometers, into the Canal. At the five kilometer mark, there will be a burning truck on each bank. When we see these markers, we turn hard a-starboard and reverse the starboard engine. We will then block the Canal. When we run aground, I will scuttle the ship."

A second gasp was heard.

"Gentlemen, please be aware this is not a game. We are simply following the guiding principle of attacking the enemy's weakness, and in this case, his weakness is his Canal. We will proceed into the Canal, scuttle the ship, disembark the ship's company and then the explosive charges will turn her into a great, impassible thorn. A thorn that will do more damage than one thousand sister ships could ever inflict. All of you will remember the difficulties we had as a massive ship of the line in rounding the Horn—the massive seas, the Roaring Forties, the Furious Fifties, the Screaming Sixties. We felt like the proverbial cork. And remember the icebergs we saw? Now think what a small, frail, common oiler, one tenth our size, will feel. Gentlemen, we are blessed.

"You have all wondered about the dry docking in Yokohama last year. And how it was done in such secrecy. How our aircraft hangars below decks were filled with the huge blocks of triangular cast steel. Blocks that are taller than two men and each weighing 50,000 kilograms. Well, now you know. As the ship explodes, these huge blocks will all settle together to create a massive barrier. Nothing will pass. You will be disembarked so we can complete our mission. Are there any questions?"

Sato felt a frisson of excitement as he finally explained to his crew what he himself had proselytized to Yamamoto two years earlier.

No one spoke.

"Dismissed, and good luck to all of you. I expect all of you to report on the first of April at noon to the bar of the Palace Hotel in Tokyo to drink sake with me and to view the cherry blossoms fall around our Emperor's palace."

The reference to the ideal of a samurai's death was a nice touch.

Ten hours later, the *Tancho* steamed at under quarter speed—six knots—into the eastern side of the Canal. The fishing agents had been modest—the *Tancho* had no difficulty in making the five kilometers into the entrance of the Canal. Sato had assigned two flagmen to stand at the front of the aircraft carrier's flight deck. In case of a premature grounding Sato had taken the precaution to have them wear harnesses attached by a rope to the deck. The flagmen were needed because it was impossible for the conning tower to see the Canal, so these two directed the way. From time to time one of the flagmen would lose his footing. Sato smiled to himself that Takashi in the battleship *Senshi* at the other end of the isthmus would be able to drive in without having to resort to using flagmen.

True to Sato's word, the five kilometer mark was indicated by a truck on fire on each side of the Canal. Upon seeing the burning beacons, Sato started the *Tancho* on the final turn of her life. At 36,000 tons, the aircraft carrier took over 16 kilometers to completely reverse direction. But because of the narrowness of the Canal at the eastern end, Sato did not have to wait long. A moment later, the *Tancho* started to run aground, her twin screws still madly turning in opposite directions doing nothing but churning the mud.

"Done with engines," Sato shouted down the voice pipe.

"Abandon ship" was the next command.

Sato had transferred the *Tancho*'s portrait of the Emperor to the *Suzume* a week before they departed; Sato abandoned his command—unheard of for an admiral—with a sense of serenity.

All the ship's skeleton company was put ashore. Four local trucks had been there and had taken them into the jungle. The jungle in Panama started 100 meters from the Canal and the U.S. troops saw it as the devil's playground—full of man-eating pythons and worse. To continue the myth, the locals would get an American soldier paralytically drunk and feed him alive, but unconscious, to a hungry male python that would then proceed to fall into a deep digestive sleep. Two weeks later they would then shoot the sleeping reptile with a simple .22 round through the eye to the reptile's brain. Then they would skin the snake and show the soldier's half-digested remains. The effect among the American troops was always the same—panic.

An hour later, safely ensconced in the jungle hamlet eating rice and udon noodles, the crew of the *Tancho* saw the night sky illuminated with a huge orange and yellow fireball—the *Tancho* had done her job.

23: Admiral Abe's Type 93

San Diego
Forenoon Watch, Sunday, 7 December 1941

IN EVERY NAVY'S LANGUAGE, the Forenoon Watch is from 8 a.m. to noon. The modern Imperial Japanese Navy followed this convention, as it was crafted by the officers seconded from the Royal Navy; to this day the uniform of Japanese school children still have the square pigtail guards of the Royal Navy from Nelson's time, embossed with three white lines, modern-day reminders of Admiral Nelson's three victories.

All this was of no importance, and of less interest, to the small trio of Japanese submarines patiently waiting outside the entrance to the San Diego naval base. For fifteen frustrating days, they had waited there submerged and quiet, surfacing only at midnight for two hours to recharge their batteries, and to quickly gasp a few breathes of fresh air. Once a week, in quiet, open seas, Admiral Abe would host the submarine captains, one at a time, on his "flag-ship"—a dirty, noisy little Mexican fishing tramp by the name of the *Anna Maria*.

"The Mexicans are noted for their intellectualism, their athleticism and their deep sense of history," Abe had said to Captain Higa on the previous Friday, in reply to Higa's question about the exotic name of the fishing boat. Or as Abe said to Higa when the two stood alone on the stern of the fishing vessel ten minutes later, smoking cigars, "They're fucking Mexicans, what did you expect, the *Chrysanthemum Throne*?" Higa laughed. Abe waved to his hosts who turned to look at the Japanese devil from under the sea.

Abe expanded,

"They're fucking children, idiots—trained monkeys could do a better job of fishing than these Mexicans. I have never met such a lazy bunch of men in my life."

Abe paused,

"But my view is generous compared to that held by their northern neighbors. That is what makes my small Mexican 'flotilla' so useful—the Americans ignore them; the Mexicans are the perfect camouflage. Actually 'ignore' is the wrong word; 'detest' is a better word. I had one of the boats in my White Stork 'flotilla' accidently—that is, deliberately—ram the port side of one of the American destroyers. I had coached the captain to say in English, 'you my starboard, you give right way.' Needless to say, the young American captain frowned and then threw this idiot off his boat. And remember, Higa, these Americans cannot see a *ruse de guerre* even when it is staring them in the face, as my 'flotilla' clearly is. I have been nosing around these waters off one of their most important naval bases with no inspections, no reviews, no surprises—nothing. Of course, any thought of inspections evaporated after the ramming incident.

"As you heard on the short-wave frequency, our agents in Bremerton signaled three days ago that the American aircraft carrier *Saratoga* has departed, and so we can expect the enemy in these waters tomorrow or Sunday. I have designed the positions of our three submarines so she should sail almost directly above you. If this does not happen, then *Imai* or *Noguchi* will surely see her."

✠ ✠ ✠

After the Great War, only the Germans and the Japanese took the submarine seriously; the English—still living in the phantasy of Nelson—dreamt of a second Trafalgar. The Americans took a more realistic view, but their torpedoes were the worst of any warring nation—"My God, even the Italians are ahead of us when it comes to torpedoes," Admiral Stark had complained to the President in '38. Stark explained that the American "fish," as he called them, ran too deep, were under-powered and—worst sin of all for any bomb—did not explode on impact.

"They do not explode on impact?" the President asked.

"They do not explode on impact—that is correct, sir."

"Well, something has to be done."

And as happens with all pronouncements from a political Olympus in any country—in this case the Oval Office of the President of the United States—nothing was done, but all vehemently agreed that something should have been done, or at the very least a complete and detailed study should be conducted, when the time was ripe, in the fullness of time, which taken at the flood.

In contrast, the Japanese Navy had spent 20 years of intensive effect to create the world's finest torpedoes. By '35, the Long Lance had been perfected. Powered by pure oxygen, it was five times more effective than conventional torpedoes that ran on air, air that contained 80% inert nitrogen. In addition to the very high-speed and tiny vapour trail on the Long Lance—technically, the "Type 93 Torpedo"—the detonator was superb: rugged, safe and, most important of all, reliable. And the "wander" was astonishing small—it was 14 times better than the American "fish."

✠ ✠ ✠

Higa had taken the risky gamble of loading and flooding the four forward and his two aft torpedo tubes—Higa's boat was now a submerged bomb with six fully loaded Long Lance torpedoes, all charged with pure oxygen. But the rewards were worth the risk—he could launch a wide spread in less than 60 seconds in either direction. Higa had gambled that he would be close to the target and had set all of the torpedoes to the maximum speed of 48 knots. While this limited the range to just under 20,000 yards, it also meant that the wander would be reduced to at most 200 yards. And like all submarine captains, Higa was a gambler.

As it happened, the *Saratoga* literally sailed over Higa's boat.

Higa had put his boat at 30 meters, the shallowest dive depth possible but one that gave him the ability to surface within 45 seconds. Which is precisely what he did. He expected a typical task force of destroyers even though his periscope man, Yako, had vehemently said there were no support vessels in sight.

Sure enough, after Higa quickly surfaced, the horizon was empty—not a destroyer in sight. But as Higa surfaced he was faced with a truly odd situation—he was too *close* to the American aircraft carrier, so he order "Emergency Reverse," probably the only time in the days of hostilities that such a command was issued.

After a minute of frantically going *away* from the enemy was Higa in a position to fire. Without hesitating, he fired the four forward torpedoes, with the widest spread. Sixteen seconds later, he and his crew were rewarded with the glorious sound that every submarine crew lives for—the sound of a torpedo exploding, and in the next five seconds the other three all registered.

With the explosion of the four Japanese torpedoes, the *Saratoga* started to immediately list to port and list dangerously. Rear Admiral Fitch, standing in the conning tower, regretted his decision to override the captain's request for General Quarters—"Bill, to run the men for over two days at the ready will not sharpen them, but it will dull them," Fitch had said to the Captain as they left Puget Sound. While this may have been true, what was also true was that without General Quarters, none of the water-tight doors were dogged.

The birth of the *Saratoga* had been a very difficult one—first as a battle cruiser, then in mothballs, then finally as an aircraft carrier. But she was superbly engineered with 18 separate water-tight compartments—"virtually unsinkable" was the verdict from Admiral King on down, but "virtually unsinkable" was concomitant with the water-tight doors being closed—that is, General Quarters having been sounded.

When the fourth Type 93 torpedo exploded at the very end of the last compartment on the *Saratoga*, the aircraft carrier's doom was sealed. As the designers could not agree on the correct approach to tapering the armor belt, they did what all engineers do in such a situation—they did nothing. So, just as a traveler sometimes sees a completed bridge that ends in space, or a suburban house with an extension that is never completed, the naval engineers poring over the blueprints of the *Saratoga* also left their work unfinished.

Normally, this action or, more accurately, inaction, would not be important. But the fourth torpedo had essentially hit a thin skinned vessel—not a man-of-war with an eight-foot belt of Specially Treated Steel armor—but a skin of one inch of mild steel plate.

The effect of this fourth torpedo was as to be expected. Although few in any navy will say it publicly, armor belts are designed to dull—not cancel—attacks. If an armor belt reduces an attack to one-tenth, then the armor belt has earned its keep. As one Captain, a former boxer said, "it's like getting your glove up to a hook to the head. You still feel it, it still hurts like hell, but you are also still conscious."

The superb Long Lance delivered a devastating 500 kilograms of TNT to the only thin-skinned area on the ship. The effect was immediate and devastating. The other three torpedoes had done little damage to the ship, but this fourth one sunk her: the first three had created fissures from one to three feet in diameter in the armor belt. In contrast, the fourth torpedo created an opening of over 26 feet in diameter. The Pacific Ocean entered like a tidal wave.

Two minutes after the staff in the conning tower had noticed the list to port, a far more ominous sight appeared—the sky was sinking, or so it appeared in the conning tower. Actually the sky was not moving, but the stern of the ship was rapidly sinking into to the ocean as the sea water filled all of the rear compartments. As the engine room was entirely under water, there was no longer power. Even the basic power—the "hotel power" in Navy parlance—had stopped.

"*Saratoga* very rapidly sinking by stern. Request Immediate Assistance," was tapped out by Morse, on the emergency batteries *en clair*.

Eight minutes later, the *Saratoga* sank beneath the waves.

24: The Polo Player

Hawaiian Islands
Sunday, 7 December 1941

MIYUKI OKINO WAS BILLETED in a tiny room along with other Officers' Club servants at the far end of the island. The billets consisted of three dreary, two-story buildings of painted cinderblock. The best of the three buildings—the one overlooking the beach—had been quickly claimed by the native Hawaiians. The other two were both far shabbier and were occupied by the Chinese, the Filipinos, the Indians, and the two Ceylonese girls. Miyuki was pleased that there were no other Japanese in the billet. She liked to do her job and in her spare time she liked to sew for the local Red Cross auxiliary.

The auxiliary was staffed by bored wives of the officers who had little to do but charity, and to drink. A few of the more adventurous wives formed a coven that helped each other and would arrange all-too-rare trysts with the gardeners' young native helpers. The arrangements were made by a simple hint being dropped to the senior lady; the senior lady who herself was known to enjoy the illicit touch of young and taut, virile, native skin. Then a few days later, a quiet young buck stud would politely knock on the servants' entrance and would be shown to the study of the lady of the house. Waiting for him would be the maid, the lady, and the elderly gardener. The lady would explain how she wanted her heavy mahogany desk moved to the window, and all four would struggle to move it. After assisting with the move, the gardener's helper would be thanked and sent to the kitchen for cake and a glass of lemonade. Before the cook had poured the lemonade, the lady would be on the telephone.

"Oh, yes. Yes, yes. He will do very nicely."

The senior lady would confide that the boy, she called him Thomas, was clean, extremely docile, and had great stamina.

"And, aah, how is his development?"

"Development?" the frown could be heard over the telephone line for an instant.

"Oh, of course. Silly me. Yes, his 'development,' as you call it. Well dear, it is no larger than usual. About the same as my husband's, but there are many differences apart from purely physical size. For one thing, I've never felt one as hard. I mean it is really like a warm stone you find when wandering on the beach in summer. It is astonishingly hard. And this deliciously warm stone is inside you. Another thing is that is stays that way even after he completes. And what I like most is the cream."

Now it was the lady's turn to frown, but the senior lady continued.

"I always tell him to forgo a prophylactic, but I am of an age I can afford to do that. For you, with your regular monthlies, this would be ill-advised. But I suggest you have him complete outside, on your face or bosom, as Thomas's greatest gift, next to his complete native docility, is the volume of his supply. Take a coffee cup filled to the brim with cow's milk, then pour that slowly over you face and body when you bathe today. That is precisely the effect of enjoying Thomas completely."

"Is that possible? Surely that is not possible. A coffee cup filled. That's not possible, is it?"

Having gotten started, the senior lady continued, ever so slightly aroused,

"Thomas is a nice boy, a little simple even as these natives go, and his face has a crude sort of handsomeness, but his arms and shoulders are exhilarating. I love him on top of me in the master bedroom, pumping away inside me while I run my hands over his huge shoulders and arms. In this position he is more like a machine than a human. Expect no conversation or cleverness. He is a native after all. But there's nothing quite like the virility of his youth to wash away the years, if only for an hour or two. And remember, he does not complete until you tell him to. There was one occasion a few months back when he accidentally lost control early and he was so apologetic that he was almost in tears. I felt it coming and rather than stop him, I just let him pump it all into me. Do remember sometimes it takes him almost half a minute to complete."

"Half a minute?" the lady sounded incredulous.

"Oh, yes. Remember, he has a coffee cup to fill."

Both giggled.

"Well, Thomas sounds ideal. Can you send him over on Wednesday, that's my maid's and cook's day off?"

The senior lady said she could.

Occasionally, Miyuki would be invited to tea at the Red Cross. A few of the ladies took sympathy on her; she seemed to them so lost—such an innocent, lost, little waif. And Miyuki was extremely dutiful, even more dutiful than when she was working at the Officers' Club on the hill. Her eyes were always down cast, she always walked very close to the wall, her head was always bowed. When a gaggle of officers' wives would meander down the hall at the Red Cross, she always stopped and stood to one side, eyes down, hands lightly clasped in front of her. Before long, her extreme modesty was noted with approval.

Sharing a rare tea, the ladies admired Miyuki's perfect English, which she explained she had learned when she was a student in the Philippines after she and her family had been expelled from Japan. The ladies consoled her about how politics were always so awful in all countries these days. After a moment or two of these niceties, the ladies would resume their private gossiping about their men and their hopes for reassignment back to the mainland and their fears of their husbands' possible assignment to ghastly Manila and the horrors there of Douglas MacArthur and his wife, which tattle had it was a half-caste.

Miyuki liked her job at the Officers' Club. She had been working there for five years. Her papers listed her as coming from Manila with excellent references from the British planter. The letters were printed on the most beautiful cream-white paper—25% cotton rag. Of course, all the Hawaiian staff hated her intensely—for her politeness; for her cleanliness and how she bathed every day; for how in the basement she never spoke ill of the officers or their odious wives. Worse, she never took part in the petty adulteration of the meals that the Hawaiians loved to do to their masters' meals. She was short, shy, modest, and quiet. Only her hair was different from the other servants—curiously she wore a flapper's bob of the Twenties, which was reminiscent of the page boys of medieval English knights—jousting and all that.

She was liked by Commander Wheeler, the commandant of the club. And she liked Commander Wheeler.

Six months earlier, she had knocked on the Commander's door and hearing no answer, entered to tidy his suite. The Commandant's suite was at the far end of the third floor, well apart from the other suites used for visiting admirals and senators. As she straightened the bed, the Commander unexpectedly entered from the bathroom, clad only in bright red silk pajama boxer shorts and wearing a gold watch. Startled, she apologized,

"Commander Wheeler, I am so sorry, sir. I did not realize you were here, sir. I will come back later, sir."

"Nonsense, Miss Okino. I'll be out of your way in just a sec," Wheeler generously drawled in his South Texas accent.

"As you wish, sir."

Miyuki had averted her eyes to the floor and had instinctively placed her right hand in front of her mouth, palm extended, with her elbow by her side. But she could not avoid admiring his muscular chest and arms, and—most important—she let him see her admiration. Wheeler was old money Texas oil, or as old as Texas oil money could be—his grandfather was one of the original wildcatters who had arrived in Texas with the clothes on his back. Commander Wheeler was a polo player and was admired—with a touch of envy—by his brother officers. But his generous nature and genuine friendliness quickly won over most officers and all the wives with whom he was both polite to the point of chivalrous and entertaining to the point of flirtatious.

Like Miyuki, not a few of the wives had also noticed Wheeler's body. A few white scars that stood out on the well-tanned body; a touch of chest hair—"to show he was a man," the wives gossiped; an exceptionally well-developed chest; and arms that women did actually talk about.

Prior to her knocking on the door, Miyuki had removed the two small squares of thin rubber sheet from between her starched white uniform and her brassiere. In her little room, Miyuki had

ANDREW BLENCOWE

amended the front of the brassiere so there was a hole on each cup about the size of her thumb, to allow her generous nipples to protrude. By using the dodge of the rubber squares, Miyuki was able to walk around the servants' basement and the club just as prim and proper as the kindergarten teacher she once was, but in Commander Wheeler's suite, her two nipples were prominent and impossible to miss.

While she was straightening the bed, she was careful to take time at the foot of the bed; the foot faced the bathroom that was in truth larger than her entire little room. While fussing, she had leaned over the bed, her legs slightly apart for balance, and, sadly, the skirt of her starched white uniform had ridden up her legs to show the bottom of the garter clips. She did not finish the bed straightening until she was sure that Commander Wheeler had a long view of her legs.

Wheeler crossed his arms to further emphasize the size of his chest. Miyuki affected a blush and was genuinely getting excited. Apart from a growing, warm dampness, she could sense her nipples swelling. Wheeler was looking directly at her nipples on her large chest—a very generous D cup. Miyuki bowed her head and looked at the floor. Her extreme passivity excited Wheeler—here was a young woman, clearly aroused and simply waiting to be taken and ravished. While looking at the floor, Miyuki could just glimpse the swelling in the silk pajamas shorts she was hoping to see.

"Miss Okino, how long have you been with us now?"

Still firmly looking at the floor, "Just under five years, sir."

"And are you happy here with us?"

"Oh yes, sir; this is so much better than my last job in the Philippines working for an English planter. The master's wife there would beat me, and they were both very cruel. I love working here and working for you, sir. Everyone is so nice. The American people are so much nicer and friendlier than the English, and the food here

240

is so much better. Oh yes, sir, I love it here; I would do anything to stay."

By this stage, Wheeler was standing directly in front of her, so she could see the top of his pajamas and his developing masculinity. He put his hand under her chin and slowly lifted it. She raised her chin and looked into his eyes, as softly as she could. He placed his hands gently on her shoulders and slowly ran his hands down her arms. She pursed her lips and opened her mouth and started a very slight panting. Her nipples were doing their part in the seduction, and were now proud of the holes in her brassiere and formed two rather large bumps on the starched white jacket.

Wheeler was an experienced hand at this, the oldest of rituals. But Miyuki knew, even better than the white man, the steps in this ritual: first the blush, then the nipples, then the slight panting, leading to more panting. All the time, Miyuki's desire was to simply have him push her onto the bed and ravish her. But, that could be a story that Wheeler might find a little too obvious when he reviewed his latest conquest later. So Miyuki simply increased the tempo of the panting.

Sure enough, Wheeler took her hand and placed it on the now fully tumescent lump in the pajamas. Without speaking, Miyuki knelt on the floor and undid the string of his pajamas. She was pleased to see he was cut—she hated uncut. The English planter was uncut and as a consequence he smelled terrible down there, and the English planter was big, and he did what all women hate most—he used her hair as if her hair was a handle, and her head as some kind of machine.

In contrast, the American was a gentleman, and an experienced gentleman at that. He knew that while ravishing an employee or servant, or even a whore, there was a certain protocol that it was polite and proper to follow. And it was more than just polite—giving the girl a good time and the noise and the arching of the back and sometimes even her legs folding under so her heels touched her hips, all this was the most enjoyable part. And he loved to see his conquests perspire as lust took over.

Miyuki was sure to use just enough teeth to elevate Wheeler's excitement, but not too much to have him complete early in her mouth. After a few moments, and without being prompted, Wheeler pushed her onto the bed.

Miyuki said,

"Sir, can I take my uniform off first? Please, sir?"

"Sure thing."

Miyuki quickly stripped to her stockings and garter belt—she was anxious for Wheeler not to see the brassiere. She folded her clothes and, for the first time, took the initiative and climbed on top of the big Texan. She rode him as hard as she could, emitting what she judged to be the best level of panting and groans—enough to keep him excited, but not too much to have him become apprehensive. (Her second concern was actually groundless—Wheeler boasted to anyone who would listen that he would "fuck any piece of ass I want, and no one was going to stop me.")

Miyuki relaxed and let herself actually climax twice before she felt Wheeler tense and finally complete inside her. He was a strong and virile man who took a good 15 seconds to complete the elemental act. She was clearly pleasing her commandant.

"Sir, let me get you a warm towel," she said jumping off the bed before he could stop her.

Wheeler smiled to himself, "this placid Asian poontang is beyond belief." He was very much of the camp that held that Asia was a man's world.

"Sir, I will return to your suite after you have dressed. I am sorry for the interruption, sir. I will dress now, I will not take long, sir."

Wheeler actually laughed at that statement, as Miyuki darted into the bathroom.

Miyuki opened the bathroom door in less than a minute. Back to prim kindergarten teacher, Miyuki bowed.

"Honey, that must be a world record for any woman to get dressed." Wheeler said.

"Please tell me if you need me again, at any time, sir. I am always available for you, sir. I love it here and will do anything to stay here, sir."

Miyuki left; after closing the Commandant's door, she replaced the two squares of thin foam rubber. Thus started an illicit affair that Miyuki had been dreaming about for five years, and it was a partnership made in heaven—the tall, rich, strapping Texan commander of the most important club in the Islands with the soft, gentle, but intensely physical, young, placid, Japanese servant girl.

More importantly, it was the activation of the Imperial Japanese Navy's single most important agent. The intelligence gathered by Miyuki from the gregarious and boastful American was so valuable, and her position so critical, that she had not one but two cut outs, and no radio traffic was ever used. She never liked radio and she especially hated radio men, who she found to be uniformly unreliable as well as congenitally nervous—what was it, the electrons? Instead, a special protocol was used whereby her coded messages were passed by the second cut out to a fishing boat that would pass the package to a submarine. And this only occurred when there were completely clear days so the "fishermen" could scour the skies with their high-powered binoculars before banging a submerged brass bell with a hammer to tell the submarine the exchange could safely be made.

Miyuki's material was of astonishing importance—she was even able to glean some of fragments of King's and Nimitz's top-level strategic thinking. In Tokyo, Yamamato himself was heard to comment that it was like having a frank, professional conversation with Admirals King and Nimitz over brandy and cigars at the Palace Hotel.

Yet this was not the most valuable achievement Miyuki performed. For that would occur on the actual day of Operation Z.

On that seminal first Sunday in December, Miyuki put on a freshly starched white uniform and took her bicycle to ride the hour to the Officers' Club. She was sure the always-late bus to the Officer's Club would not appear due to the day's mayhem, and this suited her purpose. The first part of the ride was easy, around the coast road, then the climb started and it became steeper and steeper. Half way up the climb, she dismounted and paused. Through years of training, she instinctively gasped at what she saw and drew her hand to her mouth, just as a plain person would have done when confronted with such scenes of destruction and devastation.

"You're always being watched," her trainer in Tokyo had repeated and repeated.

"Never let your guard down until you are again on Japanese soil."

So she went through the ritual of mopping her brow, of putting her arms akimbo and stretching her lower back, of tsk'ing to herself. But throughout this charade, her sole professional interest was the fuel tanks. This gargantuan farm of tanks held sufficient fuel for all ships in the U.S. Pacific Fleet for six months. Think of it, six months, or twice as much fuel as her poor homeland possessed. And through the smoke, Miyuki saw all the tanks, pristine and intact—the Japanese attack had failed.

Miyuki slowly turned her bicycle—"you are always being watched"—and rode back down the coast road. She did not stop at the three cinder block billets, but rather continued until she reached the abandoned fishing village. It was more a small hamlet of five or six tumble-down shacks where nine years ago some local fishermen with the unenthusiastic backing of some local investors planned to start a pearling operation. Of course, the combination of lack of capital and the native Hawaiians aversion to anything that even approached work doomed the cockamamie scheme from the start. But three years ago, the quietness and absolute stillness had caught the eye of an agent of the caliber of Miyuki.

She dismounted and placed her bicycle out of sight behind the first shack. She then walked to the second shack and entered. It smelled of feral cats. It was dark and dank—almost no sunlight entered. She opened the front window a fraction and sat there on a wooden crate, listening for five minutes. As her ears slowly became accustomed to the quietness, she heard nothing apart from a far-off sound of a siren wailing out the end of an era.

After ten more minutes, when she was satisfied the hamlet was deserted, she struggled to push the heavy cast iron table in the center of the room to one side. She knelt on the floor and brushed away the dirt she had placed there. She removed the outer board and was presented with the sight of a large steel padlock. Unlocking the padlock, she removed her treasure, a treasure for which she would give her life, or the life of her first son. Gently, she removed the radio set and went through the starting procedures. Machinery and radio valves always intimidated her, but she had overcome this fear; she had to succeed, so she did.

She strung the aerial wire. Once the radio set was warmed up and operational, she started typing in Morse, "181-79," over and over again. She had to get the message through and this message was so important that a code cypher was not sufficient—encrypted text could always be cracked, whereas a one-time book was infallible, albeit limited. One hundred and eighty-one was her agent number; 79 was the message—"oil tanks not destroyed." After only 30 seconds, her heart leapt, "SN"—"message understood," and the code of Yamamoto's signal ship.

Her career was over. No champagne, no syrupy speeches, no silly parties, just the satisfaction of knowing that she had done it.

She turned off the radio set, removing the radio tubes—she had to use her handkerchief because they were so hot. She smashed each one in turn. She spent ten minutes destroying the rest of the radio. She removed the two small drums of fuel she had cached in the room five months earlier and splashed all of the inside of the shack. Her final act was to remove the strike-anywhere matches from the cache. Before striking the match, she paused by the front window, more out of tradecraft than out of necessity. Hearing nothing, she opened the front door, struck the match and put it to one of the soaked rags.

Walking away without looking back, Miyuki retrieved her bicycle.

Miyuki returned to her billet. She went into the first building where the hated local Hawaiians lived. My God it was a shambles. No wonder Wheeler had fancied her—what man in his right mind would want to stick his thing into one of these native women?

To her surprise (and delight), the two girls in the common room ran to her and embraced her,

"Sister Miyuki, help us; what are we to do; are the Japanese coming? Help us sister, we love you; help us, please."

Miyuki considered a sarcastic tone, but instantly realized that would not work with this local peasant stock.

"Girls, all will be fine; let's have tea."

"Tea, yes. Tea. Why did we not think of that? Yes, tea would be wonderful."

The babbling continued and eventually tea was made.

In the ward room of his flagship *Nagato*, Japanese Marshal Admiral and commander-in-chief of the Combined Fleet, Isoroku Yamamoto, looked up at the startled junior intelligence officer.

"What is it, lieutenant?"

"Sir, 181 has signaled 79. Sir, this is the real 181, on the frequency reserved exclusively for him." (Only Yamamoto knew the truth about 181).

"Admiral, sir, this is a real 79."

"Thank you, lieutenant. Please ask Commander Genda to join me. That will be all."

Two minutes later, Commander Minoru Genda entered the ward room, smiling from ear to ear,

"Well, it's the Ginza for me when we're back next week."

Genda was referring to the 1,000 year old shopping and "entertainment" center of Tokyo. Originally a silver mine, the town had evolved to become the location of the most beautiful and also the most pliable women in Japan.

Yamamoto looked up. A small, short man, and extremely popular with his sailors, he was not quite so popular with his peers—General Tojo detested him and Tojo was not alone. Yamamoto's face was that of a 16th century Flemish portrait—stern, severe, and unsmiling.

"79."

"Really?"

"Yes, fucking really. Yes, for the sake of fuck, really. Now get the planes reloaded with bombs and let's get the job completed."

While saying this Yamamoto had been essentially polite, albeit forceful in his language. All this changed when Genda was so foolish to say without thinking, "But, Admiral, all the pilots are tired."

'I was so thoughtless', Genda later admitted in the victory party, ironically at Chuo-Ku 3-6-1, Matsuya Ginza.

Yamamoto sprang to his feet with such savagery that Genda expected the Admiral to hit him.

"Tired? Are you out of your fucking mind, tired? Oh, poor fucking babies, let's get them some warm miso soup. I am so sorry, I did not realize the babies were so tired, I am so fucking sorry."

Yamamoto did not shout this—*shout* would be far too weak, *scream* starts to approach the tone, but that's still a little weak. Think of a man using his voice with a greater volume than it is actually capable of.

All this was delivered to Genda with such proximity that Yamamoto's nose touched Genda's twice.

"I will be on deck in ten minutes and I expect to see the first flight launched."

"But what about enemy submarines?"

"Christ all-fucking-mighty." (Yamamoto had learned at his days at Harvard that Americans were some of the most creative swearers.)

"Are you a complete, total—complete—fucking retard?"

"We're in a fucking war and you're interested in the safe fucking play? Genda, you are a total fucking moron. Got it? A total moron. I want 32 'planes in the air in twenty minutes, even if I have to lead them my fucking self. Is that clear, you fucking moron?"

Genda nodded and left.

Alone, Yamamoto knew that he had just rolled his last dice with Genda. By treating Genda in this brutal manner, Genda would never trust the Admiral again, and Yamamoto had just destroyed their friendship. But, Yamamoto reflected, desperate times require desperate actions, and Genda's greatest weakness was his addiction to consensus. But, consensus in most cases was weakness.

Miyuki was lingering over tea when the first explosions were heard. Her heart leapt. All this work, all this time, putting up with the Hawaiians, and the American wives. She went outside. The sky was black with burning oil. Oil that was the life blood of any navy. And now the islands were being drained of all their precious oil and all because of her "181-79."

25: Winston's Delight

Washington
Sunday, 7 December 1941

AFTER THE EVENTS of the past week, Hopkins and Tugwell were pleased to have a quiet early lunch together in the main dining room of the Willard. Although very different men, they enjoyed each other's company and shared the bond of serving the President. Often, they had noted that he was a true bastard at times—Judge Holmes's quip about "a second-rate mind, but a first-rate disposition" was quoted.

After the young waiter had brought their coffee, Hopkins said, "Christ alive, is it possible to repeat this past week?"

Tugwell smiled and shook his head,

"Perhaps a repeat of the San Francisco earthquake of '06, that's about the only thing."

Both men laughed.

But their laughter was ended by the appearance at the entrance to the dining room by a frantic Smithers.

"Fuck, no," Hopkins muttered.

Without hesitating, Smithers raced to their table.

"The President needs you, now. Now. Right now."

Hopkins was about to say something but thought the better of it. Smithers threw a ten-dollar bill on the table.

"The car's outside."

"But it's one block," Hopkins said without thinking.

"Get in the car!" Smithers commanded.

The two men exchanged glances—for a milksop like Smithers to speak like this, well, it was clearly urgent.

Normally, they met the President alone in the Oval Office, but not today. Every minute, someone entered the Oval Office. As usual, Roosevelt was in his hated wheel chair.

It was Stimson who spoke,

"Our Isthmus Canal has been blockaded at both ends by warships of the Imperial Japanese Navy. So, all our ships in the Atlantic will need to go the long way to the Pacific."

It took Hopkins and Tugwell a second to realize he was talking about the Panama Canal.

Tugwell, with his professor's quick mind, asked Admiral King,

"Admiral, and this is the worst time of the year for the southern oceans around the Horn, isn't it?"

King answered unemotionally,

"Well, we're past the very worst time, which is the October and November period, but this is the Horn, and the weather in the southern oceans in the Forties and Fifties and Sixties is nasty year round—really, there is no 'worst time' down there. And ice is always a problem, year round. But the seas are not the only problem. The other problem is the distance—to West Coast through the Canal is 5,000 miles, but around the Horn is 13,000 miles, and this means we need oilers and the thought of fragile oilers in the Southern Ocean at any time of the year is a frightening prospect. And we have no coaling stations, I mean oil tank farms, in South America."

The phone rang.

"Henry, get that, will you please," Roosevelt said.

Stimson picked up the instrument. Listening, he frowned.

Roosevelt looked at him.

"Are you *sure*?" Stimson said, emphasizing the last word.

Stimson put the phone down. His face had not changed composure.

Stimson announced to the room with neither shock nor surprise in his voice,

"The Imperial Japanese Navy is currently attacking our naval base at Pearl Harbor in the Hawaiian Islands possessions."

Roosevelt nodded from his wheelchair, and theatrically said,

"What? What did you say?"

At this moment, King's assistant burst through the door. Forgetting all protocol, he said,

"Admiral, sir, the Japanese are attacking Pearl Harbor, the Arizona has capsized, and other of our battleships are burning out of control. All of the oil farm has been destroyed."

No one spoke for the simple reason that no one knew what to say.

King was the first to regain his composure,

"This is very, very bad. One of these two situations we could deal with. But losing both the Canal and the Hawaiian Islands' oil, this is going to make things extremely, extremely difficult."

Again, silence descended.

The old war horse, Stimson, was the first to speak.

"Young man, take my car to the War Department and bring us the latest Scapa Flow deployment please."

King looked at Stimson and nodded, "I was thinking the same."

The two young men of Roosevelt's much-vaunted Brains Trust realized how out of their depth they—and their President—were. While the two Brain Trusters were distilled almost to jelly out of fear, the two experienced men were actually thinking rationally.

King's assistant ran from the room.

253

Stimson asked King, "Are *Repulse* and *Prince of Wales* in Singapore?"

"Yes, they arrived there last Tuesday."

King said, "We might just get away with this, but it's going to be damn, damn close."

Stimson sat down on one of the yellow damask sofas. In normal times, the long-established protocol was to sit only after the President invited you to do so, but these were now no longer normal times.

The phone rang; Roosevelt lifted the receiver. There was a pause as Roosevelt listened for a great while to the instrument; finally he said,

"Yes, thank you. Thank you very much, Winston."

The President covered the mouthpiece and quietly said to the room, "He's very, very drunk and *extremely* happy."

On the sofa, Stimson looked up; King quietly sighed and said, "Shit."

Roosevelt dismissed the meeting. He requested Stimson stay behind.

✠ ✠ ✠

After the others had left the room, the President said,

"Well, Henry, I think a little celebratory tipple is in order, don't you?" Roosevelt smiled his famous broad smile that he normally reserved just for his favorite press photographers.

Stimson poured two martinis, and as was customary, he took a long look—but just a look—at the bottle of vermouth.

"I was a little surprised it took so long, Henry."

Roosevelt opened the drawer to his desk and withdrew an envelope. From inside the envelope, he withdrew four typed sheets of paper at the top of the first sheet of paper in the upper left corner was typed: "DRAFT No. 1."

"I penned these words back in January, a frigid Tuesday morning, right here in the Oval. At some stages this year, I thought I would never be able to use this glorious fiction."

The President laughed but Stimson remained unchanged.

He started reading with his fountain pen at the ready, "Yesterday," he paused,

"OK, time to finally add the date, 'December Seventh,' " he handwrote the date.

He continued,

"A date that will live in world history, the United States of America was simultaneously and deliberately attacked by naval and air forces of the Empire of Japan in the Philippines and Hawaii. Should I add 'without warning' Henry?"

Stimson shrugged, "Can if you like, Mr. President."

The President completed reading and replaced the four sheets in their envelope in the drawer.

After finishing their first of five celebratory rounds, Stimson said,

"Well, I think we've successfully 'crossed the T.' You're an old naval man, Franklin. And damn tough it was. It was harder than I thought it would be. You know in August when that fucking Konoe suggested a meeting on our possessions of Hawaii or Alaska, I feared we were in real trouble. It is very clear there are strong forces in Japan—even up to the Prime Minister—that really wanted to avoid war with us, regardless of how we tormented and provoked them. And we know Minister Kishi was also trying to maintain peace as well. We faced the delicate question of the diplomatic fencing to be done so as to be sure Japan was put into the wrong and made the first bad move—an overt move. The question was how we should maneuver them into the position of firing the first shot. Thank God we've been able to trick them into doing just that. I mean, realistically, with our rather rude closing of the Canal to them and blocking all their oil, what else could they have done?"

"Yes, I agree Henry, it was close. But finally the Goddess of Fortune has wafted by and we've been able to grasp her skirt. And just in the nick of time, I should say. Any longer and that peace faction in Tokyo may have succeeded. Of course, this war is huge benefit as it will give the U.S. economy a real boost, as young Rex—and even Hopkins, from time to time—have been suggesting. These peripatetic work projects are all well and good—but how the fuck do we make money by planting trees and creating national parks? Tell me that. We need to be constantly at war to keep our economy humming; it's a sad truth, but it is the truth—that's how the U.S. economy works. Fortunately, the Japanese are so innocent we've finally been able to force them to fire the first shot. Christ, it took enough time."

Stimson nodded enthusiastically and added,

"Yes. Absolutely. This war is a godsend. It's just what we need. We need to revitalize the core industries of the country—factories, foundries, mills, not these Namby Pamby projects—fucking writers group, oh my God. We must expand the West and get new ships built and men doing proper work. And most important of all, take complete control of the Pacific. As we have often discussed, we need to completely destroy Japan—once and for all. Dominate it. Invade it. Pacify it. And most important of all, control it. Long-term, the Japs are far more of a threat than the ragged and decrepit British, and their so-called 'Empire.' We *must* control the Pacific and the trade routes to China. And we need to starve the Japs into total and complete submission. Ideally, we could make them a colony, like the Philippines or the Hawaiian Islands, but that is probably too much to ask for. Nevertheless, we need to destroy Japan, as they really are our one true rival in the world—they have the brains and discipline and leadership to take over the Pacific, and with control of the Pacific, the Japs could control much of the world's commerce. The Japanese have a pure culture—look at what we've got—a bunch of mongrels straight off Ellis Island. And the Japanese think long-term; they plan; and they execute flawlessly."

Stimson paused and thought for a moment.

"Of course, the Brits will be a problem. But you can deal with the Lisper, Franklin."

While a classic Anglophile—weak kneed where it came to anything English—Stimson detested Churchill, who he saw as having extremely poor judgment, as being a lush, and with an unjustified air of superiority. Hadn't Churchill had the gall to correct the President's grammar at the Placentia Bay meeting, like a short, fat, condescending school master? And Stimson knew the real Churchill, the true Churchill. Not the one portrayed as the valiant bulldog, the smiling and warm father. No. Stimson knew—and hated—the real one: bitter, vindictive, too often drunk, bullying and self-centered.

"There's little to deal with. In contrast to you, I can tolerate Winston, at least in small doses. He is short, and fat, and can be entertaining at times. Of course, he does a very good job of projecting the image of the pugnacious, determined-but-friendly father figure, with his "V" for Victory signs and all that crap he goes on with. Few plain people know what a bitter and sarcastic drunk he really is. I thank my lucky stars that I can hold my liquor because it is hilarious to watch him caper nimbly around the room when he is drunk, pontificating on his many new dream projects—the Cape-to-Cairo railroad line, the overland rail link to India ('and, of course, we will allow one or two first-class American companies to offer bids, Franklin'), and adopting a common currency to replace our dollar. Combine the greenback with their so-called 'sterling'—the man must be mad."

Roosevelt burst out laughing, "The man *is* a lunatic and a drunk, but surely you see his entertainment value, Henry."

"If you say so, Franklin."

26: Somme Redux

Washington
Monday, 8 December 1941

IT HAS BEEN SAID that the difference between politicians and actors is that actors are honest in their sleight of hand. If that is so, then that Monday, the President of the United States of America would have proven the adage correct as he moved to address a joint session of the Congress. Truculent and surly, he made his way into the chamber, his face as black as thunder.

On the drive over, Roosevelt made a few last minute changes to the four typed sheets that he had prepared back in January.

"Yesterday, Sunday, December 7, 1941, a date which will live in infamy," he boomed and threatened into the microphones, as the real audience was not the Congress but rather the people glued to their radios. Roosevelt had a voice that was made for radio—a beautiful, deep baritone that was as soothing as it was sonorous; people could listen to it for hours; the gentler sex loved to listen to its glorious, strong tones projecting a virile and powerful man (if only they knew the truth). Only the little German propaganda minister could come close to matching Roosevelt but Goebbels's radio voice was more theatrical and instilled fear rather than trust; Churchill's radio voice was easily recognized and even more easily mimicked by every drunk in every pub is London; Roosevelt's radio voice was one that a person could easily listen to for hours, it was so comforting. "If President Roosevelt said it on the radio, it must be true," became the most terribly dangerous delusion of the times.

Returning to the White House, Roosevelt met with Stimson and Admiral King. The much vaulted Brains Trusters were nowhere to be seen. The three men discussed the situation and some unpleasant other developments that all seemed—at the time—to be unconnected.

Stimson read from his notes,

"Well, it seems that there is a Fifth Column operating in this country, and it's proving to be quite effective."

"Fifth Column?"

"Mr. President, saboteurs. The term "Fifth Column" is a new term from the recent war in Spain. There has been a mysterious explosion at the naval oil tanks in San Diego; there is a problem with the Northeast rail corridor—seems that the Canadian locomotives have been interfered with; both the Central Pacific and the Southern Pacific had trestle bridges destroyed out West and it could be months before they can be repaired—that means we have to depend on the Canadians, and they are not in the best of moods these days after the leaking of War Plan Red; worst of all, the fires last week in Ohio—we were desperately dependent on those stockpiles of rubber, and without them, well that rubber is worth its weight in gold."

"OK, Ernie, now you can give me some good news," the President said.

"Well, my news is not good—we lost the Saratoga yesterday, all hands I am afraid."

The President looked up; the shock on his face this time was genuine.

"Fuck."

Ever expedient, the President said, "Well, I will tell the British we need their help; that will please fat Winston no end."

He pressed the intercom, "Grace, set up a call on the scrambler for 3 p.m. today to speak to Mr. Churchill, please."

"Well, that is 15 minutes time. Ernie, plug the extensions in will you please?"

Admiral King walked over to the small bookcase in the Oval Office, opened the draw under the bookcase and extracted two earpieces that were originally part of B-25 radiomen's headphones. Attached to each earpiece was a length of wire cable covered in khaki-colored cotton; at the other end of the cable was a large brass plug, the same as used by a telephonist as she connects a caller to an extension. King plugged the two extensions into the base of the modern, Bakelite telephone instrument.

A little after three in the afternoon in Washington, the scrambler telephone rang. On the other end was the Prime Minister of the United Kingdom of Great Britain and Northern Ireland. Mr. Churchill started by expressing his regrets and the regrets of his country for the attack by the Japanese and promised to do all in his power to help. He went on to explain that he was in somewhat of a difficult position as the Japanese had not actually, formally declared war on the British Empire so he could not actually declare war on the Japanese without cause—"that would be a breach of international law." (At this, Roosevelt looked up at the two men and slowly shook his head.)

Roosevelt listened politely; both Stimson and King were taking notes.

"Well, Winston, that is what we want to talk to you about. I have Ernie King and Henry Stimson with me; they're on the extensions here in the Oval. Now, Winston, you have the *Repulse* and the *Prince of Wales* in Singapore, don't you? Who is commander of that task fleet?"

The silence was precisely what Roosevelt was hoping to not hear.

"Yes, Franklin, both of these Royal Navy ships are in Singapore at present, and it is Tom who is in command," came the unfriendly answer.

King rolled his eyes—he had met Admiral Tom Phillips, and had instantly formed a most disagreeable opinion.

"Well, Winston, I need to ask a favor. We're going to have to work together on this one. We need to have you send your ships to Manila, where we expect the Japs to attack next."

Even before Roosevelt had finished his sentence, the answer lisped down the cable,

"Not possible, Franklin. You see—and you must realize—the Empire is at risk. We must protect Singapore, and just as important, Malaya. You know Malaya is a key part of the Empire. I would like to help, but I am afraid it is completely and utterly out of the question at this time."

The two men saw the President's face redden,

"Wait a minute, Winston. Look, I have personally taken a huge gamble backing your country for the past two years—the Republicans have been after my hide, and there's Lindbergh and his American First group, and that fucking Liberty League with Al Smith and all them. I have personally put my own presidency at risk and in jeopardy to support your country. Personally. Lend-Lease, the money we've silently supplied—all of it. I think the least you can do is help us out—and it is helping both our countries—to simply divert Phillips to Manila for a week or two. That's not too much to ask, surely."

"Not possible, I am sorry Franklin. Let's speak tomorrow. Good night." The line went dead.

"That motherfucker just hung up on me. That fucking drunk. Me, the President of the United States. That motherfucker—that slimy little, fat English pompous cocksucker cunt," Roosevelt said slowly shaking his head in disbelief.

"Hung up on me. Me. The fucking President of the United States. That limey scum bag."

"Well, there goes the Special Relationship," said Stimson.

Roosevelt burst out laughing, "Henry, I do enjoy having you around at times like this for your *bon mots*."

The so-called Special Relationship was the phantasy that many countries deluded themselves into believing existed between themselves and the biggest bully on the block.

"These fucking monkeys, I cannot believe their attitude. So, Ernie, tell me about this Phillips character."

Admiral King explained how he had meet Tom Phillips,

"The first thing you notice is that he is about this tall."

King put his hand below the knot in his perfectly knotted tie.

"Because he is so short, he is called 'Tom Thumb.' And he is both shy and abrasive at the same time. I saw him standing on a wharf one time in his uniform, his hands in front of him. His right hand was holding his left thumb, as you often see shy kindergarten children do. This left a most disagreeable impression. As you know, I am a Big Ship man, but even I know in this modern era we need coverage against enemy aircraft. When I broached this subject with Phillips, his amazing answer was that gun crews on capital ships were quote, 'simply not trying hard enough' and that large capital ships had quote, 'nothing to fear from aircraft.' I was so surprised at the comment, I had him repeat himself. The man is typically English: short, smug, superior and always wrong. It is my distinct impression that Churchill is surrounding himself with yes men on the naval side—his First Sea Lord is Dudley Pound, who seems to be completely dominated by Churchill, but Pound is not as bad as this Phillips character."

"Get me a drink, will you Henry. Something for you, Ernie?"

King nodded and got himself a double tot of rum.

For minutes, no one spoke.

It was clear Roosevelt's nimble brain was hard at work. He quickly downed his martini, and Stimson provided a refill and then another. Roosevelt rubbed his chin, thinking. He leaned back in his wheelchair.

Impetuous as ever, Roosevelt said,

"I got an idea. I know it sounds crazy, but just listen for a second. Suppose, just suppose—I am not saying we do this—it's just an idea. But suppose we cut a deal with the Japs."

King exploded,

"Cut a deal; are you mad? Have you lost your senses? We lost American lives yesterday, brave American sailors, and you want to cut a deal. Are you mad? These are Americans, American lives were lost. And after your radio address."

King was so angry that all pretense of formal address and "Mr. President" had evaporated.

"OK, Ernie. First thing you need to know is we politicians simply say what our constituents want to hear—that's the essence of democracy."

The President's face beamed his broad grin while King looked stone-faced at this axiom of political expediency.

"Today, I simply gave my radio audience what they wanted to hear. But, ignoring the minutiae of a typical politician's sleight of hand for a moment, answer me this larger question. You tell me how we fight a war with them; go on, you tell me that."

Roosevelt held up his fingers and counted off each point in turn,

"We have no oil in the Hawaiian Islands; we have no oil in San Diego; we have two aircraft carriers in the Pacific, both running on fumes by now; the English are being pricks, as they always are; the Canadian rail system is broken, for how long no one knows; and to get Texas oil to California we send it by rail, but both the SP and CP roads have trestles down, and these trestles took months to build originally. And now the Canadians know all about War Plan Red. And the Canal—our Canal—is out of commission, and that could take months to clear. Oh, yes, and we don't have enough latex to make a single rubber for a randy high school boy on a Saturday night with a hot date. So you tell me, what's my next move in this chess game—what piece do I move?"

King sat and silently fumed, saying nothing. Stimson also remained silent and was drumming his fingers on the arm of his chair. An uncomfortable silence descended, which no man was eager to break.

Finally, the President spoke,

"I tell you one thing, however. Sticking it to those English pricks would feel oh so good. Fuck, yes. After all I have done and all the crap I have had put up with."

The phone rang; Roosevelt leaned forward and answered it. A broad smile spread over his generous face.

"You are *not* going to believe who is outside."

✠ ✠ ✠

The Americans called the Japanese diplomatic code, "Purple" and over the preceding two years had wildly varying degrees of success in reading the code—sometimes breaking one word in five, while a month later breaking just one word in 20. While there were many gaps in individual messages, one thing was clear—the Japanese ambassador in Washington had been dealing in good faith.

It was clear that Ambassador Nomura was an honorable man and was genuinely trying to work with Secretary Hull and his own government to resolve the two countries' differences. The common definition of an ambassador as an honest man sent to lie for this country seemed to perfectly describe Nomura.

✠ ✠ ✠

"Ernie, are you ready to speak to Nomura?" Roosevelt asked in the tones of a stern and strict school master.

"OK, let's see what he's got to say, and no insults—I suspect he is as surprised as us."

Roosevelt buzzed Miss Tully, "Grace, please send in the Ambassador."

The door opened and Nomura entered. His appearance dismissed all doubts about the Ambassador's sincerity: he had removed his top hat, and carried it in his left hand; his suit was an old-fashioned black mourning suit with tails. There are a surprising number of shades of black but the suit worn by the Japanese ambassador was the blackest any of the three men could remember ever seeing.

Upon entering the room, he bowed, and he bowed so low that his back was parallel to the floor, and he stayed bowed for ten seconds. On any day but this, a friendly American wisecrack would have been made, but this day was not one for wisecracks.

After an eternity, Nomura rose. His face showed his anguish, and it was an unhealthy white glaze.

Very slowly, he finally spoke, "Mr. President, my Emperor is very, very badly served."

Roosevelt was tempted to speak, but rather, he waved Nomura to sit. The Ambassador sadly shook his head,

"Today I do not deserve to sit, Mr. President. I have failed you and I have failed my Emperor."

Ernie King's stern Midwestern roots sensed a man in torment.

"I had heard rumors of this insanity, but foolishly dismissed them as rumors. I should have brought my suspicions to you and to Secretary Hull and to Mr. Stimson."

Stimson nervously glanced at Roosevelt who caught his glance; each could read the other's thoughts—here is an honest man trying

266

to make amends for something that Roosevelt and Stimson had themselves created.

"While Secretary Hull and I have held the differing positions of our two governments, I have always considered Secretary Hull—as I do consider you, Mr. President, and you, Mr. Stimson, as honest and honorable gentleman. I have always hoped that our two countries could work together."

"We Japanese admire the United States without limitation. It was your Commodore Perry who shook us from our incestuous complacency and thus created the modern Japan. While Japan is a very old country, we have much to learn from your country—Fordism is a religion for us, and he has helped our country immensely. It has always been my sincere hope that our two Pacific Ocean countries could jointly develop Asia, to replace the narrow-minded, bigoted European colonialists. But the fools and madmen in Tokyo have destroyed this glorious possibility."

Nomura spat out the last sentence with the contempt that Roosevelt reserved for California Republicans.

"And progressive elements in Tokyo have always talked of working with the United States and with you personally, Mr. President, to have your National Industrial Recovery Act implemented throughout all of Asia for all commodities. We Japanese could have worked with you to make this dream a reality and remove cutthroat and greedy competition with your excellent idea, and without selfish business men and foolish lawyers. But all hope of that has now been shattered. I am very truly sorry I have failed you, Mr. President."

He repeated his first, painful bow, and walked backwards leaving the room, closing the door as he left.

No one spoke.

Stimson looked at Roosevelt and finally said,

"Well there's one man in this world who was more surprised than we were."

Roosevelt nodded, "Ernie?"

"Mr. President, may I light the Smoking Lamp?"

The President smiled, and for the first time in days with a relaxed and real smile, as Roosevelt realized they were making history—or rather altering the course of history—for most of the world's inhabitants. Although the Ambassador could not see it, Roosevelt had been sitting in his hated wheelchair. He rolled it out and said to Stimson,

"Henry, fetch us that box of Cubans, will you please."

Stimson was happy to oblige and passed the box to the President who passed it to King, who in turn returned it to the Secretary of War.

After the happy ritual of cutting and teasing and lighting, all three men smoked, thinking.

"I limit myself to one per day, but one of the White House gardeners was telling me his grandfather told him that Grant smoked five per day—in this very room."

Out of nowhere Stimson said, "I like Nomura; it's a shame there's not more like him."

After a very, very long pause, Roosevelt changed the history of the world with three words, "Perhaps there are."

"My biggest problem is not the Republicans but my party—I know what those fool Republicans will do, and they know what is expected of them, but my party is full of mad dogs—some even voted against my NIRA. Perhaps, just perhaps, there are more Nomuras in Japan. Look, all three of us have experienced—all too often—the madness of our own service, be that Army or Navy, and how these mad dogs fight each other with more and more crazy schemes."

"Let me ask you one question and one question only. Just one. And think before you answer."

Stimson and King looked at the President.

"If—if—if you had to cut a deal with this fellow or the Lisper, whom would it be?"

King looked at Stimson and King simply shrugged.

"I thought as much."

Roosevelt added,

"And I agree, wholeheartedly. And the idea of a proper NIRA in all of Asia for commodities—well, I discussed precisely that idea myself with Morgenthau in '37. I could retire and become a consultant to various nations of the world. Perhaps I could correct their ailments or perhaps I would simply turn up my nose. For example, I could tell one country that she needed to move out tens of millions of her population. I could make them disarm. Now that could be of real value—and Asia has no fucking Supreme Court, and no Sutherlands, and no Brandeises, and no fucking Schechters. That's the wonderful thing about being a politician—we are the modern-day gods."

Dusk was entering the room and Roosevelt's tone softened.

"Modern mechanics are shrinking the world a little every day—when it used to take four days to travel from New York to Los Angeles by Pullman, now on the latest DC-3 it is just 17 hours and you get the pretty registered nurses as well on the modern DC-3s, not those fat, smelly and lazy Pullman porters."

Stimson reflected,

"Insane as it sounds, perhaps the Japanese have actually done us a favor. I know it sounds mad. But perhaps we've been looking through the wrong end of the telescope. Let's dissect the Asia we have today: Indochina—dead,—it's a French possession and the French are dead, the Germans have seen to that; Dutch East Indies—same; Malaya, Singapore, Hong Kong, Burma, India—well, we all know our charming Winston; and that leaves our Asian possessions of the Philippines and the Hawaiian Islands."

"Now, just suppose, just suppose for one second that we were to ally ourselves with the Japanese. Perhaps this could possibly be a dream made in heaven. Let's step backwards; what are the causes of our disagreements with the Japanese? Well, there is China; of interest to us, but it will never be truly strategic until the Chinese start acting like the Japanese and start becoming disciplined and organized. Then there is French Indochina—can either of you explain why we give a flying fuck about French Indochina, because I can't? Then there is our possession of the Philippines. We've actually been a little too clever and we've backed the Japanese into a corner; there is really not a lot that they could do but this preventive attack, and that is precisely what it is—a preventive attack. And we've done these preventive attacks ourselves. We have taunted the Japanese mercilessly—we've blocked their use of the Panama Canal, an illegal act if ever there was one; we've cut off their oil; we have totally fucked them in the ass. So we've done just about everything we can to drive them to desperate measures."

A literate fly on the wall would have noticed—likely with approval—the change of the language: "Japs" had been replaced with "Japanese" and there were no longer any bad puns about nipping the "Nips."

"Now, if, and I realize it is the world's largest 'if,' but if we come to an understanding with the likes of Nomura, perhaps, just perhaps, we can move forward."

Stimson tilted his head and looked at the other two cigar smokers.

"It will cost us nothing to try. I'm sure glad I am wearing my lucky shoes today," Roosevelt said.

"Henry, have Grace call the Embassy and get the Ambassador back here."

An hour later, a very confused Japanese Ambassador was invited to sit on one of the two yellow damask sofas and to try one of the President's excellent Cubans. Still wearing his black mourning suit, Nomura assumed he was to be executed—that the President had discussed the situation with the Secretary and the Admiral and that the decision had been made to forthwith put him up against the wall outside the Oval Office and have the Marine guard fire away. And Nomura was resigned to his fate; after all was it not Nomura who had failed both his Emperor and the emperor of his host country? Very, very slowly he came to realize that the three men were not talking about execution but about redemption.

"Kishi," the President said, even though his nickname was actually "Kichi."

"I've spent the last hour talking about the situation with Hank and Ernie, and we wanted to ask you just one question."

The President puffed on his cigar.

Feebly, Nomura nodded; it was all he could muster.

"What are your country's plans in Asia? I mean what if—and it is a huge if—what if we were to work together? How would that benefit the United States?"

Nomura nodded and then asked—actually it was more he pleaded—if he could cut and start his cigar.

Ever the gracious host, Roosevelt nodded, "Please do."

The three men saw how Nomura's hands were shaking as he tried to cut the end of his cigar. After a moment, Stimson leant forward, took the cigar from him and cut the end of his cigar for him. Nomura's eyes blinked away tears at this simple human kindness.

Roosevelt said, without sarcasm and with genuine humor, "All three of us are at your disposal this evening."

Like an old priest late for mass, Nomura quickly lit his cigar. He took precisely five puffs, and had regained just enough composure to commend the excellent quality of the cigar to his host.

Roosevelt nodded politely.

"I will not waste the time of you three gentlemen. But I must start by telling you that the government in Tokyo is riven with disagreement—many of them are like drunken samurai. Boasting, threatening, berating. Then, the next day, all apologies. It is horrible, most horrible."

"Sound like us Democrats," Roosevelt commented and Stimson and King both laughed.

Nomura did not understand the joke, but was delighted to see his American hosts laughing.

The Ambassador decided then and there not to hold back. Quietly, he started to tell the Americans all he knew, and he was a sufficiently experienced negotiator to know that starting high never hurt.

"In the next seven days, the Imperial Japanese Navy will sink the Royal Navy's *Repulse* and the *Prince of Wales*.

This really took the breath away of the three Americans, who suddenly had a new-found respect for this little Japanese man with the round face and even rounder black spectacles.

"By the Lunar New Year, the Japanese Army will have captured Singapore and Hong Kong."

As not one of the three listeners had the vaguest idea of what the hell the Lunar New Year was, King guessed and quietly asked,

"So, by the first of March?"

Nomura said, "Yes, or perhaps a little before that."

Stimson shook his head,

"I am sorry, Ambassador, but I frankly cannot see it. While the British are weak, their base in Singapore is huge and it is impregnable and it has 15 inch guns protecting it. I've been there—I've seen the guns."

Nomura said, "So have I."

"And Secretary Stimson, we have a number of our agents in Singapore. Actually, we have three Chinese agents in the quarter-master's office that keeps careful count of all the shells in the armory. Almost all of the shells for these massive guns are armor-piercing, which are extremely effective at piecing warships' armor but which are useless against infantry. The British are defending Singapore in precisely the same way that they prepared for the battles of 1916."

The penny dropped.

"Fuck," said the always verbose King.

"Of course. Yes. Fucking brilliant—Somme *redux*," King could not contain himself.

Nomura nodded.

King, like Nomura, was a diligent student of war and the all-too-common disasters caused by massive misunderstandings by distant and remote generals (and admirals)—"Send Up Three And Four Pence, We're Going To A Dance," was a message received from the British front in 1916, when the actual message had been, "Send Up Reinforcements, We're Going To Advance."

As King explained to the other two Americans, on the front line at the river Somme the British had fired over one million shells from the "heavies" in the weeks leading up to the 1st of July in 1916 (And three months later, the British armament companies who made these one million shells quietly paid two million Pounds to a Swiss bank in royalties to the German companies holding the fuse patents for these shells.).

The 25-year-old sepia films and photographs showed these shells exploding in the desolate moonscape of the northern part of the Western Front. Unfortunately for the British, the German line at the Somme was the best fortified of the entire of the Western front:

the hard, dry, chalky soil of the area—excellent for Champagne grapes—was perfect for deep fortifications. And the Germans, ever the clever engineers, had constructed massive dugouts that were impervious to the shells the British lobbed over; actually many of the second-line dugouts had carpets, "the electric," and even gramophone record players.

The two commanders—Haig and Rawlinson—had conveniently decided to ignore all reports that the German positions were still completely intact. Dozens of British raiding parties had suffered death and agony in the days and weeks leading up to the assault to find the truth. "Not possible with a million shells," was the accepted wisdom as the attitude was, "let-us-not-allow-the-facts-to-interfere-with-the-plan."

In fact, Haig described the first hours of the battle as: *"Very successful attack this morning... All went like clockwork... The battle is going very well for us and already the Germans are surrendering freely. The enemy is so short of men that he is collecting them from all parts of the line. Our troops are in wonderful spirits and full of confidence."*

But the actual outcome was what the angel of truth had always predicted: the greatest military disaster in history; according to one estimate, of the 100,000 British troops that went over the top that fateful day, only 35,000 returned.

The rest were alone, terrified and dying in horrible pain. Many of these brave young men pulled themselves into one of the countless shell holes and slowly waited for the end of their suffering, thinking of the homes and families they would never see again and of the laughter and happiness they would never again enjoy. A few got out their little Bibles and hoped for a moment of solace. When the rain started in the early afternoon on that terrible Saturday, the shell holes slowly filled with water and the final ignominy came to many of these gloriously brave—but terribly led—eager young soldiers as they slowly drowned in their shell holes, shivering from the cold, alone, discarded, and in agonizing pain for hours before a slow death ended their sufferings. And all for nothing—no ground was gained. The two commanders lied and boasted of a "limited success."

"Of course, I am now a traitor to my country—I have told you and you can call Mr. Churchill on that telephone on your desk, Mr. President."

"Yes, I could do that, Kishi."

The moment the President of the United States of America called him "Kishi" for a second time, the Ambassador suddenly realized that he could be talking to a potential ally.

Stimson asked insistently, "OK, Kishi, but what about our Philippines possessions? What guarantees can you give that they will not suffer the same fate as our Hawaiian possessions? Or that you will not attack America proper?"

Nomura decided to increase the stakes,

"Mr. President, let's go in a time machine and advance 100 years. In 2041, who will be your allies? The British Empire, the *Bolsheviks*, the Chinese Nationalists, the French, the Dutch, the Germans, the Japanese? Who?"

"What do you think, Mr. Ambassador?" Stimson asked.

"Well, that is what makes Japan last: for we Japanese, ten years is just a quarter of an hour, as we think in terms of centuries. Here is an example: there is a famous Japanese whisky maker based in Osaka. This company decided to branch out and start making and selling beer. It took this company 45 years before it made a profit from its beer making. Is there an American company that would have the patience and sense of purpose to wait 45 years before making a profit? I suspect not.

"We Japanese think that maintaining our cultural purity is the most important thing we can do. We have no colored colonies to pollute the Japanese spirit of frugality, hard work and community. Here is an example of how we Japanese work as a team: after the Great Kantō earthquake in 1923, over 95% of all wallets found were returned intact to the police so the money could be returned to its rightful owner; to do otherwise would be dishonorable for us Japanese. And the Japanese spirit of teamwork and working together is unequalled in the world. And this is solely because of the purity of our culture. Other countries hate us for this, they envy us for it, but this is the Japanese way, and we Japanese believe this is what will sustain us over the next 500 years. Remember, our Emperor's family dates from 11 February 660 BC—that's 660 years before the western Christ. Of course, there will be disasters, and defeats, and mistakes, but we Japanese work together as a team, as we always have and will always do so."

The Ambassador changed tack,

"Predicting the past is far easier than the other way, but I would say the millstone for the European countries is their colonies. As a young man, Mr. Churchill was part of the last cavalry charge of his empire. And that is the way he still thinks—as a European colonist, in spite of him being technically an American because of his American mother. But these colonies are very much a two-edged sword. In this respect, Germany was actually the winner of Versailles: by stripping Germany of all its African colonies, none of these African natives could ever claim German paternity. And looking at Africa as a single battle ground on its own, the Germans could easily have taken over all of the Dark Continent. You'll recall the brilliant hit-and-run campaign of Lettow Vorbeck. With just 15,000 men, he taunted and beat an Allied force of 400,000 men. He was a later-day John McNeill. With the likes of Lettow Vorbeck, Germany could easily have controlled most, if not all, of Africa. But, with Versailles came the complete evisceration of all these German colored colonies."

"But in these colored colonies the peoples will always be troublesome and some may actually pollute their motherland if and when they somehow settle in their motherland—can you imagine a million Mohammedans encamped in civilized England practicing their crude and primitive rituals: half-naked fakirs in the streets of London; restaurants in Cambridge next to the university colleges serving curries and spices; and even mosques next to churches in Birmingham with all those imams spouting their crazy ideas? And remember, the Mohammedans' Koran teaches there will be no peace until all the infidels are slain. I know it sounds ridiculous today, but it could possibly happen in the distant future. Who knows? And were that to happen, then these European countries will start to be overrun and destroyed, just as the Moors did to southern Europe hundreds of years ago. All these European countries will be destroyed, slowly, but ineluctably. So this is the most important unintended consequence of the madness of Versailles: Germany remains pure, while England and France now are burdened by these troublesome colored colonies; sooner or later, England and France will suffer."

"So, Kishi, you're saying the British are fucked?" King said with his usual subtlety.

Nomura answered with, "Yes, Admiral, I am. Now, Mr. Churchill is very good at talking about the English-speaking world, and the greatness of the white race, but I think this is very much overdone."

"Mr. Stimson, to answer your question, after capturing Hong Kong and Singapore, I know that the Army intends to attack your Philippines possessions. We would never dare attack the 48 states of the United States itself, but the idiots in Tokyo think the American possessions in Asia are just that—Asian possessions."

"When?"

"That I do not know, but I know the Army hotheads, so it is likely to be well before they are ready."

Nomura had just laid down four aces and he knew it.

"So how could we work together?" the President asked with real interest.

"Well, were I you, I would assume that everything I have told you this evening is a lie. Then I would wait to see how events unfold. This risks nothing for you and only takes a week or two. In the interim, we all go about our business.

"If we can come to an agreement in for the next month or two, then our two countries could work together. We Japanese could work with you to establish an American-Japanese Asia Council. As we all know, Asia is rich in resources. We need oil, and you need rubber from Malaya and other raw materials. Using a new and expanded NIRA tailored for the countries in Asia, we could stabilize prices, remove the specter of unemployment and waste, and establish new independent governments, all under the joint protection of the United States and Japan—jointly, we would be the region's policemen. Your country has made huge progress in those areas, and it is very, very unfortunate that your Supreme Court has ruled against it."

"You can say that again," Roosevelt said with real malice. "That would teach those fucks a lesson if we could do a big NIRA in Asia."

"There is one thing I can do that may be of some little assistance to you gentlemen," the Ambassador stated.

"Go on," said the President of the United States.

"I can signal Tokyo that we are speaking, and to halt all new offensive actions against your country's possessions until the first of January."

"Yes, that could be some little assistance," Roosevelt said ruefully with a smile.

Nomura took a sheet of paper from his jacket and on it wrote in clear English, "The cherry blossoms are blooming early on the Potomac."

THE GODDESS OF FORTUNE

Beneath it he wrote a short-wave frequency.

"Mr. President, can you have your naval radioman in the basement transmission center send this message now; there will be a single word reply."

Roosevelt's eyebrows rose at the mention of the secret, or as it now appeared, formerly-secret radio room.

Roosevelt nodded and Stimson rose and left the room.

Nomura withdrew a second piece of paper and wrote one word. He folded the paper, rose and stood in front of King, bowed and handed the paper to the Admiral.

"The answer code word is from a new American talking picture I enjoyed so much."

Stimson returned.

Roosevelt said, "Mr. Ambassador, you have been very forthright with us today."

Stimson's heart missed a beat fearing the always-impulsive President was about to say something he would later regret.

"Can I offer you a drink?"

Stimson's heart regained its natural rhythm.

The Ambassador smiled for the first time, and said that an American bourbon would be most pleasant.

"Like me, you're a naval man, right Kishi?" the President asked by way of small talk.

"Yes, I am sir. I have had the honor to have served my Emperor."

"See any action?"

Nomura held up his left hand, the smallest two fingers were both missing the first joint.

"Russian shell fragment when I served on the *Takachiho*, but I was luckier than the man standing next to me who was killed."

"Tsushima?" King asked.

The Ambassador nodded.

279

A moment later, the phone rang and Roosevelt listened then replaced the handset in the instrument.

"Rosebud?" the President said, more as a question than as a statement.

King unfolded the paper and nodded.

"What does this mean?" Roosevelt asked.

"This means that all offensive operations against the United States' possessions in Asia will cease, on land and at sea. A cessation of hostilities, an armistice."

"And the British?" Stimson asked.

Nomura was slightly surprised, "Sir, Mr. President, this agreement is only regarding the United States."

Roosevelt smiled, "That will piss off the gentleman in London no end."

Professional curiosity got the better of King, "So what is the plan for Malaya and Singapore, and the Royal Navy task force, and their *Force Z*?"

"I was briefed by the new adviser who arrived from Japan last week—these details are far too sensitive for cables. Well, the plan is this."

King leant forward and realized no admiral before or again would ever be in his unique position. (Yamamoto might have disputed that claim, however.)

"There are four senior Japanese submarines that have been given the task of locating and sinking the *Repulse* and the *Prince of Wales*. If they fail, then our aircraft based in the forward air fields in Saigon in French Indochina will locate and attack these two vessels. We are almost certain that Admiral Phillip will head north up, along the coast of Malaya, and as he does not think highly of aircraft attacking capital ships, he will have little or no aircraft protecting him."

This last revelation made King look very directly at Stimson. As if in answer to King's thought, Nomura said,

"Admiral King, the British Admiral Phillips has been sufficiently kind and generous to give newspaper interviews in both Pretoria and more recently in Singapore to that effect. In fact, we have the newspaper clippings of these precise interviews. In both sets of interviews, he stated that there were few Japanese aircraft in the region and quote 'they are all second-rate' and that, regardless, that 'the big ships of the Royal Navy have nothing to fear from the sky; we are, after all, the British Royal Navy, which has ruled the seas since the time of Nelson.' I also suspect that the English admiral thinks the Japanese a backward race and that 1905 was just a fluke. But he seems to conveniently forget that it was the English who created the Japanese Navy, who taught the Japanese Navy tactics, who even created the uniforms, and that my beloved *Takachiho* was built at Newcastle upon Tyne."

27: The Chamber Pot

Washington
Wednesday, 10 December 1941

KING AND STIMSON WERE WAITING for the President, seated in the small alcove in front of the main door to the Oval Office. When he buzzed Miss Tully to announce his arrival, she told him of their presence. He grunted none too enthusiastically and told her to send them in.

King started, "Well it looks Nomura was right—the *Repulse* and the *Prince of Wales* are now both at the bottom of the ocean off Malaya."

"Then it will simply be a matter of time before drunken Winston is on the scrambler. And what about Japanese activities against us?"

"It's as if they have all gone home. It's like a holiday—no submarine activity, not even over-flights, nothing, dead calm," reported Stimson.

Stimson started on a fresh tack, "Mr. President, I want to bring this report to your attention. It's from that man Dulles in Switzerland, and I think we need to review it here, the three of us."

At the mention of Allen Dulles, the President feigned no recognition of the name.

"This man Dulles—you likely know his brother, the lawyer John Dulles—got his hands on this report from the Swiss security people. The gist of the story is the Soviets executed about 20,000 men in Soviet-occupied Poland. The Soviets had first bound the men's hands behind them with barbed wire."

Looking down at the report Stimson read, "According to Swiss and Swedish Red Cross officials, the Soviet NKVD executed in excess of 22,000 men, mostly army officers and policemen. Most victims had their hands bound behind their back by barbed wire."

"Jesus. Fucking animals," Roosevelt muttered.

Calmly, King said, "The British animosity to the Germans seems solely based on the Prime Minister's views and the oleaginous clique of second-raters with which he surrounds himself. I do not understand how the British could be so blind. Frankly, the actions of the Germans in central Europe seem completely fair and reasonable as far as I am concerned in having German-speaking regions rejoin Germany or a greater German supra-nation. Now, I am just a naval person, but that gives me a perspective that I think some English lack. So while your party line plays well on the East Coast, about the 'Arsenal for Democracy,' it's actually not true, and the Americans of German descent in the Midwest are, at best, lukewarm to the idea. And it's clear from other reports that the Soviets have executed close to eight millions of their people since 1921— these are facts, not phantasies."

"And let's face some other unpleasant facts, Mr. President. Versailles was a joke—it was simply the French getting back at the Germans for 1870," the Secretary of War said.

"1870?" Roosevelt was confused, in spite of his Harvard education, where his solitary C+ was his highest grade.

Stimson explained,

"In the Franco-Prussian War of 1870, the smart money was on the French—our generals Sheridan and Sherman were there observing the French, and they both wrote glowing reports lauding the French. The *Times of London* was effusive in its praise of the French and ridiculed the Prussians—'this small war is likely to be settled in one afternoon.' But there was one critical difference—technology. While the French were using their tried and true bronze smooth bores, the Prussians were using the new rifled cast steel Krupp cannon. The Krupp cannon had essentially twice the range and could throw a far heavier shell. Actually, on the day, the Prussians used mainly what they called 'grape' or shrapnel shot that Henry Shrapnel had invented, but the point remains. That hot afternoon in 1870 was a slaughter, the French soldiers dropped like flies. They called the battlefield 'the chamber pot'—that day, they were shit on from a great height."

"So the French started a losing streak to their hated rivals that continues to this day—1870, and 1914, and last year. After 1870, and their loss of Alsace and Lorraine, the French bitterness spilled over at Versailles in 1919 and this lead to the creation of these nonsense so-called countries like *Czecho-Slovakia* and other mad artifices and constructs. And these so-called 'countries' were designed by the French solely to hem in and limit Germany. You know, in the Treaty of 1919, the Austrians—quiet reasonably—requested their country to be called 'German Austria' but the French nixed the name and the 'German' adjective was dropped. And the Slavs are even worse than the French—the Slavs in their half of the so-called 'Czecho-Slovakia' constructed 24 huge aerodromes. But the Slavs there had no bombers. However, their fellow Slavs in Russia—or the 'Soviet Union' as it is now called—had 120 squadrons of heavy bombers. No wonder the Germans were so reasonably concerned about that unsinkable aircraft carrier in 'Slovakia.' And let's not forget Gavrilo Princip in Sarajevo in 1914; we must be realistic—southern Europe needs a powerful hand and the Germans have just the temperament to control those primitive and backward peoples."

"And I agree with Ernie—the Germans do have a point. And with the sudden death of their leader this past September, who knows? From all the reports and with his comical moustache and his postman's hat, he seemed fairly nutty, but certainly no more nutty than Mr. Churchill. And let's be realistic, the Germans are a civilized race, whereas the Slavs, well, this Russian massacre just reinforces the point, and don't forget the pogroms."

Stimson's voice trailed off.

King pointed out, "The Swedes and Swiss have no real axe to grind—they make money off the Slavs as well as off the Germans."

"And speaking of the Russians, I was talking to your young Rex last week and he reminded me of Hank Whitehead's horror story that I have heard from Hank's own lips. You must remember Hank's father from your time in Cambridge."

Roosevelt frowned for a moment and then smiled his wonderful smile, remembering Hank's father's kindness,

"Oh, yes, Jack Whitehead, my Phil professor. Yes, fine man—he gave me a Gentleman's C Minus to pass the course. Had I read any of the books, I may have gotten a proper C."

Stimson continued,

"Well, young Hank volunteered for the Spanish War and went over there all piss and vinegar to help fight 'fascism,' as he called it. He was in the Lincoln Brigade, as the name suggests, mostly Yanks. As he tells it, the Soviet advisers were all animals. Treated all their troops as chattel, never enough food for the men, even though the commissars lived well in the town with their Spanish whores. Often times, no water on the battlefields when the temperature was 110 degrees. In two of the last battles, the commissars placed their machine guns *behind* the Republican troops."

Roosevelt frowned and asked why.

"So as to shoot any of the American men in the Lincoln Brigade who wanted to retreat."

Roosevelt said nothing and looked out of the windows of the Oval Office into the garden.

"So your point is that boozy Winston's blind hate of the Germans is blinding him to the natural Slav barbarism?"

Stimson nodded and said, "Before we go professing our undying love and admiration of all things Slavic, perhaps we need to think about who we're getting into bed with. We can cut a deal with the Germans in an afternoon, and the Germans are the natural rulers of central Europe, not these half-mad, mongoloid Slavs who all lack an ounce of civilization."

Over the next two weeks, the Californian newspapers, then the papers back East, all started running the same story—"The Phony War, Part 2." As the papers explained, after the invasion of Poland in 1939, "a state of eerie quiet enveloped Europe"—the English papers had called it "The Phony War," which ended in May 1940 with the sudden collapse of France.

In early afternoon, Roosevelt was amused to see the telegram Stimson had gotten from MacArthur in Manila where the General had personally had taken all the credit for the sudden calm, "I have created a sense of overwhelming trepidation in the enemy throughout Asia with the concomitant reduction of all enemy actions against the United States' possession of the Philippines."

"I am surprised Douglas is not also claiming responsibility for the sun rising every morning," was Roosevelt's terse and tart comment.

In the first week after the Japanese attack, the country had been at fever pitch to "kill all the Japs," and there were some extremely unpleasant mob lynchings in San Francisco of innocent American business men of Japanese descent. But Roosevelt's weekly radio addresses had been very, very carefully crafted to deflect this anger. And with this calm and reassuring voice, he again created a new—and better—reality.

Just as suddenly as it had erupted, the mob anger subsided.

28: Bad News For The Lisper

Washington
Wednesday, 7 January 1942

THE JAPANESE AMBASSADOR ARRIVED at the White House promptly at 9 a.m. for the meeting he had requested the previous day. Nomura was his typical Japanese self: quiet, polite and deferential. Truth be told, there was absolutely no reason for his modest demeanor.

The President and Stimson were not friendly but were also by no means frosty—they realized that the Japanese were doing precisely what they said they would do: honoring the unofficial armistice regarding the Americans while, at that same time, precisely and elegantly demolishing what was laughingly called the British "Empire."

"So, what do you have for us today, Mr. Ambassador?" the President asked.

As always, the deference of the Japanese was extreme—he had bowed deeply and solemnly before the two men before speaking quietly.

"And please take a seat."

With quiet reluctance, the ambassador sat, but unlike the sprawl of Stimson, Nomura sat, like a nervous schoolboy, on the edge of the sofa.

"Mr. President and Mr. Stimson, I am pleased to tell you that Tokyo has requested that I ask your permission to extend the armistice for another six weeks. My government feels we are making progress and they are anxious to continue this dialogue. Would it be possible for us to continue this arrangement while we continue speaking?"

The President, holding no cards, smiled and was equanimous, "That can be arranged."

The Japanese ambassador stood and bowed to the President.

"Mr. President, I can assure you that you have made my Emperor extremely happy."

Stimson said, "I see you have taken Hong Kong."

"Yes, Mr. Stimson. The British colony surrendered on Christmas Day."

The Japanese ambassador's simple reply showed none of the pride he, and his country, felt.

"But I suspect Singapore will prove to be a far tougher nut to crack."

Nomura was lost for a second until he grasped the Secretary of War's idiom.

Realizing Stimson's meaning, he said,

"Well, Admiral Yamamoto, who has spent quite a deal of time in your country, uses the American expression, 'Time Will Tell.' "

Curious, Stimson said, "You really think you can take Singapore?"

"Well, as I mentioned to you and to Admiral King, we think we may have the good fortune to do so."

Then Nomura's next question shocked the other two,

"Suppose, for a moment, that the Japanese army was able to secure Singapore, would that be grounds for a more permanent armistice between our two countries?"

The two men were not children; what Nomura was saying in essence was, with the British impotent, would a new order in Asia—a duopoly of the United States and Japan, centered on Roosevelt's beloved NIRA program—be possible? As Britain was the last of the European colonialists in the Asia, if Britain was defeated and thus made completely powerless, could a new "arrangement" be made?

"I have to be honest, Mr. Ambassador, I speak daily to Mr. Churchill, on this telephone," the President said, patting the black Bakelite instrument.

"And Mr. Churchill tells me that the Japanese cannot possibly take Singapore."

Nomura nodded, "I understand, sir. But if we Japanese were able to prove our military acumen, would it be possible for you to consider a change?"

Roosevelt showed a shard of unusual candor, "Well, Henry, what do you think?"

Stimson pulled on his ear lobe,

"Well, to be perfectly honest, Mr. Ambassador, if the Japanese were able to conquer Singapore, then yes, that would potentially change the balance of forces in Asia in a very significant way. But, as my advisers tell me, that is unlikely. And without the British defeated, an American-Japanese Asia Council would be difficult to establish. But, conversely, with a major British defeat, a vacuum of power would exist and would need to be filled by senior and responsible countries."

Nomura pressed, "But if the British were to suffer a major defeat, you would be open to considering a dialogue?"

The President pre-empted Stimson, who was about to give the same answer,

"Sure, we would consider it."

Ever the politician, Roosevelt added, "But, just consider, if and when such an event did ever occur."

Having achieved what he had wanted, Nomura followed a sacrosanct rule of selling and did not buy it back.

"Mr. President, you are being more than fair. May I return to my embassy and send this message to the government of my emperor?"

The President nodded and said that he could.

With no further ado, the ambassador rose, bowed and left.

"Henry, what the fuck just happened?"

"Well Franklin, I think we have just fucked short, fat, drunk Winston."

Roosevelt smiled, "Could be worse—could be us. Get me a drink, will you."

Stimson obliged and got himself one as well.

Sitting on the yellow sofa, Stimson said,

"You know, Franklin, we could do far, far worse than dealing with these people. Churchill goes on and on with his bullshit about 'English Speaking Peoples' and all that claptrap but we have to be realistic—our two countries border the Pacific. The French and Dutch are moribund, Chang is a toady and is completely unreliable, and if the British lose Singapore then they are finished in Asia, and that means they are finished as an empire. Let's see what happens. And I don't know about you, but I think I can work with Nomura. He's modest, reliable, sober and polite, essentially the opposite of the Lisper."

Roosevelt said nothing, but it was clear he was in agreement.

29: The Billiard Table

Nassau
Saturday, 31 January 1942

NASSAU IN JANUARY is always cool and dry—the long and glorious summer days with their delicious, lazy heat and sudden downpours have disappeared. And this January, the incessant flood of the most petty regulations from Whitehall confused the natives and annoyed the English. This morning the native head gardener asked David about *Supplementary Regulation Concerning the Washing of Farm and Gardening Implements For Cultivating Peat*. It was pure gibberish, written, no doubt, by a civil servant who had never set foot outside the British Isles.

From the next room, David's wife asked, "Darling, can you zip up, please?"

Wallis' slim body and mannish face appeared in the mirror. No one could ever be guilty of calling her beautiful, but many strong men had fallen under her spell, and the former King of England was not a strong man. And as Wallis was the always willing to admit—to herself at least—David did not come from the strong branch of the Windsor family tree. Far from it; he was weakest of her many conquests. The joke—too extensive to be mere gossip—was that she had an unequalled ability to make a man equipped with a toothpick to feel like he had a cigar.

She whispered, "there's nothing underneath, so don't dally too long tonight, darling."

These small indiscretions were all that was needed to keep him interested—he was, and he would always be, a dunderhead. She would remind him twice during the dinner, but her main message would be to the ladies after the ladies had left the men to their brandy and cigars. These ladies would all offer disapproving clucking ranging from the mild to the severe at such a meretricious trick. Of course, they all immediately adopted the practice themselves to try to rekindle a little carnal fire with their boring husbands. Much more important to Wallis would be the faithful retelling to their husbands. Among the small colony of British in the Bahamas, Wallis would always have an ample supply of English supplicants to entertain herself, and when she tired of them and their congenital lack of stamina, there were the occasional "informals" with a native helper that seemed so spontaneous, but which Wallis actually planned to the last detail—she did so love the animism of being dominated by a massive black frame of raw muscle and power sweating over her, his sweat making the grabbing of his massive arms and shoulders all the more challenging and exciting.

Wallis was buoyant as she had recently started a discreet correspondence, first by mail and then by the occasional long-distant telephone with the very polite, very proper, well-educated, and sophisticated Lord Halifax. She admired Halifax and saw him as a potential ally. She sensed Halifax could lead the charge to have her pathologically weak husband regain a position of influence. True, the terms of the Abdication had been exceedingly severe but this was after all simply a piece of paper, and new pieces of paper could always be created when the time was right. And Halifax knew that both Wallis and David were very well liked in Germany.

The previous August, Wallis had redecorated the boat house and had it painted a light cream with sky-blue trim. The boat house was far from the main house, and had the added attraction of a private winding track to the main road, and the track was very well hidden by the greenery—a man could quite easily slip down to the boat house unseen.

Actually, Wallis had been caught once and it always made her tingle when she remembered it. She had an extension added to the boat house with its glorious view of the harbor. Wallis had installed four soft, dark tan club chairs, the type David loved and that one sinks into rather than sits on. She also installed a billiard table in the far end of the room, away from the windows. It was on this table, with her legs wrapped around a stout leg, that she had been caught *in flagrante delicto.*

With her typical thoroughness and planning, Wallis had bespoke dark brown cushions made that just happened to be a little thicker than the height of the walls of the billiard table. The cushions were surprisingly firm and covered in a smooth silk. In the cupboard beneath the small bar there were four extra cushion covers, in case any of the cushions in service suffered any spontaneous but potentially embarrassing stains. One of these cushions was in use the day of the surprise discovery.

Dickie and Edwina had been David and Wallis's best friends before all the troubles started with David's mother. It was from this prim and proper archetypical upper-class English lady—and an heiress, at that—that Wallis had been educated in the glories of dark flesh.

295

"You have never experienced such a feeling. It's overwhelming—they are so big everywhere, especially down there," Edwina had stated matter-of-factly.

"Well, Edwina, I am a Southern belle and to think about having a huge, sweating Negro on top of me. And inside me. Well, I just cannot consider it."

"Pfff, don't be such a prude. I've been to Harlem a dozen times and I told you about the adventures I have had on billiard tables. You need to be open minded. After all, it's not as if you have to be seen in public with these Negro men. It's all just light-hearted fun. And remember, as you're a white woman, you're prized among these men so you get treated like royalty. Come to think of it, you are royalty."

They both giggled as Wallis was clearly warming to the idea.

Edwina had been correct. On the first few encounters with the local boys, Wallis had been thrilled to actually be nervous, as she had been in the early days working as a whore in Shanghai. The nervousness made her feel young again.

Wallis had arranged for one of the native boys who had painted the boat house earlier to return, "just to do a little touch-up work" she had explained on the telephone to the harried and rude British captain who was in charge of work details for government properties on the island.

The young man arrived wearing sandals, an old straw hat, and overalls that had once been a deep blue, but now the color had been reduced to a very pale blue with all the washing and bleaching. The bleaching had removed all the hardness of the original material so now the overalls were soft as baby flannel.

Wallis knew the seduction protocol by heart. And what excited her as much as the penetration by this strong young man was the seduction. Of course, she knew it was not really seduction, as she had complete mastery over the young man, but she loved to make all her conquests—black or white—beg.

Wallis was wearing sunglasses with a large dark brown frame, flat canvas espadrilles, and her favorite summer sun flower dress—mid-calf length white cotton with blue and yellow sun flowers; she had nothing underneath, as was her custom with the dress. She opened the door and explained to the young man that she wanted an area on the veranda painted above the main picture window. She sat in one of the white painted wicker chairs drinking a rum punch that she had made herself. Languidly the young man painted. She noted with a quiet delight that his arms were extremely well developed, as were his back and shoulders—his muscles were clearly visible, so different from the flabby white men on the Colony. She estimated his weight at 17 stone, or over twice her demure eight stone—"he will be able to throw me around like a rag doll," she dampened at the thought.

She loved the sense of complete control; ordering a man to satisfy her carnal needs was the greatest pleasure she could imagine—the sense of absolute power, of complete mastery, and the sense of not needing to ensure he was being satisfied—it was all just about her; if she was in the mood for rough, then she would simply command it that way, and she would get it that way.

The day was an unexpectedly hot. For an hour in the blazing sun, he worked. He was sweating and the armpits on his bleached overalls were dark with sweat. Wallis was perspiring and she went to the small toilet and saw with approval that her small, ruby-red nipples were starting to show through the sun flower dress. To amplify the effect and to ensure nothing was left to imagination, she daubed a little water around the top of her dress. She returned to the main room and made a cold drink of water and pineapple juice. One of the luxuries of the boat house was a small refrigerator that held three pressed-steel trays of ice cubes. And, Lord, she had to fight to get that machine—"don't-you-know-there's-a-war-on" was the standard refrain.

She took the glass to the young man, who was so passive that he would not look at her and kept his eyes on the ground. Out of the corner of her eye she saw him steal a long look at her modest chest and the two ruby-red nipples as she paused to stare absentmindedly into the harbor. Her nipples were now standing proud through the dampened white cotton. She could see the start of his excitement growing at the crux of his overalls.

Over the next hour, the young man very, very slowly became bolder. Wallis could see his boldness corresponded to the growing swelling in his overalls. Now it was time for the next step. She tossed her head back and arched her back a little. With her legs tightly crossed in English-Lady mode, she said,

"What I love most about the boat house, is that it is completely private. I am the only person with a key. It's completely deserted and no one ever comes down her. You could easily overpower me and ravish me and no one would know. You could take me here and now."

Of course, they both knew this was nonsense as she was effectively the most powerful person in the Colony. And it was also a fib that she had the only key.

The young man completely misunderstood and ever so politely asked, "Lady Wallis, should I leave now?"

"No, no, of course not. All I was saying is that I love the privacy here and how it is so peaceful. Please keep at your work."

The young man nodded.

Clearly a more direct and simpler approach was needed.

"Actually, the privacy I find extremely exciting. What with just the two of us here, and I have to say that your arms and shoulders are very big. Your muscles are so big and strong."

298

It was now time to start asking explicit questions.

"How did you get such big arms?"

The young man lost some of his tension and turning to Wallis, he looked at her for the first time. Wallis quickly stifled a gasp as she saw what looked like the outline of a baby's arm running down the inside of his right leg. In the central sweat patch, the soft material of the overalls showed the outline of a huge vein that looked as thick as Wallis's smallest finger.

"Lady Wallis, all the men in me family are the same; me father and me four brothers are all the same as me—we are all big."

"I see, and it looks like you are very fit as well, *and* very much a real man," she said in a veiled reference to the swelling in his sweat-laced overalls.

He flushed crimson red, and was lost for words.

"Don't be embarrassed, you should be happy for such gifts. Are your brothers like you in this area?"

Still flustered, he simply nodded.

"Really, all four are like you?"

Still blushing, he said, "I am the little one—me brothers are all bigger than me."

For the first time that day, Wallis was genuinely surprised, "Hell."

She held her left wrist with the thumb and forefinger of her right hand.

"Thicker than this?"

Still red, but now getting excited, he said, "Much bigger than that, Lady Wallis."

"I think me should leave now, Lady Wallis. I don't want no trouble."

She loved a little resistance. It reinforced her total dominance, her sense of power.

"No, you are to stay and answer my questions and to do precisely what I tell you to do, is that clear? You are to do precisely as I tell you to do otherwise there *will* be trouble for you. And you are to do what I tell you to do, is that clear?" she commanded.

He looked at her and her flushed face and said, "Yes, Lady Wallis. Me do as you command."

She was now starting to freely lubricate, and she uncrossed her legs and separated her knees six inches. She loved the feeling. She loved the teasing and most of all she loved the power. The summer dress still covered her knees, but the effect was still extremely exciting to the young man as it was now clear to him what this powerful white woman wanted in the quietness and privacy of the cream and sky-blue boat house.

"You know, you are very lucky as most white men are only about half that size."

He smiled, now lust was finally starting to overpower his nervousness.

"I would not know about that, but me girlfriends all like what me got down there."

Wallis approved of the plural. And the first mention of his girlfriends meant that Wallis's seduction was almost complete.

All the time he was facing her, she could see the baby's arm getting larger and firmer and now the end stood out from the leg of his overalls. Sensing he would feel less nervous if they moved to inside the boat house, she said to him,

"Let's go inside, I have something I need you to do for me. Actually, I have something you are to do *to* me."

He put down his brush and paint pot.

She led him inside and she flopped down into one of the club chairs.

"Go into the toilet and wash your hands and face, then come back here immediately," she commanded like a captain to the lowest-ranking seaman.

While doing his brief ablutions, she made herself another rum punch, this time mostly rum. And she made him one as well—she wanted to get the young man drunk as she wanted it very rough and he was far too shy a boy to do this to her if he was sober. She wanted to awaken his animal spirits.

He returned to the main room and stood in front of her. The light from the picture window was at her back and shone directly onto the young man. She stared at his little arm, which was now a good ten inches in length. And she let him watch her stare. She loved him seeing her look at him and his native masculinity. It was a crudeness, a rawness as she dominated him with her complete power over him.

"Come over here and drink all this now. It will relax you," she insisted passing him the rum. "All, now."

He did as she demanded. He loved the rum but was too frightened to comment.

"And so you are the smaller than your four brothers."

He nodded.

"Well, that is interesting," she said offhandedly.

As she later explained to two of her friends, she thought her nipples were about to explode, she was so excited, and she could feel the wetness running down her inner thighs through the sun dress and onto the chair.

She beckoned him with her finger and commanded, "Come over here."

The young man obliged.

"Now you must never tell anyone about what we are about to do, no one, ever. Is that very, very clear?"

He said it was. Actually, she didn't really care as the notion was so fantastic that no one would ever have believed him and would have simply discounted it as madness, and she knew it.

With the extended formalities over, and with the young man now standing in front of her, Wallis leaned forward and closed her right hand, extending only her small finger. Very slowly, she moved her finger to within a quarter of an inch to the end of the baby's arm. The results were precisely what she expected—the end of the little arm suddenly twitched and the material of the soft, white bleached overalls was now taut all the way to the knee. She gasped when she saw that there was a tiny dark spot of wetness on his overalls where the baby's arm ended. She loved to tease native men and she was so slowly teasing this one, her own contractions were already starting.

Like a nurse to a frightened young boy about to get an injection, she said, "Now just relax," and then smiling, "This will not hurt."

Finally, she ran her little finger the full length, stopping at the end. Through the soft material, she could see the outline of a large ridge of skin that ran the circumference, and she teased this. The teasing and the rum combined to generate a deep baritone moan from the young man who took a very deep breath and looked first at her face and then at her nipples.

Wallis continued this teasing for five minutes. At the end of this time, she simply stood and pulled the two straps of the overalls off the young man's shoulders. The top of the overalls collapsed to his waist, but the baby arm—now huge—stopped the overalls, like a shirt hanging on a nail, or, as she later explained, like a shirt attached to a branch of a young and virile dark sapling. With a little difficulty, she maneuvered the overalls to the floor. He stood there buck naked, the sapling erect. It was huge, black, and there was wetness at the end. She reveled in the size, and thought how she would feel pain. Pain that would excite her like no white man could ever excite her. Edwina, the perfect English lady, had been right—this was like nothing a white man could provide.

In the retelling to her giggling and gasping lady friends, Wallis would say,

"When you're next at dinner with us, look at David's arm from the wrist all the way to the elbow. David's forearm is thinner and smaller than what I saw that day and what went inside me. And it was all the way inside me. It was huge and so, so hard. And that went all the way inside me—God knows where."

Free from the constraints of the overalls, the young manhood was almost vertical, extending four inches past his navel.

"I could just barely get the head into my mouth," she would boast.

"Not only was it very long, it was also very thick—the girth was amazing. I thought I would not be able to take it all, but I wanted as much as I could. I wanted to mix some pain with the pleasure."

Already, she could taste some of the early cream: oily and deliciously salty.

"Lie on the floor on your back," she commanded imperiously.

Once on the floor, she straddled him and lifting her skirt with her left hand, she used her right hand to guide herself onto him. In spite of being extremely wet, she had to descend very slowly and actually had to carefully control her breathing to help get the monster inside her. All the while, the young man lay passively on his back and occasionally emitting a moan. At her suggestion, he had closed his eyes. The rum was now starting to relax her and she felt a glorious glow as she lowered herself onto the black Adonis. Further and further she descended and as she did so, she got more and more excited.

For the benefit of both of them she had started to moan and then started animal grunting—the taciturn English lady was now a raw animal with crude desires and she wanted it all the way inside her. From the experience of hundreds of men she knew that a prim and proper lady suddenly reduced to crude animal noises was always the most powerful aphrodisiac—all the middle-class pretense was stripped away as she simply got fucked and fucked very hard from this young, crude animal. As expected, she could feel the young man hardening even more; he was now like a rock. She descended two-thirds of the way but could go no further—she had reached her limit and the sensation of him hitting her inner ceiling was incandescent in the pleasure it sent coursing through her body, and she loved the pain she felt. She had rarely experienced such pleasure. Best of all, she was in complete control. She did not have to be concerned about him completing too early, as she could feel his hardness was strong but there was no signs of pulsating that she knew were the telltale signs of an early completion approaching.

She rose an inch or two to stop him from hitting her limit—it was just too strong a sensation. For minutes she slowly moved up and down, riding the monster belonging to her play thing. And her juices were doing their job. She was still wearing the sun dress, and she had the glorious feeling of being like a real whore with her white dress draping over the young man's dark black skin. Her sun dress was now sopping wet with her perspiration. She was drenched in her own perspiration and she loved the feeling. She felt young again.

Finally, she decided to reward herself with the ultimate prize, so she lowered herself so the head of his sapling started to again bang on her upper limits. All the time, she kept up a whore's tirade, and this became louder and more intense as she felt herself starting to contract uncontrollably, and then wave after wave of pleasure. After this first massive climax, she waited for a moment. Her skin felt alive; she squeezed her nipples. But she wanted more. She wanted to feel him dump inside her and dump all that load of crude animal seed inside her.

Until she started squeezing her nipples, she had been riding him holding his two hands for balance. The young man's hands were massive, and she had intertwined her fingers with his. The sight of her thin white fingers against the against the ebony fingers took her breath away, and she loved the vision of her wedding ring next to his black fingers; like the summer dress, it made her so excited to feel so terribly slutty. And his arms were so strong they did not move at all. She was in complete control.

She rose. She licked the end of him; he moaned.

Next, she put the brown cushion on the corner on the billiard table; she unbuttoned the two shoulder straps so the top of the sun dress now fell to her waist, exposing her small chest and the two hard pebbles. She pulled up her dress and sat on the cushion, her legs dangling over the side of the billiard table, six inches from the floor. She confessed that she would like to claim credit for this position, but, "alas, it was Edwina Mountbatten who told me of her adventures up in Harlem with black musicians in the Twenties."

"Do it this way, please," she said. "And I want it rough, please. Very rough, please."

The young man rose and again slid inside her. She could just get her feet behind the leg of the billiard table, and in this way she was able to brace herself against the young man's deeper and deeper thrusts. She wanted to take all of it so he was completely inside her. She did not care about the pain. She just wanted it all inside her.

"I have never experienced such a feeling—I thought something was going to rupture inside me," she would later confess.

The young man's thrusts were getting stronger and stronger and the sensations were so extreme that Wallis held her hands on each side of her head, as if wracked by a terrible migraine. The sensation was a combination of extreme pleasure mixed with a high degree of pain—pain that was almost, but not quite, too much to take.

With the young man as the active partner, the dynamics changed entirely—she was now the passive partner, out of control and being ravished, deeper and deeper by this exceptionally virile young man. In contrast to her middle-class persona, there was no need for tedious bullshit and clever words, just crude and rough and violent fucking. And she loved it. And the fucking was becoming more strident as she sensed he was getting close to completing again. She looked down and was shocked to see he was all the way inside her. At this sight and with the young man himself starting to pulsate, she had a climax the likes of which she had never had felt before.

As she completed her final climaxing, she felt him to start pumping inside her. And his paroxysm seemed not to end. This made her start all over again. Finally, he finished and withdrew from her body.

The sight of him now just a little flaccid was still exciting. She got up onto her elbows on the billiard table and looked at it. She had seen smaller ones on ponies.

"Help me up, please," she said.

He helped her stand and as she got to her feet, she felt a gush of his juice squirt out, and then a second spurt came from her—there was now a large puddle beneath her. She got to her feet and promptly collapsed; her legs were their own masters. Slightly embarrassed, she told him to carry her to the couch that looked out on the picture window. She lay there for a very long time. Finally, she swung her legs to the floor and requested him to bring her the bottle of brandy that was located on the small collection of bottles on the bar. With it, he brought her a glass—it took her a moment to have him point to all the glasses in the cabinet until he reached the snifter.

She poured herself a large tot. She marveled at the huge black thing—it was like a black arm of a baby—that had gone all the way inside her.

She sipped her brandy—it was her reward.

"I want to lick it again. Come over here and give me that thing again."

She put it again in her mouth and as she was doing so, he started to harden again. She was of two minds as to whether to have him penetrate her again. As he hardened, she kept sucking. She had both her hands around it so she could limit his penetration into her mouth. Suddenly, she was surprised as he dumped into her mouth. Amazingly, the second load was almost as great as the first load when she rode him. She simply swallowed and kept swallowing his load, and she extended the juice with some tricks she had first mastered working in Shanghai.

After the huge load, he was finally finished. She had swallowed all of it.

Primly, she sat up straight.

Without further ado, she simply said, "You may go now."

And remember, "None of this ever happened."

With a nod, the young man left.

The excitement of being able to command was almost—but not quite—as exciting as the act itself.

After ten minutes, she rose and rinsed the sun dress and hung it in the setting sun on the terrace. For the hour it took to dry, she drank two more rum punches and luxuriated in remembering what she had just done. It took another two hours for her to be able to walk, gingerly at first, then more confidently. At dusk, she went for a brief swim followed by a shower at the boat house. For a full seven days she was sore. As expected, David had not demanded any of a husband's dues, so she could recuperate in peace.

30: The American Admirer

Nassau
Saturday, 7 February 1942

DAVID STOOD OUT ON THE VERANDA of Government House. The former King of England morosely looked through the sheets of rain that drenched the green lawn that sloped down to the sea. Before the war, there were a few ships he'd see, but now almost all the freighters had been moved to convoys. Today, like so many others days, he simply stared into the empty sea. He was not looking forward to this evening's dinner—mostly Americans and mostly business talk, which he neither liked nor understood.

The dinner started promptly at eight.

The preceding hour had been spent with cocktails on the veranda and David, true to form, already imbibing too much of his favorite single malt. At dinner, a really delicious Pichon Longueville was served—the 1936, one of David's favorite years.

After dinner, the men left for cigars and brandy; Wallis entertained the ladies on the veranda.

"I must complement you on such a glorious dinner," the tall and well-spoken reporter from the *New York Herald* said.

"Well thank you, Susan. You know it's a real challenge, what with the war and such, and David is little better than a prisoner here. We're forbidden to travel, even to New York. And the Bahamas is really a third-class British colony."

"Yes, it must be truly dreadful," the American reporter said, dropping into a faux upper-class English accent that she so admired.

Susan and Wallis were left alone as the other ladies had gone inside to escape the chill and damp.

Susan looked directly at Wallis, "Yes, it's tragic the way things worked out, what with David essentially being deposed by a clique, as it were."

Susan very deliberately waited for Wallis' response. Wallis, as American herself, knew that American dinner guests could be expected to be this blunt and forward—the never-ending circumlocutions of the English in London always drove Wallis to distraction. And Wallis could sense the direction in which the conversation was moving.

"Of course, I've often told David this, but he's too blinded by loyalty, and he's far too loyal to his brother."

"I have it on good authority that Mr. Churchill threatened your husband with prison if he ever returns to England."

Wallis said nothing, but looked very directly at Susan.

"Your source of information is very good for a reporter. I don't mean this as an insult, but most of the male reporters I knew in Baltimore were simply hacks, and drunk hacks at that."

"Well, as you know, New York is the heart of the American empire and, as it happens, I grew up in Switzerland, so I have close contacts in Europe."

"I see," Wallis replied, clearly seeing more.

"So, Mr. Churchill and his clique and their antics are well known to knowledgeable Americans, and Europeans as well, Lady Wallis."

Like most Americans, Susan easily got confused with the confusing titles of the English aristocracy; it had taken Wallis over three years to master the arcane subject.

Wallis looked at Susan and asked, "What do you mean about clique?"

"Well, it's known in some circles in New York, and in Washington, too, that without massive American aid, Britain will be in for a very rough time."

"The Germans could start a second blitz—they've already liberated France."

At the word "liberated," Wallis looked at her companion very closely. Wallis was aware that reporters made the best agents for intelligences services as they have a natural cover for asking so many questions.

"And with the change of leadership in Germany last September, the Germans are now doing very, very well in Russia, at least that's what the few Foreign Office cables David is sent are saying."

"I suppose you're right, but were that to happen, and if Germany was to become a new ally to the USA, Britain would be in a jam."

"But why would Germany help out America, even if it could?"

Susan moved close to Wallis and touched her arm very lightly.

Wallis pursed her lips and said, "Go on."

"I am going to trust you and explain how you, you personally, can return to center stage. And this time, you will be in control."

At this, James the native head servant came and opened the doors at the far end of the veranda. Slowly and solemnly, he walked to Wallis, and with extreme diffidence asked if the ladies needed anything, a shawl or something, as it was getting chilly.

"No, we're fine. Thank you, James; that will be all for this evening."

James left. Wallis drank more of the wretched South African sherry, and a warm glow started.

"So I am going to put my trust in you, Mrs. Windsor," Susan went on.

"The Germans remember your visit with great affection and look forward to seeing you very soon. The late Chancellor liked and admired you and your husband. He saw something of himself in you, as he told me himself."

"You are being very trusting, aren't you Susan?"

"Perhaps, but I think we can both gain from what I am about to suggest."

The only sound came from the rain. Susan had played her hand and it was time to see the response from Wallis.

Wallis was quiet and then said,

"Yes, we met him in Germany in '36 at his mountain house, and they do seem like the natural leaders of the new order in Europe."

"Wallis, let me assure you—and I have this from the highest authority in Germany—that they have no desires on Britain. It's completely natural for the world to be divided into spheres of influence. This is the natural order of things. And with an armistice between Germany and Britain, well, one condition could be David's return to the throne."

"But why would Germany want David back as king?"

Wallis suspected she knew all too well, but wanted to hear it directly from Susan.

"Well, Wallis, it's not the English, but it's the Americans."

Wallis looked at Susan and a thrill of excitement coursed through her—perhaps it was the cheap sherry.

Susan continued,

"It's clear, actually—the current clique lead by Churchill would have to go and the more rotten and decayed elements that could be removed, the better it would be for both Germany and Britain."

At this moment, the obese wife of the American *chargé d'affaires* appeared and urged both of them to return to the warmth of the lounge. Wallis shooed the cow away with a warm and wonderful smile.

The moment the wife had been dispatched, Wallis said with true warmth,

"Susan, I am so glad you accepted the invitation."

Susan then accelerated the pace,

"France is beaten; Britain is barely surviving. Mr. Churchill is unpopular at home and abroad. The Germans have offered peace terms to Britain on three separate occasions through intermediaries, two Swedes and a Swiss. The Germans do not want to see Britain damaged. If this mad war drags on, Britain will become a pauper, and we Americans would not like to see that."

What makes most sense is for Germany and Britain to join forces."

Susan's eyes sparkled as he explained this to Wallis.

Wallis, your husband is a wonderful man who was cruelly abused.

"He's a weak fool with a small brain, and not overly endowed elsewhere."

Susan ignored this and said,

"This makes it so easy for you to regain for him his rightful place and your rightful place—Wallis Windsor, Queen of England, Scotland, Wales, and Northern Ireland."

"Well, that sounds all well and good, but I am stuck on this God-forsaken island with my dogs and that's about it."

Susan went on, "The first step is for you to consider the Germans' proposition, which I can tell you Mr. Roosevelt likes as well."

"Consider it? There is nothing to consider; I'd crawl on my hands and knees to get back to London as a somebody."

"Good, then this is what you and I need do to get this started."

They sat down at the white wrought iron table—the rain was increasing and the cold was increasing, but neither cared.

31: Brooke's Announcement

Washington
Tuesday, 17 February 1942

IT HAS BEEN SAID, "In Victory: Magnanimity." And this was never more true than by the behavior of the Japanese ambassador on this cold February Tuesday when he spoke to the small coterie in the Oval Office of the President of the United States of America. Like the other meetings, this one was held in absolute secrecy. In attendance were Admiral King; Secretary of War, Henry Stimson; the President of the United States, Franklin Roosevelt; and the Japanese Ambassador to the United States, Kichisaburō Nomura.

Twelve hours earlier, the President had received an evening call from the other side of the Atlantic on the scrambler telephone. He was surprised to hear the sober voice of Field Marshal Brooke. Roosevelt had meet Brooke twice before and had immediately liked the man—Brooke was the antithesis of his master: sober, polite and thoughtful. Roosevelt had commented to Stimson that he understood how the British could hang on with the likes of Brooke in charge.

Brooke said he was sorry to bother the President but he had been asked to call the President to tell him of the surrender of Singapore to forces of the Empire of Japan. Roosevelt feigned surprise about the rapid collapse of the supposedly impregnable fortress. It was clear from Brooke's tone that Roosevelt was not alone in his surprise. While it was three in the morning for Brooke he sounded completely awake and alert. From the depths of the room, Roosevelt could hear the Prime Minister's loud and sometimes violent shouting, which the Field Marshal tried to do his best to ignore and to hide from his listener. There was a long pause and then the familiar voice of the Prime Minister was on the line. As he later said to King and Stimson, he had never heard the Prime Minister so drunk. Churchill's ramblings were a bizarre mixture of maudlin and threatening, the low point of which was when Churchill said,

"I know personally from Marshal Stalin—that he told me—himself to me, to me, personally to me—he has plans to retake Alaska and that you need me to talk him out of it."

When Roosevelt told King and Stimson of this, King simply shook his head.

"That pompous drunk has no place in high office; he has to go, and go sooner rather than later," was Stimson's only comment.

In the meeting in the now-familiar Oval Office, King kept his professional admiration in check, but Roosevelt was more forthcoming,

"Mr. Nomura, I have to congratulate your country on the surprising events of yesterday."

Nomura thanked the President.

"Well, Mr. President, it was a hard and tough battle, and we were very fortunate and our tough opponents, the British, were very unlucky.

The four men knew the reality was very different from this modest statement. The reality was that the Japanese had been outnumbered by three-to-one: 35,000 Japanese troops to 115,000 British troops. And the British had all the benefits of defense. The classic ratio was four-to-one in favor of defense—according to von

Clausewitz, an attacker needs four times as many troops as the defender.

But, all during the hot December of '41, the Japanese troops in Malaya made daring raids, often using the Malay jungle as an ally. The British commanders—all safely cocooned and pampered and perfumed in distant Singapore—considered the jungle in Malaya to be horrible, hateful and impenetrable, in spite of the Japanese repeatedly using it to outflank them. All though that hot and humid December, the Japanese bicycle infantry rode south, often times on just the rims of their bicycles—the tires on their bicycles having all been punctured, so the Japanese troops simply cut off and discarded the tires. The noise of the Japanese bicycle infantry clattering along the cobble stone roads on the bicycles' steel rims terrified their enemy, especially during those hot and still summer nights.

Once at the causeway that linked Singapore to Malaya, the Japanese commander Yamashita made the Sultan's palace at the tip of Malaya his headquarters, and from it he could very clearly see the British troop dispersal on the island of Singapore. By now, the Japanese were masters at flexible, modern mobile warfare, while the British commanders' dogma was still stuck in the mud of the Western Front of the Great War.

Low on supplies and ammunition, Yamashita was contemplating withdrawing. But, rolling the dice—as all truly great commanders do—Yamashita sent a message to the British and called on the British General Percival to "give up this meaningless and desperate resistance to save further bloodshed."

What Yamashita did not know at the time was that the complete air supremacy of the Japanese over the skies of Singapore had terrified the local population and much of this fear had quickly seeped into the troops themselves. Once the troops caught the fear, both civilian and military discipline collapsed—very soon, drunken allied troops were looting stores and deserting in droves.

The deplorable behavior of the British troops had been reported to Stimson by cables from the American *chargé d'affaires* in Singapore since early February. The phantasy of the superiority of the British army evaporated in a trice—they were seen for what they really were: pompous, hide-bound and useless.

Nomura politely asked if the Secretary of War had received any reports of any "events" as he called it by Japanese forces against any American troops or ships.

Stimson said,

"I have heard nothing. Admiral King, have you had any reports?"

King shook his head.

Then Nomura raised, as delicately as he could, the purpose of his visit.

"Mr. President, Mr. Stimson, Admiral King, my government is most anxious to put the recent past behind us. As you know, there are many of us who were horrified by the events of last December, and for this monstrous mistake I can tell you that we are extremely sorry. And I can assure you the hotheads in Tokyo now are no longer in power."

Roosevelt said,

"Ambassador Nomura, that is all well and good, but the fact of the matter is you have blood—American blood—on your hands. We're not talking about a *Ruben James* here with one hundred sailors, but a massive death toll; many American people are still baying for blood. Now, they have calmed a little but vengeance is still sought by many."

While literally true, Roosevelt had to walk a very fine line—with the fall of Singapore, the Japanese now effectively controlled all of Asia, and all four men knew that America was powerless to do anything about it, at least not for two years.

After a pause, Roosevelt asked, "So what do you suggest?"

The reply was painfully long in coming.

"Well, Mr. President, my Emperor is extremely concerned to protect the honor of the United States. This is his first and only concern. It is the honor of your country, so it has been suggested to my Emperor that the Japanese ring leaders of this callous attack be put on trial for all the world to see, and hear with radio broadcasts, in neutral Switzerland in a specially convened court consisting of an American judge, a Japanese judge, and a Swiss judge. This court's verdict would need a simple majority, and the government of my Emperor is willing to accept any punishment."

Stimson asked, "Any punishment?"

Nomura nodded.

"Ambassador, thank you for your visit, I think it's time we discussed your suggestion," Roosevelt said.

Nomura rose, bowed, and left.

"Get me a drink, will you Henry and get one for yourself and Ernie."

Roosevelt sipped his martini and looking at his drink remarked, "This is about the last pleasure left to me, you know."

"Well, there we have it. I mean we have completely underestimated the Japanese all along. And as the events of the past days have shown, we're not the only ones."

Stimson added, "The biggest mistake we made was that fucking oil embargo. We knew it would hurt them, but who would have thought that they would be so effective in their fucking response— just the Hawaiian fiasco and we could have gotten by. OK, by the skin of our teeth, but add the Canal and San Diego and that fucking rubber fire and the Canadian trains and the attacks on the trestles bridges. Jesus Christ, the list is endless. And frankly, I am shocked by Singapore."

King added thoughtfully, "And Nomura seems a natural ally. Yes, he is duplicitous, but what politician isn't? No offense, Mr. President."

Roosevelt smiled, "None taken—it comes with the territory, Ernie."

Roosevelt requested another drink and then said,

"And let's be realistic: we cannot mount an offensive and we can't really mount a defense. With Singapore as a base, the Japanese can take the Philippines any time they like. And an attack on war ships is one thing, but losing an American possession like the Philippines, then Christ, that would make Hawaii pale by comparison."

"I discussed with Henry Morgenthau my idea of a Super-NIRA for Asia and he told me something very interesting: Jacob Schiff, through Kuhn, Loeb on Wall Street, actually financed Japan in 1904 with a loan of 200 million dollars for their war against the Russians. With this money the Japanese were able to buy munitions and war materiel. Of course, Schiff hated the Russians because of their never-ending pogroms. Well, it's just a thought but we could do the same in Asia. Why, we can even build dirigibles to fly from California."

The odd mention of airships confused Stimson and King until Roosevelt explained,

"You may not know this but I was running a dirigible company that planned to establish a service from New York to Chicago. It was an idea before its time, but it has more merit today than ever before. And with a partnership with the Japanese, why I could even restart that business."

After a pause to let this idea sink in, Roosevelt said, "Anyway, let's sleep on it and meet tomorrow."

In reality, the decision had been made by a pronoun: when Roosevelt referred to Nomura's suggestion on a pan-Asia NIRA as "my idea," the old snake had inadvertently shown his hand.

But the scheduled meeting with Nomura was preempted by another shock.

32: The Burning And Third Manassas

Washington
Wednesday, 18 February 1942

AT PRECISELY 8:00 A.M. on Wednesday, the German ambassador's secretary rang Miss Tully and asked for an appointment for the German ambassador to see the President of the United States, "on a matter of extreme urgency." As the German ambassador was known to be quiet and modest and normally never made any stronger requests than for a second glass of champagne at the interminable round of diplomatic parties, Miss Tully immediately penciled in the appointment for 10 a.m. that morning.

The ambassador arrived accompanied by a rather sharp-eyed individual by the name of Schneider.

The two men were shown into the Oval Office where they were greeted by the President and Secretary Stimson.

"How can I help you, gentlemen?" asked the President as he sat behind his desk in his wheelchair.

It was Schneider who spoke as his English was perfect; the elderly ambassador had wisely decided that the message was so important that translation errors had to be avoided at all costs.

"Well, sir, Mr. President, we want to inform you and Mr. Stimson that my country and the Soviets have earlier today been meeting in Geneva and are speaking about the possibilities of discussing arrangements and the extended modalities for a potential armistice."

In spite of the painfully convoluted language, the last word jumped out at Roosevelt and Stimson, but both man said nothing.

"After our country's tragic loss this past September, there have been certain, how shall I say, 'rearrangements' made, whereby General Jodl and Field Marshal Milch have made significant military, as well as political changes. Chief among the military changes is what we Germans are calling the new Brest-Litovsk-Kiev-Crimea line. I have it here on a map. If I may, sir?"

Schneider very carefully laid out the map on the old desk from the President's uncle, taking extreme pains not to notice the President's wheel chair.

"As you can see with the broad red line on the map, the goal of the German army is to cut off the oil to the Soviets. And we have been extremely successful in doing this, while at the same time protecting our own fields at Ploesti in Romania. This new line was put in place in the second week of September, and now it is achieving what it was designed to do."

"In addition to the German army's new line, the British RAF has been largely neutralized."

Stimson, who had a week earlier briefed the President on the details of this denuding of the British air arm, simply asked, "What do you mean?"

"Well, we do not have all the details, but the *Luftwaffe* has destroyed many of the Britishers' air fields and fuel supplies. And now there are no longer any bombing raids on the *Reich*. This has meant that our aircraft have been freed to fly sorties into Russia to destroy the Russian tanks with our new 45 millimeter cannons.

These new cannons reportedly open a Russian tank as if it was a tin can."

"As a consequence, the Soviets have realized their position is now untenable. So our two sides are speaking about an accommodation in Geneva."

"What kind of accommodation?" Stimson asked.

"We two are just diplomats, but it is the understanding of my ambassador as well as myself that the Soviets will grant German control of the Ukraine, and that Germany will hold the Baku fields and will supply the Russians with 100,000 tons of oil per month at no cost. In return, Germany will grant the Soviets autonomy in the Baltics. Finland will become a free, sovereign nation."

"You're in that strong a position?" Stimson asked candidly.

Schneider nodded, "Gentlemen, please do remember that all of the ill-conceived notions about how to attack Soviet Russia—'you have merely to kick in the front door' and all that gibberish—have been washed away with the sudden death of our Chancellor last September."

The reference to the dead Chancellor alerted both the President and Stimson that there was as much discord in the German ranks as there was in their own.

Roosevelt asked, "So how does this affect your two allies in the agreement?"

Schneider replied, "Well, sir, regarding the Tripartite Agreement, we have been in very close consultations with our Japanese allies and have completely ignored the Italians."

Schneider answered Roosevelt's frown, "They are Italian."

For a second there was silence then Roosevelt erupted in laughter; Stimson joined him.

While the ambassador was a little lost with the proceedings, seeing the two Americans roaring with laughter removed his concerns.

Schneider winked at the old man.

"And to be completely honest and forthright, gentlemen, the Japanese put in a surprising request, which in all propriety I am not sure I should disclose."

This stopped the laughter.

"Our Japanese allies explicitly requested that the *Reich* not declare war on the United States, in spite of the *Reich* being legally bound to do so. It struck us as odd and unusual at the time, but perhaps it is the workings of the Japanese mind."

Ever the diplomat, Stimson said, "Is that a fact?"

Schneider—his turn to play the fool—just nodded.

"Well, Mr. President and Secretary Stimson, you are both very busy men. I think it is time the Ambassador and I stopped wasting your time. We bid you good day."

With this the two Germans stood, clicked their heels, and left.

"Hmm," was the President's sole comment.

Twenty minutes later, at precisely ten minutes past noon, Admiral King entered the Oval Office. Ten minutes later, Miss Tully buzzed the intercom to tell the President that Ambassador Nomura had arrived.

Quietly the Japanese ambassador entered the room, bowed, as was his custom, and waited for the President of the United States to offer him a seat.

The previous evening, Roosevelt had sent Stimson to the Hill to speak to two of the three most vociferous critics of Roosevelt's apparent inactivity. Only last month, the Senator from California made mention on the floor of the Senate of a "Second Munich."

Oddly, Stimson found both Senators oddly quiet and curiously accommodating. As Stimson joked to Roosevelt on the telephone, "We should have the water checked up there on the Hill."

Under mysterious circumstances, the third Senator—the one from Oregon—had died in an automobile accident a week earlier when one night he tragically drove his car off a bridge into Bull Run Creek outside of Washington.

The Senator from California always returned home to California by Pullman rather than airplane. It was not so much that he disliked flying, but rather that he had an addiction to the young Pullman porters. And—sadly—while relaxing after a tenuous month of law making and speechifying just two weeks earlier during a special session, he had the terrible misfortune to be walked in on by a Presbyterian minister and the minister's two maiden aunts. All three were returning from an ecumenical conference in Chicago. The look of horror and disgust on their faces was seared into the Senator's memory. And the minister looked as though he was straight out of Central Casting—white hair, tall, honest and open face, forthright, and with a slight stoop.

Actually, he *was* straight out of Central Casting, as where the two "aunts," and the young porter had been paid ten $100 bills— "more money than I will ever have," was his comment to another porter, as the young man boasted of his plans to return to Mississippi. The three actors tsk'ed and quickly disappeared. The Senator's mood was gray as he knew he would have to resign, so a visit from Stimson was actually a welcome diversion. The Senator was remembering the look on the minister's face all the while as he spoke to Stimson.

Only three years later, sitting in a hot and stinking movie house dive in south San Diego, did the now-disgraced former Senator start to see the truth. Sitting in the back row, while being serviced by a 50-cent-an-hour male escort and sipping lukewarm Thunderbird, he saw the self-same "minister" on the silver screen, paradoxically playing a man of the cloth who had failed the temptation of the flesh.

The burning of the other two Senators was far more straight-forward. And both happened in the same house on K Street. The house was well known and highly regarded, both for the freshness of the young ladies and the absolute discretion of the proprietress.

The proprietress herself was from the South—Richmond, as it turns out, the former capital of the Stars and Bars. She took very pretty girls from Richmond and "introduced" them to Washington. She would tell the parents all about her Lee Finishing School Of Deportment For Young Southern Ladies, and how a few young ladies were sometimes selected to attend diplomatic parties in Washington where they could be introduced to young European princes and other nobles of royal lines.

Why, only two weeks ago the young crown prince of Sweden announced his intention to marry one of her girls. Gasps always resulted in the six years she has told this story. Occasionally, the parents would sense the possibility of a deflowering, and in these cases the proprietress would simply thank her hosts for the tea and, "Thank you for seeing me, I will see myself out."

The young girls themselves were all eager to escape the dull back water that Richmond had become after the surrender in Wilmer McLean's parlor. Alone with the young ladies, the proprietress was more frank—the work was entertaining and relaxing the overworked public servants who labored so long and hard in the public good in the alphabet soup that was the New Deal. And with the huge legislative agenda of the Roosevelt administration there were new agencies to create almost every month. The proprietress explained to the girls—always with very limited success—how the Roosevelt administration had added over 10,000 pages of new laws for his New Deal, and how the complete Federal legal structure before the current president had consisted of less than 8,000 pages.

"So you can see the lawmakers are working very, very hard," she would intone.

The girls all nodded, most just pretending to understand to be polite to the lady they saw as their salvation from the perpetual boredom of Richmond and from their dates on Saturday nights who were generally drunk and always inept in their groping.

The proprietress explained that many of these older men were rich and were always interested in pretty, friendly young southern belles. The best outcome was the girl would find herself in the Washington papers' wedding announcements; the worst outcome was the girl would make some very good money, have a good time for a year or two, make some very useful contacts, and have some very good times in bed—not all the politicians were titans, but quite a few of these men, especially the southerners, were experienced and surprisingly adept at satisfying a young lady's more primitive desires.

The proprietress elaborated how these most powerful men in the country's capital had equally powerful appetites. At this she would produce a list of eligible senators, representatives and high officials. Generally, there was often much excited giggling by the young ladies as the proprietress explained the names in red had an "understanding" with their wives (divorce was politically unacceptable); the ones with the green mark by their names were unmarried and only looking for mistresses. Of course, the list was a pure fabrication, but it served its purpose.

The proprietress was never short of willing girls and had more than sufficient clients. Nevertheless, when a man asked for a very special arrangement—he called it "burning"—the proprietress was open, so long as the rewards were worth the risk to her hard-earned reputation. When the man brought an old-fashioned brown leather

Gladstone bag filled with one-hundred-dollar bills—"all used, none serial, and none traceable"—the proprietress was interested; actually, she was very interested. Afterwards, she personally counted (she could hardly trust the girls) well over one million dollars.

For a large fortune like this, the proprietress would have burned herself. The technical detail of the burn was simplicity itself. Over the past three years, the proprietress had taught herself the rudiments of photography and simple developing. On the two nights in question, the proprietress closeted herself in the tiny, hot, stuffy nook behind the largest bedroom and happily clicked away for two hours taking photos of the Senator being burned through the large two-way mirror at the head of the bed. For the benefit of the annals of photographic history, she was happy that on each of the two nights the politicians were using more than the bland-and-boring one-girl missionary position; in one case, it was two girls and the very naughty Senator being spanked; the other Senator wanted it very rough with all three girls he had selected that night, and the second Senator was very rough after drinking so much bourbon.

The proprietress's benefactor collected the photographs and the negatives the next day and provided an extra small satchel—"just a token of thanks for a job well done."

The final step was to drop off a few sample snaps to each of the Senators' offices with a note inside to meet at a dull and dirty bar seven blocks from the White House—seven blocks from the center of power, with sawdust on the floors and spittoons in abundance. The sharped-eyed man met each Senator on consecutive nights in February at the bar. At the start of the second meeting, the Senator, who, like his peers, was used to getting his way, actually started with threats; the man tersely replied with,

"Shut the fuck up or I walk out now, and feel free to shoot me now, for if I do not return by 10 p.m., a fresh and pristine set of all the photos—not just the sample five you got—go to all the

Washington papers and a set will be delivered by hand to your wife at your home in Portland."

The Senator from Portland sulked.

"Now, Senator, I represent a very large employer who has interests in your state and who is very interested in expanding his business with his Japanese partners."

At the mention of Japan, the corrupt Senator was trying to revive his grumbling.

"Shut up, you old fool! You will now take a benign line and say 'I have reconsidered my position, and I now think we should work to expand our ties with the Japanese who, after all, are our Pacific neighbors.' "

"I cannot and I will not say that; the Japs are sneaky yellow cunts who should be eliminated from the face of the fucking planet—every last one of them."

"Have it as you will," said the man as he rose; he went to the bar, paid the tab, and left.

Two hours later, all the Washington papers were calling the Senator's Washington home and the apartment of the Senator's chief aide. And there was a message for the Senator that said, "Call your wife immediately."

At 10:10 p.m., the Senator had realized his career and his life were over. He backed out his car and drove towards Virginia.

Nomura had been insulated from the cloak-and-dagger melodrama regarding the three Senators, not out of concern for the moral turpitude it involved, but for the rather more simple point of queering the pitch—it would not profit Nomura to know any of the details, and it may have altered his performance in the Oval Office.

When Nomura, politely as ever, quietly entered the Oval Office, he greeted his host with his formal bow. Roosevelt was seated in his hated wheelchair, discretely hidden from view by the recent additions to his uncle's desk.

"Mr. President, the government of my Emperor sends its greetings to you and to Mr. Stimson."

While Stimson may have had his differences with the Japanese in the past, particularly over China, if they had any more like Nomura, then he could easily change his position—politics, especially at this highest level, was a very personal business; liking a protagonist was half the battle, as Stimson had learned.

"And my Emperor is very concerned about your country's honor as the United States is the most important and powerful country in the world."

Both Roosevelt and Stimson compared this sentiment with the one that came from the too-often intoxicated British Prime Minister and his bankrupt country—never in a thousand years would Churchill have been so thoughtful and so courteous.

"Your concern and that of your Emperor are very considerate and we in this country are very thankful for them and for your presence."

There was a very long pause that Nomura was happy to let continue.

"Now, regarding your recent proposition, I think we may be able to reach an accord. Please have a seat."

Nomura sat on one of the now-familiar yellow damask sofas.

For the next two hours, the three men knocked out a crude plan, whereby the Japanese would ask the Swiss to broker an Armistice and the Americans would agree, but only under certain strict conditions that the criminals responsible for the horrible acts of December would be tried and convicted.

Roosevelt smiled,

"I love how these political promulgations always start by assuming guilt and conviction."

Nomura concurred.

"I understand from my staff that the two key Senators opposing this arrangement have moderated their tone and that the Senator from Oregon has been tragically killed in a traffic accident."

Roosevelt explained the details of the parochial politics and how time was the best remedy.

After another hour, Roosevelt looked up and smiled, "That, gentlemen, looks like a decent plan."

"Drinks all round please, Henry."

Stimson obliged and then for Roosevelt the most interesting part of the day's conversation started,

"Gentlemen, my government sees the Pacific as the future of the world, and it also sees Japan and the United States of America as the two countries, in partnership, to manage and develop it. In simple terms, we see it with we Japanese as the administrators and controllers, while the United States develops the region by implementing the President's brilliant NIRA in Asia. We Japanese are very good at governing and organizing, but we do not have the raw materials and we frankly lack the financial skills to build nations. You have Mr. Ford and hundreds of like-minded leaders of industry."

Stimson in particular listened to this explanation, and for the first time understood the concepts of the Greater East Asia Co-Prosperity Sphere: Japan Manages, America Sells. And this suited Stimson down to the ground.

Roosevelt—at Nomura's urging—painted the developments as Japan's contrite surrender, and as the Japanese desire to make amends. The use of the word "surrender" knocked the wind of out the sails of Roosevelt's critics. And the photographs of the glum faces of Tojo and Yamamoto in the dark, dank cells of the Geneva police department made for exceptionally good press coverage in the United States. And so it should have—it had taken over an hour of careful lighting at Tokyo's biggest movie lot and even more careful makeup to create these illusions. For both men, it was their first experience with actor's makeup and both detested it, but for the greater good of the country and for the Emperor, well, this was a small price to pay.

As with most political theater, like politics in general, the effect was powerful but very short-lived. By some quite legal maneuvers, the Japanese defendants were permitted to be replaced by proxies. The drafting of the court's basic documents extended well beyond the three months originally allocated. The Swiss judge fell ill and was incapacitated for four months with a mysterious rash. The Japanese judge's father died and he had to return to Japan. And then the American judge decided to take early retirement.

Initially, the world press, and particularly the American press, took a rabid interest in the proceeding, but as the months dragged on, the observation that delay is the finest form of denial took hold. And even for the American press, the endless delays were no longer news—there was fresh news with the President extolling almost daily the benefits the country would gain with his new pan-Asian NIRA. And Roosevelt revved up the country with his vision for the new Asia, freed from the tyranny of colonialism. He even had mockups of his fleet of PANIRA airships created with Old Glory on one side and the Rising Sun on the other. Next to Roosevelt, it was his faithful Rex Tugwell who was most energized.

And as Roosevelt told Joe Alsop one evening after far too many martinis,

"And, Joe, no fucking Supreme Court to push us back to the horse and buggy era, so you may have to revise your *168 Days*. Mark my words, in Asia I have a completely free hand thanks to Nomura and the Japanese. And remember the Japanese had us completely by the balls—they were the pros and we were like high school players with leaky water buckets. Keep this to yourself, but the Japanese were far more generous than we would have been if we had such total mastery. I guess it must be the four thousand years of civilization that makes them so polite and civilized. And the Japanese are polite even when they are in complete control. You can imagine how boorish we Americans would be if we had such power. And compared to that drunk in London, the contrast is night and day; Churchill does not speak, he pontificates as if his words are direct from God. What a bore."

33: Halifax's New Job

Washington
Thursday, 19 February 1942

ON THE WET THURSDAY AFTERNOON, immediately after lunch and a very large postprandial martini, Roosevelt took particular delight at breaking the news of the armistice with the Japanese to the British Prime Minister. At one stage in the proceedings, Churchill bellowed at the American President words to the effect that "Ambassador Halifax will take a very dim view on that point," to which Roosevelt suavely replied,

"I am not so sure about that Winston, but you can ask him yourself as he is sitting in front of me now."

That sentence told Churchill that his reign of drunken diatribes and ill-considered strategies (dating back to 1915) was over— the President had consulted with Churchill's old rival before speaking to him. Even more important, Roosevelt had not even deigned it necessary to tell Churchill that Halifax was present in the Oval Office. Well, that had torn it.

"And with the recent understanding in Geneva and the cessation of hostilities between the Soviets and the Germans, well there is no need for us to provide any more war matériel or gold or credit. Actually, Winston, it makes no sense at all. You know in time you will come to an understanding with the Germans."

Roosevelt looked at Halifax who in return slowly nodded.

After the call, Roosevelt said to the British ambassador,

"The Germans are extremely eager for an understanding with your country. I know I could broker that in a day. I take it that Churchill is the only roadblock?"

"Mr. President, you are correct. As you know I was considering the job myself, but I think the country needs more of a figurehead who is well liked. We could consider David Windsor."

"Do you really think that would work? I don't know much of the machinations of Westminster but the former King seems very unlikely to a Yank like me as PM: isn't that extremely far-fetched?"

Roosevelt's natural political instincts showed a very deep, visceral understanding of politics, regardless of the country. And Roosevelt realized with the impracticality of the suggestion that Halifax was weak and a man easily dominated.

Lord Halifax reluctantly agreed.

"But what if you take the PM job and David takes your job? Wouldn't that work?"

Halifax said nothing.

"What is Windsor's mood at the moment? And what about this wife, Wallis, right?"

Halifax ever so slightly winced at the mode of address; yes, David Windsor was a disgraced regent, but he still was a former King of England.

"I believe he is in good spirits, Mr. President."

"So, Eddie, you take the PM job and send David here."

Being referred to as "Eddie," even by a personage as high as the President of the United States, did make Halifax's blood boil.

Misreading Halifax's response, Roosevelt added,

"What, don't you want it?"

Halifax opened his mouth to reply, but was cut off by the American,

"So how do we actually do this—I mean I know how to do it here, but what are the mechanics in London?"

The effects of the double Scotch Halifax had poured himself when he served the President were finally taking effect, and the inadvertent crudeness of the President seemed somehow to be less grating. Halifax pondered.

"Well, Franklin, we would need a vote of no confidence. In times like this, that is easy to arrange. Um, a few choice snippets to Geoffrey to get into the *Times.*"

"Geoffrey?"

"Geoffrey Dawson, a pal of mine and just retired as editor of the *Times*, but he is still the force behind the paper."

"So, Ed, where do we start? And who do you think as your deputy, Butler or Anthony? Who?"

Halifax shot back,

"Well, Rab is possible. Actually, Rab is completely suitable, but Anthony is equally unsuitable. 'Half a mad baronet, and half a beautiful woman' is what Rab calls Eden, and I am inclined to agree."

Roosevelt roared with laughter.

"No, no, Anthony would be a complete disaster; you know, he actually paints his finger nails with clear nail polish?"

Roosevelt frowned, but before he could ask for an explanation, Halifax asked,

"Franklin, did you have anything to do with the Russian armistice?"

Roosevelt said that he did not.

"Pity. That could have been useful."

"Wait just a second."

Impetuous as always and without thinking, Roosevelt picked up the telephone and called the German Embassy, "Herr Schneider, please."

After a moment, Schneider came on the line,

"Schneider, hello, it's Franklin here. Look, I think I can get you a deal with the Brits, but we're going to have to gild the lily a little. Look, you know Eddie Halifax, right? Well, he's with me now and he thinks—and I agree—that we can change the London government to a more, how shall I say, friendly one, if we put it about that the Oval was involved in the settlement with you and the Soviets. Is that reasonable to you?"

Schneider said it was.

Roosevelt said, "Great, leave it to me and Eddie."

At the embassy, Schneider put down the phone and looked at a naked Louise on the couch, her long, long legs draped along the length of the couch wearing nothing but her favorite pair of nude high heels. (Schneider, like so many other men, loved sex with a woman wearing nothing but heels.)

"Who was that?" she asked.

"You would not believe me if I told you."

"OK, Eddie, the game's afoot," the President said.

34: Rab's Delight

London
Friday, 20 February 1942

THE GOVERNMENT WHIPS LOOKED NERVOUS as the division was called. Their nervousness was well justified—the government was short a staggering 102 votes. Earlier that day, the MPs—and indeed all of educated England—had read in the *Times* an account of the tireless and strenuous efforts of the American president in securing the peace accord between the Germans and the Soviets, and how the Germans had first resisted the entreaties of the American president as the Germans were is such an overwhelmingly strong position, but, finally, the Germans had come around.

But, it was on page three that the phantasy of Churchill's reputation as the savior of democracy was destroyed. An article, based on information supplied by the Swiss and Swedish Red Cross organizations, listed the details of the gruesome discoveries in the Katyn forest in Poland. Even the Anglican churchmen—ever the bedrock of the British Establishment—were making noises about the "Soviet Massacre," as it came to be known.

As the roll was called, Churchill stormed from the chamber, an act as imperious as it was insulting.

Rab Butler, who detested Churchill, enjoyed the ultimate pleasure in visiting Number 10 later that afternoon with the message that Butler had personally arranged for Halifax to return to "help the country recover from the insanity you have put it through." Butler simply laughed as Churchill screamed at him from the top of the stairs at Number 10, as Colville tried to restrain his boss.

"You are a half-American bankrupt whore who should have been shot after Gallipoli. I am here to reclaim the post for a rational and reasonable, pure Englishman."

After his mocking, Rab left. Churchill turned to his often-abused secretary, and said,

"Jock, it's not true. Tell me it's not true. Please."

Colville drew in his breath, and slowly said, "Well, sir, I am afraid it is true."

The next day witnessed one of the most astonishing events in the long life of the oldest parliament—the new Deputy Prime Minister, Rab Butler, sought a meeting with the King to seek permission to form a new government, as Prime Minister Elect Halifax would not land at Heston until that evening.

The King was not informed that his elder brother would replace Halifax in Washington—"the King is a very busy man, and I did not want to bother him with the minutiae of the democratic process," Butler would remark later to Halifax over whiskies when Halifax was comfortably ensconced in his new residence at Downing Street.

Epilogue

ONE OF THE MOST TELLING of all photos taken in the early post-European war period was snapped by a young *Life* photographer on an early May morning in the Rose Garden.

Glorious bright sunlight, so loved by photographers the world over, streamed down on the White House, the primrose yellow of the roses contrasted so perfectly with the green of the lawn mowed the previous day for the benefit of the mob of photographers.

And there in the middle of the lawn, looking very bonny, and almost smug, stood the heads of state and their wives: Franklin Roosevelt, President of the United States of America; on his left, Albert Speer, the new *Reich* Chancellor; Nobusuke Kishi, Prime Minister of Japan; and on his right, Lord Halifax, Prime Minister of the United Kingdom of Great Britain and Northern Ireland.

Nervously fiddling behind Albert was David Windsor, the British Ambassador to the United States, who had less than six weeks life remaining—he was assassinated leaving the Cafe Royale in London by three officers of the Grenadier Guards still loyal to Churchill. After shooting the former king, the three politely waited for the police and to be arrested; the start of a rebellion Rab Butler was to so brutally—and successfully—suppress.

David's wife, having once been denied the throne, was again bitterly denied the limelight she so adored. On this glorious May day, the smoke still rose from the English Oval cigarette reluctantly dropped by the new British Prime Minister at the insistence of the young *Life* photographer.

The overall impression was of three very satisfied men.

The End

Bibliography

While obviously a work of fiction, the history is accurate.

This brief bibliography lists some of the more useful books and authors. All books mentioned are available online.

In addition, both YouTube and Wikipedia are useful—the Yokohama sword story is based on a YouTube video.

This list is not meant to be complete and comprehensive, but it does cover some of the major points.

Finally, I would like to thank Dean Lekos whose tireless fact-checking and proof-reading removed countless errors; the errors that remain are due to me alone.

- **Shlaes, Amity. *The Forgotten Man: A New History of the Great Depression*. New York: HarperCollins, 2007.**

This novel is inspired by *The Forgotten Man*, by Amity Shlaes. In fact, the seven words of the dedication are based on the first paragraph of the introduction to Shlaes's book. *The Forgotten Man* destroys many myths and shibboleths and as such it is highly recommended.

I happened on this book from a review in the *Economist*. Before reading this book, I had the standard-issue regular commonsense view: the naughty and wicked Republicans caused the Great Depression, helped largely in part by the boozy excesses of the Twenties—flappers, Jay Gatsby, and all that; then the wonderful FDR saved the day.

Unfortunately, this view conveniently ignored all the facts, such as the Chicago School aphorism that all bubbles are monetary bubbles: the Dow's rise from 200 to 381 between Spring 1927 and Summer 1929 was caused solely by the Fed's printing presses; and the disaster of 1937—the infamous Depression Within A Depression—was caused by the ill-advised Excess Profits tax, much along the lines of the today's policies of "Super Tax The 1%" (France has already implemented this. *Plus ça change...*).

A survey a few years ago showed that of 900 college history teachers surveyed in the U.S., 830 were registered Democrats; it's likely Europe is even more unbalanced. With this bias, it is very unlikely that the truth will ever be told about "the wise old bird" (Roosevelt's self-serving description of himself).

The photographs Rex shows Louise are depicted in Shlaes's book.

- **Tooze, J. Adam. *The Wages of Destruction: The Making and Breaking of the Nazi Economy.* New York: Viking, 2007.**

This book is seminal—most of the thousands of books about the Second World War in Europe speak in terms of battles and armies, and mostly focusing on the wrong battles at that (the five leading battles were all on Russian territory).

Tooze's book is how all history should be written—starting with the most important aspect first, namely the <u>money</u>. This is the major theme of *The Goddess*—Sasaki's printing press, etc. *Wages* is both engrossing and well written. The Notes section alone is pure gold dust. *Wages* suggests the obvious question: how did the Third *Reich* survive until 1945? It certainly wasn't because of the leadership from the top. It is clear that Germany could have won had Jodl, Model, Rundstedt, *et al*, done the strategic planning rather than the mad-cap Alice-in-Wonderland nonsense that actually occurred. It's one thing to be an opportunist, it's another thing to confuse beginner's luck with professional acumen, and very short-lived luck at that (Greece in summer 1941 was the Austrian's last victory).

- **Keegan, John. *The First World War*. New York: A. Knopf, 1999.**

  All books by the late John Keegan are a pleasure to read; his book on the World War I is no exception. The description of terror and misery of the British soldiers during the Somme is an abstraction from this book. (I was in Bermuda three years ago and read a gravestone in a Hamilton churchyard for a soldier who died on August 15, 1916, "From wounds received on the river Somme.")

- **Beevor, Antony. *The Spanish Civil War*. New York: P. Bedrick, 1983.**

  Fat Herman's double-dealing via the *Bramhill* is described in Beevor's book, as is the description of the horrors of the Lincoln Brigade, and the Battle of Brunete.

- **Manchester, William. *The Arms of Krupp*. Boston: Little, Brown & Co., 1968.**

  Jodl's comments of 1870 are based on Manchester's description of the effects of the rifled cast steel Krupp cannon, as is the presence of the two American generals. (Burnside and Sheridan are changed to Sherman and Sheridan—better alliteration.)

  The Kaiser's horror-filled evening in 1901 is described in detail by Manchester; Jules Verne's submarine is converted to a space ship, "the engine is constructed of the finest steel in the world, cast 'by Krupp in Prussia.' "

- **Heller, Anne Conover. *Ayn Rand and the World She Made*. New York: Nan A. Talese/Doubleday, 2009.**

This book is an extremely interesting description of Ayn Rand and her acolytes. It is the basis of Speer's visit to Barcelona. The train conversation is based on two likely candidates for the U.S. Presidency in 2016; I will let the reader deduce who they are; there are more than sufficient hints.

Other Sources

The *Esquire* article is F. Scott Fitzgerald's "The Crack-Up" (*Esquire*, February, March, and April 1936). I learned of this from a quote in a John le Carré novel—Smiley is asked by Roy Bland, "who said 'the test of a first-rate intelligence is the ability to hold two opposed ideas in the mind at the same time?'" The article is available online.

The Confederate one hundred dollar bill was bought on eBay for six U.S. dollars; good Union money.

Senator Beveridge's 1900 speech is quoted verbatim and the complete speech is available online.

"Tim" is, of course, the English traitor Harold Adrian Russell "Kim" Philby.

Secretary of War Henry Stimson's diaries are quoted verbatim.

Morgenthau's notes, quoted verbatim, are from his appearance in front of the House Ways and Means Committee in May 1939.

"Cigar" and "The Diplomat" were nicknames of Curtis LeMay, Milch's counterpart.

The "hairy hand in the ice bowl" is taken from a description of Lord Beaverbrook.

A "damn close run" is a slight misquoting of Wellington's comment on Waterloo.

"{W}here bed and boys were also not expensive" is from Michael Holroyd's *Lytton Strachey: A Critical Biography*, London: Heinemann, 1967.

The "ovaries rattling" quote is from the Austrian's driver, commenting about Magda Goebbels.

The Caudillo's mortgage plan is actually the HUD dictate, starting in 1992, to direct 30% of Fannie Mae's and Freddie Mac's mortgages to borrowers who were at or below the median income in their communities—the start of "Cov-lite." It ended at 55% in 2007; what happened next is now ancient history.

"Whole thing goes arse over tit" is from the book *A Bridge Too Far*, describing a glider's landing on soft ground.

"I don't want to have to eat a broomstick" was a boast from the Reichsmarshall that "If any enemy bomber ever attacks Germany then I will eat a broomstick."

Tex Wheeler and his much-displayed gold watch, a gift from Prisoner Number 1 at Nuremburg, are transposed to Hawaii.

ARB

About the Author

Originally from Melbourne, Australia, Andrew Blencowe discovered at an early age what it was like to live on the edge of life. During his high school years he dropped out to become a motorcycle racer. Smitten by computers in his early twenties, he went on to become founder and CEO of an international software company with offices on five continents. It is his international perspective and a drive to challenge assumptions that influence his writing interests.

Learn more at **AndrewBlencowe.com** including details about Blencowe's forthcoming *The Last Bastion of Civilization: Japan 2041* scheduled for Fall 2015.

Made in the USA
Lexington, KY
28 December 2016